# MURDER IMPOSSIBLE

# MURDER IMPOSSIBLE

## AN EXTRAVAGANZA OF MIRACULOUS MURDERS FANTASTIC FELONIES & INCREDIBLE CRIMINALS

EDITED AND INTRODUCED BY

Jack Adrian + Robert Adey

Carroll & Graf Publishers, Inc.
New York

First published in Great Britain by Xanadu Publications Limited
1990
First published in the United States of America by Carroll & Graf
Publishers, Inc. 1990, by arrangement with Xanadu Publications
Ltd

Carroll & Graf Publishers, Inc.
260 Fifth Avenue
New york, NY 10001

Library of Congress Cataloging-in-Publication Data
  Murder impossible: the book of locked-room mysteries and other
  impossible crimes/edited and introduced by Jack Adrian and
  Robert Adey. – 1st Carroll & Graf ed.
      p. cm.
    ISBN 0–88184–641–4: $18.95
    1. Detective and mystery stories. 2. Crimes and criminals-
  -Fiction. I. Adrian, Jack II. Adey, Robert.
  PN6120–95-D45M8 1990
  808.83'872—dc20                                    90–43442
                                                         CIP

Manufactured in Great Britain

# Contents

# Introduction

'Politics,' said Disraeli, thrice prime minster of Great Britain and a man of shrewd, manipulative intelligence, 'is the art of the possible.'

This is not only true but acute, like a good many other things the great Tory said. Clever and memorable phrases pepper his novels (still readable today, incidentally) and political speeches—'Little things please little minds' . . . 'Time is the great healer' (actually 'great physician', but never mind) . . . 'Peace with honour' . . . 'Two nations' . . . 'Dark horse' . . . 'I am on the side of the angels' (he wasn't; that was mere political expediency at the time of the great Darwin debate, but it sounded good) . . . 'Lay flattery on with a trowel'.

In this anthology will be found something of the Art of the *Im*possible—for surely there is an art in making a reader believe that a grown woman, say, has vanished in circumstances where it is just not possible that she could have done—or a large oil painting has disappeared when that simply could not have happened—or a dead man can drive a car. All of these events (and others, even stranger) occur in the pages that follow. Yet, patently, they could not have occurred; there has to be a rational explanation—this is, after all, detective, not science or fantasy, fiction.

Just as a great politician is a manipulator who identifies key people and spots then seizes opportunities and uses both to advantage (whether or not for the public weal is hardly the point), so your common-or-garden crime writer is in roughly the same line of business; and a great crime writer is a manipulator *par excellence*, one who has the ability to take readers by the nose and lead them right up the garden path.

Of all the multifarious sub-divisions in the detective fiction genre the Impossible Crime—or Locked Room Mystery or Miracle Problem—is surely the ultimate manifestation of the writer pitting his or her wits against the reader. It is also, to be sure, the most mechanical, for in it the puzzle is all. Characterisation and scene description are often shoved ruthlessly aside as largely irrelevant, although mood and atmosphere are still useful weapons in the writer's armoury (think of the best novels of John Dickson Carr, or Hake Talbot's *Rim of the Pit*).

Perhaps this is why the Impossible Crime is to a certain extent frowned on now. In some ways the pure puzzle is a relic of the Golden Age along with all its attendant impedimenta: the X-ed sketch-map of a country house; an itemised list of the contents of the corpse's pockets; whole chapters of train-times from Bradshaw; a bumbling official detective; a silly-ass sleuth one would like to take a pickaxe handle to oneself, never mind the murderer. Nowadays, we are far more likely to encounter harrowing details of the detective's current domestic crises than a floorplan of the murder building or pages of correlated railway timetables. And, frankly, a good thing too.

Yet the puzzle still has its place and there are writers around today who, while eschewing utterly all forms of Golden Age flummery and even utilising a mean-streets milieu, still delight in detailed clueing, a meticulously unravelled denouement, and (more importantly) much artful misdirection. Misdirection, of course, is the essential ingredient of the Impossible Crime story. The classic Miracle Problem situation—the hermetically sealed room, the corpse lying in the middle of an acre of unmarked snow, the train disappearing from a stretch of observed line, and so on—only seems miraculous because at some stage in the proceedings the author has skilfully contrived to pull the wool over the reader's eyes.

At its best, the Impossible Crime can be brilliant, outrageous, bizarre, spectacularly ingenious . . . profoundly infuriating. It can encompass a dazzling piece of verbal or situational legerdemain or a simple and obvious (indeed thumpingly obvious) explanation that the reader can hardly believe he or she has missed. At its worst, it can be trite, silly, or well beyond any rational imaginings, taking in the unmentioned (and often searched-for in vain, by both detective and reader) secret passage or sliding panel; mass hypnosis; berserk chimpanzees; trained rats; or even (yes, indeed) the failure to provide any solution or explanation at all.

It can, in short, cause the reader to leap out of his chair bellowing 'That's ludicrous!' (although here it must be confessed that one of your editors has a fondness for the kind of stories that include, say, deranged knife-wielding pygmies hiding in the false humps of ersatz hunchbacks, than which, surely, there is nothing more ludicrous), or smite his brow with the palm of his hand while muttering through gritted teeth, 'Of *course.*'

In *The Art of the Impossible* demented dwarves are (alas) notable by their absence, although there are one or two illusionists who might be said to be borderline cases (mentally, anyhow). Otherwise, here are nineteen short stories (including two fine parodies), one playlet and a 30,000-word novella. John Dickson Carr appears twice—but that is only right and proper. One story has no solution, though for a very good reason. As far as we are aware, only four of the stories have appeared in bookform before, the rest having been chosen from various periodicals or stumbled across serendipitously; not a few may be classed as rarities. One story was set from the original typescript, since it was never sold to a magazine in its author's lifetime.

When all is said and done, the Impossible Crime is indeed pure manipulation. We cordially invite you to be manipulated.

JACK ADRIAN/ROBERT ADEY
May, 1990

# The House in Goblin Wood

John Dickson Carr *was never a prolific short story writer—no more than forty all told. They included youthful romances and a couple of chilling ghost stories, but quite the majority were detective stories.*

*A few of them were one-offs such as the excellent 'The Gentleman From Paris'; nine more, and by far the biggest grouping, featured Colonel March of the Department of Queer Complaints (though he never figured in a novel), while six were the Sherlock Holmes pastiches penned with Adrian Conan Doyle. Which left precious few to be shared out between Carr's main protagonists—Bencolin, Dr Gideon Fell and Sir Henry Merrivale.*

*Henri Bencolin, the French prefect of police and Carr's earliest detective, graced the pages of* The Haverfordian *(a college literary magazine) and there solved five cases, one of which, 'Grand Guignol', was expanded into Carr's first novel* It Walks By Night *(1930). Dr Fell rumbled and harrumphed his Chestertonian way through five more stories from 'The Proverbial Murder' to 'King Arthur's Chair', virtually the last short story Carr wrote.*

*So what then of Sir Henry—'H.M.', 'The Old Man'—favourite sleuth of those pre-eminent critics Torquemada (E. Powys Mathers) and Howard Haycraft? How many villains did Sir Henry lay by the heels, taking less than a novel to do it? The surprising answer (and we're talking novelettes here, not villains) is only two. Others were probably planned—a tantalisingly tentative title for a never-written volume was* Commander Sir Henry Merrivale—*but two, alas, is all we have.*

*The later story, 'Ministry of Miracles', better known as 'All in a Maze', is a typical rumbustious H.M. romp, but somehow doesn't linger in the memory. The earlier tale is another matter entirely. In it, after a knockabout opening, Sir Henry has to find an explanation for the disappearance of a strange, fey girl from a woodland cottage, where he himself was present and her voice could still be heard after her corporeal being had vanished. This is Sir Henry in a much grimmer and darker mood than normal, and a story that will stay with you long after you have read it . . . right down to the very last word.*

ROBERT ADEY

In Pall Mall, that hot July afternoon three years before the war, an open saloon car was drawn up to the kerb just opposite the Senior Conservatives' Club.

And in the car sat two conspirators.

It was the drowsy post-lunch hour among the clubs, where only the sun remained brilliant. The Rag lay somnolent; the Athenaeum slept outright. But these two conspirators, a dark haired young man in his early thirties and a fair haired girl perhaps half a dozen years younger, never moved. They stared intently at the Gothic-like front of the Senior Conservatives'.

'Look here, Eve,' muttered the young man, and punched at the steering wheel. 'Do you think this is going to work?'

'I don't know,' the fair-haired girl confessed. 'He absolutely *loathes* picnics.'

'Anyway, we've probably missed him.'

'Why so?'

'He can't have taken as long over lunch as that!' her companion protested, looking at a wrist-watch. The young man was rather shocked. 'It's a quarter to four! Even if . . .'

'Bill! There! Look there!'

Their patience was rewarded by an inspiring sight.

Out of the portals of the Senior Conservatives' Club, in awful majesty, marched a large, stout, barrel-shaped gentleman in a white linen suit.

His corporation preceded him like the figurehead of a man-of-war. His shell-rimmed spectacles were pulled down on a broad nose, all being shaded by a Panama hat. At the top of the stone steps he surveyed the street, left and right, with a lordly sneer.

'Sir Henry!' called the girl.

'Hey?' said Sir Henry Merrivale.

'I'm Eve Drayton. Don't you remember me? You knew my father!'

'Oh, ah,' said the great man.

'We've been waiting here a terribly long time,' Eve pleaded. 'Couldn't you see us for just five minutes?—The thing to do,' she whispered to her companion, 'is to keep him in a good humour. Just keep him in a good humour.'

As a matter of fact, H.M. was in a good humour, having just triumphed over a fellow-member in an argument. But not even his own mother could have guessed it. Majestically, with the same lordly sneer, he began in grandeur to descend the steps of the Senior Conservatives'. He did this, in fact until his foot encountered an unnoticed object lying some three feet from the bottom.

It was a banana skin.

'Oh dear!' said the girl.

From the pavement, where Sir Henry Merrivale landed in a seated position, arose in H.M.'s bellowing voice such a flood of invective as had seldom before blasted the holy calm of Pall Mall. It brought the hall-porter hurrying down the steps, and Eve Drayton flying out of the car.

Heads were now appearing at the windows of the Athenaeum across the street.

'Is it all right?' cried the girl, with concern in her blue eyes. 'Are you hurt?'

H.M. merely looked at her. His hat had fallen off, disclosing a large bald head; and he merely sat on the pavement and looked at her.

'Anyway, Sir Henry, get up! Please get up!'

'Get up?' bellowed H.M., in a voice audible as far as St. James's Street. 'Burn it all, how *can* I get up?'

'But why not?'

'My behind's out of joint,' said H.M. simply. 'I'm hurt. I'm probably goin' to have spinal dislocation for the rest of my life.'

'But, sir, people are looking!' said the hall-porter.

H.M. explained what these people could do. He eyed Eve Drayton with a glare of indescribable malignancy over his spectacles.

'I suppose, my wench, *you're* responsible for this?'

Eve regarded him in consternation.

'You don't mean the banana skin?' she cried.

'Oh yes, I do,' said H.M., folding his arms like a prosecuting counsel.

'But we—we only wanted to invite you to a picnic!'

H.M. closed his eyes.

'That's fine,' he said in a hollow voice. 'All the same, don't you think it'd have been a subtler kind of hint just to put mayonnaise over my head, or shove ants down the back of my neck? Oh, lord love a duck!'

'I didn't mean that! I meant . . .'

'Let me help you up, sir,' interposed the calm, reassuring voice of the dark-haired and blue-chinned young man who had been with Eve in the car.

'So you want to help too, hey? And who are *you*?'

'I'm awfully sorry,' said Eve. 'I should have introduced you! This is my *fiancé*, Dr. William Sage.'

H.M.'s face turned purple.

'I'm glad to see,' he observed, 'you had the uncommon decency to bring along a doctor. I appreciate that, I do. And the car's there, I suppose, to assist with the examination when I take off my pants?'

The hall-porter gave a gasp of horror.

Bill Sage, either from jumpiness and nerves or from sheer inability to keep a straight face, laughed loudly. 'I keep telling Eve a dozen times a day,' he said, 'that I'm not to be called "doctor." I happen to be a surgeon'—(here H.M. really did look alarmed)—'but I don't think we need operate. Nor, in my opinion,' Bill gravely addressed the hall-porter, 'will it be necessary to remove Sir Henry's trousers in front of the Senior Conservatives' Club.'

'Thank you very much, sir.'

'We had an infernal nerve to come here,' the young man confessed to H.M. 'But I honestly think, Sir Henry, you'd be more comfortable in the car. What about it? Let me give you a hand up?'

Yet even ten minutes later, when H.M. sat glowering in the back of the car and two heads were craned round towards him, peace was not restored.

'All right?' said Eve. Her pretty, rather stolid face was flushed; her mouth looked miserable. 'If you won't come to the picnic, you won't. But I did believe you might do it to oblige me.'

'Well . . . now!' muttered the great man uncomfortably.

'And I did think, too, you'd be interested in the other person who was coming with us. But Vicky's—difficult. She won't come either, if you don't.'

'Oh? And who's this other guest?'

'Vicky Adams.'

H.M.'s hand, which had been lifted for an oratorical gesture, dropped to his side. 'Vicky Adams? That's not the gal who . . .'

'Yes!' Eve nodded. 'They say it was one of the great mysteries, twenty years ago, that the police failed to solve.'

'It was, my wench,' H.M. agreed sombrely. 'It was.'

'And now Vicky's grown up. And we thought if you, of all people, went along, and spoke to her nicely, she'd tell us what really happened on that night.'

H.M.'s small, sharp eyes fixed disconcertingly on Eve.

'I say, my wench, what's your interest in all this?'

'Oh, reasons.' Eve glanced quickly at Bill Sage, who was again punching moodily at the steering wheel, and checked herself. 'Anyway, what difference does it make now? If you won't go with us . . .'

H.M. assumed a martyred air.

'I never said I *wasn't* goin' with you, did I?' he demanded. 'Even

after you practically made a cripple of me, I never said I *wasn't* goin'?'
His manner grew flurried and hasty. 'But I've got to leave now,' he
added apologetically. 'I got to get back to my office.'

'We'll drive you there, H.M.'

'No, no, no,' said the practical cripple, getting out of the car with
surprising celerity. 'Walkin' is good for my stomach if it's not so good
for my behind. I'm a forgivin' man. You pick me up at my house
to-morrow morning. G'bye.'

And he lumbered off in the direction of the Haymarket.

It needed no close observer to see that H.M. was deeply abstracted.
He remained so abstracted, indeed, as to be nearly murdered by a
taxi at the Admiralty Arch; and he was halfway down Whitehall before
a familiar voice stopped him.

'Afternoon, Sir Henry!'

Burly, urbane, buttoned up in blue serge, with his bowler hat and
his boiled blue eyes, stood Chief Inspector Masters.

'Bit odd,' the Chief Inspector remarked affably, 'to see you taking
a constitutional on a day like this. And how are you, sir?'

'Awful,' said H.M. instantly. 'But that's not the point. Masters,
you crawlin' snake! You're the very man I wanted to see.'

Few things startled the Chief Inspector. This one did.

'You,' he repeated, 'wanted to see *me*? What about?'

'Masters, do you remember the Victoria Adams case about twenty
years ago?'

The Chief Inspector's manner suddenly changed and grew wary.

'Victoria Adams case?' he ruminated. 'No, sir, I can't say I do.'

'Son, you're lyin'! You were sergeant to old Chief Inspector
Rutherford in those days, and well I remember it!'

'That's as may be, sir. But twenty years ago . . .'

'A little girl of twelve or thirteen, the child of very wealthy parents,
disappeared one night out of a country cottage with all the doors and
windows locked on the inside. A week later, while everybody was
havin' screaming hysterics, the child reappeared again: through the
locks and bolts, tucked up in her bed as usual. And to this day
nobody's ever known what really happened.'

There was a silence, while Masters shut his jaws hard.

'This family, the Adamses,' persisted H.M., 'owned the cottage;
down Aylesbury way, on the edge of Goblin Wood, opposite the lake.
Or was it?'

'Oh, ah,' growled Masters. 'It was.'

H.M. looked at him curiously.

'They used the cottage as a base for bathin' in summer and iceskatin' in winter. It was black winter when the child vanished, and the place was all locked up inside against draughts. They say her old man nearly went loopy when he found her there a week later, lying asleep under the lamp. But all she'd say, when they asked her where she'd been, was "*I don't know.*" '

Again there was a silence, while red buses thundered through the traffic press of Whitehall.

'You've got to admit, Masters, there was a flaming public rumpus. I say, did you ever read Barrie's "Mary Rose"?'

'No.'

'Well, it was a situation straight out of Barrie. Some people, y'see, said that Vicky Adams was a child of faërie who'd been spirited away by the pixies . . .'

Masters removed his bowler hat and wiped his forehead. He made remarks about pixies in detail, which could not have been bettered by H.M. himself.

'I know, son, I know.' H.M. was soothing. Then his big voice sharpened. 'Now, tell me. Was all this talk strictly true?'

'What talk?'

'Locked windows? Bolted doors? No attic-trap? No cellar? Solid walls and floor?'

'Yes, sir,' answered Masters, regaining his dignity with a powerful effort, 'I'm bound to admit it *was* true.'

'Then there wasn't any jiggery-pokery about the cottage?'

'In your eyes there wasn't, said Masters.

'How d'ye mean?'

'Listen, sir.' Masters lowered his voice. 'Before the Adamses took over that place, it was a hide-out for Chuck Randall. At that time he was the swellest of the Swell mob; we lagged him a couple of years later. Do you think Chuck wouldn't have rigged up some gadget for a getaway? Just so! Only . . .'

'Well? Hey?'

'We couldn't find it,' grunted Masters.

'And I'll bet that pleased old Chief Inspector Rutherford?'

'I tell you straight: he was fair up the pole. Especially as the kid herself was a pretty kid, all big eyes and dark hair. You couldn't help trusting her.'

'Yes,' said H.M. 'That's what worries me.'

'Worries you?'

'Oh, my son!' said H.M. dismally. 'Here's Vicky Adams, the spoiled daughter of dotin' parents. She's supposed to be "odd" and "fey." She's even encouraged to be. During her adolescence, the most impressionable time of her life, she gets wrapped round with the gauze of a mystery that people talk about even yet. What's that woman like now, Masters? What's that woman like now?'

'Dear Sir Henry!' murmured Miss Vicky Adams in her softest voice.

She said this just as William Sage's car with Bill and Eve Drayton in the front seat, and Vicky and H.M. in the back seat, turned off the main road. Behind them lay the smokey-red roofs of Aylesbury, against a brightness of late afternoon. The car turned down a side road, a damp tunnel of greenery, and into another road which was little more than a lane between hedgerows.

H.M.—though cheered by three good-sized picnic hampers from a famous provisioner's, their wickerwork lids bulging with a feast— did not seem happy. Nobody in that car was happy, with the possible exception of Miss Adams herself.

Vicky, unlike Eve, was small and dark and vivacious. Her large light-brown eyes, with very black lashes, could be arch and coy; or they could be dreamily intense. The late Sir James Barrie might have called her a sprite. Those of more sober views would have recognized a different quality: she had an inordinate sex-appeal, which was as palpable as a physical touch to any male within yards. And despite her smallness, Vicky had a full voice like Eve's. All these qualities she used even in so simple a matter as giving traffic directions.

'First right,' she would say, leaning forward to put her hands on Bill Sage's shoulders. 'Then straight on until the next traffic light. Ah, clever boy!'

'Not at all, not at all!' Bill would disclaim, with red ears and rather an erratic style of driving.

'Oh yes, you are!' And Vicky would twist the lobe of his ear, playfully, before sitting back again.

(Eve Drayton did not say anything. She did not even turn round. Yet the atmosphere, even of that quiet English picnic-party, had already become a trifle hysterical).

'Dear Sir Henry!' murmured Vicky, as they turned down into the deep lane between the hedgerows. 'I do wish you wouldn't be so materialistic! I do, really. Haven't you the tiniest bit of spirituality in your nature?'

'Me?' said H.M. in astonishment. 'I've got a very lofty spiritual nature. But what I want just now, my wench, is grub—Oi!'

Bill Sage glanced round.

'By that speedometer'—H.M. pointed—'we've now come forty-six miles and a bit. We didn't even leave Town until people of decency and sanity were having their tea. Where are we goin'?'

'But didn't you know?' asked Vicky, with wide-open eyes. 'We're going to the cottage where I had such a dreadful experience when I was a child.'

'Was it such a dreadful experience, Vicky dear?' inquired Eve.

Vicky's eyes seemed far away.

'I don't remember, really. I was only a child, you see. I didn't understand. I hadn't developed the power for myself then.'

'What power?' H.M. asked sharply.

'To dematerialize,' said Vicky. 'Of course.'

In that warm sun-dusted lane, between the hawthorn hedges, the car jolted over a rut. Crockery rattled.

'Oh yes. I see,' observed H.M. without inflection. 'And where do you go, my wench, when you dematerialize?'

'Into a strange country. Through a little door. You wouldn't understand. Oh, you *are* such Philistines!' moaned Vicky. Then, with a sudden change of mood, she leaned forward and her whole physical allurement flowed again towards Bill Sage. '*You* wouldn't like me to disappear, would you, Bill?'

(Easy! Easy!)

'Only,' said Bill, with a sort of wild gallantry, 'if you promised to reappear again straightaway.'

'Oh, I should have to do that.' Vicky sat back. She was trembling. 'The power wouldn't be strong enough. But even a poor little thing like me might be able to teach you a lesson. Look there!'

And she pointed ahead.

On their left, as the lane widened, stretched the ten-acre gloom of what is fancifully known as Goblin Wood. On their right lay a small lake, on private property and therefore deserted.

The cottage—set well back into a clearing of the wood so as to face the road, screened from it by a line of beeches—was in fact a bungalow of rough-hewn stone, with a slate roof. Across the front of it ran a wooden porch. It had a seedy air, like the long yellow-green grass of its front lawn. Bill parked the car at the side of the road, since there was no driveway.

'It's a bit lonely, ain't it?' demanded H.M. His voice boomed out against that utter stillness, under the hot sun.

'Oh yes!' breathed Vicky. She jumped out of the car in a whirl of skirts.

'That's why *they* were able to come and take me. When I was a child.'

'They?'

'Dear Sir Henry! Do I need to explain?'

Then Vicky looked at Bill.

'I must apologise,' she said, 'for the state the house is in. I haven't been out here for months and months. There's a modern bathroom I'm glad to say. Only paraffin lamps, of course. But then,' a dreamy smile flashed across her face, 'you won't need lamps, will you? Unless . . .'

'You mean,' said Bill, who was taking a black case out of the car, 'unless you disappear again?'

'Yes, Bill. And promise me you won't be frightened when I do.'

The young man uttered a ringing oath which was shushed austerely by Sir Henry Merrivale. Eve Drayton was very quiet.

'But in the meantime,' Vicky said wistfully, 'let's forget it all, shall we? Let's laugh and dance and sing and pretend we're children! And surely our guest must be even more hungry by this time?'

It was in this emotional state that they sat down to their picnic.

H.M., if the truth must be told, did not fare too badly. Instead of sitting on some hummock of ground, they dragged a table and chairs to the shaded porch. All spoke in strained voices. But no word of controversy was said. It was only afterwards, when the cloth was cleared, the furniture and hampers pushed indoors, the empty bottles flung away, that danger tapped a warning.

From under the porch Vicky fished out two half-rotted deck-chairs, which she set up in the long grass of the lawn. These were to be occupied by Eve and H.M., while Vicky took Bill Sage to inspect a plum tree of some remarkable quality she did not specify.

Eve sat down without comment. H.M., who was smoking a black cigar opposite her, waited some time before he spoke.

'Y'know,' he said, taking the cigar out of his mouth, 'you're behaving remarkably well.'

'Yes.' Eve laughed. 'Aren't I?'

'Are you pretty well acquainted with this Adams gal?'

'I'm her first cousin,' Eve answered simply. 'Now that her parents are dead, I'm the only relative she's got. I know *all* about her.'

From far across the lawn floated two voices saying something about wild strawberries. Eve, her fair hair and fair complexion, vivid against the dark line of Goblin Wood, clenched her hands on her knees.

'You see, H.M.,' she hesitated, 'there was another reason why I invited you here. I—I don't quite know how to approach it.'

'I'm the old man,' said H.M., tapping himself impressively on the chest. 'You tell me.'

'Eve, darling!' interposed Vicky's voice, crying across the ragged lawn. 'Coo-ee! Eve!'

'Yes, dear?'

'I've just remembered,' cried Vicky, 'that I haven't shown Bill over the cottage! You don't mind if I steal him away from you for a little while?'

'No, dear! Of course not!'

It was H.M., sitting so as to face the cottage, who saw Vicky and Bill go in. He saw Vicky's wistful smile as she closed the door after them. Eve did not even look round. The sun was declining, making fiery chinks through the thickness of Goblin Wood behind the cottage.

'I won't let her have him,' Eve suddenly cried. 'I won't! I won't! I won't!'

'Does she want him, my wench? Or, what is more to the point, does he want her?'

'He never has,' Eve said with emphasis. 'Not really. And he never will.'

H.M., motionless, puffed out cigar smoke.

'Vicky's a faker,' said Eve. 'Does that sound catty?'

'Not necessarily. I was just thinkin' the same thing myself.'

'I'm patient,' said Eve. Her blue eyes were fixed. 'I'm terribly, terribly patient. I can wait years for what I want. Bill's not making much money now, and I haven't got a bean. But Bill's got great talent under that easy-going manner of his. He *must* have the right girl to help him. If only . . .'

'If only the elfin sprite would let him alone. Hey?'

'Vicky acts like that,' said Eve, 'towards practically every man she ever meets. That's why she's never married. She says it leaves her soul free to commune with other souls. This occultism—'

Then it all poured out, the family story of the Adamses. This repressed girl spoke at length, spoke as perhaps she had never spoken before. Vicky Adams, the child who wanted to attract attention, her father, Uncle Fred, and her mother, Aunt Margaret, seemed to walk in vividness as the shadows gathered.

'I was too young to know her at the time of the "disappearance," of course. But, oh, I knew her afterwards! And I thought . . .'

'Well?'

'If I could get *you* here,' said Eve, 'I thought she'd try to show off with some game. And then you'd expose her. And Bill would see what an awful faker she is. But it's hopeless!'

'Looky here,' observed H.M., who was smoking his third cigar. He sat up. 'Doesn't it strike you those two are being a rummy-awful long time just in lookin' through a little bungalow?'

Eve roused out of a dream, stared back at him. She sprang to her feet. She was not now, you could guess, thinking of any disappearance.

'Excuse me a moment,' she said curtly.

Eve hurried across to the cottage, went up on the porch, and opened the front door. H.M. heard her heels rap down the length of the small passage inside. She marched straight back again, closed the front door, and rejoined H.M.

'All the doors of the rooms are shut,' she announced in a high voice. 'I really don't think I ought to disturb them.'

'Easy, my wench!'

'I have absolutely no interest,' declared Eve, with the tears coming into her eyes, 'in what happens to either of them now. Shall we take the car and go back to Town without them?'

H.M. threw away his cigar, got up, and seized her by the shoulders.

'I'm the old man,' he said, with a leer like an ogre. 'Will you listen to me?'

'No!'

'If I'm any reader of the human dial,' persisted H.M., 'that young fellar's no more gone on Vicky Adams than I am. He was scared, my wench. Scared.' Doubt, indecision crossed H.M.'s face. 'I dunno what he's scared of. Burn me, I don't! But . . .'

'Hoy!' called the voice of Bill Sage.

It did not come from the direction of the cottage.

They were surrounded on three sides by Goblin Wood, now blurred with twilight. From the north side the voice bawled at them, followed by crackling in dry undergrowth. Bill, his hair and sports coat and flannels more than a little dirty, regarded then with a face of bitterness.

'Here are her blasted wild strawberries,' he announced, extending his hand. 'Three of 'em. The fruitful (excuse me) result of three-quarters of an hour's hard labour. I absolutely refuse to chase 'em in the dark.'

For a moment Eve Drayton's mouth moved without speech.

'Then you weren't . . . in the cottage all this time?'

'In the cottage?' Bill glanced at it. 'I was in that cottage,' he said, 'about five minutes. Vicky had a woman's whim. She wanted some wild strawberries out of what she called the "forest." '

'Wait a minute, son!' said H.M. very sharply. 'You didn't come out of that front door. Nobody did.'

'No, I went out of the back door. It opens straight on to the wood.'

'Yes. And what happened then?'

'Well, I went to look for these damned . . .'

'No, no! What did *she* do?'

'Vicky? She locked and bolted the back door on the inside. I remember her grinning at me through the glass panel. She—'

Bill stopped short. His eyes widened, and then narrowed, as though at the impact of an idea. All three of them turned to look at the rough-stone cottage.

'By the way,' said Bill. He cleared his throat vigorously. 'By the way, have you seen Vicky since then?'

'No.'

'This couldn't be . . .?'

'It could be, son,' said H.M. 'We'd all better go in there and have a look.'

They hesitated for a moment on the porch. A warm moist fragrance breathed up from the ground after sunset. In half an hour it would be completely dark.

Bill Sage threw open the front door and shouted Vicky's name. That sound seemed to penetrate, reverberating, through every room. The intense heat and stuffiness of the cottage, where no window had been raised for months, blew out at them. But nobody answered.

'Get inside,' snapped H.M. 'And stop yowlin'.' The Old Maestro seemed nervous. 'I'm dead sure she didn't get out by the front door; but we'll just make certain there's no slippin out now.'

Stumbling over the table and chairs on the porch, he fastened the front door. They were in a narrow passage, once handsome with parquet floor and pine-panelled walls, leading to a door with a glass panel at the rear. H.M. lumbered forward to inspect this door and found it locked and bolted, as Bill had said.

Goblin Wood grew darker.

Keeping well together, they searched the cottage. It was not large, having two good-sized rooms on one side of the passage, and two small rooms on the other side, so as to make space for bathroom and kitchenette. H.M., raising fogs of dust, ransacked every inch where a person could possibly hide.

And all the windows were locked on the inside. And the chimney-flues were too narrow to admit anybody.

And Vicky Adams wasn't there.

'Oh, my eye!' breathed Sir Henry Merrivale.

They had gathered, by what idiotic impulse not even H.M. could have said, just outside the open door of the bathroom. A bath-tap dripped monotonously. The last light through a frosted-glass window showed three faces hung there as though disembodied.

'Bill,' said Eve in an unsteady voice, 'this is a trick. Oh, I longed for her to be exposed! This is a trick!'

'Then where is she?'

'Sir Henry can tell us! Can't you, Sir Henry?'

'Well . . . now,' muttered the great man.

Across H.M.'s Panama hat was a large black handprint, made there when he had pressed down the hat after investigating a chimney. He glowered under it.

'Son,' he said to Bill, 'there's just one question I want you to answer in all this hokey-pokey. When you went out pickin' wild strawberries, will you swear Vicky Adams didn't go with you?'

'As God is my judge, she didn't,' returned Bill, with fervency and obvious truth. 'Besides, how the devil could she? Look at the lock and bolt on the back door!'

H.M. made two more violent black handprints on his hat.

He lumbered forward, his head down, two or three paces in the narrow passage. His foot half-skidded on something that had been lying there unnoticed, and he picked it up. It was a large, square section of thin, waterproof oilskin, jagged at one corner.

'Have you found anything!' demanded Bill in a strained voice.

'No. Not to make any sense, that is. But just a minute!'

At the rear of the passage, on the left-hand side, was the bedroom from which Vicky Adams had vanished as a child. Though H.M. had searched this room once before, he opened the door again.

It was now almost dark in Goblin Wood.

He saw dimly a room of twenty years before: a room of flounces, of lace curtains, of once-polished mahogany, its mirrors glimmering against white papered walls. H.M. seemed especially interested in the windows.

He ran his hands carefully round the frame of each, even climbing laboriously up on a chair to examine the tops. He borrowed a box of matches from Bill; and the little spurts of light, following the rasp of the match, rasped against nerves as well. The hope died out of his face, and his companions saw it.

'Sir Henry,' Bill said for the dozenth time, 'where is she?'

'Son,' replied H.M. despondently, 'I don't know.'

'Let's get out of here,' Eve said abruptly. Her voice was a small scream. 'I kn-know it's all a trick! I know Vicky's a faker! But let's get out of here. For heaven's sake, let's get out of here!'

'As a matter of fact,' Bill cleared his throat, 'I agree. Anyway, we won't hear from Vicky until to-morrow morning.'

'*Oh yes, you will,*' whispered Vicky's voice out of the darkness.

Eve screamed.

They lighted a lamp.

But there was nobody there.

Their retreat from the cottage, it must be admitted, was not very dignified.

How they stumbled down that ragged lawn in the dark, how they piled rugs and picnic-hampers into the car, how they eventually found the main road again, is best left undescribed.

Sir Henry Merrivale has since sneered at this—'a bit of a goosey feeling; nothin' much'—and it is true that he has no nerves to speak of. But he can be worried, badly worried; and that he was worried on this occasion may be deduced from what happened later.

H.M., after dropping in at Claridge's for a modest late supper of lobster and *Peach Melba*, returned to his house in Brook Street and slept a hideous sleep. It was three o'clock in the morning, even before the summer dawn, when the ringing of the bedside telephone roused him.

What he heard sent his blood pressure soaring.

'Dear Sir Henry!' crooned a familiar and sprite-like voice.

H.M. was himself again, full of gall and bile. He switched on the bedside lamp and put on his spectacles with care, so as adequately to address the 'phone.

'Have I the honour,' he said with dangerous politeness, 'of addressin' Miss Vicky Adams?'

'Oh yes!'

'I sincerely trust,' said H.M., 'you've been havin' a good time? Are you materialized yet?'

'Oh yes!'

'Where are you now?'

'I'm afraid,' there was a coy laughter in the voice, 'that must be a little secret for a day or two. I want to teach you a really *good* lesson. Blessings, dear.'

And she hung up the receiver.

H.M. did not say anything. He climbed out of bed. He stalked up and down the room. Then, since he himself had been waked up at three o'clock in the morning, the obvious course was to wake up somebody else; so he dialled the home number of Chief Inspector Masters.

'No, sir,' retorted Masters grimly. 'I do *not* mind you ringing up. Not a bit of it!' He spoke with a certain pleasure. 'Because I've got a bit of news for you.'

H.M. eyed the 'phone suspiciously.

'Masters, are you trying to do me in the eye again? What's the news?'

'Do you remember mentioning the Vicky Adams case to me yesterday?'

'Sort of. Yes.'

'Oh, ah! Well, I had a word or two round among our people. I was tipped the wink to go and see a certain solicitor. He was old Mr. Fred Adams's solicitor before Mr. Adams died about six or seven years ago.' Here Masters's voice grew suave with triumph. 'I always said, Sir Henry, that Chuck Randall had planted some gadget in that cottage for a quick getaway. And I was right. The gadget was . . .'

'You were quite right Masters. The gadget was a trick window.'

The telephone, so to speak, gave a start. 'What's that?'

'A trick window,' H.M. spoke patiently. 'You press a spring. And the whole frame of the window, two leaves locked together, slides down between the walls far enough to let you climb over. Then you push it back up again.'

*'How in lum's name do you know that?'*

'Oh, my son! They used to build windows like it in the country houses during the persecution of Catholic priests. It was a good enough *second* guess. Only . . . it won't work.'

Masters seemed annoyed. 'It won't work now,' Masters agreed. 'And do you know why?'

'I can guess. Tell me.'

'Because, just before Mr. Adams died, he discovered how his darling daughter had flummoxed him. He never told anybody except his lawyer. He took a handful of four-inch nails, and sealed up the top of the frame so tight an orangoutang couldn't move it, and painted 'em over so they wouldn't be noticed.'

'Did he. You can notice 'em now.'

'I doubt if the young lady herself ever knew. But, by George,' Masters said savagely, 'I'd like to see anybody try the same game now!'

'You would, hey? Then will it interest you to know that the same gal has just disappeared out of the same house AGAIN?'

H.M. began a long narrative of the facts, but he had to break off because the telephone was raving.

'Honest, Masters,' H.M. said seriously, 'I'm not joking. She didn't get out through that window. But she did get out. You'd better meet me,' he gave directions, 'to-morrow morning. In the meantime, son, sleep well.'

It was, therefore, a worn-faced Masters who went into the Visitors' Room at the Senior Conservatives' Club just before lunch on the following day.

The Visitors' Room is a dark sepulchral place, opening on an air-well, where the visitor is surrounded by pictures of dyspeptic-looking gentlemen with beards. It has a pervading mustiness of wood and leather. Though whisky and soda stood on the table, H.M. sat in a leather chair far away from it, ruffling his hands across his bald head.

'Now, Masters, keep your shirt on!' he warned. 'This business may be rummy. But it's not a police matter yet.'

'I know it's not,' Masters said grimly. 'All the same, I've had a word with the Superintendent at Aylesbury.'

'Fowler?'

'You know him?'

'I know everybody. Is he goin' to keep an eye out?'

'He's going to have a look at that ruddy cottage. I've asked for any telephone calls to be put through here. In the meantime, sir—'

It was at this point, as though diabolically inspired, that the telephone was heard to ring. H.M. lumbered out and reached the telephone box before Masters.

'It's the old man,' he said, unconsciously assuming a stance of grandeur. 'Yes, yes! Masters is here, but he's drunk. You tell me first. What?'

The telephone talked thinly.

'Certainly I looked in the kitchen cupboard,' bellowed H.M. 'Though I didn't honestly expect to find Vicky Adams hidin' there. What's that? Plates? Cups that had been . . .'

An almost frightening change had come over H.M.'s expression. All the posturing went out of him. He was not even listening to the voice that still talked thinly, while his eyes and his brain moved to put together facts. At length (though the voice still talked) he hung up the receiver and blundered back to the Visitors' Room, where he drew out a chair and sat down.

'Masters,' he said very quietly, 'I've come close to makin' the silliest mistake of my life.'

Here he cleared his throat.

'I shouldn't have made it, son. I really shouldn't. But don't yell at me for cuttin' off Fowler. I can tell you now how Vicky Adams disappeared. And she said one true thing when she said she was going into a strange country.'

'How do you mean?'

'She's dead,' answered H.M.

The words fell with heavy weight into that dingy room, where the bearded faces looked down.

'Y'see,' H.M. went on, 'a lot of us were right when we thought Vicky Adams was a faker. She was. To attract attention to herself, she played that trick on her family with the hocussed window. She's lived and traded on it ever since. That's what sent me straight in the wrong direction. I was on the alert for some trick Vicky Adams might play. So it never occurred to me that this elegant pair of beauties, Miss Eve Drayton and Mr. William Sage, were deliberately conspirin' to murder *her*.'

Masters got slowly to his feet.

'Did you say . . . murder?'

'Oh yes. It was all arranged before-hand for me to witness. They knew Vicky Adams couldn't resist a challenge to disappear, especially as Vicky always believed she could get out by the trick window. They wanted Vicky to *say* she was goin' to disappear. They never knew anything about the trick window, Masters. But they knew their own plan very well.

'Eve Drayton even told me the motive. She hated Vicky, of course. But that wasn't the main point. She was Vicky Adams's only relative; she'd inherit an awful big scoopful of money. Eve said she could be patient. (And, burn me, how her eyes meant it when she said that!) Rather than risk any slightest suspicion of murder, she was willing to wait seven years until a disappearing person can be presumed dead.

'Our Eve, I think, was the fiery drivin' force of that conspiracy. She was only scared part of the time. Sage was scared all the time. But it was Sage who did the real dirty work. He lured Vicky Adams into that cottage, while Eve kept me in close conversation on the lawn . . .'

H.M. paused.

Intolerably vivid in the mind of Chief Inspector Masters, who had seen it years before, rose the picture of the rough-stone cottage against the darkling wood.

'Masters,' said H.M., 'why should a bath-tap be dripping in a house that hadn't been occupied for months?'

'Well?'

'Sage, y'see, is a surgeon. I saw him take his black case of instruments out of the car. He took Vicky Adams into that house. In the bathroom he stabbed her, he stripped her, and *he dismembered her body in the bath tub.*—Easy, son!'

'Go on,' said Masters.

'The head, the torso, the folded arms and legs were wrapped up in three large square pieces of thin transparent oilskin. Each was sewed up with coarse thread so the blood wouldn't drip. Last night I found one of the oilskin pieces he'd ruined when his needle slipped at the corner. Then he walked out of the house, with the back door still standin' unlocked, to get his wild strawberry alibi.'

'Sage went out of there,' shouted Masters, 'leaving the body in the house?'

'Oh yes,' agreed H.M.

'But where did he leave it?'

H.M. ignored this.

'In the meantime, son, what about Eve Drayton? At the end of the arranged three-quarters of an hour, she indicated there was hanky-panky between her *fiancé* and Vicky Adams. She flew into the house. And what did she do?

'She walked to the back of the passage. I heard her. *There she simply locked and bolted the back door.* And then she marched out to join me with tears in her eyes. And these two beauties were ready for investigation.'

'Investigation?' said Masters. '*With that body still in the house?*'

'Oh yes.'

Masters lifted both fists.

'It must have given young Sage a shock,' said H.M., 'when I found that piece of waterproof oilskin he'd washed but dropped. Anyway, these two had only two more bits of hokey-pokey. The "vanished" gal had to speak—to show she was still alive. If you'd been there, son, you'd have noticed that Eve Drayton's got a voice just like Vicky Adams's. If somebody speaks in a dark room, carefully imitating a coy tone she never uses herself, the illusion's goin' to be pretty good. The same goes for a telephone.

'It was finished, Masters. All that had to be done was to remove the body from the house and get it far away from there . . .'

'But that's just what I'm asking you, sir! Where was the body all this time? And who in blazes *did* remove the body from the house?'

'All of us did,' answered H.M.

'What's that?'

'Masters,' said H.M., 'aren't you forgettin' the picnic hampers?'

And now, the Chief Inspector saw, H.M. was as white as a ghost. His next words took Masters like a blow between the eyes.

'Three good-sized wickerwork hampers, with lids. After our big meal on the porch, those hampers were shoved inside the house where Sage could get at 'em. He had to leave most of the used crockery behind, in the kitchen cupboard. But three wickerwork hampers from a picnic, and three butcher's parcels to go inside 'em. I carried one down to the car myself. It felt a bit funny . . .'

H.M. stretched out his hand, not steadily, towards the whisky.

'Y'know,' he said, 'I'll always wonder whether I was carrying the—head.'

HAKE TALBOT

# The Other Side

*Astonishingly, Hake Talbot does not appear in any edition (thus far) of
20th Century Crime And Mystery Writers. To be sure, he published
only two novels and one short story that qualify, all in the 1940s—but I
can think of one or two (or more: come to think of it, many more) writers
who are featured in that monumental reference tome who don't deserve
to be included on four or even five times that output.*

*As my co-editor once remarked, Hake Talbot 'produced the only books
that challenged Carr on his own terms and earned a draw'. Those books
were* The Hangman's Handyman *(1942) and* Rim of the Pit *(1944).
Actually, if Talbot had only written* Rim of the Pit *he would still have
merited inclusion in* 20th Century, *for* Rim of the Pit *is an out-and-out,
no-holds-barred masterpiece. Not that* The Hangman's Handyman, *a
masterly mélange of hocus-pocus, intricate plotting, and brilliantly dabbed-
in touches of the macabre, is that far behind—but* Rim of the Pit, *which
features necromancy, flying creatures, ghostly voices and an Impossible
murder, is truly in a class of its own. In 1981 a panel of experts (plus
your two editors) judged it to be second only to Carr's* The Hollow Man
*(a.k.a.* The Three Coffins*) in a poll of Best Impossible Crimes.*

*Oddly, Talbot—whose real name was Henning Nelms—did not seem
to care for his extraordinary excursions into fiction, preferring his non-fiction
(what he called his 'serious writings'): books such as* Play Production
*(1950),* Scene Design *(1975), and (based on his love of conjuring)* Magic
And Showmanship *(1969). For many years he taught drama (mainly at
Pennsylvania State University) and was a professional director for amateur
theatres.*

*The short story presented here, 'The Other Side', is something of a coup
for* The Art of the Impossible, *since it was never sold commercially during
Talbot's lifetime and has only ever appeared in print once, in Swedish,
to fill out the last few pages of a Swedish reprint of* Rim of the Pit. *Talbot
wrote other short stories, all featuring his professional gambler and ex-
convict (two years in Sing Sing) detective Rogan Kincaid, but all, save
'The Other Side', remained unsold and were either destroyed by their author
or simply disappeared (a fate also reserved, horrifyingly, for an entire novel,*
The Affair of the Half-Witness*). The mouth-watering possibility that
there may be other Kincaid manuscripts in existence should have all true
Impossible Crime enthusiasts hurrying to Arlington, VA, where Talbot
died (in 1986), and ransacking every attic in town—for those manuscripts,*

*should they still exist, might well feature Talbot's other detective, the wonderful, and wonderfully sinister, Svetozar Vok, who triumphed in* Rim of the Pit. *And triumphs here.*

JACK ADRIAN

---

Six shots rang out. Svetozar Vok peered at the target at the far end of the shooting gallery and lowered his revolver with a sigh.

'It is no use, my friend. I take careful aim; you point a pistol as a man points his finger; yet you always win. I lack the Kincaid touch.'

Rogan Kincaid laughed. 'Why not apply a touch of your own? A professional magician like you should be able to use a little magic in his target practice.'

'I am working on that,' Vok replied with perfect gravity. 'Already I have a bullet in my dressing-room whom I am training to shoot round corners.' He glanced at his wrist. 'I must be getting back to him. In forty-five minutes it will be time for my afternoon show.'

A coin appeared from nowhere between his bony fingers. He tossed it on the counter and started for the door, speaking over his shoulder to Kincaid.

'If you do not find someone foolish enough to play poker with you before 6:30, pick me up at the theatre and I will buy you dinner.'

The magician pushed open the door and held it while a girl entered with two men. She looked barely sixteen. Her nimbus of pale gold hair and her rose-leaf complexion might have proclaimed her a princess out of fairyland had it not been for her two escorts. They were elderly military men in mufti—one tall and portly, the other short and merely fat. The two men labelled the girl. She was, Mr. Kincaid decided, no fairy princess.

As the girl passed Vok she turned back to stare at him. That was to be expected. His gaunt height and his mummy's face took the eye. But there was more to this girl's interest. When the door closed behind him, she seized the arms of her companions and began whispering excitedly. Although Kincaid caught no word, the pantomime of the little group was perfectly clear. The girl had formed some belief about Vok, and the two men were assuring her that she was mistaken.

Then, as the girl turned from one of her escorts to the other, her eyes met Kincaid's. She broke off in the middle of a word—and blushed.

If she had suddenly put forth wings, she could not have surprised him more. He had been smugly sure of her classification as a bit of dainty bric-a-brac. Before he had time to revise his opinion, she mumbled something to the men with her and fled.

They turned, saw Kincaid watching her and started to frown. Then the prominent blue eyes of the larger man lit with recognition.

'Good Lord, aren't you Rogan Kincaid? I'm Colonel Boyd Lathrop. Played poker with you in Shanghai before the war.'

Kincaid, who now recognized Colonel Lathrop as a man from whom he'd taken some three hundred dollars in two hours of play, politely expressed the hope that the colonel would soon find time to give him his 'revenge'.

Colonel Lathrop was flattered by the suggestion that he had been the victor in Shanghai and promised vaguely that he would try to arrange a game. He introduced the shorter man as his brother, Major Clifford Lathrop. 'I'm . . . ah . . . sorry our niece, Daphne, was unable to remain, but . . .'

The gambler was now prepared to accept the relationship. Daphne's blush proved it.

'She's heard stories,' the major put in, 'about these fool religious cults. California's full of 'em. Took the skinny man for some sort of high priest.'

He seemed to lose the thread of his thought. With a mumbled leave-taking the two harmless old soldiers drifted to the counter. There they opened a walnut box, which the major carried, and produced a set of matched target pistols. These they proceeded to shoot with fair accuracy but with impractical deliberation.

Kincaid decided that he could best promote his poker game by biding his time. So while his prospective victims fired at targets, he discussed a case of war trophies with the attendant.

'The Walther P38's the gun, though,' said that worthy. 'Best thing the Heinies made. You ought to see one of them. I sold mine to your friend Colonel Lathrop. He'd be glad to show it to you, wouldn't you, Colonel?'

That gave Kincaid all the opening he needed. Ten minutes later he was in a taxi between the two brothers.

In the cab they seemed ill at ease. They could ignore Kincaid as a casual acquaintance, but now that he was their guest, they felt called upon to explain their niece's interest in Vok.

'It was not mere idle curiosity, I can assure you,' said the colonel. 'You see, Daphne has . . . ah . . . heard something about a cult leader named Ergon.'

'Picked the skinny fellow as the right type,' added the major. 'Thought he was Ergon. Wasn't, of course. Told her so.'

Daphne's mistake was, Colonel Lathrop declared, quite natural. Of course the man she had seen at the shooting gallery was not the cult leader but . . .

'Might have been, though,' the major put in. 'Weird-looking devil.'

Colonel Lathrop smiled apology for his brother's tactlessness and continued hastily. 'Neither is there anything strange about the child's interest in this Ergon. After all, she worshipped her aunt.'

The gambler began to find his companions amusing. They were almost pitifully anxious to keep their family affairs private, but they seemed to feel that their niece's conduct demanded an explanation. In their efforts to provide it they floundered from one revelation to another.

By the end of the ride Kincaid had learned that Daphne had been orphaned in babyhood and brought up by her aunt and guardian, Miss Imogene Lathrop. The brothers were also guardians but only by courtesy. In fact Daphne's father had placed so little reliance on them that he had given Miss Lathrop power to name her own successor in her will.

When the girl reached sixteen, she had been left in an eastern school while the elder Lathrops wintered in California. There Imogene had met Ergon, who had an apartment in the next building. To her brother's amazement, the previously level-headed Imogene had fallen immediately under Ergon's spell and gone to live at a temple he maintained on the borders of Hollywood. Three months later she was dead, but not until she had made a will appointing Ergon as guardian in her place and instructing her brothers to obey him without question.

Daphne had flown in for the funeral, but her uncles, alarmed at the idea of her meeting Ergon, had managed to have it held some hours before she arrived. Now they encouraged her to spend her time with friends and away from their apartment. They seemed to hope that they might get her back east without letting her come into connection with Ergon at all.

There was no doubt that they considered their apartment the danger zone, not only for Daphne but for themselves. As the cab drew near it, they grew more apprehensive. Kincaid wondered if they expected to find their enemy waiting on the front steps.

That was exactly where they did find him. The brothers paid off the taxi and started up the walk, marching close together as though it took all their courage to go in front instead of shielding themselves behind Kincaid. The gambler was inclined to be contemptuous until he drew close enough to see Ergon's eyes.

Kincaid had expected the usual unctuous fraud, but this man looked like an apostate angel. His great mane of pale hair exactly matched the unbleached linen of his robe. The face was a mask cast in bronze, but the eyes were like living things. They were enormous and so dark that pupil and iris blended into one. Kincaid found them drawing his attention like a magnet.

Ergon stood motionless until the three were within six feet of him. Then he spoke one word, like a single stroke of a great bell.

'Come!'

Without waiting for an answer, he turned and led the way to the elevator. The Lathrop apartment was on the second floor. Ergon led the way across a small hall and into the luxurious living room, where he took up his position on the hearth. The brothers followed like men going under fire. Colonel Lathrop shifted from one foot to the other. Then in a gesture of defiance he marched to a small table that stood under a light bracket beside the mantel and placed his case of pistols squarely in the centre of it. With an almost military about-face he returned to stand beside his brother.

Ergon spoke. 'We must be alone.'

Major Lathrop glanced unhappily at Kincaid. 'Damn it all,' he protested to Ergon. 'This man's our guest.'

'We must be alone.'

Kincaid offered to leave, but the brothers refused to hear of such a thing. Finally they compromised by suggesting that he wait in their bedroom and examine their collection of firearms until they were free.

If Ergon believed that banishing Kincaid to the bedroom would insure secrecy, he was mistaken. The apartment was impressive to the eye, but of such flimsy construction that every word came through one wall.

'I have come,' Ergon announced, 'as guardian of the child Daphne. I have communed with the Forces. It is their decision that she shall be dedicated to the Temple.'

The brothers were aghast. Ergon's plan was worse than anything they had imagined. Indignantly they refused. They also were Daphne's guardians. Their consent would be necessary to such a thing and they would not give it.

The great bell of Ergon's voice took on a tone of sadness. Daphne's dedication was the decision of the Forces. The two men might not share their sister's enlightenment, but surely they would regard the directions in her will as a sacred trust.

Major Lathrop assured him that they regarded Daphne herself as a damn sight more sacred trust.

The last shreds of the colonel's poise deserted him. He broke into an incoherent tirade from which Kincaid gathered only that the colonel believed Ergon was scheming to gain control of the fortune left Daphne by her father.

Ergon's reply was scornful. A servant of the Forces had no need of money, and no more temptation to steal it than a man had to steal the playthings of a child.

Apparently the contempt in Ergon's tone stung the colonel, for Kincaid heard him step forward angrily. The step was followed by a long pause as if a battle of wills was being fought out in the next room. Then the colonel's feet shuffled on the carpet and Ergon spoke softly.

'I am glad you were able to conquer yourself. All truth is one. In your own sacred book it is written that he who lives by the sword must die by the sword. You were about to threaten me, but I tell you that he who voices a threat against a servant of the Forces shall himself suffer what he threatens.'

The colonel took his courage in both hands. 'I don't care what happens to me, but I do care what happens to Daphne. I'm on the retired list and not much good for anything, but I can still knock the pips out of a playing card at twenty yards. If any harm comes to Daphne through you, I am going to take one of those guns on the table and shoot you dead.'

'Oh blind, and worse than blind!' The magnificent voice struck a note of infinite pity. 'You have spoken your doom. Unless I can intercede for you, you will die by your own hand.'

With that warning he left them. Kincaid could not hear his footsteps, but the click of the latch as the outer door opened and closed told that he had gone, and the rattle of glassware announced that the brothers had turned to the decanter for comfort.

When they joined Kincaid in the bedroom they were still frightened and still defiant. They glanced apprehensively at the wall opposite the door. The gambler followed their gaze but saw nothing. Then a bronze gong spoke from behind the wall and Ergon's great voice echoed it. Each syllable was a separate bell note as if he were chanting in some forgotten tongue.

'*Lerd ferbeh mahgaad*!'

Major Lathrop mopped his bald head. 'Fellow lives next door. Whole row of apartments is one long building really. Only partitions between. Hear every word he says.' The major chose one of the pistols and made a brave effort to explain its merits.

The strange words had an even more disquieting effect on his brother. The colonel moved restlessly from one gun to another, picking each up and laying it down almost by an effort of will.

The chant went on and on, each syllable beautifully distinct, and always returning to the same refrain.

'*Lerd ferbeh mahgaad!*'

The major turned to stare at the wall. 'Intercession be damned! Sounds more like a curse.'

Colonel Lathrop sat down beside Kincaid. The fingers of his right hand closed around the butt of a revolver and his left moved toward the box of cartridges lying beside it. The gambler picked up the box and began tossing it idly in the air. For a moment the colonel seemed fascinated by the movement and the little click the cartridges made as the box fell in Kincaid's hand. Slowly Ergon's chant died away. Colonel Lathrop appeared to come out of his daze.

'You should see our target pistols. I left them in the living room.' He rose and passed through the door. The man seemed shrunken inside his clothes. All his pompousness had gone.

Afterward Kincaid was to remember the situation in detail. He followed the departing colonel with his eyes and sat staring across the tiny hall at the lock on the outside door.

Colonel Lathrop's footsteps crossed to the table near the fireplace. There was a moment's pause—followed by the bark of a pistol.

Kincaid's reflexes carried him into the living room. He was through the doorway before Colonel Lathrop's body thudded on the carpet. Major Lathrop pushed past the gambler and knelt to feel his brother's wrist, but it was a meaningless gesture. The wound above the colonel's eye already told the story.

The major rose and shook himself like a dog coming out of water. 'By God, I don't believe it. Boyd wouldn't have shot himself, not for all the damn chants in the world! Besides, where's the gun?'

'Under the edge of the sofa.' Kincaid pointed. 'Don't touch it. The police will want to examine it for fingerprints.'

'Mine are on it anyway. It's one we shot with this afternoon. Do you mind calling the police? I'd like to stay here with Boyd.'

The telephone was in the hall. Kincaid dialled Headquarters and asked for Lieutenant Nichols, whom he knew to be shrewd and energetic and who had already learned the futility of trying conclusions with Rogan Kincaid.

While the gambler waited, someone rapped on the door. When it was opened Ergon stalked past without speaking and entered the living room.

The major saw him and began to curse with heartfelt intensity.

Ergon interrupted him. 'Profanity in the presence of your dead brother is impious.'

'Damn you, you killed him!'

'No. He killed himself. I do not mean with the pistol. That was merely the means. His threat against me was the cause. I tried to intercede for him but it was hopeless.'

'And now you've come to gloat.'

'I have come to take the child Daphne to the Temple.'

'I'll see you in hell first!'

'Resistance to the will of the Forces is vain. They will brush you aside as they did your brother. Then, as Daphne's sole guardian, I shall be free under human law to carry out the will of my Masters.'

The phone squawked in the gambler's ear. 'Lieutenant Nichols speaking.'

'Hello, Al. This is Rogan Kincaid. I have a homicide for . . . No, I had no motive. Besides, I have an alibi. Unfortunately the man responsible has one too, so if there's anybody down there with brains, bring him along.'

'Ergon must have known I could hear him,' Kincaid argued to Lieutenant Nichols an hour later. 'If a man's really planning to kill someone, he doesn't usually talk about it in front of witnesses.'

'That part's easy enough,' Nichols replied. 'If this Ergon had a way to murder the colonel and get away with it, he *wanted* witnesses. That would give him the sweetest racket on earth. Daphne and her money would be chicken feed. He could go around to rich guys and say, "Shell out or I'll put the Indian sign on you like I did on Colonel Lathrop." With a threat like that he'd rake in money faster than the boys from the IRS could take it away from him.'

The lieutenant ran his fingers through his thick black hair. 'On the other hand, if this Ergon did bump the colonel, how did he do it? You were watching the hall, the windows were latched and the screens were stuck to the paint.'

'What about the fireplace?'

'It's just a fireplace. We tested every brick. Unless we can figure a way Ergon shot the old boy, it's suicide.'

'Why should he kill himself? Even colonels don't do things without a reason.'

'I'm not a mind-reader. That's your speciality.' Nichols rose. 'We're taking Ergon and the major down to headquarters for further questioning. I don't suppose you'd like to come along?'

'No. Daphne Lathrop will be home soon, and someone a little less heavy-footed than your harness bulls should be here to break the news.'

The lieutenant cocked his head on one side. 'I bet she's pretty.'

'Very, but only sixteen. Besides, seduction in Hollywood is carrying coals to Newcastle.'

'Don't tell me you've turned Galahad.'

'No, but I keep strict accounts. I misjudged her once. I owe her something for that.'

At 6:30 Nichols lifted the phone in his office, recognized Kincaid's voice and asked, 'How's Daphne?'

'Safe. I sent her to stay with friends, but she still needs her Uncle Clifford. If we don't provide Ergon with a berth in the gas-chamber, Cliff will put a bullet through that bald head of his one fine day and the girl will wind up in Ergon's Temple.'

'You're tearing my heart out, but it's no dice, friend. The laboratory evidence is in. Ergon didn't shoot Colonel Lathrop.'

'You don't doubt he's responsible for the colonel's death, do you?'

'How could he be?'

'I'll tell you how—if you have your men take him to his apartment. You bring Major Lathrop with you and pick me up in front of the Public Library at seven sharp.'

'The Public Library!'

'That's right—and bring a police stenographer so he can take down a confession.'

The phone clicked in Nichols' ear.

The watch on the lieutenant's wrist stood at one minute to seven as the big police car rolled to a stop in front of the Public Library. Kincaid greeted Nichols and Major Lathrop and introduced the man standing beside him on the curb.

'This is Svetozar Vok. He's doing a magic act at the Paramount and he has another show to play tonight so tell your driver not to dawdle.'

As the car roared away, the Lieutenant turned to Vok.

'I saw your show and it's good, but if Kincaid brought you to look for hanky-panky in this case, he's wasting your time. The colonel used the gun this afternoon and his prints would be on it anyway, so we can't actually prove he shot himself. What we can prove is that he was alone in the room and nobody else could've got in or out. The gun was beside him, and the bullet was fired from that gun. What's more, three people saw Ergon come out of his own apartment within half a minute after they heard the shot. That gives him a holeproof alibi, so there isn't any trick for you to find.'

'Mr. Kincaid did not seek my aid as conjuror,' said Vok, 'but as hypnotist.'

'Hypnotist? What the hell's that got to do with it?'

'Perhaps everything. Mr. Kincaid and I have made discovery about this Ergon. When he left the Lathrop apartment this afternoon he promised to "intercede with the Forces" in an effort to preserve the colonel's life. However, the chant which he actually made was not an intercession but rather an incantation—something in the nature of a curse.'

Major Lathrop nodded. 'Said so myself.'

'Your instinct was right, but we have proof. Kincaid has a keen ear for sound and he remembered the refrain. I recognized it as '*Lödd fobe magad!*', which is Hungarian for "You will blow out your brains!" I myself am Czech, but I speak Hungarian, and that also may be important.'

'None of it's important to me,' said Nichols. 'This Ergon sure as hell didn't kill the colonel with any Hungarian curse.'

'Of course not. The words merely show that Ergon lied and that his intentions were evil. His talk of the "the Forces" and "intercession" was a blind. I suggest that what he actually did was to hypnotize the colonel and force him to shoot himself.'

'Baloney! You can't hypnotize a guy into shooting anybody else, let alone himself. Everybody knows that.'

'Everybody except the men who know something about hypnosis.' Vok produced a slim volume and handed it to the lieutenant. 'I borrowed that for you at the library. Read it when you have time. It is by a professor at the college of Cornell named Esterbrook. In it he makes clear that it is impossible to know whether a hypnotized subject will commit a crime unless you actually have him commit a real one. Naturally no students of hypnosis will take that responsibility.'

'You could load a gun with blanks and . . .'

'Then it would cease to be a real crime, and the subject would be aware of that fact. Our friend Kincaid is an expert at reading men's minds from tiny clues which most men do not notice, but even Kincaid is a novice at that compared with the most stupid hypnotic subject. What the hypnotist knows, the subject may know, so experiments with mock crimes are meaningless. We shall not be certain whether a man can be forced to commit a real crime by hypnotism until someone actually uses a real crime for experiment.'

'And you think Ergon's done it?'

'What other explanation is there?'

'I don't know, but hell, even if you're right, we'd never get an indictment.'

'We may, if we approach the matter properly. I myself am not without hypnotic experience. I propose to match my power against Ergon's and force him to confess his guilt.'

'What good'll that do? If you mesmerize a guy into confessing, it won't stand up in court any more than if you beat it out of him with a rubber hose.'

The lieutenant was still arguing when the car pulled up before the row of apartment buildings, but Kincaid silenced him. 'Come on, Al. You can't be any worse off than you are now, and at least Vok will find out the facts.'

When the elevator left them on the second floor, Vok turned to Nichols. 'This Ergon is evidently an experienced hypnotist—stronger than I, it may be. If I am to succeed I must gain at the outset the advantage. You four shall go first and leave the door open. I will come suddenly and address him in Hungarian. He will not expect that. It may throw him off balance. Then perhaps I can force him to confess in English.'

'Suppose you miss?'

'Then, my friend, you will have to use every means in your power to prevent me killing myself. For rest assured, Ergon will try to force me to do so.'

They traversed the corridor on tiptoe, not quite knowing why.

Nichols rapped on the door. When one of the two policeman set to watch Ergon responded, Vok stepped back and the others filed into the apartment.

The living room was identical to the one in the Lathrop apartment but reversed as in a mirror. Even the light brackets on either side of the mantel were duplicated. However, this room contained neither furniture nor pictures, only a carpet of coarse matting which reached from wall to wall. Ergon sat cross-legged before the fireplace, his linen robe breaking in stiff folds and his hands hidden in his wide sleeves. The eyes in the motionless face were wide open but they stared straight ahead without even a glance at the newcomers.

'Csirkefogo!' Suddenly Vok was in the room. The Hungarian caught Ergon unawares. His eyes flicked upward and in that moment Vok was standing before him with bony hands outstretched.

'Gazember!' Ergon rose to his feet as if lifted by an unseen power. The great bell notes of his voice boomed out with calm dignity.

The man radiated power. Lieutenant Nichols had to dig his fingernails into the palms of his hands to keep them from trembling.

He was certain that Vok was beaten, and if he were, God alone knew what would happen to the rest of them.

For a full minute Czech and Hungarian stood face to face. Vok took full advantage of his great height, but he lacked the other's calm, and now that Ergon had recovered his poise Vok's words seemed to have no more effect than a dust storm might have upon the great pyramid.

Nichols' hands grew wet, but whether from perspiration or from blood drawn by his nails he did not know, nor could he take his eyes from the strange duel in the centre of the room for long enough to find out.

Neither of the antagonists moved, but if they had blasted each other with machine-guns the strain on the watchers could hardly have been greater. Little by little Ergon appeared to gain the upper hand. His voice became richer and more confident while Vok's showed a tendency to waver. Nichols expected the Czech to break at any moment. Then suddenly Vok said something in a new tone, and his long arm pointed to the wall behind the other man. Ergon's poise cracked and he stole a quick glance over his shoulder in the direction indicated by the magician's outstretched hand. Vok laughed in triumph and spoke three more words in measured accents like a man driving nails into a coffin.

The result was a kind of satanic miracle. Ergon's face changed for the first time, but it was merely a new expression. The bronze features seemed to run together as though melted in a crucible. The power that supported him had left him, and he seemed to collapse before their eyes.

Vok turned his back scornfully on Ergon, and spoke in English.

'You may take this despoiler of orphans and destroy him, Lieutenant. He killed Colonel Lathrop.'

'You mean he hypnotized him?'

'Not he. He is a poor fraud with no power—only effrontery. This afternoon he insisted that Mr. Kincaid leave the room. The box of matched target-pistols which the brothers shot every day was on a table beside the fireplace. Ergon took two of these pistols. One he kept, the other he placed on the floor out of sight in the shadows under the edge of the couch.'

'With the colonel and the major both looking at him?'

Vok smiled. 'My friend, I do a hundred more difficult things every day with a thousand people looking at me, and I do not wear a loose robe under which anything may be hidden, nor do I conceal my hands like this poor fraud who wore gloves so that he would not mar the colonel's prints on the revolvers. The gun he left on the floor served only as a dummy. He knew Mr. Kincaid and Major Lathrop would not touch it before the police arrived. The other gun he brought here, to his own apartment where he used it to shoot the colonel. Afterwards he went back to the Lathrop apartment, put the gun with which he had murdered the colonel on the floor, and returned the gun he had used as a dummy to its box.'

Nichols exploded. 'Are you trying to tell me Ergon shot Colonel Lathrop from this apartment?'

'Precisely.'

'Sure, right through the wall without leaving a hole.'

'That is true. He shot through the wall and he left no hole. Do you see that light fixture to the right of the fireplace? There is another just opposite it in the Lathrop apartment, and the walls are thin. Ergon could remove the one on this side at will, and it would be easy to rig the other so that it could be swung out of the way to leave a hole large enough for a pistol barrel to pass through—a barrel whose muzzle was less than a foot from the forehead of Colonel Lathrop as he bent to pick up his walnut box from the table by the fireplace.'

While Vok talked, Ergon had been gathering himself together. Now, without warning, he launched himself at the magician's throat.

Rogan and the two policemen caught him. In his rage he seemed hardly to notice them, but strained forward, cursing Vok in gutter English and convicting himself with every word, while the police stenographer's flying fingers raced to keep pace with him.

When Ergon stopped from sheer weariness, Vok stepped back and gestured to Nichols.

'There is your man, Lieutenant—confession and all.'

'I told you the confession was no good if he's hypnotized.'

'Oh, he's not—merely hysterical. Mr. Kincaid saw through Ergon's murder trick at once. However, Kincaid was afraid there would not be any positive evidence, so he brought me in to see if I could not draw our friend out.'

Nichols stared. 'You mean you didn't mesmerize him? That was just a gag?'

'Exactly. We wanted you and your men to play your parts well and we could not rely on your acting ability.' Vok smiled. 'You see, Lieutenant, a confession obtained by either hypnotism or the third degree would be thrown out of court, but there is no law against using showmanship.'

VINCENT CORNIER

# The Courtyard of the Fly

*Vincent Cornier (1898-1976) clearly had a most unusual mind. Something of a polymath, he threw all kinds of arcane knowledge into his fiction— mainly written for British magazines of the 1920s and 1930s—and tended to produce stories that verged on the strange, the bizarre, the outré, sometimes straying over into sheer fantasy.*

*A Yorkshireman by birth (though manifestly not by inclination, Yorkshiremen being famously a hard-headed and down-to-earth breed, not given to extravagant flights of fancy), he had a lively youth. Gassed in the First World War after spending ten months in France, he was discharged from the BEF but then re-enlisted in the RAF in 1918. A short period in Ireland just prior to the main Troubles was followed by four years prowling round Middle Europe and the Near East reporting for the Press Association on the various post-War political and military upheavals, including the bloody riots in Vienna (where he attended the university) and the failed attempt of ex-Emperor Karl of Austria to regain his throne.*

*Yet although he sometimes wrote of Secret Service work his stories were surprisingly un-action-oriented, Cornier preferring pure puzzles to physical conflict and the harsh clamour of automatic weaponry. And what puzzles! In 'The Shot That Waited' a man is shot by a 200-years old bullet coming from nowhere; in the breathtaking 'Dust of Lions' spontaneous combustion occurs simultaneously in Transylvania, at the North Pole, and in a secluded London Square, and is, moreover, explained away effortlessly.*

*Sometimes Cornier relied on perfectly fair general knowledge. In a story I stumbled across, 'The Million Water', the explanation of the impossibility depends on knowing a simple geographical fact of the kind printed on the backs of match-boxes or (for those whose memories stretch back that far) at the tops of most pages in the* Wizard, Rover *and* Adventure. *On other occasions—as Cornier authority Dr Stephen Leadbeatter has pointed out— there is a strong suspicion that imagination supplied an answer where dull reality has failed to come up with the goods.*

*In the 1940s Ellery Queen discovered Cornier and printed a number of his stories, some old, some new. Then he faded into obscurity. A volume of his dazzling tales is long overdue.*

JACK ADRIAN

Some thirty-seven years ago, when the pages of the *Almanac de Gotha* were slim passports to the narrowest society civilization has yet produced, a cartouche with the word 'Labordien' appeared within its yellow backing. Around and about the name were seven royal escutcheons. None of your 'by appointment to—'; not even the indiscretion of an address.

Those were unnecessary. Everyone knew that Henri Labordien was a master-artist in the craft of pearl mounting. Henri Labordien and pearls were not to be thought of apart. Nations, through their rulers, trusted him with awesome treasures; and trust continued until that night which was marked by the appearance of the fly and the subsequent loss of a Russian Grand Duchess's rope of superbly matched pearls.

The fly (according to Henri Labordien and Tobias Lockwood, the only other man to see it) was a black and orange monstrosity as large as a mouse. It darted with a rapidity that was swifter than the bolt of a swallow. It hissed.

Oh, yes, it hissed—a tremulous and poignant sound like a horny finger slashed across silk. Henri Labordien heard the noise coming to him; Tobias Lockwood had heard it going away, yet each agreed that this was its nature.

Now here was a fly that was unlike one's ordinary experience of flies, in appearance and faculty. The police, investigating the mystery of the vanished Russian treasure, paid a great deal of attention to it. One of their company, a constable called Hamilton—afterwards destined to become Superintendent Hamilton of the C.I.D.—went so far as to roughen his finger-tips with pumice and to draw them, a hundred times, over silken fabric, until his ears were educated to the sound these other men had heard.

What he could not experiment with was any known species of the insect world capable of clawing up a rope of pearls weighing a quarter of a pound and flying away with it.

According to Henri Labordien and Tobias Lockwood, that was what this fly had done.

Labordien had been sitting at his bench by an open window in his riverside house—the June evening was glowering and sultry with impending storm—when out of the sombre twilight the big fly darted into his workroom. He heard it hiss past him and turned to follow its flight. Before he could take the jewellers' eyeglass from his right eye, the fantastic insect went out again into the open air. Somewhat startled, Labordien got to his feet and picked up a welt of leather in order to crush the thing if it came back. It was loathsome and it looked deadly, as though it carried venom. In his opinion it was a phenomenon hatched from some cargo of sub-tropical fruit—bananas or such—carried by the Thames barges that were always passing this suburb of London. That was, of course, his later and considered opinion. At the moment of reaching out for the piece of leather he had no time for ordered thought.

Even as his hand touched the sheepskin, the big fly came back. This time it alighted on the long string of pearls laid upon his workbench. For a second or so it quivered, then it rose and went out of the window for the last time. The Dmitrioevitsch pearls went with it, and the world-famous Henri Labordien was ruined.

Stuttering with astonishment, shaking his head, he saw the glitter of the gems and the sullen mass of the great fly going into evening space. Among some plane trees, at the end of his courtyard, fringing the narrow road before the river embankment, fly and necklace disappeared.

He could not lean out of the window at once, since the littered expanse of the bench prevented him; but after a moment, when he had swept aside his tools and cabinets and gold and soldering-plant, he clambered up and shrieked for aid. So urgent was his call that half a dozen people were thronging his little courtyard in a matter of two to three minutes. Among them were his next-door neighbour Colonel Brough, the constable Hamilton, and Tobias Lockwood—a shabby and pallid-faced man who clawed at P.C. Hamilton even as that officer came towards the door.

To a heterogeneous crowd, then, Henri Labordien told of his loss. Therein lay his greatest mistake. It might have been possible, had his tale not been given such publicity, for him to carry on with his craft for years to follow. The affair might have been hushed up. Peculiarly enough, Labordien's story was corroborated by this out-of-work clerk, Tobias Lockwood. After P.C. Hamilton had cleared the courtyard of all save Labordien, Colonel Brough, Lockwood and himself, he listened to a second narrative of the hideous fly.

It appeared that Lockwood was sauntering along the embankment, beneath the gently stirring planes, when a rattle on the pavement attracted his attention. To his amazement he looked down to see a lane of shimmering jewels—undoubtedly the lost pearls—almost at his feet. For a time all conscious action ebbed from Lockwood's body. He simply halted, petrified with astonishment, and gaped at the fortune. Before he could find it in himself to pick up the necklace, the fly was in the air again. Straight for his face it came.

*　　*　　*

It stung him. Lockwood showed P.C. Hamilton the bleeding little wound in his ear where the thing had attacked him. The fly had stung and, while its victim had danced with the sudden agony of that sting, the insect alighted on the pearls. A momentary quivering, then again the monstrous creature took itself into the air, carrying the pearls.

Which way had it gone? Towards the river or along the embankment? Tobias Lockwood could not tell. Hadn't he enough to put up with, him with his stung ear, without watching the damned thing?

P.C. Hamilton, Colonel Brough—a frankly suspicious and guffawing sceptic—and the distracted Labordien listened to Lockwood with growing amazement. The colonel bluntly grunted that the proper place to harken to Lockwood's fat-headed tale was in the local police charge-room. Whereat P.C. Hamilton looked up from his notebook and asked the dapper military officer if by any chance he also doubted Mr. Labordien's story. To that question Colonel Brough had no answer.

All was entered up and all was done that could be done, but the pearls were never traced nor the mystery cleared up in its slightest facet.

The twentieth century dawned. The colonel moved from the house next door to Labordien and the stricken little jewel expert was left without any old friend at hand. Since his grotesque story about the fly was never accounted anything but a ridiculous camouflage for his own appropriation of the forty-thousand-guinea necklace (Lockwood's corroboration was conveniently treated as the yarning of a well-paid accomplice) Labordien found every door closed against him. In the place of his former fame he had the friendship of P.C. Hamilton.

The solid young man never rested from his task of attempting to solve the wild mystery. On duty and off duty, he was a constant caller at Labordien's lonely house. Gradually a friendship sprang up between the men—growing as the years grew, throughout the War—until Superintendent Hamilton's retirement.

It was nearly thirty-seven years later—Labordien was now old and bald and very gentle in his ways; Hamilton a sturdy and iron-grey man inclined to excessive fatness—when the fly once again came across the courtyard from the direction of the river.

Labordien's workroom had long been converted to a sort of study—a bookish place with a Whistleresque view of the bending river. As of old, the window facing the courtyard and the plane trees was wide open. And, as of old, the night was in June—sultry and overcast by massing thunder-clouds.

Labordien dropped the book he had been reading. Every vestige of colour went out of his face. He could not mistake that curiously abrupt hissing; no more could he deny his eyes their certitude that they had looked on the grisly insect once more. Trembling and suddenly terrified, he got up out of his chair.

'All right, Henri,' a hearty voice boomed up to him from some place not discoverable. 'Don't you get alarmed. It's only Hamilton, you know.'

'*Hamilton!* Where—where are you? What are you doing? That fly— that beastly thing's been in here!'

'I know that.' Still the voice came from the courtyard, but there was no sighting the speaker. 'I sent it.'

The jocular tone faded and an earnest ring came into Hamilton's voice.

'Be careful, Henri. Stand to one side, well away from the window, and put your spectacles on the table. Turn 'em broadside on, facing the river, and keep back.'

Mechanically, Henri Labordien did as he was bidden to do.

The silken hiss sounded quite distinctly. A big orange and black fly rushed through the opening. Lightly it fell—across the spectacles. For a second it hovered and was still, then it darted like a coloured bolt from the room. The spectacles went with it.

Weakly, Labordien sat down and covered his face with his hands. Whatever Hamilton's devilry was, it was too violently akin to the experience of years ago for comfort.

Without his glasses he could not see very clearly, but he could hear a lot of rustling of leaves from the plane trees. Then a rough and guttural coughing, as of a man clearing his throat from dust. After that, steps which he recognized as those of Hamilton came across the courtyard and to the lower door. Without ceremony Hamilton clumped in and rapidly mounted the stairs. There was a rattle on the table and a laugh.

'There are your specks, Henri! Sorry I risked 'em. But now our old friend Brough is nicely settled in chokey with a few years penal staring him in the face, hang him!'

'*Brough*—you mean, Colonel Brough?'

'That's the gentleman! Got him at last. He stole those pearls, you know. I was always dead certain of it, but never could get proof. That's the charge . . . half a lifetime old, but none the less certain.'

'Brough stole—stole those pearls?' Old Labordien was pitifully shaken. He gulped his drink and blinked. 'Am I still in command of my senses?'

'You are! Listen, Henri, don't talk.' The ex-superintendent rubbed his big hands together jubilantly. 'The mystery of that theft is solved at last and I'm only sorry that poor Toby Lockwood isn't alive to be vindicated. Brough stole those pearls, and it was the cunningest job I ever knew.

'Remember how you used to sit by the open window, day in and day out, on your jewel work?' Labordien nodded. 'And Brough could not fail to see what treasure you had in your hands every now and then. The open window lured him; the devil suggested means. For more years than I care to recollect I've tried to find out what those means were.'

'And have you succeeded?'

'Yes! When I was in Scotland the other day I walked along a river bank and I heard a sound. It was that finger-on-silk sound I've had in my ears for years. Not only that but, with the sound, a big silver blue fly came whizzing past my face. "Sorry," a voice called out; "my fault for not watching the bank—carry on!" The fly had been thrown by a salmon angler just below me. And lo and behold! the mystery of the stolen pearls was solved.

'The fly was, I learned a "Silver Doctor." I betook myself to various authorities, practical and otherwise, until I learned that a good salmon fisher could drop such a fly into a floating coco-nut shell at thirty yards' range, nine times out of ten.

'I went into Colonel Brough's history. He was adept at salmon fishing. Among his possessions we've found a beautiful rod and a cabinet of flies—double-hooked 'uns—one of which clawed those pearls out of your possession.

'He was up one of those plane trees. He cast out his fly, lengthening and ever lengthening his line, until he had just the amount out he required. The first fly you saw was a false cast—the second was dead accurate. The twin hooks got across the necklace and hauled the thing up into the tree.

'Unfortunately for him he excitedly dropped the necklace, or else it fell off the hooks at the last minute, right under Lockwood's eyes. Brough cast again—a short cast now and infinitely more accurate. He tore Lockwood's ear, again crossed the fallen necklace and finally secured the treasure. He probably pocketed it then, leaving his rod hidden among the plane tree branches. No one dreamed of searching up there. He just had time to drop to earth and look as though he'd come out of his front door before the courtyard was filled up.

'The fly he used was a "Durham Ranger"—black and orange and

vermilion. It ranged all right for him, eh? The silken hiss was the noise of the almost invisible gut-cast, to which the artificial fly was fastened. It cuts through the air with that precise sound.'

'But surely this is all mere surmise—theory?'

'Not on your life, Henri. You noticed how I, the veriest tyro in fly-casting, managed to grab your glasses in two shots? After only a month's practice I could do that, out of the tree where he lurked. You may be sure that Brough did the job just like that. Your good name will be restored and my professional pique will be ended and all things are satisfactory.'

'If only I could hope,' Labordien's old voice quavered to a half-fearful, half-joyful note, 'that all you say is true, I'd be a happy man after all these years of loss.'

Deliberately ex-Superintendent Hamilton poured drinks into two glasses. He passed one to Labordien.

'Then drink to happiness, Henri, old friend. Brough confessed within an hour of his arrest. Here's to better days!'

# Coffee Break

---

*No one could accuse Arthur Porges of creating unforgettable characters. Yet from the late-1950s to the mid-1970s (plus an occasional later offering), this unassuming author produced getting on for a hundred and fifty short stories of crime and detection in a range of mystery digests, from* Bizarre!, Fear! *and* Terror Detective Story *via* Alfred Hitchcock *and* Mike Shayne *through to that pillar of the establishment* Ellery Queen.

*Quite a lot of the stories are one-of-a-kind, many of them yarns of vengeance and retribution with cunning little kinks in the tail. For the rest: well, they certainly had detectives—or, more properly, 'problem-solvers', as Porges himself sometimes referred to them—usually quiet little men with academic backgrounds to whom perplexed and pressured police officers brought apparently unsolveable problems.*

*There was Cyriack Skinner Grey, a brilliant research chemist confined to a wheelchair as a result of a climbing accident, with Lieutenant Trask of the local police to bring him the problem, and Grey's fourteen-years old son, Edgar, to do some of the legwork. Grey appeared in thirteen stories. Just behind Grey, at least in terms of quantity, was Ulysses Price Middlebie, Professor Emeritus of the History and Philosophy of Science, a helpmate on no less than ten occasions to police detective Sergeant Black. Next we have Joel Hoffman, a pathologist on the staff of Pasteur Hospital, and thereby specially enabled to solve the murders, five in all, brought to him by his friend Lieutenant Ader. One of the Hoffman stories incidentally, 'No Killer Has Wings', earned a rightful place in the 1961* Best Detective Stories of the Year. *Julian Morse Trowbridge, once a child prodigy in mathematics, now retired following a breakdown, provided the cerebral assistance, to Captain Gregg, in four criminal cases. Chester Payne Middleton solved one murder; so did Professor Charles Westmore Norton, and pathologist John Holland, and George Fort Elgin . . . You're beginning to get the picture?*

*The fact is that in Porges's stories (and I leave aside his splendid parodies involving Stately Homes and Celery Green) the detectives are not important. It is the problem that matters—and, indeed, the problem at which the author excels.*

*If you're looking for a tale of unusual ingenuity, look no further. Porges will show you how to conceal a valuable painting on a yacht so that no one can find it, obtain a sample of blood from a murder suspect when he refuses to give it, cause a house to burn down six weeks after it was locked and barred. And here he is, through the medium of Professor Middlebie, solving a locked room poisoning—and showing how it's possible to put another wrinkle on the oldest of walnuts.*

ROBERT ADEY

'I always thought that locked room cases occurred only in detective novels.' Sergeant Black's tone was plaintive, as if he accused the universe of unfairness to the police.

Ulysses Price Middlebie, object of the remark, and former professor of the history and philosophy of science, but now a sometime crime consultant, looked thoughtful.

'Undoubtedly they began with mystery fiction,' he said evenly. 'But life does imitate art. To put it otherwise, I'm sure that many bright and imaginative crimes have been suggested—even guided step by step—by ingenious stories.'

'Which means in addition to out-guessing dumb apes with lengths of pipe, we now have to keep two jumps ahead of the best mystery story writers!' the sergeant grumbled. 'I don't suppose *you* ever read such stuff,' he added.

'To the contrary,' Middlebie said. 'I've always enjoyed a good crime story, especially of the puzzle variety. And now even more so.' He glanced down at his heavily taped ankle, which was propped up on a hassock.

'As much my bad luck as yours,' Black said. 'It's the kind of case where you'd come in very handy. But you can't get around, even to watch birds, and anything that stops you from galloping over hill and dale with binoculars is pretty bad.'

'Tell me about it, anyhow,' Middlebie suggested. 'I may still be of some help.' Then he added drily: 'My head isn't taped.'

Black had the grace to redden slightly.

'You're right of course,' he said. 'It's your brains I've picked, mostly. But you must admit,' he persisted, 'that often I just miss seeing things that are significant to you because of your scientific background.'

'True, but I'll try to pry out of you even the things you saw without noticing them. So go ahead, and give me all the facts.'

The sergeant paused to organize his thoughts for a moment, and then began the recital.

'The dead man is Cyrus Denning, a bachelor of sixty-two. He's supposed to have poisoned himself with cyanide. His prints, and only his, are on the cup. He was found dead in a locked room. Nobody had been near him for at least half an hour before his death. From here on in,' Black suggested, 'we'd better change to that method— Socratic, wasn't it?—you liked so much in college, because I don't really know what to tell you or in what order.'

'All right,' the professor said amiably. 'That's as good an approach as any. You say the door was locked. How?'

'Bolted on the inside; a heavy brass bolt.'

'That's not such an impossibility. Such a door can often be locked by attaching a string or wire to the bolt, and shooting it home from the outside.'

'Not this time,' Black said grimly. 'The door is recessed, and fits too tightly. Besides, no such string was found, and my suspect had no chance to remove it.'

'Very well. What about a window?'

'One, at the back. It's been nailed shut for years, and undisturbed; that I guarantee. I went over every inch with a good magnifying glass.'

'Could the glass have been cut out and re-puttied in?' There was a twinkle in the old man's grey eyes. 'That's one from a mystery story I read some months ago.'

'Not a prayer. It was old, crumbly putty; dry and hard, but still holding tight.'

'Why nailed down?'

'Denning didn't care much about fresh air, and he was very secretive. Fancied himself a scientist and inventor. The place was a one room cabin by Lake Bradley, converted into a workroom and lab. The front door—the only one—he used to padlock on the outside when he left. When he was working there, he usually bolted it from the inside.'

Middlebie frowned slightly. 'Perhaps I should ask why, in the face of all this, you doubt he killed himself.'

Black's lips narrowed. 'Instinct—plus the fact that he left no note. In my experience, a suicide almost always leaves some explanation. Then there's the fact that Denning was filthy rich. When there's enough money as bait, the greedy rats can be inferred.'

'Do you have a particular rodent in mind?'

'You bet. The old man's nephew. He was right there when they found him, and he's the lad to inherit two hundred thousand bucks, and who knows how to spend it fast.'

'So he was at the cabin. Let's have the details.'

'The boy—his name's Jerry Doss—admits seeing his uncle in the lab at noon. Sometimes he helped Denning, and managed to borrow a few bucks each time; not much because the old boy was tighter than a new girdle.

'Anyhow, he left Denning at 1:30, alive, he claims. The old man promptly bolted the door behind him. Then Doss went across the lake—that's about a hundred yards—to chat for a bit with the man at the dock, who rents boats in season. Things are quiet there now, of course.

'Well, he stayed there for half an hour, then left. But he asked the boatman to keep an eye on Denning's front door, which to me is one sign of a plot. The boy was obviously setting up an alibi.'

'What reason did he give for such an odd request?'

'He told the fellow that Denning had been bothered by some of the kids—that they hammered at the door and ragged him. Doss said that if the boatman could catch them at it, and identify them, his uncle would be glad to slip him ten bucks.'

'Very plausible,' Middlebie said, with a wry grin. 'The boy has imagination—*if* he invented the story.'

'I'm betting he did. Anyhow, at this point all is clear. Doss left Denning half an hour before, and didn't go near the door, as the boatman can testify. He never took his eyes off the area, watching for the kids, and hoping to earn ten bucks the easy way.

'Then, about fifteen minutes after the boy left the dock, the man sees him at the front door, hammering away and ye...ing. Finally, he turns and motions to the boatman to join him. When the guy gets there, Doss tells him that he looked in the window, and saw that his uncle was either dead or unconscious. The window's in back, remember, so nobody could have seen the boy look in.

'Well, they break down the door—it takes both of them, because of the heavy brass bolt—and find Denning dead, with a cup of poison at his hand. He's slumped over the table near the window.'

'Couldn't he have been killed when Doss first left? Before going across the lake to the boatman?'

'That's what bugs me,' Black groaned. 'There was a cup of coffee on the table, boiling hot. It must have been recently poured—and that's where the cyanide was. Cold water wasn't good enough for this suicide. He has to have his poison in fresh, hot coffee!

'And that isn't all,' the detective almost shrieked. 'A cigarette was burning on the edge of an ash tray. It couldn't have been lit more than a few minutes earlier.' He looked at the professor, his whole face one agonized question mark.

'Hmmm,' Middlebie murmured. 'I begin to see what you're upset about.'

'So it has to be suicide, and I'm an idiot,' Black said, more quietly, 'only I don't like the smirk of that nephew, or the little spark in his beady eyes. He engineered this deal some way, and I want to nail him!'

The professor was lost in thought for the moment. Then he said absently: 'You must have read about Sherlock Holmes.'

Black gaped at him.

'I'm thinking of his brother, Mycroft,' Middlebie said, smiling.

'Mycroft?'

'Like me, he was immobilized. In his case, sheer laziness and bulk. But he solved some very puzzling cases from his armchair, with brother Sherlock doing the leg work.' He gave Black a quizzical stare. 'Why don't we try that, eh?'

'I'll try anything,' the sergeant said. 'I'm good at leg work. Sometimes I think that's all I'm good at.'

'Nonsense. You have brains and imagination,' The professor assured him a in a gruff voice. 'No, here's what I'd like you to do. Get me large, clear photos of the lab, inside and out, all four sides. And of the view from the place in all directions.' His eyes clouded briefly, and he said: 'Are you sure the bolt is brass, and not just painted that colour?'

'Painted? No, but why—' He bit the question off short. 'I'll certainly find out,' he promised, his voice hard.

'You do that, and let me know. Is there a phone in the lab?'

'Yes.'

'Then call me from there. And bring the pictures as soon as they're available.'

'I'll phone you in three hours. We should have pictures by tomorrow afternoon.'

'Good.' Middlebie watched the sergeant stride to the door. When Black had left, the old man opened a drawer in his desk, took out a fifth of bourbon, and after some painful limping about, made his favourite tipple of whisky, beer, and brown sugar. He sipped it appreciatively, his brow knitting with thought every few moments.

Two hours and forty-eight minutes later Black phoned.

'The bolt seems to be brass,' he said. 'At least, it's not iron, steel, aluminum, or lead.'

'Hmph,' Middlebie said, his voice indicating some disappointment. 'That's a pity.' After a moment's silence, he spoke again, his tone sharper. 'I want you to scrape that bolt all over, and study it with that magnifying glass you were bragging about. Call me back if you spot anything interesting.'

'What am I looking for?' the sergeant demanded irritably.

'Just make a careful examination and see what develops,' the professor said. And he hung up.

Half-an-hour later, Black called back; there was a hum of excitement in his voice.

'I don't know how you knew,' he said, 'but somebody's been at the bolt, all right. Looks as if he drilled a hole, and put in a plug of some kind.'

'Ahh,' Middlebie purred. 'Soft iron, I'll bet anything. First hypothesis verified.'

'What's it all about?' Black queried eagerly.

'Tell you when we get those pictures,' the professor said. 'Bring 'em over tomorrow, will you?'

'Damn right, I will. But tell me—'

'Tomorrow,' was the firm reply. 'It's not all clear yet. Not at all.' Again he hung up.

The next day, early in the afternoon, the sergeant appeared with a stack of glossy eight-by-tens. Middlebie took them, and shuffled through the pile in an impatient way, finally fishing out a shot of the interior. He peered at it, and groaned.

'S'matter?' Black demanded.

'The table.' Middlebie's voice was full of disgust. 'It's too far from the window. If only it had been right next to it . . . I don't suppose,' he said wistfully, 'there was any way to introduce the coffee and cigarette after the door was bolted.'

'None,' the sergeant declared. 'Oh, there is a chimney from the fireplace, but I'd like to see the man dexterous enough to get a nearly-full cup of hot coffee and a lighted cigarette down that. And with the chimney in plain sight of Wilson—he's the boatman.'

'Another good theory gone to pot,' the professor said. Then he asked: 'By the way, was the coffee pot also hot?'

'Had to be,' Black said. 'It was still on a tiny gas fire.'

Middlebie shook his head in admiration.

'That killer, whoever he was—and *if* he was—has brains. Pity he's warped. The lad even avoided anybody's finding a discrepancy between boiling hot coffee in a cup, and a pot only lukewarm. He just left the coffee on the flame—damned foresighted.'

A bit dubious now, he studied the pictures. Suddenly his gaze grew sharp.

'What's that behind the cabin—this thing on the pillar. It looks like an astronomical telescope.'

'That's just what it is,' the sergeant said. 'Denning dabbled in astronomy, too. They say he even found a new comet.'

'This seems to be a refractor.'

'Could be. I didn't pay much attention.'

'You'd better pay more. I want the name of the manufacturer. But don't touch it; there may be prints.'

'Whose prints? And what difference? I wish I knew what was going on in your head these last few days.' The sergeant was obviously exasperated.

'I'll tell you when I'm sure myself,' the old man soothed him. 'Wouldn't want you to think I'm senile. Be a good lad, and check that scope. Get the maker's name, and if that isn't on it, measure the diameter of the objective—the big lens at the end. But hands off. Got it?'

'All right,' Black said. Then he smiled briefly. '. . . Mycroft!'

Middlebie blinked. That was the first time the sergeant had ever dared come back at him. Good! It was time they had a less formal relationship.

'Before I go,' Black said, gazing directly into the grey eyes. 'Please explain that bit about the bolt. Certainly you're sure of that part.'

'Oh, yes. I didn't mean to conceal anything,' the professor said. 'Open that right hand cabinet, and take out what's on the second shelf up.'

The sergeant obeyed him, and was amazed at his own former incomprehension.

'Right,' Middlebie said. 'That's a magnet; a big one. It weighs five pounds, and has a two thousand gauss rating. Which means, I would guess, that even through a thick wooden door it has enough pull on a bit of iron imbedded in a brass bolt to slide the thing into its socket. Did you notice if the assembly was smooth-working—oiled, perhaps?'

'You bet it was!' Black exclaimed. 'So that's it. What a chump I've been. All Doss had to do was step out, shut the door on his dead uncle, and move this kind of magnet from left to right at the proper height against the door.' He flipped the piece of heavy metal from hand to hand in his enthusiasm. Then his face darkened. 'But we're still up the creek on that coffee and cigarette bit. We know he was away from the cabin for over half an hour. The coffee would have cooled by then, and the smoke gone out.'

'I am aware of the difficulty,' the professor said. 'That's why I hoped the table would be nearer the window. By the way,' he asked, 'what kind of a day was it—the weather, I mean?'

'Nice one; cool, clear, sunny. Anybody but an old idiot would have been outside, or at least had a window open to enjoy the fresh air.

'It takes all kinds,' Middlebie said. 'Go check on that telescope like a good lad.'

Black seemed about to ask more questions, but the old man's face was forbiddingly wooden. With a sigh, the detective left.

When he returned that evening, Middlebie was working with a binocular microscope, and seemed almost reluctant to shift his line of thought. He shoved his chair back, gave a grunt of resignation, and raised one eyebrow questioningly.

'Well?' he demanded.

'No maker's name that I could find. But the objective was five inches across.'

'Good. A five incher could have a focal length of from sixty to ninety inches.'

'What does that mean?' Black's voice was querulous. He was tired of driving up and back, and almost sorry he hadn't certified the case as suicide. Only sheer persistence—plus the nature of a good cop—made him stay with it.

'Here's how it must have happened,' Middlebie said, sounding the least bit smug. 'Doss visits his uncle; maybe works with him a bit in the lab. Then they have coffee, either as normal routine, or at the boy's suggestion. There are cases of standard chemicals against the south wall; your pictures show them plainly. It's easy for Doss to put cyanide in the old man's cup. The moment his uncle collapsed, the boy wiped his own prints off the cup, pressed Denning's on, and left, closing the door behind him. But first he put an unlighted cigarette on the edge of the ceramic ashtray.

'Once outside, he unobtrusively—in case somebody was watching—stood facing the door, and with a magnet taken probably from his uncle's lab, shot the bolt. I assume that at some earlier visit, when left alone by the old man, he drilled out some of the brass and inserted an iron plug so the magnet would work.

'Now, then. He went to the dock and established that half hour alibi. After that, Doss approached the cabin from the rear, where neither the boatman nor anybody else could see him, took the objective glass—already loosened, I imagine, the boy being so thorough—and stood a foot or two from the window. There, he focused the bright sunlight—'

'By God!' Black exclaimed, almost in a whisper, and Middlebie frowned at the interruption.

'An ordinary magnifier wouldn't work unless the table was only inches from the glass, but this thing focuses at from sixty to ninety inches. The window glass would cut a lot of the heat, but there would be plenty to bring the coffee cup to boiling, and then light the cigarette.'

'Then, very quickly, to the front door, there to pound and finally hail the boatman. Very neat!'

'You've got it,' Black said. 'No doubt of that.' He shook his head gloomily. 'But how to prove anything in court.'

'Well,' the old man said. 'The drilled bolt has some evidential value.'

'Not enough, I'm afraid.'

'Prints on the telescope?'

'Weak,' the sergeant said crisply. 'After all, the boy helped out in the scientific stuff.

'Ah,' Middlebie said. 'But if you're lucky, there'll be some on the *inside* of the objective. They would be harder to explain; much harder, since few astronomers ever dismount the objective. There are realignment problems, and dust—all sorts of reasons to leave it alone. But frankly, I think if you go at it right, the boy may crack. He doesn't dream we're onto him. Feeling plenty smug, I imagine.'

Black looked at the lean face and seemed to see cats' whiskers twitching.

He's not the only one who feels that way, the sergeant reflected with amusement. But aloud he said only, 'In any case, you've done your share. No Mycroft could have done better.'

# W. HOPE HODGSON

# Bullion!

*It is as the possessor of an extraordinary and fantastic imagination, a writer of powerful and disturbing weird tales, that William Hope Hodgson (1877–1918) will be remembered.* Two novels stand out: The House on the Borderland *(1908), in which the narrator is besieged by hideous swine-like beings from a bottomless abyss and experiences an awesome journey through time and space (prompting the thought that Hodgson may have experimented with hallucinogens), and* The Night Land *(1912), a 200,000-word epic of an odyssey into absolute nightmare, billions of years hence when the sun is dead and darkness shrouds the dying earth.*

*He was equally imaginative in his short stories, many of which reveal a profound horror of the sea, although a horror more than tinged with fascination. Hodgson spent eight years before the mast, twice circling the globe, before returning to England to write for his living.*

*Some of his finest tales were set in the Sargasso Sea, in Hodgson's lively imagination a nightmarish place alive with giant rats, giant octopi, giant sea-lice, giant poisonous mushrooms and slug-like Weed-men with tendrils for arms. He also wrote love stories, a Western or two, science-fantasy, and mysteries such as 'Bullion!'*

*'Bullion!' itself is, in a sense, a lost story, its finding as perfect an example of serendipity as has ever happened to me. In 1989 I was doing some research on the* Strand Magazine *in the Bodleian Library, Oxford. On the final day, with—quite literally—half an hour to spare before the Stack was locked up for the night, I began strolling along the narrow tome-lined alleyways, idly pulling out volumes that took my eye, in much the same way that Adelaide Proctor's organist's fingers meandered over the noisy keys. The chord he struck Ms Proctor likened to the sound of a great Amen. It has to be admitted that my own vocal reaction, on tugging down a tall thin volume labelled* Everybody's Weekly *(a title unknown to me, at least from this pre-Great War period) and opening it in the middle of the first issue, fell somewhat short of that, since what shattered the hush of G Floor in the Bodleian Stack was a yelped four-letter word an Anglo Saxon midden-forker would have had no difficulty in recognizing. Never mind.*

*Here, in cold print, was the story Hodgson arch-votary Sam Moskovitz had assumed had never been published (probably because he'd been looking in the wrong place: the American* Everybody's Magazine*). Not only that, but it featured an Impossible Vanishment.*

JACK ADRIAN

This is a most peculiar yarn. It was a pitchy night in the South Pacific. I was the second mate of one of the fast clipper-ships running between London and Melbourne at the time of the big gold finds up at Bendigo. There was a fresh breeze blowing, and I was walking hard up and down the weather side of the poop-deck, to keep myself warm, when the captain came out of the companionway and joined me.

'Mr James, do you believe in ghosts?' he asked suddenly, after several minutes of silence.

'Well, sir,' I replied, 'I always keep an open mind; so I can't say I'm a proper disbeliever, though I think most ghost yarns can be explained.'

'Well,' he said in a queer voice, 'someone keeps whispering in my cabin at nights. It's making me feel funny to be there.'

'How do you mean whispering, sir?' I asked.

'Just that,' he said. 'Someone whispering about my cabin. Sometimes it's quite close to my head, other times it's here and there and everywhere—in the air.'

Then, abruptly, he stopped in his walk and faced me, as if determined to say the thing that was on his mind.

'What did Captain Avery die of on the passage out?' he asked quick and blunt.

'None of us knew, sir,' I told him. 'He just seemed to sicken and go off.'

'Well,' he said, 'I'm not going to sleep in his cabin any longer. I've no special fancy for just sickening and going off. If you like I'll change places with you.'

'Certainly, sir,' I answered, half pleased and half sorry. For whilst I had a feeling that there was nothing really to bother about in the captain's fancies yet—though he had only taken command in Melbourne to bring the ship home—I had found already that he was not one of the soft kind by any means. And, so, as you will understand, I had vague feelings of uneasiness to set against my curiosity to find out what it was that had given Captain Reynolds a fit of the nerves.

'Would you like me to sleep in your place to-night, sir?' I asked.

'Well,' he said with a little laugh 'when you get below you'll find me in your bunk, so it'll be a case of my cabin or the saloon table.' And with that it was settled.

'I shall lock the door,' I added. 'I'm not going to have anyone fooling me. I suppose I may search?'

'Do what you like,' was all he replied.

About an hour later the captain left me, and went below. When the mate came up to relieve me at eight bells I told him I was promoted to the captain's cabin and the reason why. To my surprise, he said that he wouldn't sleep there for all the gold that was in the ship; so that I finished by telling him he was a superstitious old shellback.

When I got down to my new cabin I found that the captain had made the steward shift my gear in already, so that I had nothing to do but turn in, which I did after a good look round and locking the door.

I left the lamp turned about half up, and meant to lie awake a while listening; but I was asleep before I knew, and only waked to hear the 'prentice knocking on my door to tell me it was one bell.

For three nights I slept thus in comfort, and jested once or twice with the captain that I was getting the best of the bargain.

Then, just as you might expect, on the fourth night something happened. I had gone below for the middle watch, and had fallen asleep as usual, almost so soon as my head was on the pillow. I was wakened suddenly by some curious sound apparently quite near me. I lay there without moving and listened, my heart beating a little rapidly; but otherwise I was cool and alert. Then I heard the thing quite plainly with my waking senses—a vague, uncertain whispering, seeming to me as if someone or something bent over me from behind, and whispered some unintelligible thing close to my ear. I rolled over, and stared around the cabin; but the whole place was empty.

Then I sat still, and listened again. For several minutes there was an absolute silence, and then abruptly I heard the vague, uncomfortable whispering again, seeming to come from the middle of the cabin. I sat there, feeling distinctly nervous; then I jumped quietly from my bunk, and slipped silently to the door. I stopped, and listened at the keyhole, but there was no one there. I ran across then to the ventilators, and shut them; also I made sure that the ports were screwed up, so that there was now absolutely no place through which anyone could send his voice, even supposing that anyone was idiot enough to want to play such an unmeaning trick.

For a while after I had taken these precautions I stood silent; and twice I heard the whispering, going vaguely now in this and now in that part of the air of the cabin, as if some unseen spirit wandered about, trying to make itself heard.

As you may suppose, this was getting more than I cared to tackle, for I had searched the cabin every watch, and it seemed to me that there was truly something unnatural in the thing I heard. I began to get my clothes and dress, for, after this, I felt inclined to adopt the captain's suggestion of the saloon table for a bunk. You see, I had got to have my sleep, but I could not fancy lying unconscious in that cabin, with that strange sound wandering about; though awake, I think I can say truthfully I should not really have feared it. But to lie defenceless in sleep with that uncanniness near me was more than I could bear.

And then, you know, a sudden thought came blinding through my brain. The bullion! We were bringing some thirty thousand ounces of gold in sealed bullion chests, and these were in a specially erected wooden compartment, standing all by itself in the centre of the lazarette, just below the captain's cabin. What if some attempt were being made secretly on the treasure, and we all the time idiotically thinking of ghosts, when perhaps the vague sounds we had heard were conducted in some way from below! You can conceive how the thought set me tingling, so that I did not stop to realize how improbable it was, but took my lamp and went immediately to the captain.

He woke in a moment, and when he had heard my suggestion he told me that the thing was practically impossible; yet the very idea made him sufficiently uneasy to determine him on going down with me into the lazarette, to look at the seals on the door of the temporary bullion-room.

He did not stop to dress, but, reaching the lamp from me, led the way. The entrance to the lazarette was through a trapdoor under the saloon table, and this was kept locked. When this was opened the captain went down with the lamp, and I followed noiselessly. At the bottom of the ladder the captain held the lamp high, and looked round. Then he went over to where the square bulk of the bullion-room stood alone in the centre of the place, and together we examined the seals on the door; but of course they were untouched, and I began to realize now that my idea had been nothing more than unreasoned suggestion. And then, you know, as we stood there silent, amid the various creaks and groans of the working bulkheads, we both heard the sound—a whispering somewhere near to us, that came and went oddly, being lost in the noise of the creaking woodwork, and again coming plain, seeming now to be in this place, and now in that.

I had an extraordinary feeling of superstitious fear; but the captain was unaffected. He muttered in a low voice that there was someone inside the bullion-room, and began quickly and coolly to break the sealed tapes. Then telling me to hold the lamp high, he threw the door wide open. But the place was empty, save for the neat range of bullion-boxes, bound sealed, and numbered, that occupied half the floor.

'Nothing here!' said the captain, and took the lamp from my hand. He held it low down over the rows of little chests.

'The thirteenth!' he said, with a little gasp. 'Where's the thirteenth —No. 13?'

He was right. The bullion-chest which should have stood between No. 12 and No. 14 was gone. We set to and counted every chest, verifying the numbers. They were all there, numbered up to 60, except for the gap of the thirteenth. Somehow, in some way, a thousand ounces of gold had been removed from out of the sealed room. In a very agitated but thorough manner the captain and I made a close examination of the room; but it was plain that any entry that had been made could only have been through the sealed doorway. Then he led the way out, and having tried the lock several times, and found it showed no signs of having been tampered with, he locked and sealed up the door again, sealing the tape also right across the keyhole. Then, as a thought came to him, he told me to stay by the door whilst he went up into the saloon.

In a few minutes he returned with the purser, both armed and carrying lamps. They came very quietly, and paused with me outside the door, and examined the old seals and the door itself. Then, at the purser's request, the captain removed the new seals, and unlocked the door.

As he opened it the purser turned suddenly and looked behind him. I heard it also—a vague whispering; seeming to be in the air, then it was drowned and lost in the creaking of the timbers. The captain had heard the sound, and was standing in the doorway holding his lamp high and looking in, pistol ready in his right hand, for to him it had seemed to come from within the bullion-room. Yet the place was as empty as we had left it but a few minutes before—as, indeed, it was bound to be— of any living creature. The captain went to where the bullion-chest was missing, and stooped to point out the gap to the purser.

A queer exclamation came from him, and he remained stooping, whilst the purser and I pressed forward to find what new thing had happened now. When I saw what the captain was staring at, you will understand that I felt simply dazed, for there right before his face, in its proper place, was the thirteenth bullion-chest, as, indeed, it must have been all the while.

'You've been dreaming,' said the purser, with a burst of relieved laughter. 'My goodness, but you did give me a fright!'

The captain and I stared at the rematerialized treasure-chest, and then at one another.

'That chest was not there a few minutes ago!' the captain said at length. Then he brushed the hair off his forehead, and looked again at the chest. 'Are we dreaming?' he said at last, and looked at me.

He touched the chest with his foot, and I did the same with my hand; but it was no illusion, and we could only suppose that we had made some extraordinary mistake.

I turned to the purser.

'But the whispering!' I said. '*You* heard the whispering!'

'Yes,' said the captain. 'What was that? I tell you there's something queer knocking about, or else we're all mad.'

The purser stared, puzzled and nodding his head.

'I heard something,' he said, 'The chief thing is, the stuff is there all right. I suppose you'll put a watch over it?'

'By Moses! Yes!' said the captain. 'The mates and I'll sleep with that blessed gold until we hand it ashore in London!'

And so it was arranged. We three officers took it in turn to sleep actually inside the bullion-room itself, being sealed and locked in with the treasure. In addition to this, the captain made the petty officers keep watch and watch with him and the purser, through the whole of each twenty-four hours, trapesing round and round that wretched bullion-room until not a mouse could have gone in or out without being seen. In addition, he had the deck above and below thoroughly examined by the carpenter once in every twenty-four hours, so that never was a treasure so scrupulously guarded.

For our part, we officers began to grow pretty sick of the job, once the touch of excitement connected with the thought of robbery had worn off. And when, as sometimes happened, we were aware of that extraordinary whispering, it was only the captain's determination and authority which made us submit to the constant discomfort and breaking of our sleep; for every hour the watchman on the outside of the bullion-room would knock twice on the boards of the room, and the sleeping officer within would have to rouse, take a look round and knock back twice, to signify that all was well.

Sometimes I could almost think that we got into the way of doing this in our sleep, for I have been roused to my watch on deck, with no memory of having answered the watchman's knock, though a cautious inquiry showed me that I had done so.

Then, one night when I was sleeping in the bullion-room, a rather queer thing happened. Something must have roused me between the times of the watchman's knocks, for I wakened suddenly and half sat up, with a feeling that something was wrong somewhere. As in a dream, I looked round, and all the time fighting against my sleepiness. Everything seemed normal; but when I looked at the tiers of bullion chests I saw that there was a gap among them. Some of the chests had surely gone.

I stared in a stupid, nerveless way, as a man full of sleep sometimes will do, without rousing himself to realize the actuality of the things he looks at. And even as I stared I dozed over and fell back, but seemed to waken almost immediately and look again at the chests. Yet it was plain that I must have seen dazedly and half-dreaming, for not a bullion-chest was missing, and I sank back again thankfully to my slumber.

Yet when at the end of my 'treasure watch' (as we had grown to call our watch below) I reported my queer half-dream to the captain, he came down himself and made a thorough examination of the bullion-room, also questioning the sail-maker, who had been the watchman outside. But he said there had been nothing unusual, only that once he had thought he heard the curious whispering going about in the air of the lazarette.

And so that queer voyage went on, with over us all the time a sense of peculiar mystery, vague and indefinable; so that one thought a thousand strange weird thoughts which one lacked the courage to put into words. And the other times there was only a sense of utter weariness of it all, and the one desire to get to port and be shut of it and go back to a normal life in some other vessel. Even the passengers—many of whom were returning diggers—were infected by the strange atmosphere and of uncertainty that prompted our constant guarding of the bullion, for it had got known among them that a special guard was being kept, and that certain inexplicable things had happened. But the captain refused their offers of help, preferring to keep his own men about the gold, as you may suppose.

At last we reached London and docked; and now occurred the strangest thing of all. When the bank officials came aboard to take over the gold, the captain took them down to the bullion-room, where the carpenter was walking round as outside watchman, and the first mate was sealed inside, as usual.

The captain explained that we were taking unusual precautions, and broke the seals. When, however, they unlocked and opened the door, the mate did not answer to the captain's call, but was seen to be lying quiet beside the gold. Examination showed that he was quite dead; but there was nowhere any mark or sign to show that his death was unnatural. As the captain said to me afterwards, 'Another case of "just sickening and going off." I wouldn't sail again in this packet for anything the owners liked to offer me!'

The officials examined the boxes, and, finding all in order had them taken ashore up to the bank, and very thankful I was to see the last of it. Yet this is where I was mistaken, for about an hour later, as

I was superintending the slinging out of some heavy cargo, there came a message from the bank to the effect that every one of the bullion-chests was a dummy filled with lead, and that no one be allowed to leave the ship until an inquiry and search had been made.

This was carried out rigorously, so that not a cabin or a scrap of personal luggage was left unexamined, and afterwards the ship herself was searched, but nowhere was there any signs of the gold; yet as there must have been something like a ton of it, it was not a thing that could have been easily hidden.

Permission was now given to all that they might go ashore, and I proceeded once more to supervise the slinging out of heavy stuff that I had been 'bossing' when the order came from the bank. And all the time, as I gave my orders, I felt in a daze. How could nearly seventeen hundredweight of gold have been removed out of that guarded bullion-room? I remembered all the curious things that had been heard and seen and half-felt. Was there something queer about the ship? But my reason objected: there was surely some explanation of the mystery.

Abruptly I came out of my thoughts, for the man on the shore-gear had just let a heavy case down rather roughly, and a dandy-looking person was cursing him for his clumsiness. It was then that a possible explanation of the mystery came to me, and I determined to take the risk of testing it. I jumped ashore and swore at the man who was handling the gear, telling him to slack away more carefully, to which he replied, 'Ay, ay, sir.' Then, under my breath, I said:

'Take no notice of the hard talk, Jimmy. Let the next one come down good and solid. I'll take the responsibility if it smashes.'

Then I stood back and let Jimmy have his chance. The next case went well up to the block before Jimmy took a turn and signalled to the winch to vast heaving.

'Slack away handsome!' yelled Jimmy and he let his own rope smoke round the bollard. The case came down, crashing from a height of thirty feet, and burst on the quay. As the dust cleared I heard the dandy cursing at the top of his voice.

I did not bother about him. What was attracting my attention was the fact that among the heavy timbers of the big case was a number of the missing bullion chests. I seized my whistle and blew it for one of the 'prentices. When he came I told him to run up the quay for a policeman. Then I turned to the captain and the third mate, who had come running ashore, and explained. They ran to the lorry on which the other cases had been placed, and with the help of some of the men pulled them down again on to the quay. But when they came to search for the swell stranger, who had been looking after the unloading of the stolen gold, he was nowhere to be found; so that, after all, the policeman had nothing to do when he arrived but mount guard over the recovered bullion, of which, I am glad to say, not a case was missing.

Later, a more intelligent examination into things revealed how the robbery had been effected. When we took down the temporary bullion-room we found that a very cleverly concealed sliding panel had been fitted into the end opposite to the door. This gave us the idea to examine a wooden ventilator which came up through the deck near by from the lower hold. And now we held the key to the whole mystery.

Evidently there had been quite a gang of thieves aboard the ship. They had built the cases ashore, and packed them with loaded dummy bullion chests, sealed and banded exactly like the originals. These had been placed in the hold at Melbourne as freight, under the name of 'specimens.' In the meanwhile some of the band must have got our carpenter, who had built the bullion-room, and promised him a share of the gold if he would build the secret panel into one end. Then, when we got to sea, the thieves got down into the lower hold through one of the forrard hatches, and, having opened one of the cases, began to exchange the dummies for the real chests, by climbing up inside the wooden ventilator shaft, which the carpenter had managed to fit with a couple of boards that slid to one side, just opposite to the secret panel in the wooden bullion-room.

It must have been very slow work, and their whispering to one another had been carried up the ventilator shaft, which passed right through the captain's cabin, under the appearance of a large ornamental strut, or upright, supporting the arm-racks. It was this unexpected carrying of the sound which had brought the captain and me down unexpectedly, and nearly discovered them; so that they had not even had time to replace the thirteenth chest with its prepared dummy.

I don't think there is much more to explain. There is very little doubt in my mind that the captain's extraordinary precautions must have made things difficult for the robbers, and that they could only get to work then when the carpenter happened to be the outside watchman. It is also obvious to me that some drug which threw off narcotic fumes must have been injected into the bullion-room, to ensure the officer not waking at inconvenient moments, so that the time that I did waken, and felt so muddled I must have been in a half-stupefied condition, and did *really* see that some of the chests were gone; but these were replaced so soon as I fell back asleep. The first mate must have died from an over-prolonged inhalation of the drug.

I think that is all that has to do with this incident. Perhaps, though, you may be pleased to hear that I was both handsomely rewarded for having solved the mystery. So that, altogether, I was very well satisfied.

# Proof of Guilt

---

*When I first began collecting material for this anthology some time ago (it feels like a century but is only a decade), there were three stories I noted down at the top of a sheet of pink A4 paper which, come hell or high water, had to go in. Numbers two and three were Barry Perowne's 'The Blind Spot' and Alex Atkinson's 'Chapter The Last' (to the earnest Impossible Crime buff this may well reveal an attitude towards the genre little short of frivolous, but I am unrepentant). At the top of the list, number one, was Bill Pronzini's 'Proof of Guilt' which I still, even now, over ten years and a few thousand other short stories later, regard as one of the very best Impossible shorts written over the past 50 years.*

*It's so simple. And witty. But hellishly ingenious. And it could work. That's the beauty of it:* it could work.

*I'm no puritan in this matter. I've read Impossible Crime stories whose plots are absurd, gimmicks are ludicrous, solutions are preposterous—and still thoroughly enjoyed them. I've even had my doubts. A few of John Dickson Carr's solutions, to me, seem perilously close to incomprehensibility. And quite often one wonders (perhaps traitorously): Why on earth did the murderer go to all that trouble? Even allowing for all the sub-plots and side-issues, why didn't he just fell the guy with a monkey-wrench in a back alley and have done with it?*

*It's all down to the writers, of course. The best writers can get away with murder . . . can sometimes come up with what, if one stopped to think about it, is really a farrago of nonsense from beginning to end; yet with the magic of their narrational power they can force one to ignore the absurdities and go with the flow of their own enthusiasm for—not to mention enjoyment of—the task in hand: which is to delude and baffle. Thus, in a sense, with some writers one is happily in collusion with one's own deceiver!*

*Not here, though. This is a plain, no-nonsense tale which just happens to have a brilliant and perfectly logical twist to it—the sort of twist which probably came to Bill Pronzini while he was shaving, or taking a bath, or feeding the cat: the way these ideas do come. And I'll bet it hit him like a bolt of lightning.*

JACK ADRIAN

---

I've been a city cop for 32 years now, and during that time I've heard of and been involved in some of the weirdest most audacious crimes imaginable—on and off public record. But as far as I'm concerned, the murder of an attorney named Adam Chillingham is *the* damnedest case in my experience, if not in the entire annals of crime.

You think I'm exaggerating? Well, listen to the way it was.

My partner Jack Sherrard and I were in the Detective Squadroom one morning last summer when this call came in from a man named Charles Hearn. He said he was Adam Chillingham's law clerk, and that his employer had just been shot to death; he also said he had the killer trapped in the lawyer's private office.

It seemed like a fairly routine case at that point. Sherrard and I drove out to the Dawes Building, a skyscraper in a new business development on the city's south side, and rode the elevator up to Chillingham's suite of offices on the sixteenth floor. Hearn, and a woman named Clarisse Tower, who told us she had been the dead man's secretary, were waiting in the anteroom with two uniformed patrolmen who had arrived minutes earlier.

According to Hearn, a man named George Dillon had made a 10:30 appointment with Chillingham, had kept it punctually, and had been escorted by the attorney into the private office at that exact time. At 10:40 Hearn thought he heard a muffled explosion from inside the office, but he couldn't be sure because the walls were partially sound-proof.

Hearn got up from his desk in the anteroom and knocked on the door and there was no response; then he tried the knob and found that the door was locked from the inside. Miss Tower confirmed all this, although she said she hadn't heard any sound; her desk was farther away from the office door than was Hearn's.

A couple of minutes later the door had opened and George Dillon had looked out and calmly said that Chillingham had been murdered. He had not tried to leave the office after the announcement; instead, he'd seated himself in a chair near the desk and lighted a cigarette. Hearn satisfied himself that his employer was dead, made a hasty exit, but had the presence of mind to lock the door from the outside by the simple expediency of transferring the key to the outside—thus sealing Dillon in the office with the body. After which Hearn put in his call to Headquarters.

So Sherrard and I drew our guns, unlocked the door, and burst into the private office. This George Dillon was sitting in the chair across the desk, very casual, both his hands up in plain sight. He gave us a relieved look and said he was glad the police had arrived so quickly.

I went over and looked at the body, which was sprawled on the floor behind the desk; a pair of French windows were open in the wall just beyond, letting in a warm summer breeze. Chillingham had been shot once in the right side of the neck, with what appeared by the size of the wound to have been a small-calibre bullet; there was no exit wound, and there were no powder burns.

I straightened up, glanced around the office, and saw that the only door was the one which we had just come through. There was no balcony or ledge outside the open windows—just a sheer drop of 16 stories to a parklike, well-landscaped lawn which stretched away for several hundred yards. The nearest building was a hundred yards distant, angled well to the right. Its roof was about on a level with Chillingham's office, it being a lower structure than the Dawes Building; not much of the roof was visible unless you peered out and around.

Sherrard and I then questioned George Dillon—and he claimed he hadn't killed Chillingham. He said the attorney had been standing at the open windows, leaning out a little, and that all of a sudden he had cried out and fallen down with the bullet in his neck. Dillon said he'd taken a look out the windows, hadn't seen anything, checked that Chillingham was dead, then unlocked the door and summoned Hearn and Miss Tower.

When the coroner and the lab crew got there, and the doc had made his preliminary examination, I asked him about the wound. He confirmed my earlier guess—a small-calibre bullet, probably a .22 or .25. He couldn't be sure, of course, until he took out the slug at the post-mortem.

I talked things over with Sherrard and we both agreed that it was pretty much improbable for somebody with a .22 or .25 calibre weapon to have shot Chillingham from the roof of the nearest building; a small calibre like that just doesn't have a range of a hundred yards and the angle was almost too sharp. There was nowhere else the shot could have come from—except from inside the office. And that left us with George Dillon, whose story was obviously false and who just as obviously had killed the attorney while the two of them were locked inside this office.

You'd think it was pretty cut and dried then, wouldn't you? You'd think all we had to do was arrest Dillon and charge him with homicide, and our job was finished. Right?

Wrong.

Because we couldn't find the gun.

Remember, now, Dillon had been locked in that office—except for the minute or two it took Hearn to examine the body and slip out and relock the door—from the time Chillingham died until the time we came in. And both Hearn and Miss Tower swore that Dillon hadn't stepped outside the office during that minute or two. We'd already searched Dillon and he had nothing on him. We searched the office—I mean, we *searched* that office—and there was no gun there.

We sent officers over to the roof of the nearest building and down onto the landscaped lawn; they went over every square inch of ground and rooftop, and they didn't find anything. Dillon hadn't thrown the gun out the open windows then, and there was no place on the face of the sheer wall of the building where a gun could have been hidden.

So where was the murder weapon? What had Dillon done with it? Unless we found that out, we had no evidence against him that would stand up in a court of law; his word that he *hadn't* killed Chillingham, despite the circumstantial evidence of the locked room, was as good as money in the bank. It was up to us to prove him guilty, not up to him to prove himself innocent. You see the problem?

We took him into a large book-filled room that was part of the Chillingham suite—what Hearn called the 'archives'—and sat him down in a chair and began to question him extensively. He was a big husky guy with blondish hair and these perfectly guileless eyes; he just sat there and looked at us and answered in a polite voice, maintaining right along that he hadn't killed the lawyer.

We made him tell his story of what had happened in the office a dozen times, and he explained it the same way each time—no variations. Chillingham had locked the door after they entered, and then they sat down and talked over some business. Pretty soon Chillingham complained that it was stuffy in the room, got up, and opened the French windows; the next thing Dillon knew, he said, the attorney collapsed with the bullet in him. He hadn't heard any shot, he said; Hearn must be mistaken about a muffled explosion.

I said finally, 'All right, Dillon, suppose you tell us why you came to see Chillingham. What was the business you discussed?'

'He was my father's lawyer,' Dillon said, 'and the executor of my father's estate. He was also a thief. He stole three hundred and fifty thousand dollars of my father's money.'

Sherrard and I stared at him. Jack said, 'That gives you one hell of a motive for murder, if it's true.'

'It's true,' Dillon said flatly. 'And yes, I suppose it does give me a strong motive for killing him. I admit I hated the man, I hated him passionately.'

'You admit that, do you?'

'Why not? I have nothing to hide.'

'What did you expect to gain by coming here to see Chillingham?' I asked. 'Assuming you didn't come here to kill him.'

'I wanted to tell him I knew what he'd done, and that I was going to expose him for the thief he was.'

'You tell him that?'

'I was leading up to it when he was shot.'

'Suppose you go into a little more detail about this alleged theft from your father's estate.'

'All right.' Dillon lit a cigarette. 'My father was a hard-nosed businessman, a self-made type who acquired a considerable fortune in textiles; as far as he was concerned, all of life revolved around money. But I've never seen it that way; I've always been something of a free spirit and to hell with negotiable assets. Inevitably, my father and I had a falling-out about fifteen years ago, when I was twenty-three, and I left home with the idea of seeing some of the big wide world—which is exactly what I did.

'I travelled from one end of this country to the other, working at different jobs, and then I went to South Africa for a while. Some of the wanderlust finally began to wear off, and I decided to come back to this city and settle down—maybe even patch things up with my father. I arrived several days ago and learned then that he had been dead for more than two years.'

'You had no contact with your father during the fifteen years you were drifting around?'

'None whatsoever. I told you, we had a falling-out. And we'd never been close to begin with.'

Sherrard asked, 'So what made you suspect Chillingham had stolen money from your father's estate?'

'I am the only surviving member of the Dillon family; there are no other relatives, not even a distant cousin. I knew my father wouldn't have left me a cent, not after all these years, and I didn't particularly care; but I *was* curious to find out to whom he had willed his estate.'

'And what did you find out?'

'Well, I happen to know that my father had three favourite charities,' Dillon said. 'Before I left, he used to tell me that if I didn't "shape-up," as he put it, he would leave every cent of his money to those three institutions.'

'He didn't, is that it?'

'Not exactly. According to the will, he left two hundred thousand dollars to each of two of them—the Cancer Society and the Children's

Hospital. He also, according to the will, left three hundred and fifty thousand dollars to the Association for Medical Research.'

'All right,' Sherrard said, 'so what does that have to do with Chillingham?'

'Everything,' Dillon told him. 'My father died of a heart attack— he'd had a heart condition for many years. Not severe, but he finally expected to die as a result of it one day. And so he did. And because of this heart condition his third favourite charity—the one he felt the most strongly about—was the Heart Fund.'

'Go on,' I said, frowning.

Dillon put out his cigarette and gave me a humourless smile. 'I looked into the Association for Medical Research and I did quite a thorough bit of checking. It doesn't exist; there *isn't* any Association for Medical Research. And the only person who could have invented it is or was my father's lawyer and executor, Adam Chillingham.'

Sherrard and I thought that over and came to the same conclusion. I said, 'So even though you never got along with your father, and you don't care about money for yourself, you decided to expose Chillingham.'

'That's right. My father worked hard all his life to build his fortune, and admirably enough he decided to give it to charity at his death. I believe in worthwhile causes, I believe in the work being done by the Heart Fund, and it sent me into a rage to realize they had been cheated out of a substantial fortune which could have gone toward valuable research.'

'A murderous rage?' Sherrard asked softly.

Dillon showed us his humourless smile again. 'I didn't kill Adam Chillingham,' he said. 'But you'll have to admit, he deserved killing— and that the world is better off without the likes of him.'

I might have admitted that to myself, if Dillon's accusations were valid, but I didn't admit it to Dillon. I'm a cop, and my job is to uphold law; murder is murder, whatever the reasons for it, and it can't be gotten away with.

Sherrard and I hammered at Dillon a while longer, but we couldn't shake him at all. I left Jack to continue the field questioning and took a couple of men and re-searched Chillingham's private office. No gun. I went up onto the roof of the nearest building and searched that personally. No gun. I took my men down into the lawn area and supervised another minute search. No gun.

I went back to Chillingham's suite and talked to Charles Hearn and Miss Tower again, and they had nothing to add to what they'd already told us; Hearn was 'almost positive' he had heard a muffled explosion inside the office, but from the legal point that was the same as not having heard anything at all.

We took Dillon down to Headquarters finally, because we knew damned well he had killed Adam Chillingham, and advised him of his rights and printed him and booked him on suspicion. He asked for counsel, and we called a public defender for him, and then we grilled him again in earnest. It got us nowhere.

The F.B.I. and state check we ran on his fingerprints got us nowhere either; he wasn't wanted, he had never been arrested, he had never even been printed before. Unless something turned up soon in the way of evidence—specifically, the missing murder weapon—we knew we couldn't hold him very long.

The next day I received the lab report and the coroner's report and ballistics report on the bullet taken from Chillingham's neck—.22 calibre, all right. The lab's and coroner's findings combined to tell me something I'd already guessed: the wound and the calculated angle of trajectory of the bullet did not entirely rule out the remote possibility that Chillingham had been shot from the roof of the nearest building. The ballistics report, however, told me something I hadn't guessed— something which surprised me a little.

The bullet had no rifling marks.

Sherrard blinked at this when I related the information to him. 'No rifling marks?' he said. 'Hell, that means the slug wasn't fired from a gun at all, at least not a lawfully manufactured one. A home-made weapon, you think, Walt?'

'That's how it figures,' I agreed. 'A kind of zipgun probably. Anybody can make one; all you need is a length of tubing or the like and a bullet and a grip of some sort and a detonating cap.'

'But there was no zipgun, either, in or around Chillingham's office. We'd have found it if there was.'

I worried my lower lip meditatively. 'Well, you can make one of those zips from a dozen or more small components parts, you know; even the tubing could be soft aluminum, the kind you can break apart with your hands. When you're done using it, you can knock it down again into its components. Dillon had enough time to have done that, before opening the locked door.'

'Sure,' Sherrard said. 'But then what? We *still* didn't find anything—not a single thing—that could have been used as part of a home-made zip.'

I suggested we go back and make another search, and so we drove once more to the Dawes Building. We re-combed Chillingham's office—we'd had a police seal on it to make sure nothing could be disturbed—and we re-combed the surrounding area. We didn't find so much as an iron filing. Then we went to the city jail and had another talk with George Dillon.

When I told him our zipgun theory, I thought I saw a light flicker in his eyes; but it was the briefest of reactions, and I couldn't be sure. We told him it was highly unlikely a zipgun using a .22 calibre bullet could kill anybody from a distance of a hundred yards, and he said he couldn't help that, *he* didn't know anything about such a weapon. Further questioning got us nowhere.

And the following day we were forced to release him, with a warning not to leave the city.

But Sherrard and I continued to work doggedly on the case; it was one of those cases that preys on your mind constantly, keeps you from sleeping well at night, because you know there has to be an answer and you just can't figure out what it is. We ran checks into Chillingham's records and found that he had made some large private investments a year ago, right after the Dillon will had been probated. And as George Dillon had claimed, there was no Association for Medical Research; it was a dummy charity, apparently set up by Chillingham for the explicit purpose of stealing old man Dillon's §350,000. But there was no definite proof of this, not enough to have convicted Chillingham of theft in a court of law; he'd covered himself pretty neatly.

As an intelligent man, George Dillon had no doubt realized that a public exposure of Chillingham would have resulted in nothing more than adverse publicity and the slim possibility of disbarment—hardly sufficient punishment in Dillon's eyes. So he had decided on what to him was a morally justifiable homicide. From the law's point of view, however, it was nonetheless Murder One.

But the law still had no idea what he'd done with the weapon, and therefore, as in the case of Chillingham's theft, the law had no proof of guilt.

As I said, we had our teeth into this one and we weren't about to let go. So we paid another call on Dillon, this time at the hotel where he was staying, and asked him some questions about his background. There was nothing more immediate we could investigate, and we thought that maybe there was an angle in his past which would give us a clue toward solving the riddle.

He told us, readily enough, some of what he'd done during the 15 years since he'd left home, and it was a typical drifter's life: lobster packer in Maine, ranch hand in Montana, oil worker in Texas, road construction in South America. But there was a gap of about four years which he sort of skimmed over without saying anything specific. I jumped on that and asked him some direct questions, but he wouldn't talk about it.

His reluctance made Sherrard and me more than a little curious; we both had the cop's feeling it was important, that maybe it was the key we needed to unlock the mystery. Unobtrusively we had the department photographer take some pictures of Dillon; then we sent them out, along with a request for information as to his whereabouts during the four blank years, to various law enforcement agencies in Florida—where he'd admitted to being just prior to the gap, working as a deckhand on a Key West charter-fishing boat.

Time dragged on, and nothing turned up, and we were reluctantly forced by sheer volume of work to abandon the Chillingham case; officially, it was now buried in the Unsolved File. Then, three months later, we had a wire from the Chief of Police of a town not far from Fort Lauderdale. It said they had tentatively identified George Dillon from the pictures we'd sent and were forwarding by airmail special delivery something which might conceivably prove the nature of Dillon's activities during at least part of the specified period.

Sherrard and I fidgeted around waiting for the special delivery to arrive, and when it finally came I happened to be the only one of us in the Squadroom. I tore the envelope open and what was inside was a multicolored and well-aged poster, with a picture of a man who was undeniably George Dillon depicted on it. I looked at the picture and read what was written on the poster at least a dozen times.

It told me a lot of things all right, that poster did. It told me exactly what Dillon had done with the home-made zipgun he had used to kill Adam Chillingham—an answer that was at once fantastic and yet so simple you'd never even consider it. And it told me there wasn't a damned thing we could do about it now, that we couldn't touch him, that George Dillon actually had committed a perfect murder.

I was brooding over this when Jack Sherrard returned to the Squadroom. He said, 'Why so glum, Walt?'

'The special delivery from Florida finally showed up,' I said, and watched instant excitement animate his face. Then I saw some of it fade while I told him what I'd been brooding about, finishing with, 'We simply can't arrest him now, Jack. There's no evidence, it doesn't exist any more; we can't prove a thing. And maybe it's just as well in one respect, since I kind of liked Dillon and would have hated to see him convicted for killing a crook like Chillingham. Anyway, we'll be able to sleep nights now.'

'Damn it, Walt, will you tell me what you're talking about!'

'All right. Remember when we got the ballistics report we talked over how easy it would be for Dillon to have made a zipgun? And how he could make the whole thing out of a dozen or so small component parts, so that afterward he could break it down again into those small parts?'

'Sure, sure. But I still don't care if Dillon used a hundred components, we didn't find a single one of them. So what, if that's part of the answer, did he do with them? There's not even a connecting bathroom where he could have flushed them down. What did he do with the damned zipgun?'

I sighed and slid the poster—the old carnival side-show poster—around on my desk so he could see Dillon's picture and read the words printed below it: STEAK AND POTATOES AND APPLE PIE IS OUR DISH; NUTS, BOLTS, PIECES OF WOOD, BITS OF METAL IS HIS! YOU HAVE TO SEE IT TO BELIEVE IT: THE AMAZING MR GEORGE, THE MAN WITH THE CAST-IRON STOMACH.

Sherrard's head jerked up and he stared at me open-mouthed.

'That's right,' I said wearily. 'He *ate* it.'

# JACQUES FUTRELLE

# An Absence of Air

*Jacques Futrelle (1875–1912) was the first author to write prolifically in the Impossible Crime genre. A working journalist, for many years on the staff of the Boston-based* American, *he wrote a good, clean, crisp prose and was an 'ideas' man at a time of great scientific and technological change. Fascinated by the rapid advances made in the worlds of applied and experimental science, he created one of the best of the early scientific detectives, Professor Augustus S.F.X. Van Dusen, the 'Thinking Machine', who brings his own brand of icy and remorseless logic to bear on all the problems presented to him. To Van Dusen there is nothing, however bizarre or impossible, that cannot be rationally explained.*

*Van Dusen was not in the same league as R. Austin Freeman's Dr John Thorndyke (it's doubtful that Futrelle actualized his plots in the same way that Freeman personally carried out many of the experiments later used in the Thorndyke stories) although, while often utilizing the new technology, he was certainly more realistic in his approach than the only other contemporary scientific sleuth of any note, Arthur Reeve's wholly sensational and gadget-addicted Craig Kennedy (just a few of whose exploits go rather a long way). Where the Thinking Machine does stand out is that he's one of the rudest, most misanthropic sleuths from the Classic era.*

*Ironically, in 1912 Futrelle perished with the* Titanic, *then, supposedly, the most advanced liner in the world and a triumph of modern technology. In London, Futrelle had written ten Thinking Machine stories, the manuscripts of six accompanying him on the* Titanic's *maiden voyage (and thus lost for ever). The remaining four stories were left in London.*

*In the early-1940s Ellery Queen published one of the four as 'The Case of the Mysterious Weapon'. The impression given was that this was its first appearance in print, and perhaps it was—in America, and in the version printed. But the same story—the story that follows—had already appeared in England twenty years earlier, in an issue of* The Storyteller, *although in a somewhat different form.*

*In* The Storyteller *version an editorial hand has altered the location of the story from America to England so that, for instance, Detective Mallory, a member of New York's Finest, is now an officer in Scotland Yard's CID (this sort of thing was always happening to second-rights material: in a series of paperbacks published during the First World War, the great Nick Carter was transplanted across the Atlantic to, of all places,*

*Manchester). I have changed the locale back to America. However, I have also indulged in a little editorial scene-shifting myself. In the original version, Futrelle, for some inexplicable reason, has placed the solution to the mystery (or at least given the game away) half-way through the story, thus effectively sabotaging the denouement. With a modicum of tinkering (and I suspect I'm following in Ellery Queen's own footsteps here) I've moved this crucial scene to the end, with the addition of only one word. I hope the shade of Jacques Futrelle is nodding its head and not gnashing its teeth. I suspect—good journalist that he was—the former.*

JACK ADRIAN

Certainly no problem that ever came to the attention of Professor Augustus Van Dusen required in a greater degree subtlety of mind, exquisite analytical sense, and precise knowledge of the marvels of science than did that singular series of events which began with the mysterious death of Miss Violet Danbury, only daughter and sole heir of the late Charles Duval Danbury, of Boston, in the state of Massachusetts.

In this case Professor Van Dusen brought to bear upon an extraordinary mystery of crime that remarkable genius of logic which had made him the Court of Last Appeal in his profession. 'Logic is inexorable,' he has said; and no greater proof of his assertion was possible than in this instance where, literally, he seemed to pluck a solution of the riddle from the void.

Shortly after eleven o'clock on the morning of Thursday, May 4, Miss Danbury was found dead, sitting in the drawing-room of apartments she was temporarily occupying in a big family hotel in Beacon Street. She was richly gowned, just as she had come from the opera the night before, her marble white bosom and arms a-glitter with jewels. On her face, dark in death as are the faces of those who die of strangulation, was an expression of unspeakable terror. Her parted lips were slightly bruised, as if from a light blow; in her left cheek was an insignificant, bloodless wound. On the floor at her feet was a shattered goblet. There was nothing else unusual, no disorder, no sign of a struggle. Obviously she had been dead for several hours.

All these things considered, the first judgment of the police— specifically, the first judgment of Detective Mallory, of the Criminal Investigation bureau—was suicide by poison. Miss Danbury had poured some deadly drug into a goblet, sat down, drained if off, and died. Simple and obvious enough. But the darkness in her face? Oh, that! Probably some effect of a poison he didn't happen to be acquainted with. But it looked as if she might have been strangled! Pooh! Pooh! There were no marks on her neck of fingers or anything else. Suicide, that's what it was—the autopsy would disclose the nature of the poison.

Cursory questions of the usual nature were asked and answered. Had Miss Danbury lived alone? No; she had a companion upon whom, too, devolved the duties of chaperon—a Mrs Cecelia Montgomery. Where was she? She'd left the city the day before to visit friends in Boston; the manager of the hotel had telegraphed the facts to her. No servants? No. She had availed herself of the service in the hotel. Who had last seen Miss Danbury alive? The hotel lift attendant the night before when she had returned from the opera, about half-past eleven o'clock. Had she gone alone? No. She had been accompanied by Professor Charles Meredith of the University. He had returned with her and left her at the lift.

'How did she come to know Professor Meredith?' Mallory inquired. 'Friend, relative—'

'I don't know,' said the hotel manager. 'She'd only been in the city two months this time, but once, three years ago, she spent six months here.'

'Any particular reason for her coming to town? Business, for instance, or merely a visit?'

'Merely a visit, I imagine.'

The front door swung open, and there entered at the moment a middle-aged man, sharp-featured, rather spare, brisk in his movements, and distinctly well-groomed. He went straight to the inquiry desk.

'Will you please 'phone Miss Danbury and ask her if she will join Mr Herbert Willing for luncheon at the country club?' he requested. 'Tell her I am below with my motor.'

At mention of Miss Danbury's name both Mallory and the hotel manager turned. The boy behind the inquiry desk glanced at the detective blankly. Mr Willing rapped upon the desk sharply.

'Well, well?' he demanded impatiently. 'Are you asleep?'

'Good morning, Mr Willing,' Mallory greeted him.

'Hallo, Mallory!' and Mr Willing turned to face him. 'What are you doing here?'

'You don't know that Miss Danbury is'—the detective paused a little—'is dead?'

'Dead!' Willing repeated incredulously. 'What are you talking about?' He seized Mallory by the arm and shook him.

'Dead,' the detective assured him again. 'She probably committed suicide. She was found in her apartments two hours ago.'

For half a minute Mr Willing continued to stare at him as if without comprehension; then he dropped weakly into a chair with his head in his hands. When he glanced up again there was deep grief in his keen face.

'It's my fault,' he said simply. 'I feel like a murderer. I gave her some bad news yesterday, but I didn't dream she would—' He stopped.

'Bad news?' Mallory urged.

'I've been doing some legal work for her,' Mr Willing explained. 'She's been trying to sell a huge estate in the country, and at the moment when the deal seemed assured it fell through. I—I suppose it was a mistake to tell her. This morning I received another offer from an unexpected quarter, and I came to inform her of it.' He stared tensely into Mallory's face for a moment without speaking. 'I feel like her murderer!' he said again.

'But I don't understand why the failure of the deal—' the detective began; then 'She was rich wasn't she? What did it matter particularly if the deal did fail?'

'Rich, yes, but land poor,' the lawyer elucidated. 'The estates to which she held title were frightfully involved. She had jewels and all those things, but see how simply she lived. She was actually in need of money. It would take me an hour to make you understand. How did she die? When? What was the manner of her death?'

Detective Mallory placed before him those facts he had, and finally went away with him in his motorcar to see Professor Meredith at the University. Nothing bearing on the case developed as the result of that interview. Mr Meredith seemed greatly shocked, and explained that is acquaintance with Miss Danbury dated some weeks back, and friendship had grown out of it through a mutual love of music. He had accompanied her to the opera half a dozen times.

'Suicide!' the detective declared as he came away. 'Obviously suicide by poison.'

On the following day he discovered for the first time that the obvious is not necessarily true. The autopsy revealed absolutely no trace of poison, either in the body or clinging to the shattered goblet, carefully gathered up and examined. The heart was normal, showing neither constriction nor dilation, as would have been the case had poison been swallowed, or even inhaled.

'It's the small wound in her cheek then,' Mallory asserted. 'Maybe she *didn't* swallow or inhale poison—she injected it directly into her blood through the wound.'

'No,' one of the examining physicians pointed out. 'Even that way the heart would have shown constriction or dilation.'

'Oh, maybe not,' Mallory argued hopefully.

'Besides,' the physician went on, 'that wound was made after death. That is proven by the fact that it did not bleed.' His brow clouded in perplexity. 'There doesn't seem to be the slightest reason for that wound, anyway. It's really a hole, you know. It goes straight through her cheek. It looks as if it might have been made with a large hatpin.'

The detective was staring at him. If that wound had been made after death, certainly Miss Danbury didn't make it; she had been murdered, and not murdered for robbery, since her jewels had been undisturbed.

'Straight through her cheek!' he repeated blankly. 'By George! If it wasn't poison, what killed her?'

The three examining physicians exchanged glances.

'I don't know that I can make you understand,' said one. 'She died of absence of air in her lungs, if you follow me.'

'Absence of air—well, that's illuminating!' the detective sneered heavily. 'You mean she was strangled or choked to death?'

'I mean precisely what I say,' was the reply. 'She was not strangled—there is no mark on her throat; or choked—there is no obstruction in her throat. Literally she died of absence of air in her lungs.'

Mallory stood silently glowering at them. A fine lot of physicians, these.

'Let's understand one another,' he said at last. 'Miss Danbury did not die a natural death?'

'No'—emphatically.

'She wasn't poisoned? Or strangled? Or shot? Or stabbed? Or run over by a truck? Or blown up by dynamite? Or kicked by a mule? Nor,' he concluded, 'did she fall from an aeroplane?'

'No.'

'In other words, she just stopped living?'

'Something like that,' the physician admitted. He seemed to be seeking a means of making himself more explicit. 'You know the old nursery theory that a cat will suck a sleeping baby's breath?' he asked. 'Well, the death of Miss Danbury was like that, if you understand. It is as if some great animal or—or thing had—' He stopped.

Detective Mallory was an able man, the ablest, perhaps, in the Criminal Investigation bureau, but a yellow primrose by the river's brim was to him a yellow primrose, nothing more. He lacked imagination, a common fault of that type of sleuth who combines, more or less happily, a No. 11 shoe and a No. 6 hat. The only vital thing he had to go on was the fact that Miss Danbury was dead— murdered in some mysterious, uncanny way. Vampires were something like that, weren't they? He shuddered a little.

'Regular vampire sort of thing,' the youngest of the three physicians remarked, echoing the thought in the detective's mind. 'They're supposed to make a slight wound, and—'

Detective Mallory didn't hear the remainder of it. He turned abruptly and left the room.

On the following Monday morning, one Henry Sumner, a longshoreman, was found sitting in his squalid room. On his face, dark in death as are the faces of those who die of strangulation, was an expression of unspeakable terror. His parted lips were slightly bruised, as if from a light blow; in his left cheek was an insignificant bloodless wound. On the floor at his feet was a shattered drinking-glass!

'Twas Hutchinson Hatch, newspaper reporter, long, lean, and rather prepossessing in appearance, who brought this double mystery to the attention of Professor Van Dusen. Martha, the eminent scientist's one servant, admitted the newspaper man, and he went straight to the laboratory. As he opened the door Professor Van Dusen turned testily from his work table.

'Oh, it's you, Mr Hatch. Glad to see you. Sit down. What is it?' That was his idea of extreme cordiality.

'If you can spare me five minutes—' the reporter began apologetically.

'What is it?' repeated Professor Van Dusen, without raising his eyes.

'I wish I knew,' the reporter said ruefully. 'Two persons are dead— two persons as widely apart as the poles, at least in social position, have been murdered in precisely the same manner, and it seems impossible that—'

'Nothing is impossible,' Professor Van Dusen interrupted in the tone of perpetual irritation which seemed to be part of him. 'You annoy me when you say it.'

'It seems highly improbable,' Hatch corrected himself, 'that there can be the remotest connection between the crimes, yet—'

'You're wasting words,' the crabby little scientist declared impatiently. 'Begin at the beginning. Who was murdered? When? How? Why? What was the manner of death?'

'Taking the last question first,' the reporter explained, 'we have the most singular part of the problem. No one can say the manner of death, not even the physicians.'

'Oh!' For the first time the little professor lifted his petulant, squinting, narrowed eyes and stared into the face of the newspaper man. 'Oh!' he said again. 'Go on.'

As Hatch talked the lure of a material problem laid hold of the master mind, and after a little Professor Van Dusen dropped into a chair. With his great grotesque head tilted back, his eyes turned steadily upward, and slender fingers placed precisely tip to tip, he listened in silence to the end.

'We come now,' said the newspaper man, 'to the inexplicable after-developments. We have proven that Mrs Cecelia Montgomery, Miss Danbury's companion, did not go to Boston to visit friends; as a matter of fact, she is missing. The police have been able to find no trace of her, and to-day are sending out a general alarm. Naturally, her absence at this particular moment is suspicious. It is possible to conjecture her connection with the death of Miss Danbury, but what about—'

'Never mind conjecture,' the scientist broke in curtly. 'Facts, facts!'

'Further'—and Hatch's bewilderment was evident on his face— 'mysterious things have been happening in the rooms where Miss Danbury and this man, Henry Sumner, were found dead. Miss Danbury was found dead last Thursday. Immediately after the body was removed Detective Mallory ordered her room to be locked, his idea being that nothing should be disturbed, at least for the present, because of the strange circumstances surrounding her death. When the nature of the Henry Sumner affair became known, and the similarity of the cases recognized, he gave the same order regarding Sumner's room.'

Hatch stopped and stared vainly into the pallid, wizened face of the scientist; a curious little chill ran down his spinal column.

'Some time Tuesday night,' he continued after a moment, 'Miss Danbury's room was entered and ransacked; and some time that same night Henry Sumner's room was entered and ransacked. This morning, Wednesday, a clearly defined hand-print in blood was found in Miss Danbury's room. It was on the wooden top of a dressing-table. It seemed to be a woman's hand. Also, an indistinguishable smudge of blood, which may have been a hand-print, was found in Sumner's room!' He paused. Professor Van Dusen's countenance was inscrutable. 'What possible connection can there be between this young woman and this—this longshoreman? Why—'

'What chair,' questioned Professor Van Dusen, 'does Professor Meredith hold in the University?'

'Greek,' was the reply.

'Who is Mr Willing?'

'One of our leading lawyers.'

'Did you see Miss Danbury's body?'

'Yes.'

'Did she have a large mouth or a small mouth?'

The irrelevancy of the questions, to say nothing of their disjointedness, brought a look of astonishment to Hatch's face, and he was a young man who was rarely astonished by the curious methods of the little professor. Always he had found that the scientist approached a problem from a new angle.

'I should say a small mouth,' he ventured. 'Her lips were bruised as if—as if something round, say the size of a two-shilling piece, had been crushed against them. There was a queer, drawn, caved-in look to her mouth and cheeks.'

'Naturally,' commented Professor Van Dusen enigmatically. 'And Sumner's was the same.'

'Precisely. You say "naturally." Do you mean—' There was eagerness in the reporter's question.

It passed unanswered. For half a minute or so the little scientist continued to stare into nothingness. Finally:

'I dare say Sumner was not a foreigner? His name is English?'

'Yes, and a splendid man physically—a hard drinker, I hear, as well as a hard worker.'

Again a pause.

'You don't happen to know if Meredith is now or ever has been particularly interested in physics—that is, in natural philosophy?'

'I do not.'

'Please find out immediately,' the scientist directed tersely. 'Willing has handled some legal business for Miss Danbury. Learn what you can from him to the general end of establishing some connection—a relationship, possibly—between Henry Sumner and Miss Violet Danbury. That, at the moment, is the most important thing to do. Neither of them may have been aware of the relationship, if relationship it was, yet it may have existed. If it doesn't exist, there's only one answer to the problem.'

'And that is?' Hatch asked.

'The murders are the work of a madman,' was the tart rejoinder. 'There's no mystery of course, in the manner of the death of these two.'

'No mystery?' the reporter echoed blankly. 'Do you mean you know how—'

'Certainly I know, and you know. The examining physicians know, only they don't know that they know.' Suddenly his tone became didactic. 'Knowledge that can't be applied is utterly useless,' he said. 'The real difference between a great mind and a mediocre mind is only that the great mind applies its knowledge.' He was silent a moment. 'The one problem remaining here is to find the person who was aware of the many advantages of this method of murder.'

'Advantages?' The newspaper man was puzzled.

'From the view point of the murderer there is always a good way and a bad way to kill a person,' the scientist told him. 'This particular murderer chose a way that was swift, silent, simple, and sure as the march of time. There was no scream, no struggle, no pistol shot, no poison to be traced; nothing except—'

'The hole in the left cheek, perhaps?'

'Quite right, and that leaves no clue. As a matter of fact, the only clue we have at all is the certainty that the murderer, man or woman, is well acquainted with physics, or natural philosophy.'

'Then you think'—the newspaper man's eyes were about to start from his head—'that Professor Meredith—'

'I think nothing,' Professor Van Dusen declared briefly. 'I want to know what he knows of physics, as I said; also, I want to know if there is any connection between Miss Danbury and the longshoreman. If you'll attend to—'

Abruptly the laboratory door opened, and Martha entered, pallid, frightened, her hands shaking.

'Something most peculiar, sir,' she stammered in her excitement.

'Well?' the little scientist questioned.

'I do believe,' said Martha, 'that I'm a-going to faint!'

And as an evidence of good faith she did, crumpling up in a little heap before their astonished eyes.

'Dear me! Dear me!' exclaimed Professor Van Dusen petulantly. 'Of all the inconsiderate things. Why couldn't she have told us before she did that?'

It was a labour of fifteen minutes to bring Martha round, and then, weakly, she explained what had happened. She had answered a ring of the telephone, and someone had asked for Professor Van Dusen. She inquired the name of the person talking.

'Never mind that,' came the reply. 'Is he there? Can I see him?'

'You'll have to explain what you want, sir' Martha had told him. 'He always has to know.'

'Tell him I know who murdered Miss Danbury and Henry Sumner,' came over the wire. 'If he'll receive me I'll be right up.'

'And then, sir,' Martha explained to Professor Dusen, 'something must have happened at the other end, sir. I heard another man's voice, then a sort of a choking sound, sir, and then "Damn you!" just like that, sir. I didn't hear any more. They hung up the receiver or something, sir.' She paused indignantly. 'Think of him, sir, a-swearing at me that way!'

For a moment the eyes of the two men met; the same thought had come to them both. Professor Van Dusen voiced it.

'Another one!' he said. 'The third!'

With no other word he turned and went out; Martha followed him grumblingly. Hatch shuddered a little. The hand of the clock went on to half-past seven, to eight. At twenty minutes past eight the scientist re-entered the laboratory.

'That fifteen minutes "Martha was unconscious probably cost a man's life, and certainly lost to us an immediate solution of the riddle,' he declared peevishly. 'If she had told us before she fainted, there is a chance that the operator would have remembered the number. As it is, there have been fifty calls since, and there's no record.' He spread his slender hands helplessly. 'The manager is trying to find the calling number. Anyway, we'll know to-morrow. Meanwhile, try to see Mr Willing to-night and find out what relationship, if any, exists between Miss Danbury and Sumner; also see Professor Meredith.'

The newspaper man telephoned to Mr Willing's home in Melrose to see if he was in; he was not. On a chance he telephoned to his office. He hardly expected an answer, and he got none. So it was not until four o'clock in the morning that the third tragedy in the series came to light.

The scrub women employed in the great building where Mr Willing had his law offices entered the suite to clean up. They found Mr Willing there, gagged, bound hand and foot, and securely lashed to a chair. He was alive, but apparently unconscious from exhaustion. Directly facing him, his secretary, Maxwell Pittman, sat dead in his chair. On his face, dark in death as are the faces of those who die of strangulation, was an expression of unspeakable terror. His parted lips were slightly bruised, as if from a light blow; in the left cheek was an insignificant bloodless wound. At his feet was a shattered drinking-glass.

Within less than an hour Detective Mallory was on the scene. By that time Mr Willing, under the influence of stimulants, was able to talk.

'I have no idea what happened,' he explained. 'It was after six o'clock, and my secretary and I were alone in the offices finishing up some work. He had stepped into another room for a moment, and I was at my desk. Someone crept up behind me and held a drugged cloth to my nostrils. I tried to shout, to struggle, but everything grew black, and that's all I know. When I came to myself poor Pittman was there, just as you see him.'

Searching about the offices Mallory came upon a small lace handkerchief. He seized upon it tensely, and, as he raised it to examine it, he became conscious of a strong odour of drugs. In one corner of the handkerchief there was a monogram.

' "C. M." ' he read. His eyes blazed. 'Cecelia Montgomery!'

In the grip of an uncontrollable excitement Hutchinson Hatch butted in upon Professor Van Dusen in his laboratory.

'There was another,' he announced.

'I know it,' said Professor Van Dusen, still bent over his work table. 'Who was it?'

'Maxwell Pittman.' And Hatch related the story.

'There may be two more,' the scientist remarked. 'Be good enough to call a cab.'

'Two more?' Hatch gasped in horror. 'Already dead?'

'There may be, I said. One, Cecelia Montgomery; the other the unknown who called on the telephone last night.'

Together they were driven straight to the University and shown into Professor Meredith's study. Professor Meredith showed his astonishment plainly at the visit, and astonishment became indignant amazement at the first question.

'Mr Meredith, can you account for every moment of your time from mid-afternoon yesterday until four o'clock this morning?' Professor Van Dusen queried flatly. 'Don't misunderstand me—I mean every moment covering the time in which it is possible that Maxwell Pittman was murdered?'

'Why, it's a most outrageous—' Professor Meredith exploded.

'I'm trying to save you from arrest,' the scientist explained curtly. 'If you can account for all that time, and prove your statement, believe me, you had better prepare to do so. Now, if you could give me any information as to—'

'Who the devil are you?' demanded Professor Meredith belligerently. 'What do you mean by daring to suggest—'

'My name is Van Dusen,' said the little professor mildly; 'Augustus S. F. X. Van Dusen. Long before your time I held the chair of philosophy in this university. I vacated it by request. Later the university honoured me with a degree of LL.D.'

The result of the self-introduction was astonishing. Professor

Meredith, in the presence of the master mind in the sciences, was a different man.

'I beg your pardon,' he began.

'I'm curious to know if you are at all acquainted with Miss Danbury's family history,' the scientist went on. 'Meanwhile, Mr Hatch, take the cab and go straight and measure the precise width of the bruise on Pittman's lips; also see Mr Willing, if he is able to receive you, and ask him what he can give you as to Miss Danbury's history—I mean her family, her property, her connections; all about everything. Meet me at my house in a couple of hours.'

Hatch went out, leaving them together. When he reached the scientist's home Professor Van Dusen was just coming out.

'I'm on my way to see Mr George Parsons, the so-called Copper King,' he volunteered. 'Come along.'

From that moment came several developments so curious and bizarre and so widely dissociated that Hatch could make nothing of them at all. Nothing seemed to fit into anything else. For instance, Professor Van Dusen's visit to Mr Parsons' office.

'Please ask Mr Parsons if he will see Mr Van Dusen?' he requested of an attendant.

'What about?' the query came from Mr Parsons.

'It is a matter of life and death,' the answer went back.

'Whose?' Mr Parsons wanted to know.

'His!' The scientist's answer was equally short.

Immediately afterwards Professor Van Dusen disappeared inside. Ten minutes later, he came out, and he and Hatch went off together, stopping at a toy shop to buy a small high-grade, rubber ball, and later at a department store to purchase a vicious-looking hatpin.

'You failed to inform me, Mr Hatch, of the measurement of the bruise.'

'Precisely one and a quarter inches.'

'Thanks. And what did Mr Willing say?'

'I haven't seen him as yet. I have an appointment to see him in an hour from now.'

'Very well'—and Professor Van Dusen nodded his satisfaction— 'when you see him will you be so good enough to tell him, please, that I know—I *know*, do you understand?—who killed Miss Danbury, and Sumner, and Pittman. You can't make it too strong. I *know*, do you understand?'

'*Do* you know?' Hatch demanded quickly.

'No'—frankly. 'But convince him that I do, and add that to-morrow at noon I shall place the extraordinary facts I have gathered in possession of the police. At noon, understand; and I know.' He was thoughtful a moment. 'You might add that I have informed you that the guilty person is a person of high position, whose name has been in no way connected with the crimes—that is, unpleasantly. You don't know that name; no one knows it except myself. I shall give it to the police at noon to-morrow.'

'Anything else?'

'Drop in on me early to-morrow morning, and bring Mr Mallory.'

Events were cyclonic on that last morning. Mallory and Hatch had hardly arrived when there came a telephone message for the detective from police headquarters. Mrs Cecelia Montgomery was there. She had come in voluntarily, and asked for Mr Mallory.

'Don't rush off now,' requested Professor Van Dusen, who was pottering around among the retorts and microscopes and what not on his work table. 'Ask them to detain her until you get there. Also, ask her what relationship existed between Miss Danbury and Henry Sumner.' The detective went out; the scientist turned to Hatch. 'Here is a hatpin,' he said. 'Some time this morning we shall have another caller. If, during the presence of that person in this room, I voluntarily put anything to my lips—a bottle, say—or anything is forced upon me and I do not remove it in just thirty seconds, you will thrust this hatpin through my cheek. Don't hesitate.'

'Thrust it through—' the reporter repeated. An uncanny chill ran over him.

'I say if I don't remove it,' Professor Van Dusen interrupted shortly. 'You and Mallory will be watching from another room; I shall demonstrate the exact manner of the murders.' There was a troubled look in the reporter's face. 'I shall be in no danger,' he said simply. 'The hatpin is merely a precaution if anything should go wrong.'

After a little Mallory entered, with clouded countenance.

'She denies the murders,' he announced, 'but admits that the handprints in blood are hers. According to her yarn she searched Miss Danbury's room and Sumner's room after the murders to find some family papers which were necessary to establish claims to some estate—I don't quite understand. She hurt her hand in Miss Danbury's room, and it bled a lot—hence the hand-print. From there she went straight to Sumner's room, and presumably left the smudge there. It seems that Sumner was a distant cousin of Miss Danbury's—the only son of a younger brother who ran away years ago after some wild escapade, and later returned home. George Parsons, the Copper King, is the only other relative in this country. She advises us to warn him to be on guard—seems to think he will be the next victim.'

'He's already warned,' said Professor Van Dusen, 'and he has gone away on important business.'

Mallory stared.

'You seem to know more about this case that I do,' he sneered.

'I do,' asserted the scientist; 'quite a lot more.'

'I think a cross-examination will change Mrs Montgomery's story soon,' the detective declared. 'Perhaps she will remember better—'

'She is telling the truth.'

'Then why did she run away? How was it we found her handkerchief in Mr Willing's office after the Pittman affair? How was it—'

The little scientist shrugged his shoulders and was silent. A moment later the door opened and Martha appeared, her eyes blazing with indignation.

'That man who swore at me over the telephone,' she announced distinctly, 'wants to see you, sir.'

Mallory's keen eyes swept the faces of the scientist and the reporter, trying to fathom the strange change that came over them.

'You are sure, Martha?' asked Professor Van Dusen.

'Indeed, I am, sir.' She was positive about it. 'I'd never forget his voice, sir.'

For an instant her master merely stared, then dismissed her with a curt: 'Show him in,' after which he turned to the detective and Hatch.

'You will wait in the next room,' he said tersely. 'If anything happens, Mr Hatch, remember.'

Professor Van Dusen was sitting when the visitor entered—a middle-aged man, sharp-featured, rather spare, brisk in his movements, and distinctly well-groomed. It was Mr Herbert Willing, solicitor. In one hand he carried a small bag. He paused an instant and gazed at the diminutive scientist curiously.

'Come in, Mr Willing,' Professor Van Dusen greeted. 'You want to see me about—' He paused questioningly.

'I understand,' said the lawyer suavely, 'that you have interested yourself in these recent—er—remarkable murders, and there are some points I should like to discuss with you. I have some papers in my bag here which'—he opened it—'may be of interest. Some—er—newspaper man informed me that you have certain information indicating—'

'I know the name of the murderer,' said Professor Van Dusen.

'Indeed? May I ask who it is?'

'You may. His name is Herbert Willing.'

Watching tensely, Hatch saw the little scientist pass his hand slowly across his mouth as if to stifle a yawn; saw Willing leap forward suddenly with what seemed to be a bottle in his hand; saw him force the scientist back into his chair, and thrust the bottle against his lips. Instantly came a sharp click, and some hideous change came over the scientist's wizened face. His eyes opened wide in terror, his cheeks seemed to collapse. Instinctively he grasped the bottle with both hands.

For a scant second Willing stared at him, his countenance grown demoniacal; then he swiftly took something else from the small bag and smashed it on the floor. It was a drinking-glass! After which the scientist calmly removed the bottle from his lips.

'The broken drinking-glass,' he said, 'completes the evidence.'

Hutchinson Hatch was lean and wiry and hard as nails; Detective Mallory's bulk concealed muscle of steel; but it took both of them to overpower the solicitor. Heedless of the struggling trio, Professor Van Dusen was curiously scrutinising the black bottle. The mouth was blocked by a small rubber ball which he had thrust against it with his tongue a fraction of an instant before the dreaded power the bottle held had been released by pressure upon a cunningly concealed spring. When he raised his squinting eyes at last, Willing, manacled, was glaring at him in impotent rage. Fifteen minutes later the four were at police-headquarters; Mrs Montgomery was awaiting them.

'Mrs Montgomery, why'—and the petulant pale blue eyes of the little scientist were fixed upon her face—'why didn't you go to Boston, as you had said?'

'I did go there,' she replied. 'It was simply that when the news came of Miss Danbury's terrible death I was frightened. I lost my head; I pleaded with my friends not to let it be known that I was there, and they agreed. If anyone had searched their house I would have been found; no one did. At last I could stand it no longer. I came to the city, and straight here to explain everything I knew in connection with the affair.'

'And the search you made of Miss Danbury's room? And of Sumner's room?'

'I've explained that,' she said. 'I knew of the relationship between poor Harry Sumner and Violet Danbury, and I knew each of them had certain papers which were of value as establishing their claims to a great estate in the country now in litigation. I was sure those papers would be valuable to the only other claimant, who was—'

'Mr George Parsons, the Copper King,' interposed the scientist. 'You didn't find the papers you sought because Willing had taken them. That estate was the thing he wanted, and I dare say by some legal jugglery he would have got it.' Again he turned to face Mrs

Montgomery. 'Living with Miss Danbury, as you did, you probably held a key of her apartments? Yes. You had only the difficulty, then, of entering the hotel late at night, unseen, and that seemed to be simple. Willing did it the night he killed Miss Danbury, and left it unseen, as you did. Now, how did you enter Sumner's room?'

'It was a terrible place,' and she shuddered slightly. 'I went in alone, and entered his room through a window from a fire-escape. The newspapers, you will remember, described its location precisely, and—'

'I see,' Professor Van Dusen interrupted. He was silent a moment. 'You're a shrewd man, Willing, and your knowledge of natural philosophy is exact if not extensive. Of course, I knew if you thought I knew too much about the murders you would come to me. You did. It was a trap, if that's any consolation to you. You fell into it. And curiously enough, I wasn't afraid of a knife or a shot; I knew the instrument of death you had been using was too satisfactory and silent for you to change. However, I was prepared for it, and—I think that's all.' He arose.

'All?' Hatch and Mallory echoed the word. 'We don't understand—'

'Oh!' And Professor Van Dusen sat down again. 'It's logic. Miss Danbury was dead, neither shot, stabbed, poisoned, nor choked—"absence of air in her lungs," the physicians said. Instantly the vacuum bottle suggested itself. That murder, as was the murder of Sumner, was planned to counterfeit suicide; hence the broken goblet on the floor. Incidentally the murder of Sumner informed me that the crimes were the work of a madman, else there was an underlying purpose which might have arisen through a relationship. Ultimately I established that relationship through Professor Meredith, in whom Miss Danbury had confided to a certain extent; at the same time, he convinced me of his innocence in the affair. But come back to the laboratory with me, both of you, and I'll explain.'

In the laboratory Professor Van Dusen turned to his work-table.

'Let me show you a simple experiment,' he said, and he held aloft a thick glass vessel closed at one end and with a stopcock at the other. 'I place this heavy piece of rubber over the mouth of the tube and then turn the stopcock.' He suited the action to the word. 'Now take if off.'

The reporter tugged at it with all his strength, then took a long breath and tried again. He was unable to move it. Detective Mallory also tried, and was equally unsuccessful. They looked at the scientist in perplexity.

'What holds it there?' asked Hatch.

'Vacuum,' replied Professor Van Dusen. 'You may tear it to pieces, but no human power can pull it away whole.' The little man with the yellow hair picked up a steel bodkin and thrust it through the rubber into the mouth of the tube. As he withdrew the bodkin there came a sharp, prolonged, hissing sound. A few seconds later the rubber fell off. 'The vacuum was practically perfect—something like one-millionth of an atmosphere. The pin hole permitted the air to fill the tube, the tremendous pressure against the rubber was removed, and—' he waved his slender hands.

In that instant Mallory and Hatch comprehended. Hatch suddenly remembered some of his college experiments.

'If I should place that tube to your lips, Mr Hatch—or to yours, Mr Mallory—you would never speak again, never scream, never even struggle. It would jerk every particle of air out of your body, paralyse you. Within two minutes you would be dead. To remove the tube I should simply thrust the bodkin through your cheek—say, your left one—and withdraw it.

'Now,' he continued after a moment, 'we come to the murder of Pittman. Pittman learned, and tried to 'phone me, who the murderer was. Willing heard that message. He killed Pittman, then bound and gagged himself and waited. It was a clever ruse. His story of being overpowered and drugged is absurd on the face of it; yet he asked us to believe that by leaving a handkerchief of Mrs Montgomery's on the floor. That was reeking with drugs. Mr Hatch can give you more of these details.' He glanced at his watch. 'I'm due at a luncheon where I am to make an address to the Society of Psychical Research. If you'll excuse me—'

He went out; the others sat staring after him.

JOHN F. SUTER

# The Impossible Theft

*John F. Suter is by no means a prolific writer, his short story output mainly directed at Ellery Queen (with one or two excursions into Alfred Hitchcock territory, long, long ago). But when his name crops up on a Contents page it's worth reading the rest of the issue first and keeping his story until the end—on the principal that one always saves the best till last.*

*The first story he sold, 'A Break in the Film' (EQ, September 1953) won him a Queen Special Award, deservedly. It's a wonderfully nostalgic trip into his own past—to the kind of slightly ramshackle, small-town movie-house of his youth in the 1920s that showed Westerns and actioners and serials and funnies; the kind of semi-fleapit that never showed the 'Big Films' and had a piano instead of an organ. Against that backdrop he wove a compelling tale of certain events that took place during a long hot summer which lead, inevitably, to murder.*

*After that came other stories, spread out over the years; but certainly not enough—not nearly enough—to gratify lovers of neatly-constructed and finely-written tales of crime. Happily (since retirement, I suspect) he now not only seems to be appearing more regularly but has acquired for himself a series character. And the character he's acquired proves that John Suter isn't averse to taking appalling risks, for he's taken on the mantle of Melville Davisson Post and dared to continue the saga of possibly the second greatest detective in American fiction (needless to specify the first): that 'protector of the innocent and righter of wrongs' Uncle Abner.*

*Taking on another author's character is surely the most arduous task in a writer's life (all that checking, all that getting-it-right), and you have to be a masochist or at least deeply besotted with your subject to want to do it at all, since however you handle the character someone out there will hate it, and thus you. Some pastiches are good, some are bad (some, like J.T. Edson's additions to Edgar Wallace's J.G.Reeder, for instance, are unspeakable). I suspect John Suter is deeply besotted with Uncle Abner, though in the nicest possible way, and to my mind he's succeeded triumphantly in recreating the style, mood and atmosphere of the originals.*

*One of John Suter's Uncle Abner tales, 'The Fairy Ring', is an Impossible, and a good one too. But good as it is 'The Impossible Theft', included here, is even better. It's the sort of story that makes one jump out of one's chair with a whoop of glee at the author's ingenuity—which is precisely what occurred to both your editors when we first read it.*

JACK ADRIAN

Robert Chisholm's palms were faintly damp. He had less confidence in his ability to persuade than in the probability of his accomplishing the theft. Still, he hoped that theft would be unnecessary.

Donald Tapp looked up at him sardonically as he turned the second key to the double-locked room.

'Robert,' he said in a voice that had been hoarse all his life, 'you still haven't told me how you found out about my collection.'

Chisholm's shrug was the smooth practised action of a man who knows and controls every muscle. He permitted his smile to be open and frank, instead of the faintly diabolical one which his lean face wore on certain occasions.

'I told you,' he said. 'A mutual friend. He just doesn't want to be identified.'

Tapp reached around the metal doorframe and pressed a switch. Fluorescent lights hesitated, blinked, then came on.

He pursed his thick lips. 'Mutual friend? I don't advertise what I own. There is always a clamour to have such items as these placed in a museum. Time enough for that when I'm dead.' He studied Chisholm quizzically. 'Would it have been Perry?'

Chisholm became poker-faced. 'Sorry, Don.'

Tapp still waited before ushering him into the room.

'Robert, I haven't seen you in—how many years? Even though we played together as boys and went to school together—clear through college. Now you arrive in town for a convention and after all these years you look me up. I'm delighted, Robert, delighted. I don't see old friends much any more. Chiefly my own fault. But, Robert, you arrive and make small talk and then, in the middle of it, you ask to see the collection.'

Chisholm said, just a shade too casually, 'If you'd rather not—'

*Ask yourself, Don,* he thought; *when you were a kid and somebody asked 'Whatcha got?' you'd always hide it, make a big secret of it.*

Tapp stepped away from the door, lifting a stubby right hand. 'Come and look. I'll be honest and say I'm particular. Not everybody can get into this room. But you're an old friend. At least, you were never grabby like the other kids.'

*If you only knew,* Chisholm thought, entering the strongroom which Tapp devoted to his collection of rare historical documents.

It was a windowless room, about 12 feet by 20, lighted only by two rows of fluorescent tubes overhead. The only door was at the end of one long wall. To the left on entering, the wall was decorated with a large rectangular mirror in a gilded frame. The borders of the glass itself were worked in elaborate scrolls and tracery. Ranged against the two long walls and the far end of the room were nine exhibition cases, four along each wall, one at the end. The cases were of beautifully grained wood, with glass tops.

Tapp beckoned Chisholm across the room.

'We'll begin here.' He snapped a switch on the side of one cabinet, and the interior became evenly illuminated, showing a frayed yellowed paper on a background of black velvet.

As Chisholm bent his lean shoulders to look at the descriptive card, Tapp began to explain. 'The last page of a letter by James Garfield. Identity of recipient unknown, but signature authenticated. Can you read it? It says, *As to your wish that I make a Fourth of July address in your community, this would give me the greatest of pleasure. I must defer my answer, however, because I feel that there is some prior commitment which I cannot identify at this moment. Should this prove to be only faulty memory, I shall be pleased to accept . . .* Of course, when you realize this was written just prior to that fatal July 2, it makes for interesting speculation, doesn't it?'

As Chisholm murmured an appropriate reply, Tapp switched off the light and moved to the right. 'In this cabinet I have a receipt from William Tecumseh Sherman to Braxton Bragg for money that Bragg asked Sherman to invest for him in San Francisco in 1854, when Sherman was in the banking business. The accompanying letters have great historical significance.'

Chisholm stared with a fascination he did not need to pretend as Tapp led him from case to case, showing him exceptionally valuable documents signed by George Washington, Abraham Lincoln, Andrew Johnson, Alexander Graham Bell, John C. Fremont, William H. Seward, and Carry Nation. This last brought a chuckle from Tapp.

'Simple, isn't it? *No truce with Demon Rum! Carry Nation.*'

He snapped off the light in the eighth case and turned toward the last one, at the end of the room. He paused and glanced at Chisholm.

'Robert, what was it you told me you were doing these days?'

'Area man for Shaw and Pontz Lock Company.' Chisholm reached toward his left lapel with supple, slender fingers and tapped the identity which was stuck to his coat by the adhesive on the back of the tag. 'The convention is one of hard-ware dealers. I'm showing a new line of passage sets.'

Tapp shrugged off a faint air of perplexity. 'Well! Let's look at my prize exhibit.' He illuminated the last cabinet.

In it lay a scrap of paper no bigger than the palm of the average-sized hand. It was even more yellowed than the other documents, the ink slightly more faded. It was charred along the top edge.

Tapp said nothing. Chisholm bent to look closely.

'Some kind of register or ledger?'

'That's right. From an inn.'

'Three names. James—Allen? Samuel Green. That one's clear. But—*Button Gwinnett?*'

Tapp rubbed his stubborn chin with his solid-fleshed left hand. The tip of his broad nose wrinkled in amusement.

'You're amazed, Robert. Yes, the rarest of all signatures in United States history. Your amazement is justified. But it's genuine, I assure you—absolutely genuine.'

'But how did you—? Where did you—?'

Tapp shook his head. 'When I am dead, all information on these documents will be released to the museum which will inherit them. In the meantime, that information is my secret.'

Chisholm glanced around the room. 'I hope you have these well protected. And adequately insured.'

'Both, you may be sure.'

'What protection, Don? This interests me, since I'm in the lock business.' He bent over the case containing the Button Gwinnett signature.

'I'm satisfied with it,' said Tapp bluntly.

'Are you?' Chisholm drew a key ring from his pocket. It bristled with keys—and other odd-looking objects. His supple fingers gripped something which Tapp could not see, and inserted it quickly into the lock on the edge of the glass top. Something clicked and he lifted the lid of the case. 'You see?'

Instantly a clamour began somewhere in the big house.

'I see. And do you hear?' Tapp gave his old friend an exasperated look. 'Come on. I'll have to shut off the alarm.'

'Might I remain here, Don? I'd like to look some more. I promise I won't touch anything.'

Tapp shook his head. 'Nobody looks unless I'm here. But if you don't want to come with me, you may stand by the door, outside, until I come back.'

After Tapp had locked both locks from the outside, Chisholm stood by the door thinking about the strongroom. All the cases were obviously wired to alarms. He had seen no wires. This meant that the wiring probably went through the legs of the cases, where it would be difficult to reach. Did each case activate a separate alarm, or trip a separate indicator, to show exactly which cabinet a burglar had attacked? Probably.

And the mirror on the left wall? What was the mirror doing in a room of this sort?

Tapp came bustling back, his chunky frame still radiating annoyance.

'Now, Robert,' he said, unlocking the door for the second time, 'I ask you, *please* don't try to sell me any locks—not this time.'

'We have some things which would help you, if you'd let me demonstrate,' Chisholm said, as he began to scan the room closely on re-entering.

'All right, all right—but show me a little later. In my den or in my office. Of course, I'm always interested in improving my safeguards. But not just now.'

Chisholm moved slowly from case to case, keeping up a running conversation to distract Tapp's attention. But he could discover nothing other than alarms and the puzzling mirror. There were, of course, the two locks in the door—which would be impossible to jimmy, or to pick. Then two tiny air passages, high in the end walls, protected by a fine, strong mesh caught his roving eye; but he dismissed them as irrelevant.

Finally he straightened and looked directly at Tapp.

'There's a lot of money represented here, Don.'

Tapp nodded soberly. 'I'd hate to tell you how much, Robert.'

'And you'll put even more documents in this room, won't you?'

'If something good comes along.'

'This, of course, means that you have the money to spend.'

Tapp's expression grew pained. 'You're being a bit ingenuous, Robert. Of course I have the money.'

'Have you ever considered putting some of that money into something more worthwhile?'

Tapp grinned without humour. 'I should have known there was more to this visit than a chat with an old friend. Now comes the touch. How much do you need?'

Chisholm shook his head. 'The need isn't mine, Don. It's Green Meadows Hospital. A check for §50,000 from you would put their new equipment drive over the top.'

Tapp grimaced. 'Green Meadows! I've heard their pitch. A corny one, too. Green Meadows—even the name's corny. No, thanks, Robert. Why did you have to spoil our first meeting in years?'

Chisholm said seriously, 'I don't consider geriatric problems corny, Don. Are you sure you just don't like to think of the kind of future any one of us might have to face? Look here: I've contributed §20,000 myself, and believe me, it'll hurt for a while. If I could give twenty, surely you can give fifty?'

Tapp grimaced again. 'I don't like people telling me what I can or can't give to charity.'

'It would be a deduction on your income tax return.'

'Thanks. I know all the possible deductions upside down and backwards.'

'Is there any way I can reach you on this, Don? Could I tell you some details of their program—'

Tapp shook his head firmly. 'No way at all—not even for an old buddy. Especially not for an old buddy. I can't stand corn.'

Chisholm's eyes narrowed, and his brows slanted up in a manner familiar to many people who had met him.

'All right, Don. You won't listen to a rational argument, so I'll make you an irrational proposition. Is your gambling blood still what it used to be?'

Tapp's smile was grim. 'If it's a sure thing, I'll still bet.'

'Would you bet a check for §50,000 that I can't steal something of value from this room?'

Shock and amazement crossed Tapp's heavy features. 'Why, that's idiotic. I won't listen.'

Chisholm held out a restraining hand. 'No, wait. You have complete confidence in your safeguards. Let's see just how good they are. I don't know a thing about them except there are locks on the door and alarms connected with the cabinets. Yet I am willing to bet I can beat your system.'

Tapp pondered. 'There's nothing in the world which can't stand improvement. But $50,000—'

Chisholm pressed on. 'Here's what I propose: shut me in this room for fifteen minutes—no more. In that short time I guarantee to steal one of these documents—*and get it out of here in spite of all your safeguards*. If I get that paper *out* of this room, you'll make the contribution to the hospital.'

'And if you fail? What is your stake?'

'I'll guarantee to increase the efficiency of your safeguards one hundred per cent.'

'That's hardly worth fifty thousand.'

'I own a quarter interest in my company. I'll assign it to you.'

Tapp eyed him shrewdly. 'You seem pretty confident.'

'I might be betting on a sure thing, Don. The way you like to do. Or I might be willing to take a bigger risk than you.'

Tapp mused, 'Fifteen minutes. And you have to get it *out* of the room by the end of that time. You know, I could just leave you locked in here.'

'No, you must come and let me out. But I must agree to let you search me or put any reasonable restrictions on me until it's absolutely clear that you've lost.'

'When do you want to do this?'

'Right now.'

Tapp studied Chisholm speculatively. 'Chisel—remember how we used to call you that?—when we were kids a lot of the others had contempt for me because I wouldn't take chances. I've done pretty well in life because of caution. But don't be misled: I *will* take a risk. I'll take this one.'

Chisholm smiled broadly, but this time his smile had a Mephistophelian look. 'Fine. Shall we begin?'

Tapp held out his wrist silently and they compared watches.

'Fifteen minutes from the time you close the door,' said Chisholm.

Tapp went out. As he pushed the door shut, he called through the narrowing crack, 'Not that I think you have a snowball's chance, Chisel.'

The door had scarcely closed before Chisholm was examining the mirror on the long wall with minute attention. He would have to proceed as though it were a two-way mirror, with only a thin layer of silver. He doubted that this was true, but he could not ignore the possibility. Finally he located what he was looking for: a circular loop in the border decoration on the glass. The glass within the loop looked subtly different.

His smile grew even more diabolical. He quickly stripped the convention badge from his left lapel and pasted it over the circle in the glass.

He then turned swiftly to the cases, taking out his keyring. Before he started to use it, he took a pair of thin rubber gloves from another pocket and put them on. Then, at a pace only a little slower than a walk, he went from case to case and opened the locks, which he had studied while looking at the documents the second time.

When he lifted all the lids, he laughed at the thought of nine alarms ringing simultaneously in Tapp's ears, or nine position lights flashing at one time in Tapp's face. He then went from case to case and reached inside each. All his movements were swift. Most of them were intended as pure misdirection.

Finally he had what he wanted. Now all he had to do was to make sure—doubly sure—that he was not being observed. To provide a cloak, he removed his jacket and slipped it over his shoulders backward, with the back of the jacket hanging in front of him and concealing his hands. His fingers made several rapid movements beneath the protection of the jacket. Then he suddenly reversed the process and put the coat back in its normal position.

He looked at his watch. Only eight minutes had passed.

For the remainder of the time Chisholm lounged against the door-frame singing slightly ribald songs in a clear, but not overloud, voice.

Precisely at the end of fifteen minutes, first one, then the other of the door locks was opened. The door itself, which was covered with a panelling of steel, swung back.

As Tapp stepped in, his glance already darting around the room, Chisholm clapped him lightly on the back.

'I hope you brought the cheque with you, Don.'

Tapp half turned, and Chisholm felt a hard object bore into his ribs. He looked down. Tapp had shoved a pistol into his side.

'I have the cheque, Chisel, but you're going to earn it—if you get it at all. Step back.'

Chisholm obeyed.

'Now, go over there to the opposite wall and sit on the floor by that first case. Fine. Extend your arms so that one is on either side of the leg of the case. Very good.'

Chisholm, from his position on the floor, saw Tapp take a pair of handcuffs from his pocket. Warily, the shorter man approached him.

'Wrists out, Chisel. Good.'

Tapp leaned over and snapped the cuffs on Chisholm's wrists. The tall diabolical-looking man had not ceased to smile.

'A lot of trouble, Don, just to find out what I did take. A lot of trouble to keep me from confusing you even more while you look. But I'll be glad to tell you without all this melodrama.'

'Just be quiet, Chisel,' Tapp said calmly. 'If you aren't, I'll slug you with the butt of this gun.'

'Violence wasn't in our agreement, Don.'

'You were not completely honest with me, Chisel. After you put all your misdirections into action, the hunch I'd had about you came out into the open. I remembered your hobby when you were a boy. I made one phone call to a local convention delegate I happen to know, and he told me you still practice your hobby. You're still an amateur magician, aren't you, Chisel?'

Chisholm shrugged. 'I do a little routine to catch the buyer's attention, then I work it into a sales talk for our products. It often helps.'

'Spare me,' Tapp muttered, peering into cases. His face darkened. 'You lied to me, Chisel. You said you would take only one document. I count three of them: the Garfield letter we read, the Seward I mentioned, and the Button Gwinnett.'

'I didn't lie,' Chisholm replied calmly. 'Figure it out for your-self.'

'Misdirection again.' Tapp turned and stared at him, but it was clear that his thoughts were elsewhere. In a moment he turned back to the cabinets and carefully lifted the velvet in the bottom of each. He found nothing.

He stood in thought for a few more minutes.

'The Garfield and the Alexander Graham Bell are the same size, and so are the Seward and the Lincoln. The Button Gwinnett doesn't match any, but it is *smaller* . . .'

Once more he went from case to case, this time lifting each of the remaining documents. When he had finished, he was smiling. He had found two of the missing papers carefully placed beneath others of the same size. He restored the Garfield and Seward documents to their proper cases.

'That leaves only the Button Gwinnett, Chisel. But this was what you had in mind all along. It's obvious. And if you're worth your salt as a magician, its hiding place won't be obvious. So let's eliminate the commonplace.'

Tapp went over the cases carefully, first lifting out all the documents, then each piece of velvet. When he had replaced everything, he closed and locked the cases. Then he dropped to his knees and inspected the under sides of the cabinets.

He found nothing.

He walked to each end of the room in turn and reached up to the tiny air passages. The mesh in both was still firmly in place, and he could not budge it at either opening.

Then his eye caught the mirror.

'Oh, and another thing—' He walked to the mirror and stripped off the convention tag. 'You're a sharp fellow, Robert.'

Chisholm laughed. 'Was my guess right? Closed-circuit TV? Did I cover the lens?'

'You put a patch on its eye, I must admit.'

'No two-way mirror?'

'I considered it, but with several receivers on the TV, I can be at any one of several places in the house. A two-way mirror would only restrict me.'

He walked over and stood in front of Chisholm. 'Two possibilities still remain. One is that you might have slipped it into my own pocket at the door. So I'll check that out now.'

He searched through all his pockets, but found nothing which had not been in them before.

He now stopped and unlocked the handcuffs, but made no move to take them from Chisholm's wrist.

'Drop the cuffs there, get up, and go to that corner,' he said, motioning with the gun to the bare corner furthest away from the door.

Chisholm obeyed. When he had moved, Tapp inspected the area where the magician had been sitting. 'All right. Now take off your clothes—one garment at a time—and throw them over to me.'

Chisholm complied, beginning with his coat jacket, until he stood completely stripped.

Tapp went over each item minutely, crushing cloth carefully, listening for the crackle of paper, inspecting shoes for false heels and soles and the belt for a secret compartment. From Chisholm's trousers he extracted a handkerchief and an ordinary keyring. In the pockets of the coat jacket he found a larger collection. The inside breast pocket yielded a wallet and two used envelopes with jottings on the back. The outside pockets contained the unusual keyring, the rubber gloves, a nearly full packet of cigarettes, a crumpled cigarette packet, a ballpoint pen, and a rubber band.

Tapp examined all these things with intense concentration. In the wallet he found money, a driver's license, a miscellany of credit and identification cards, and a small receipt for the purchase of a shirt at a local department store. He searched for a hidden compartment in the wallet, but found none. He then shook the cigarettes from the pack, but neither the pack itself nor the individual cigarettes was the least out of the ordinary. Replacing them, he then smoothed out the crumpled pack. Several items inside it he dumped on the top of one of the cases: a twist of cellophane; two wadded bits of brownish, waxy-looking paper; a fragment of wrapper from a roll of peppermints; and part of a burned match. He snorted and swept this trash back into its container.

He drew in his breath with an angry hiss. 'All right, Chisel, let's look *you* over. Turn round. Raise your arms. All right, now sit down on the floor and raise your feet.'

'Nothing on the soles of my feet except dust from the floor. You should clean this place oftener,' said Chisholm, leaning back on his arms.

Tapp's only answer was a growl.

'Have you checked the ceiling?' Chisholm asked.

Tapp looked up involuntarily. The ceiling was bare.

'See, you wouldn't have thought of that, would you?' Chisholm mocked.

Tapp leaned against one of the cabinets and aimed the pistol at Chisholm's midriff.

'Chisel, playtime is over. I want that Button Gwinnett back.'

'Or else, eh? You forget a number of things. We haven't yet established whether the paper is in this room or out of it. We haven't exchanged your cheque for §50,000 for the stolen document. I haven't even put my clothes back on. And, incidentally, I give you my word: the missing paper isn't in my clothing.'

Tapp tossed the clothing to Chisholm. 'It doesn't matter. You're going to tell me where that piece of paper is.'

Chisholm began to dress. 'How do you propose to make me tell? Shoot me? On the grounds that I broke into your house to steal? A respected businessman like me—steal? If you killed me, then you'd never find your paper. If you only wounded me, I'd refuse to talk. So where are we, old friend?'

Tapp said grimly, 'This bet of yours is just a stall. Once you get out of this room you'll take off with the signature to certain other collectors I could name. Why else won't you admit who told you about my collection. Only a handful of people know about it.'

Chisholm was tempted to yield on this point and reveal to Tapp that it was the district manager of Tapp's own insurance company who had mentioned the collection to him in strict confidence. Had he not wished to show even the slightest sign of weakness, he would have told this.

'The whole thing was strictly honourable,' Chisholm said. 'This stunt was my own idea.'

'And my idea,' said Tapp heavily, 'is to lock you in here without food and water until you return the paper. When you finally get out, I could always claim that I thought you had left the house and had locked you in without knowing.'

Chisholm shook his head. 'I had more respect for you, Don. If you did that, you'd either have to leave the other documents with me— and risk my destroying them—or take them out and have their absence disprove your story.'

Inwardly, Chisholm was beginning to have qualms. If Tapp should abandon reason in favour of a collector's passion, as he seemed about to do, anything might happen. The best course was an immediate distraction.

'How do you know,' he said challengingly, 'that the paper isn't *already* outside the room?'

Tapp snorted. 'Impossible!'

'Is it, now? There is a small trick I often do at dinner gatherings *which depends entirely on the victim's being too close to me to see what my hands are really doing.* I move a handkerchief from hand to hand near the victim's face, then throw it over his shoulder when my hand is too close for him to see exactly what I've done.'

Tapp said warily, 'But at no time were you outside this room.'

'I didn't have to be.' Suddenly Tapp understood. 'You mean when I came in!' He moved back and reached behind him to open the door. 'Stay where you are.' He stepped out and pushed the door shut again.

Chisholm waited tensely.

The door opened to a pencil-wide crack. 'There's nothing out here, Chisel.'

Chisholm answered evenly. 'I didn't say there was. But if you'll use the brains I've always given you credit for, you'll realize that I don't *want* to steal your precious piece of paper. If I had, why make the bet? Let me out of here and give me the §50,000 cheque for the hospital, and I'll tell you where the Button Gwinnett signature is.'

A silence followed his words. Seconds dragged by. Minutes.

Finally Tapp spoke. 'You swear that this will end here? That you won't even tell anyone about this incident? I used to think your word could be relied on, Chisel.'

'I'll swear on anything you name.'

'That won't be necessary.' The door opened wide. 'Now, where is it?'

Chisholm smiled and shook his head. 'First, the §50,000 cheque.'

Tapp eyed him shrewdly. 'I don't know that the paper is out of the room. I don't owe you anything unless it *is* outside, and you're still *inside*. But you agreed to tell me where it is.'

Chisholm kept smiling. 'I'll swear again, if you like. The paper is outside the room, according to the conditions of our bet.'

Tapp studied him. 'Very well, come up to my den and I'll give you the cheque. You have my word I'll keep my part of the bargain. Now—where is that paper?'

Chisholm stepped to Tapp's side and clapped him affectionately on the back. Then he held out his right hand.

'Here.'

As Tapp all but snatched the document from him, Chisholm fished in his own jacket pocket. He took out the crumpled cigarette pack, opened it, and shook out the contents.

'Remember the convention badge I stuck over your TV camera lens? Such badges are only strips of cardboard coated on the back with a permanently tacky adhesive—the way surgical adhesive tape is coated. From the cigarette pack he took the two scraps of brownish, waxy paper. 'That gave me the idea. It's easy to obtain tape with such an adhesive on *both* front and back. This brown paper protects the adhesive until it's peeled off, making the tape ready for use. In this case I kept a small bit of such tape in my pocket, removed the Button Gwinnett signature from the cabinet, exposed the adhesive on one side of the tape, and stuck the Button Gwinnett to that exposed side. Then I made the other side of the tape ready and palmed the whole thing.'

Chisholm repeated an earlier gesture. A look of comprehension spread over Tapp's face.

'When you came into the room at the end of the fifteen minutes,' Chisholm explained, 'I simply put the Button Gwinnett paper in the one place you couldn't see—*on your back!*'

JOHN LUTZ

# It's a Dog's Life

*If you're a mystery writer, budding or well-established, watch out for John Lutz. You may think you've carved out a piece of turf that's peculiarly your own and where you can't be challenged. Don't believe it. Here's a writer whose versatility is a watchword and whose regular standard is that of excellence.*

*Perhaps you specialize in offbeat thrillers? Lutz can do them. Take* Bonegrinder—*only his third book but already with the hallmark of a master of suspense as he pits Sheriff Billy Wintone against the unseen, perhaps unseeable, Bigfoot monster that prays relentlessly on a rural community. Or there's* The Shadow Man, *the eponymous, multi-personalitied Martin Karpp who, despite being under close guard, seems to have the ability to project one of his personae beyond his prison walls to carry out a series of brutal murders.*

*Then again, you may earn your bread-and-butter writing PI novels. Many do—and John Lutz is one of them. Even better (or worse, if you're the opposition) he doesn't have just one series, he has two. The longer-running features Nudger (six books so far), a sensitive man with a dyspeptic stomach. His speciality is the re-taking of children taken out of state in custody cases, but Nudger is frankly not the world's most successful detective. Much more on the ball is Lutz's second PI, Fred Carver (four books), an ex-cop with a gimpy leg, invalided out of the Orlando, FL, force and inclined to a more aggressive line.*

*And if you write police procedurals—well, there's Lutz again. Only two so far (and one of those co-authored with Bill Pronzini) but the later one,* Shadowtown, *came out as recently as 1988, and all the evidence is that once John Lutz gets his teeth into something he keeps on chewing.*

*Fine, I hear you say (a faint note of desperation in your voice), I'll switch to short stories. Forget it. Lutz has been there, done it all, bought the T-shirt! Or, more accurately, about 150 different T-shirts. So what is there left? Impossible Crime. That has to be it. But no—for here, before your very eyes (no pun intended) Lutz sets a neat little Impossible problem . . . which has an equally neat solution.*

ROBERT ADEY

Sam growled beside me, as if he didn't like the looks of the rambling mansion beyond the car's windshield. The place didn't seem particularly forbidding to me, maybe because there was a fee involved in our coming here.

I pulled my Beetle into the circular drive and stopped in the shadow of one of the house's many gables. Parked on the other side of the driveway was a plain grey sedan I recognized and wasn't at all surprised to see. As I held the door open for Sam, I glanced at the miles of wooded hills surrounding the house and wondered how much of them the Creel family owned.

I rang the bell. A butler opened the door six inches and peered down an aristocratic nose at me. 'Milo Morgan to see Vincent Creel,' I said.

The nose dipped a few degrees as the butler took in Sam's low, squat frame. 'Come in, sir. But the, er . . .'

'Mr Creel hired both of us,' I said.

Lieutenant Jack Redaway, whose unmarked police car was parked outside, was in a large Victorian room talking to the Creel family. Vincent Creel shook my hand and introduced me to the other family members. There was tall and elegant Robert, short and muscular James, short and almost as muscular Millicent. Like Vincent Creel, who was silver-haired, urbane, and very rich, they were all the brothers and sister of homicide victim Carl Creel.

It had been Carl Creel who had replenished the family coffers with his bestselling book on how to survive the ravages of inflation. The Creel family, struggling along on dwindling wealth from the oil dealings of their forebears, had no further financial problems after a big movie studio bought the rights to Carl Creel's book and made it into a successful comedy.

'Mr Morgan and I have met all too often,' Lieutenant Redaway said. He glanced at Sam. 'I heard you had a new partner.'

'This is Sam,' I said. 'He doesn't bite or make a mess.'

'The gentleman of the firm. As a private detective, Morgan, I would think you'd have noticed that "Sam" doesn't suit that animal's gender.'

'It's short for Samantha,' I explained. 'Since Sam's been neutered, we use the male pronoun for the sake of convenience. But we have impressive, and accurate, business cards.'

'Don't tell me. I already heard. Sam Spayed.'

'Correct. And he's got a bloodhound nose.' Which was true. Sam is a drab brown animal who looks like a mixture of a hundred breeds, the last generation of which might have been a bulldog, but his nose is one hundred percent pedigree bloodhound. 'We'd like to examine the death scene,' I said, to both Vincent Creel and Redaway, 'before the scent grows any colder or is obliterated by official bungling.'

Vincent led me, Sam and Redaway to a ground floor study. 'I've heard you employ unusual methodology,' he said to me. 'I've also heard you get results. I want this stigma removed from our family at any cost. As we agreed at your office, I will give you carte blanche in every respect to solve my brother's murder.'

I nodded. Sam shoved his pushed-in bloodhound nose against Creel's pants leg, snuffled, and gave Creel his weird kind of canine grin that might mean anything.

When Vincent had left us in the study, Redaway rolled out the hostility. 'I hate to see you here,' he said. 'You can muddle a case more thoroughly than any shamus I know.'

'If the case weren't muddled to begin with,' I replied, 'Sam and I wouldn't have been hired by Vincent Creel.' I looked down at the large oval bloodstain that Sam already was sniffing. 'That's where Carl Creel's body was discovered, I suppose.'

'Your deductive powers are at full strength,' Redaway said. He was as mean as his hatchet face and tiny glittering black eyes suggested.

'Fill us in,' I told him, knowing he couldn't refuse. Vincent Creel had hired me, and like any smart cop, Redaway respected the Creel family's political clout.

'Carl was working here in his study the night before last,' Redaway said around a smelly cigar he was lighting, 'when the other family members heard a shot. They all rushed in from various places in the house. Carl was lying on the carpet, having died from a single .22 bullet to the brain. Those French windows were wide open, and the family dog, Caster, a big Irish setter, was seen running up that hill as if chasing someone into the woods. It was obvious to all that Carl was dead, so Vincent phoned the police first, then a doctor.' Redaway crossed his arms and pretended to be a smokestack.

'That's it?' I asked.

'That's a quick overview,' Redaway said. He looked down and grinned as Sam coughed at the cigar smoke and glared at him.

I looked around the study. Not a large room, it was furnished expensively with a desk, small sofa, velvet chair, bookshelves, oak filing cabinets. Besides the French windows there were two other windows. The door to the hall was spring-loaded and had no latch.

'Not your locked-room type of crime,' I said. 'What about the motive?'

'Carl had announced his intention of donating all his movie and book sale profits to the Insomniacs Society, a research group in New York. Creel himself was a chronic insomniac. The rest of the family were losing sleep because they might lose the money.'

'What you're saying is—'

'That everyone in the house at the time of Carl Creel's death had a motive. Furthermore, everyone had opportunity.'

Sam sighed and stretched out where a sunbeam cast a bar of light across the floor. He gets discouraged easily. I have to do the heavy thinking.

'One of the Creels in that other room did the killing,' Redaway said, 'but there's no way we can get an indictment as long as they claim it was the work of an intruder whom Carl Creel surprised.'

'A jury won't buy that old intruder line,' I told him.

'They will if we can't produce a weapon. And no gun was found. The Creels were all here together less than a minute after the shot was fired, so there was little or no time to hide the weapon. We've searched this house and the surrounding grounds thoroughly. No gun. The defense attorney can say, quite logically, that the intruder took it with him.'

'So maybe it was an intruder after all. A burglar surprised by an unlucky Creel.'

Redaway sneered around his cigar. 'Maybe the butler did it?'

Sam and I exchanged glances. 'What *about* the butler?'

'Bart—that's the butler—was off that night and has a concrete alibi. He was at the racetrack with Jenny, the Creel's cook. Witnesses confirm.'

'What about footprints outside? And you said the dog chased someone.'

'We're in the middle of a drought; the ground was too hard for footprints. And Caster wandered home after an hour or so, empty pawed.'

Sam seemed to smile, baring his teeth for an instant in that quick, good-natured snarl of his.

'If there was no intruder,' I asked, 'what do you suppose the dog was chasing into the woods?'

Redaway shrugged. 'A squirrel, a rabbit—who knows? Dogs are always running after something.'

Still grinning, Sam got up and sat by the door. He had an uncanny sense of timing in a case.

'It's time for me to talk to each of the suspects,' I said.

'Sure,' Redaway said. 'Especially the butler.'

*     *     *

The family members told Sam and me what they'd already told the police. Not one of them didn't complain about having to tell the story again.

Millicent Creel had been in the sewing room, talking on the phone to a friend, when she'd heard the shot. The friend had verified Millicent's story, and had even heard the shot herself over the phone. Millicent had excused herself and rushed to investigate. She'd reached Carl's study at almost the same time as her brothers. They knocked several times in quick succession, then threw open the door to find Carl dead on the floor. The French windows were standing open, and in the distance they saw Caster running into the woods as if in pursuit of something or someone.

Robert Creel had been in his upstairs bedroom taking a late afternoon nap. James, having just returned from hunting with Caster, had been showering in the bath adjoining his own bedroom. Wearing only a towel, he had rushed from his room and seen Robert already running down the stairs. They had reached the study door in time to see Vincent Creel burst onto the scene from the basement, where he had been engaged in his hobby of woodworking, and they'd seen Millicent scurrying along the hall from the direction of the sewing room.

'Calculate the distances,' Redaway said when we were again alone. 'Any one of them could have shot Carl Creel, then made it back to where he or she could pretend to be rushing to the study with the rest of the Creels.'

'After stashing the gun,' I added.

'Now if you'll just tell me where,' Redaway said, 'we'll simply pick up the gun, make an arrest, and wind this thing up.' He was the only man I knew who could gnash his teeth and smoke a cigar simultaneously.

Sam stretched out near the sofa and made a sound somewhere between a growl and a chortle.

'Is that dog laughing at me?' Redaway demanded, seriously.

'The smoke bothers him, is all,' I said. 'I'd like to speak to the butler and the cook.'

Redaway rolled his eyes, but he sent for Bart and Jenny.

Bart the butler told me he'd been at the racetrack at the time of the murder. At the moment the trigger was pulled, he was losing ten dollars on the daily double and he had the witnesses and worthless stubs to prove it. He said Jenny had been with him, using her complicated system of astrology in conjunction with the names of exotic spices to place her bets. She had won twenty-seven dollars; Bart had lost fifty. They often went to the track together, usually with similar results.

Jenny was busy preparing lunch so I went to the kitchen to question her, and to see what sort of exotic spices she used. The Creel kitchen was as large and efficient looking as the kitchen of a good-sized restaurant. There were food grinders, heavy-duty processors, a commercial-size freezer, and a gas double oven that covered half of one wall. Something smelled good.

Jenny was a middle-aged, round-shouldered woman with her blonde hair pinned in a bun above a wary frown. Sam whiffed the aroma of cooking and sidled right up to her as I introduced us. Also in the kitchen was a tall, gangly Irish setter I took to be Caster. Sam and Caster ignored each other, which didn't strike me as odd. That was Sam's way, and apparently Caster's.

'I'm told you were at the track at the time Carl Creel was murdered.'

Jenny nodded. She was adjusting the temperature on the eye-level oven.

'What did you think of Carl Creel?'

'Did you ask the others that?' She fixed her shrewd, gambler's eyes on me.

'No. Their alibis aren't as good as yours and Bart's. They'd be less likely to give an honest answer.'

She smiled faintly. 'I didn't like him,' she said. 'Carl Creel was a vicious and miserly man. No one liked him.'

'Do you think anyone here disliked him enough—'

'I wouldn't know. I'm a cook, not a psychologist.' She reached into the sink and picked up a steak bone. 'You have a nice dog.' She offered the bone to Sam, who turned his head away in refusal. He was poisoned on the Hatfield case and has since been leery of food from strangers.

'The hell with you,' Jenny said, and gave the bone to Caster, who promptly took it out the back door.

'Sam's independent,' I said.

'Bad mannered is what he is.' She began chopping onions.

'Is this the daily menu?' I asked. A list was attached to the refrigerator with a magnet.

'It is.'

'The same every week?'

'Every other week,' Jenny said, 'for variety.'

'Roast beef on Mondays? Ham on Thursdays? Steak on Fridays?'

'On odd weeks,' Jenny told me acidly.

'Who does the shopping?'

'Either me or Bart.'

'What do you do with garbage?'

'We put it outside in a can with a plastic liner. It's picked up once a week and taken to the dump.' *Chunk!* went the knife through the onion.

Sam and I got out of there. Sam's eyes were watering.

I talked to James again, next. He told me he hadn't really been hunting on the day of his brother's death, merely walking in the woods and shooting at various objects for target practice. I went down to see Vincent, in the basement. He had his power tools out; he was making a handsome walnut plaque featuring the Creel family crest of two crossed oil derricks on a field of green. Nothing illuminating in that conversation. When I left Vincent, I hunted up Lieutenant Redaway.

'Making any progress?' he asked sarcastically.

Sam glared at him.

'I think I have this one about wrapped up,' I said. 'Will you arrange for everyone to meet in Carl Creel's study after lunch?'

Redaway stood staring at me with an expression of hostile incredulity. 'Okay,' he said, 'but if you ask me, it's all a ruse so you can stay for lunch.'

'Steak and salad today,' I said.

'Now how would you know that?'

I smiled. 'A little detective work, lieutenant.' Sam gave his chortling little growl and we moved on. I had a few things to do before lunch.

After lunch, the household, including Bart and Jenny, gathered in Carl Creel's study as I'd suggested. We were joined by a tall, stoic police sergeant named Evans, sent for by Redaway at my request. Everyone stood about uneasily, trying to avoid stepping on the bloodstain. Caster sat near Robert Creel, enjoying an ear rub.

'It's time for the Milo Morgan show,' Redaway said with a sneer. All eyes in the room rotated in my direction, even Sam's.

Since I already had everyone's attention, I figured I'd keep it. 'I know who the killer is,' I said, 'and I will set about proving it.'

Sam ambled over and sat by the door, wearing his stern expression.

'The key to the case is Caster,' I said. 'When he was seen dashing into the woods, everyone assumed he might be chasing someone. But perhaps he was running *from* someone, or, more accurately, *to* someplace. When I saw him leave the kitchen with a bone this morning, it occurred to me that many dogs have special area, where they bury their bones or go to chew on them, and usually the instant they're given a bone they dash for that place. It's an instinctive thing involving protection of food, and dogs are such slaves to instinct that their behaviour seldom varies.' Sam seemed to be frowning at me. 'Most dogs,' I added.

'Murderers are not as predictable as dogs,' Redaway said. 'Unless you think Caster shot Carl Creel, get to the point.'

'Your story, James,' I said to the youngest Creel, 'is that you were out shooting the day of the murder, and that Caster was with you.'

James nodded, his grey eyes cool and unblinking.

'That indicated to me that Caster, who was in the room when Carl Creel was shot, was not gunshy.'

An expression of disbelief suddenly transformed Redaway's narrow face. 'You're not saying that Caster was trained to get rid of the gun!'

'A dog couldn't be reliably trained to do that—not to the point where anyone would make a murder charge on it. Not to mention that the gun still might be found.'

'This seems to be leading us nowhere, then,' Millicent Creel said impatiently, her podgy features in a frown. When she subsided, I turned to Vincent.

'I've been down to the basement to examine your woodworking tools,' I said calmly. 'I found what I was looking for.'

'Which was?'

'Bone,' I said. 'Minute fragments of bone.' Vincent's feet edged him a little towards the door. Sam growled and Redaway moved over to stand by Vincent. Redaway, though still disbelieving, was catching on.

'You used your skill with tools to fashion a simple gun out of bone,' I said. 'Something like the home-made zipguns street gangs carry. Only instead of using a metal barrel, you drilled a hole in the bone the exact diameter of the bore of a .22 pistol, then created a functional hammer and firing pin. Oh, the weapon was crude, and you probably had to use both hands to aim and fire it, but it only had to fire one shot, and at very close range. After you fired the shot, you handed the gun to Caster, knowing he'd run off with it, gnaw on it, and bury it. You hurried to the basement. From there you pretended to be dashing upstairs to investigate the shot that you yourself had fired.'

Vincent was obviously flustered. 'Morgan, if this is some pathetic attempt of yours to . . .'

'To what, Mr Creel?' Redaway asked, finally on top of things.

'You have no proof, Morgan!'

That's when I pulled a jar of horseradish from my pocket and rubbed some on Caster's hind paws. I put a leash on Sam and handed the end of it to Sergeant Evans. 'Sam is an excellent tracker,' I said, 'and he loves horseradish. The scent should make it easier.' From another pocket I withdrew my steak bone from lunch and handed it to Caster. The big setter clamped his jaws on it, scrambled for traction, and dashed away through the French windows I'd made sure were open.

'If you'll just follow Sam following Caster's scent,' I said to Sergeant Evans, 'I'm sure you'll come to the spot where a little of your own snooping around will uncover the murder weapon.'

Sam had his gnarled nose to the carpet and was already snuffling and snorting like a steam engine straining uphill. Evans was stumbling, holding onto the leash, and leaning backward to keep his balance as Sam yanked him across the room and out the French windows.

'Why don't we go into the den,' I suggested.

The atmosphere in that den was cool, I can tell you. Cool and tense. No one said five words until, half an hour later, Sergeant Evans and Sam walked in. I don't know which of those tenacious crimefighters was grinning the widest.

Evans showed us the bone he'd found a few inches beneath freshly turned earth. It was a neat job, all right, a big ham bone tooled into the rough shape of a handgun. A neat round hole had been drilled slightly off centre, to avoid the marrow. The empty shell was still stuck inside the drilled hole, which was of larger diameter for about four inches near the butt end, to allow for a tooled cylinder of bone to be propelled, probably by a powerful rubber strap, up to the cartridge to strike with a firing pin fashioned from a filed-down pointed screw. That screw was the only metal part of the gun itself; a little more gnawing by Caster and it would have dropped off, along with the spent shell, leaving the whole apparatus to look like any dog-mistreated bone unless someone examined it and noticed the drilled hole. I figured Vincent Creel had shot his brother, slid the rubber strap up his arm out of sight beneath his sleeve, given Caster the bone-gun, and thought he was home free. A precision-tooled perfect crime. Almost.

Vincent Creel, his face now nearly Chinese red, snarled at me and started up from his big leather armchair. But Redaway and Sam both snarled back at him, and he settled down.

Redaway got out a little card and read Creel his rights, then nodded to Evans, who put the cuffs on Creel and led him away. The rest of the family looked on in a state of shock, except for Millicent, who was dabbing at her potato nose with a handkerchief.

'What I don't get,' Robert Creel said, 'is why Vincent hired a private detective if he was the murderer.'

'To divert suspicion,' I explained. 'And he thought he was safe anyway.'

'He also hired the most incompetent private detective he could find.' Redaway was his obnoxious self again. He knew he'd be credited with the arrest.

'He wouldn't be the first to underestimate our firm,' I said pointedly.

Figuring why should we stay around to be insulted, Sam and I made for the door. Redaway was in our path. Sam walked right at him and he moved. I turned. 'I'm sorry it couldn't have been an intruder,' I said to the still stunned Creel family. To Redaway I said nothing, not even goodbye. Sam and I let ourselves out and didn't look back.

It wasn't until we'd got back to the office, Sam gazing out the window at the city skyline, me at my desk sorting through the mail, that it occurred to me. Since we'd hung the crime on our client, there was nobody to pay our fee. This was some business! I cursed, crumpled the half-written bill into a compact wad and hurled it into the wastebasket.

I couldn't see Sam's face, but his shoulders were shaking as though he might be laughing. It's a dog's life. It really is.

SAX ROHMER

# The Death of Cyrus Pettigrew

*The definitive biography of Sax Rohmer (or Arthur Henry Ward as the Inland Revenue and passport office knew him) has yet to be written. The scrappy (and one is tempted to strike out that initial consonant) life which came out nearly 20 years ago,* Master of Mystery, *was a dog's breakfast of highly dubious anecdotes, lazily written and facetious Sunday newspaper-style showbiz reminiscence, and absurd hyperbole (its principal author Cay Van Ash regarded Rohmer as 'the last great master of the English language'). Too, the book suffered from the iron hand of its co-author, Rohmer's wife Elizabeth, and thus, despite Rohmer's extra-marital shenanigans and not-infrequent disappearances, there is a highly unrealistic* Mills & Boon *gloss over all. Brought in as editor, Rohmer authority Robert Briney tried his hardest to pull the whole farrago together (his notes, interpolations and bibliography are the only bright spots), but on the whole it was a hopeless task.*

*Should another, and more critical, biography be contemplated? It ought to be. Rohmer was a fascinating figure who created a hero—or anti-hero—of extraordinary, indeed mythic, proportions. Dr Fu Manchu is one of a rare breed of fictional characters (Sherlock Holmes, Bulldog Drummond, James Bond, Billy Bunter are just a few more) who have acquired over the years an independent cultural identity quite divorced from their origins. In Fu Manchu's case he was, in his time, the embodiment of a particular class's view of a particular race and, rightly or wrongly, Rohmer's books, even though fiction (perhaps because they were fiction), influenced the ideas and prejudices of an entire generation. An in-depth analytical life is sorely needed.*

*There are, in any case, so many foggy areas in his life, especially the period from 1903, when he sold what seems to be his first story, 'The Mysterious Mummy' (which appeared in* Pearson's Weekly Xmas 'Xtra*), to 1911, when he started writing the first episodes of the initial Fu Manchu series. His early stories were all published under the name A. Sarsfield Ward (the Sarsfield from an heroic Irish ancestor, or so his mother claimed), from 1903 through to at least 1909.*

*When exactly he became Sax Rohmer is something of a mystery. It's generally assumed the pseudonym arrived with the publication of the first of the Séverac Bablon stories in* Cassell's Magazine *(June, 1912), but, as I only very recently discovered, 'Sax Rohmer' had already appeared over a year earlier, by-lining the first of his four 'Narky' tales in*

Everybody's Weekly *in early March, 1911. As far as is known the last use of the Sarsfield Ward name (apart from when he had two stories in a magazine in the same issue) was in mid-1909, so there may well be lost stories by Rohmer in obscure, and perhaps not so obscure, periodicals in between those two dates.*

*Some of which may well be Impossible, for at least three of Rohmer's early tales contain 'miracle' crimes, including 'The Mysterious Mummy' (possibly the very first story to hinge on a thief escaping detection by donning a policeman's uniform). In the 1900s Rohmer knew many artists who worked in the music halls and variety theatres, including illusionists and magicians (much later he became friendly with Harry Houdini), and these associations almost certainly sparked off story-ideas. The gimmick he uses here was new in 1909, but has been utilized pretty extensively by numerous writers since.*

JACK ADRIAN

---

'**R**ugby in two minutes!' said Saxham glancing at his watch.

As if to belie his words, at that moment the brakes were smartly applied, and, with a great rattling, the train was brought to a standstill.

'Signals against us!' muttered my friend, settling himself more comfortably in his corner. "Beastly night! Shouldn't like to be out in it!'

But Fate had ordained that he should go out in it, for the words had barely left his lips when, above the hissing from the locomotive and the pattering of the rain, we heard the sound of voices, and a guard came running along the metals, crying: 'Is there a doctor on the train?'

'Just my luck!' growled Saxham, dropping the window. 'All right, guard. What's the trouble?'

'Don't know, exactly, sir,' said the man, as my friend and I descended from the footboard; 'but I think somebody's been killed! This way gentlemen!'

Muffling ourselves in our greatcoats, for the rain was pouring down in torrents, we followed the evidently excited official to the door of a first-class compartment, and making our way through the knot of passengers whom even the inclement weather did not suffice to keep in their seats, climbed in and surveyed a scene which I shall never forget.

The one occupant of the compartment crouched on the floor against the further door, with his head upon the seat. I judged him to be a man of sixty, and somewhat obese; but a closer inspection showed that his features and limbs were swollen to much more than their normal size. His clean-shaven face was covered with singular blotches, and his lips showed a pale grey-white against the purple.

'Only a few minutes, in my opinion,' declared Saxham. 'Who gave the alarm?'

'The young lady that always travels with him, sir. They're regular passengers. She's in the next carriage, being attended to. After pulling the communication-cord, she fainted.'

'What steps do you propose taking?'

'Is it murder, sir?' asked the guard, in horrified tones.

'I should not like to express an opinion at present,' Saxham said. 'Were they alone in the carriage?'

'Yes, sir. The poor gentleman always preferred to get a carriage to himself, as he liked to travel with the window open; and, the train not being very full, I locked the door at Euston. If you'll step in and see what you can do for the young lady, we'll get on to Rugby, else there'll be trouble.'

The increasing group of curious passengers was warned to board the train, and, leaving Dr Saxham to attend to the lady in the next compartment, we all returned to our seats. At Rugby I immediately hurried back to see of what assistance I could be to my friend, arriving just as he assisted to the platform a stylishly dressed and, in a colourless fashion, rather pretty girl, whose pallid face and frightened eyes looked out of a frame of light hair.

I learned that she was a Miss Pettigrew, niece of the dead man, to whose house, near Harborne, on the outskirts of Birmingham, they had been journeying. Mr Cyrus Pettigrew had been a wealthy collector of pictures and curios, and he and his ward spent a great deal of time in London. They had that day been to attend a big auction.

Learning that she had friends in Rugby, Saxham prevailed upon her to remain there for the night, since he feared that a continuance of the journey so tragically interrupted might lead to a more serious breakdown. Before she could leave the station, however, she had to submit to a brief examination at the hands of two detectives.

'Sorry to trouble you at such a time, miss,' said the elder of the officers, a bluff, kindly looking man; 'but my colleague and myself are taking charge of the case, and we shall have to make our report.'

'Have you any idea who might have done the thing?' inquired the younger man, from which remark I concluded that murder was assumed.

'There was no one else in the carriage all the way,' declared Miss

Pettigrew, who spoke and looked as though she were half dazed. 'I fell asleep before the train left Northampton, and did not awake until I heard a loud shriek and a hand suddenly clutched me. I started up, to find my uncle tearing at his throat, with his face purple, and his eyes glaring most horribly.'

She shuddered at the recollection, and became so deadly pale, that we feared she was about to faint again. Exercising a great effort, however, she succeeded in recovering herself.

'To what do you attribute death, doctor?' asked the elder officer.

'To poison!' said Saxham promptly.

We were all very much amazed at the reply.

'Might it not be a case of suicide?' I suggested.

'There was no trace of a phial of any kind in his possession, or anywhere in the carriage,' said the detective.

'It was not *swallowed*,' explained Saxham vaguely. 'Owing, however to the state of the body, I am unable to make a definite statement.'

I was greatly puzzled by that guarded assertion, as was the officer.

'Tell me, miss,' he inquired: 'did you notice anything in his hand when you woke?'

'Nothing at all. I immediately ran to the communication-cord, pulled it and remembered nothing more.'

'How were you seated in the carriage?'

'I was in the right-hand corner, facing the engine, and my uncle sat opposite to me. The window on that side was closed, but the farther one was open. It was a peculiarity—'

She broke off, with a stifled sob.

'He would never travel with both windows up, even in the coldest weather, if he could avoid it,' she added.

The detectives were clearly nonplussed.

'I understand that both doors were locked,' said the elder reflectively; 'and he was sitting in the corner farthest from the open window, so how—'

'Both doors were locked when the guard arrived,' confirmed the station official who had come up. 'So if you're working on the idea that anyone got in from another carriage and then slipped out again, it's a wrong track you're on. There wouldn't be time, apart from the practically insurmountable difficulty of locking and re-locking a carriage-door from the footboard while the train was in motion. The unfortunate gentleman evidently cried out at the moment he was injured, and there was no one in the carriage then, nor was either door open. Isn't that so, Miss Pettigrew?'

She nodded silently.

'You're sure about the poison not being swallowed, doctor?' asked the elder detective.

'Certain,' said Saxham. 'I merely withhold my opinion respecting the means whereby it was administered.'

I could see that his words set both the men pondering, and I think they would have liked to have asked another question but the warning came that the delayed 9.5 for London was off, and they both left us hurriedly.

A message had been sent to Miss Pettigrew's friends; so, leaving the unhappy girl in charge of the courteous station-master, my friend and I rejoined our train, which had also, of course, been delayed for the detaching of the car containing the body, and resumed our interrupted journey to Birmingham.

Saxham was not very communicative on the subject of this gruesome episode; and, since the business wherein we were mutually interested, and which was responsible for our visit to the Midlands, entirely occupied our attention throughout the following day, the matter was not again discussed between us until the evening. Before entering the London train, we provided ourselves with a bundle of newspapers, and naturally turned to those columns devoted to the mysterious crime.

My friend seeming still unwilling to talk about the case, I asked no questions, but occupied myself with the newspapers, several of which, after giving more or less inaccurate accounts of the tragedy, offered theories which were principally notable for their extraordinary absurdity.

One of the more reputable evening journals published an interview with Inspector Pepys, in whom I recognized the younger of the officers that had taken charge of the case at Rugby.

I drew the doctor's attention to this interview; but, having read it with apparent interest, he returned the paper, without offering any comment. In one of the half-penny evening journals I also came across a curious item. This was an account, by a passenger on the train, of an eccentric person who shared the carriage with him from Euston to Willesden.

It was a second-class compartment, said this dubious witness, and, he *thought*, next to that in which the tragedy subsequently occurred. He entered it at the moment that the train was leaving the London terminus, to find that it had one other occupant, a stranger who would seem to have principally impressed him by reason of his peculiarly livid complexion. Auburn-haired, and wearing pincenez, this young man—for, according to the story, he was about thirty years of age—

had nothing alarming in his appearance, seeming to be a poor student.

He was reading a book; but, as the other got in, he put it down and fixed his eyes upon him. His eyes were very dark and penetrating, as the passenger could see through the pebbles, and when, having looked up several times from his paper, the latter gentleman found, on each occasion, this disconcerting gaze still fixed upon him, he began to grow nervous.

Hoping to relieve the situation, he addressed a commonplace remark to his strange companion, which the other answered with a smile that occasioned the gentleman much alarm.

'The night, as you truly remark, is wet,' said this singular young man, still smiling; 'but blood is thicker than water!'

This peculiarly significant, if somewhat irrelevant, observation seems to have closed the conversation; and, enduring the horrible stare until the first stop, the other passenger, by then in a state of deplorable nervousness, hastened from the compartment into one already well filled.

He did not report the episode to the guard, as, after all, he might have been mistaken in assuming the young man to be insane. Such, at any rate, was the explanation offered to the Press man by this witness.

Saxham and I shared chambers in Carey Street at this time, and, on our return there that night, we were both too tired to talk much, almost immediately retiring to our rooms. On the following morning, directly breakfast was dispatched, my friend went out, giving me to understand that he proposed making a few inquiries respecting certain points of the case that were dark to him.

He did not join me at lunch, as was his usual custom; and during my solitary meal I gathered from the early editions that the inquest would be adjourned for the attendance of the Home Office expert. Saxham did not put in an appearance until late in the evening, and even then offered no explanation as to how and where he had spent the day.

At the inquest, he declined to express any opinion as to the cause of death, but the delayed report from the Government analysts served to confirm his earlier statements. In fact, there appeared to be but little doubt that Cyrus Pettigrew had succumbed to the action of some subtle poison. There were a series of minute punctures in the skin of the right wrist and lower forearm, which might, said the experts, result from the bite of a small reptile.

The local conditions rendered it extremely difficult to express any definite opinion. Since there was always the possibility that some such creature had escaped from the possession of a collector, and remained concealed in an unsuspected corner until disturbed by the unfortunate man, this testimony put a fresh complexion on the case; and an open verdict was returned.

Passengers by the line travelled in constant alarm during the days that followed; for, since the hypothetical snake remained undiscovered, its appearance from some dark nook amid the cushions was to be expected at any moment. Such was the purport of more than one letter appearing in the Press. Naturally enough, the railway authorities prompted a thorough search for the creature, and the public eagerly awaited the confirmation of the lost-snake theory which would be afforded by the advent of the reptile's owner.

No one who had lost such a reptile put in an appearance, however, nor were the searchers successful in unearthing this hidden menace to travellers. The alarm and excitement which the case created throughout the country were already subsiding, and people beginning to forget the matter, when a new and unforeseen development occurred.

As I was about to turn from Chancery Lane into Carey Street one night, about ten o'clock, I met a boy running with an armful of papers, and displaying a glaring bill, which read as follows:

RUGBY TRAIN MURDER
SENSATIONAL DEVELOPMENT
ARREST OF MISS PETTIGREW

Hastily securing a copy, I found in the Stop Press News a brief paragraph which simply stated that Miss Pettigrew had that afternoon been apprehended in London for the murder of her guardian. There were no details, but this, in itself, was sufficiently astounding; and I almost ran into Carey Street and upstairs to our rooms, so eager was I to communicate the news to Saxham, whom I had left earlier in the evening at work upon some intricate analysis.

I found him still busily absorbed at the plain deal table, with the green-shaded electric lamp suspended just above his head and throwing a circle of light upon the scientific disorder that surrounded him. His neat, black Velasquez beard almost touched the chemical litter as he bent over his work like some Mephistophelian necromancer.

'Look at this!' I cried, holding the paper before his eyes.

He glanced up absently and read the paragraph, scratching his head with a bone spatula the while. But as the truth percolated through the density of the obscure equations that doubtless occupied his mind at that moment, he forgot his experiments in face of this human problem.

'Good heavens, Barton!' he said, with an instant return to his brisk, consulting-room manner, 'what a horrible error! If I could only have been present at the post-mortem!' he added regretfully.

Temporarily he seemed undecided what to do, taking down and lighting his corncob, with some return to the preoccupation which marked a reflective mood. I, for my own part, failed to see how we were to concern ourselves in the case; and I was idly watching Saxham as he lent upon the corner of the mantelpiece, enveloping himself in clouds of tobacco-smoke, when the door-bell rang violently, and some late visitor could be heard impatiently shuffling upon the landing.

I went out and opened the door, to find a man of medium height, slim and carefully dressed. He was of conspicuously tawny complexion, and had lank, black hair.

'Dr Saxham?' he inquired, with a slight accent.

'He is in,' I said. 'Have you business with him?'

'I come about Miss Pettigrew,' explained the visitor, in whose manner I detected a suppressed excitement.

He proffered at the same time a card bearing the words:

'J. Goree Bachoffner, B. A., B.Sc.(Lond.), No.—, Fig Tree Court.'

At that I invited him to step inside, where Saxham, who had overheard the brief conversation, was still standing by the fireplace.

'My dear sir,' he assured our visitor, as we entered and I mentioned his name, 'I had really expected to see you!'

'I am surprised,' was Bachoffner's reply. 'I was unaware that you knew of my existence.'

'Miss Pettigrew spoke of you on the night of the dreadful occurrence that is, doubtless, responsible for your present visit,' explained Saxham. 'She desired that a telegram be dispatched to you. I at once recalled the name.'

'Ah,' said the other, 'now I understand. That wire reached me at my chambers in time for me to catch the midnight train for Rugby. I called them up at nearly three o'clock in the morning.'

Saxham made no reply, so Bachoffner continued slowly:

'I came straightaway in search of you, on hearing of this astounding arrest, knowing that you viewed the body immediately after death. Tell me frankly: do you consider it possible, apart from the unthinkable nature of such a crime, that Miss Pettigrew could have murdered her uncle?'

The doctor paused for a moment, as though to carefully select his words, surrounding himself with smoke-clouds.

'Judging from what I saw,' he admitted cautiously, 'I do not for a moment believe that she was in any way concerned.'

Bachoffner passed his tongue over his dry lips, and clutched the arm of his chair nervously. He leant forward, his dark face wearing a curiously set expression.

'You have a theory?' he suggested softly. 'Now that a woman's life is at stake, tell me what it is.'

I saw Saxham glance sharply towards him and then turn his eyes away again from the concentrated gaze of the visitor.

'Having had no means of verifying any theory which I may have formulated,' he answered, never for a moment committing himself, 'I really cannot make any definite statement.'

That seemed to irritate Bachoffner. He shrugged his shoulders and smiled almost contemptuously.

'Is she, then, to hang,' he harshly demanded, 'when there is one man who can save her and who yet declines to speak?'

'Why do you assert,' asked Saxham, 'that I can save her?'

'Because,' said Bachoffner tensely, 'you *know* that a hypodermic syringe was not used to inject the venom!'

Some fleeting expression showed upon my friend's face. An instant later it had gone, and he was calmly puffing at his corncob.

'I am afraid,' he replied, 'you are better informed than I. Is it alleged that a hypodermic syringe was employed?'

'It is because such an instrument has been found in her possession that she is now under arrest,' was the answer. 'Yet I know well that she has had the instrument for a long time. Being a victim to neuralgia, she has, unhappily, become addicted to the morphia habit. I had hoped to cure her, when my position justified such stern measures as alone could prove effective; but unless her innocence can speedily be proved, the cure will be brought about in another way!'

Saxham nodded, and screwed the wooden stem firmly into the yellow bowl of his pipe.

'In your opinion,' he remarked 'a hypodermic syringe was *not* employed?'

'Heavens!' cried Bachoffner, springing from his chair. 'I, with my poor knowledge of such things, can answer that question! I, who but saw the body for a moment! I, who have no M.D. after my name! Do you, a man that professes to be read in medicine, to be qualified in the science of poison and antidote, stand here and plead ignorance on such a point?'

My friend was in no way perturbed. Bachoffner stood before him, with his black brows drawn into one continuous straight line, and his deep-set eyes blazing furiously. He was obviously a hot-tempered man, and Saxham's seeming callousness had fired him to passion.

'You see,' said the doctor, 'I was not present at the post-mortem.'

'Post-mortem!' rapped the other. 'You saw the body directly after death—only a few minutes after! If you knew anything of snake poisons, that would be enough.'

'Snake poisons?' queried Saxham.

'I said snake poisons!' Bachoffner repeated furiously. 'I am of half Indian parentage; I have lived in a country where many hundreds die every year as Mr Pettigrew died. When a man has been bitten by a snake, I can tell that it is so. I do not talk nonsense of hypodermic syringes!'

'I must apologize,' Saxham said soothingly, 'if I have unintentionally ruffled you; but may I venture to point out the improbability of your theory? Where could such a creature have come from? Where have gone?'

Bachoffner's foot tapped the floor impatiently.

'You are not prepared to stake your professional reputation upon the point?' he asked fiercely.

'I fear not,' replied the doctor.

At that our visitor, with some muttered remark, clapped his soft hat upon his head, and went out without a word of apology or farewell.

This strange termination of the interview greatly surprised me; but Saxham merely smiled, and knocked out the smoking ashes from his pipe. He was quietly reloading, when again the bell rang, and I turned to him with the words:

'He's come back!'

'Perhaps,' said my friend, and went out to the door.

A moment later Inspector Pepys stood in the room.

'Good-evening, gentlemen,' he began. 'I'm sorry to trouble, so late; but I wanted to ask, if it isn't private, what Mr Goree Bachoffner came about?'

Saxham proffered a box of cigarettes.

'Thinking of arresting him?' he inquired genially. 'Nothing like a broad mind in these matters—a really comprehensive outlook.'

Pepys made a slight grimace, detecting the irony in this remark.

'Well, sir,' he said, 'the case is a very extraordinary one, and I was coming to you, anyway; but seeing our German friend running up here, I waited till he came out again, not wishing to interrupt.'

For the second time that evening Saxham's opinion was solicited upon the matter of Cyrus Pettigrew's death, on this occasion he being invited to testify that a hypodermic syringe *had* been employed!

'It's a funny thing for a young woman to carry about,' continued the inspector; 'and, when you come to think of it, no one else could very well have got into the carriage and out again. She inherits all his money, too.'

'There are several objections to the theory,' Saxham assured him, after a pause. 'It is not likely, for instance, that she would carry such incriminating evidence about with her after the crime. Also, she is addicted to morphia. Any physician will tell you that.'

Inspector Pepys did not seem too well pleased.

'But a hypodermic syringe must have been used!' he persisted.

'There were several punctures,' said the doctor; 'that rather militates against the idea. What's the evidence against Bachoffner?'

Pepys started slightly.

'Excuse me, sir,' he explained, 'but I didn't say I had any. As he's engaged to Miss Pettigrew, I've been keeping an eye on him, thinking he might be in her confidence. Even if I'd an atom of evidence against him, which I've not, the fact that he was in his rooms in Fig Tree Court when Miss Pettigrew's wire came from Rugby would clear him. I certainly thought they might be in it together, she doing the dirty work, and so I looked into the matter. He took in the telegram himself.'

'Ah!' commented Saxham thoughtfully. 'He seemed very cut up this evening. In his opinion, Mr Pettigrew died from snake-bite.'

'Snake-bite be hanged!' responded Pepys. 'Of course *he'd* try to clear her. He's marrying a cool five thousand a year there! You may depend he's not anxious to see a big fortune slip through his fingers.'

'You don't credit him with very exalted motives,' I said.

'No, I don't,' replied the inspector. 'From all I hear, he's no great catch. I'm surprised at any girl standing him; but she seems to be more afraid of him than anything else. I wonder if he had influence enough over her mind—'

'That's hypnotism,' Saxham interrupted. 'You're getting in a bit deep.'

The Inspector rose from his chair, with something very like a sigh.

'Then you're not of opinion that a hypodermic syringe was used?' he asked.

'No,' said Saxham slowly, and with the air of a man who has come to a momentous decision. 'I think a very extraordinary thing was responsible for Mr Pettigrew's death. Mr Bachoffner, I believe, could assist us, if he felt so disposed.'

'But,' cried Pepys, 'he'd move heaven and earth to prove her innocent!'

'I believe you,' admitted the doctor; 'but suppose we take the liberty of calling upon him, as time is precious, and putting a few plain questions.'

This suggestion came as a great surprise to me. 'Why didn't you put the questions when he was here?' I demanded.

'Because I had not made up my mind,' was the vague reply.

Pepys and I, the inspector as mystified as myself, accompanied the doctor into Fleet Street and to Goree Bachoffner's rooms in Fig Tree Court. After some little delay, our knocking and ringing was answered by Bachoffner in person. He gave a start of surprise at seeing us, but almost immediately invited us to step inside. His room was very disorderly, being a litter of books and papers, with a few strange-looking Oriental ornaments, and very little furniture. A handsome cabinet, apparently of Burmese work, stood against the wall between the windows.

Bachoffner was far from cordial, but stood leaning against a chair, never asking us to be seated. Saxham, however, opened the conversation blandly.

'My friend Inspector Pepys,' he said, 'is going fishing. We thought you might be so good as to lend him a rod.'

This singular remark amazed the inspector and myself; but its effect on Bachoffner was truly astonishing. It might have been his death-sentence, so ghastly was the hue that crept over his tawny skin. His face assumed a mottled appearance, while he stared glassily at the smiling speaker.

'You're mad!' he gasped hoarsely, his eyes straying first to the big cabinet and then towards a corner in which I noticed, for the first time, the joints of a fishing-rod. 'You're mad! I was here in my rooms when—'

He checked himself suddenly, and stood there staring, a picture of terror-stricken humanity.

'When the telegram arrived?' suggested Saxham softly. 'Quite so. You have already been good enough to tell us that. But, as I chance to know, owing to Miss Pettigrew being taken ill again, the said telegram was not dispatched from Rugby until considerably after ten o'clock. It probably did not reach Fleet Street until eleven or later; and I would point out—a circumstance that my friend the inspector has somehow overlooked—that even allowing for five minutes' delay at Rugby, the 9.5 would reach Euston before eleven o'clock. In fact, there is no doubt that you got back in your rooms in time to provide yourself with this excellent alibi.'

Bachoffner grasped the chair fiercely.

'It's a lie!' he almost screamed. 'A cursed ingenious lie! I was not on the train when it reached Rugby.'

'Neither was the queer-complexioned, auburn-haired young man who so alarmed a certain nervous passenger,' Saxham pursued. 'That particular grease-paint known as "two-and-a-half," well rubbed into such a skin as yours, would produce a highly interesting effect, and would moreover, be imperceptible at night. A fair wig, too, will do wonders, particularly in conjunction with pincenez.'

The man who was thus accused, after a rapid glance around the room, sank into a chair like one half stunned, still keeping his strange gaze fixed upon the doctor. I saw Pepys sidle to the door and take up his stand there, while Saxham's manner suddenly changed, and he strode forward, standing before Bachoffner with blazing eyes.

'You cowardly, callous hound!' he said quietly. 'You trapped that poor girl into an engagement to marry you, and then, finding her guardian's objections insurmountable, and his niece wise enough to decline marriage without his consent, you determined to remove the only barrier that stood between you and a fortune. Had you been successful in this instance, probably your wife would have been the next victim.'

Bachoffner did not move.

'How many times you travelled, disguised, between London and Birmingham in the next carriage to Mr Pettigrew, waiting your chance, I cannot tell; but when, at last, only one nervous passenger stood between you and the achievement of your murderous scheme, you even took the risk of arrest as a madman and inevitable discovery, rather than let this opportunity go by. Shall I tell you how you took advantage of your victim's habit of travelling with one window open? How you risked your wretched life on the footboard of the train outside Northampton? How, having accomplished your purpose, you returned to the second-class compartment, to leave the train and slip away when the alarm was given? How you so timed the murder that by hurrying on foot into Rugby you caught the 9.5 for Euston, quietly sitting there whilst the car containing the dead man was detached from the Birmingham train?'

'Good God!' cried the accused man, throwing wide his arms in a frenzied gesture. 'How do you know!'

'I did not know,' said Saxham. 'Certain data, I collected; the rest I assumed. But you have confessed now. You all but did so in Carey Street to-night. It has been, perhaps, for the best that Miss Pettigrew was arrested. To see the very perfection of your plans leading to the ruin of the scheme proved too complex a situation even for you. You betrayed yourself, Mr Goree Bachoffner, making a certainty of a suspicion that I had hardly hoped to confirm.'

There was no doubt whatever that Bachoffner was guilty; but lacking the singular penetration and abnormal reasoning powers of my scientific friend, I was still hopelessly in the dark respecting the actual mode of Mr Pettigrew's death. I was soon enlightened.

'So confident were you in your own devilish cunning,' Saxham resumed suddenly, 'that you even left *this* here—where it struck my eye directly I entered the room, supplying the missing link and suggesting my opening remark.'

As he spoke, he stepped to the cabinet, and took in his hand the top-joint of a fishing-rod, evidently a part of that which I had noted in the corner. A loop of black silk ran through the little brass ring at the top.

'What thing was it that you attached to this and held through the open carriage window so that it settled on your victim's arm?' he demanded.

Bachoffner looked up, with a face dreadful to see, and then laughed with an ever-rising cadence. The shocking peals rang through the building.

'You shall see!' he shrieked, springing past Saxham to the cabinet. 'You shall see!'

Before we had time to conceive what he was about to do, he opened a drawer and threw back a glass lid, thrusting in his hand and withdrawing a length of black silk.

At sight of the hideous thing which hung suspended at the end a sudden nausea came upon me. It was a huge insect of a dirty grey colour—a loathsome thing with great hairy, clutching legs and a bloated, scaly body the size of a small hen-egg.

'This is my sweet friend that kissed the poor Pettigrew!' he cried, his eyes glaring madly; and suddenly jerking the unclean creature into his hand, he ran through an open door that evidently led to his bedroom, laughing discordantly.

'After him,' said Saxham; 'but don't let that fearful insect spring upon you! It is a Burmese spider, of a species related to the tarantula. Its bite is certain death.'

The inner room was in darkness, but the doctor took the shaded lamp in his hand and entered. Pepys and I followed, to find Bachoffner writhing on the bed, with his fearful pet in his right hand. It was striking at his bare wrist again and again.

As he caught sight of Saxham standing in the door with the lamp uplifted, he gave a maniacal shriek, tore the infuriated insect from his hand and hurled it across the room. A shudder of revulsion ran through me as the thing fell, with a dull thud, almost at my feet—dead.

When we turned again to the bed, a glance sufficed to show that the master, in the throes of an agonizing death which he had so callously visited upon a fellow-being, had but a few minutes to outlive his venomous servant.

JOSEPH COMMINGS

# Ghost in the Gallery

*In the annals of Impossible Crime fiction, Joe Commings is a very
underrated writer. Strike that. In the annals of Impossible Crime fiction
Joe Commings is the* most *underrated writer.*

*Consider the evidence. Starting with his first published short story,
'Murder Under Glass', in March, 1947, Joe produced a series of
beautifully crafted tales of Impossible Crime which had stretched to almost
forty by the time the last appeared in November, 1984. And whereas some
authors can, like Joe, hit on clever and inventive plotlines, they rarely
augment them with punchy dialogue, knockabout action and three-
dimensional characters—all of which are to be found in Joe's entertaining
and ingenious tales.*

*Take his main series detective for instance, US Senator Brooks U.
Banner. His entry in* Detectives' Who's Who *lists among his past careers
auctioneer, sideshow barker and county sheriff, while his hobbies include
magic tricks, mechanical toys, watching sport and reading comicbooks . . .
and solving locked room murders. It doesn't, naturally enough, mention
that he weighs near as damn it 300 pounds, smokes vile-smelling Pittsburgh
stogies, eats like a horse and sports a line in clothing—frock-coat as big
as a pup-tent, string tie, peppermint-striped shirt, baggy britches and braces
(being American, Banner calls them suspenders)—which, once seen, is never
forgotten, no matter how hard his startled clients may try. Very much a
Renaissance man, Banner is cut from the same bolt as Sir Henry Merrivale
and Dr Fell, the creations of John Dickson Carr, a writer Commings much
admired.*

*You might be forgiven for thinking that Banner's career was perhaps
somewhat short-lived since only four of his cases have seen the inside of
a book, and two of those only in the last three years. But the facts are
otherwise. Banner appeared, from 1947 to 1984, in no less than thirty-
two stories and all but three of them were Impossibles. But the comparative
obscurity of most of the magazines in which the stories themselves originally
appeared has resulted in even the most eagle-eyed of anthologists missing
out on one of the genuine treats of post-War detective fiction. Here is an
early Banner, a gem of a story—and only the fifth, out of thirty-two, ever
to appear in bookform.*

ROBERT ADEY

That afternoon Linda Carewe poisoned her husband. She poisoned him with arsenic.

As an afternoon, it was a rainy, dreary one in late fall. The downpour made the Honeywell Art Galleries gleam in the wet like a dark green marble tomb.

Linda Carewe stumbled inside with a throbbing heart right past McPherson, the front door attendant. McPherson stopped talking to the newsboy with his sodden bundle of papers and stared into the gloomy interior after her.

She was wearing a black plastic raincoat and Russian boots. Her folded, dripping transparent umbrella was squeezed in her pale hand. Later when Senator Banner was investigating the murder, he described her as having a fascinating frame and head full of brown follow-me-lad curls. Her eyes, as long as an Egyptian queen's, darted with fright.

Borden Argyll was waiting for her in their usual nook. He was an anaemic artist with tortoise shell glasses and a scrubbed face. But he was young. That was all that mattered to Linda.

When she saw him she went to pieces emotionally. He raised his arms too slowly as she rushed into them and she caught him full on the narrow chest, almost knocking him backward into the T'ang Dynasty vase.

'I killed him!' she sobbed. 'I'm rid of him. Borden! I did! I did!'

He jerked his head around to see if anybody was within earshot. There was no one else there at all. At that moment he was as near to panic as he had ever been in his life.

It had all started eight months ago when Linda married DeWitt Carewe. The marriage was the culmination of a hasty romance that began in the woods four months before. It had been a gusty day when they'd met. The earth and the sky had the same unnatural, lurid glow. And Linda, out for a Sunday stroll, was lost. A man appeared suddenly on the path. The wild wind in the trees seemed to shout and try to tell her things to warn her.

The man showed her the way back to the bus line. As they walked, they talked. Linda became intrigued by DeWitt Carewe. There was not too great a difference between their ages. He looked about forty and she was twenty-three. And he had money. In finance he led Wall Street by the nose. Where others failed he begot riches. He had inhuman drive.

She married him.

There were whisperings about Carewe. Whisperings about his connection with unspeakable things that went on behind certain locked doors in Washington Square. Things that had to do with werewolves and vampirism. Some people even went so far as to say that Linda had married Lucifer himself.

During the last three months Linda had repeatedly and incautiously fled to someone 'more human'—Borden Argyll. She had been introduced to Argyll by Carewe himself. Argyll, a laborious workman with the brush, had been using Carewe as a subject in one of his art series called *Studies in the Supernormal*. Aside from going with another man's wife, smoking a calabash, and matching pennies, Argyll had few vices.

Now in that dim, dreary gallery he tried to console Linda. Bit by bit, she told him about the noon meal and the five grains of arsenic in the milk and how she had hurried out of the house after she'd seen him drink it. She couldn't witness his death agony.

'He was a monster,' muttered Argyll. 'I realize that now.' The tattoo of the rain on the stained glass window blurred their voices. 'But, sweetheart, what shall we do? The police will find—' The tortured look on her face at the mention of police made him hesitate.

Neither of them wanted to think about the police. And they clung to each other quivering with doubt and apprehension in the long shadowy gallery.

Someone was walking toward them. Walking with a slow tantalizing deliberate tread. They both turned their heads in that direction to see who was coming.

Out of the streaming grey light leered a triangular face. A full-lipped mouth was drawn back exposing sharp animal teeth in a cruel grin.

Linda made a sound as if she'd been struck.

Argyll gasped, 'Carewe!'

'My dear sweet wife'—the voice sounded sepulchral—'murdered me this noon. Do you believe in ghosts, Argyll?'

Argyll was lead-coloured. But he stood his ground. 'No, damn you! You're alive!'

'Follow me and see—if you dare!' came the taunt.

The apparition wheeled and went back rapidly the way he had come.

Linda stared dazedly at Argyll. 'Then I didn't—'

He reached for her hand. 'No, you didn't poison him. Come on. We'll follow him.'

'Oh no, Borden. No. He's up to something terrible. You don't know him as I do.'

They started off blindly, trailing Carewe to the first elbow of the deserted gallery. As they turned the corner, they saw the flitting form mingling with the shadows a good distance ahead.

The whole building was deadly still save for their footsteps, their quick breathing, and the steady rain.

The man ahead had whisked around the next corner. They heard his footsteps break into a sharp run. They heard the opening and closing of a glass door.

On the wall near them a small sign with gilt lettering and an arrow said: *Administrative Offices.*

Argyll drew cautiously to the turn around which Carewe had vanished. Linda panted at his collar. They halted.

Now they could see down the next wide hall and across it as far as the first office door, which was marked: *Trustees.* It was diagonally fifteen feet from the corner where they stood. The closed door was, except for its wooden frame, sheer plate glass. They could look clearly into the room.

They saw a lighted floor lamp set to the left and rear. Standing beside the lamp, grinning out at them, was Carewe. They saw him reach out his arm and yank the lamp chain. The room and the hall became one vast shadow.

Argyll fumbled for a box of wooden matches and struck one. He took a step toward the Trustees' office door.

Linda caught him restrainingly by the arm. 'No, Borden! Don't go in!'

'Please, Linda!' he snapped, nerves ragged. 'Let's get this nonsense over with.'

She let go. Like a will o' the wisp, he crossed the space in a half dozen steps. The doorknob rattled loosely in his fingers and he swung the door open. 'Don't come in, Linda,' he warned her over his shoulder.

The same match in his hand was still burning when he groped for the lamp chain. His hand brushed against the bulb. It was warm. He found the chain and jerked it. Flinging away the twisted black match stump, he swung around. His arms were upraised, half protectingly.

He saw Linda standing squarely in the office doorway. He saw— *nobody else!*

Carewe had vanished with the turning out of the light!

Then Linda's rasping intake of breath made the short hairs at the nape of Argyll's neck bristle. He peered around the edge of a maple desk to where she was pointing.

A girl's body was spilled there. Her skull had been crushed with one blow of the silver statuette that was lying by her. The statuette was an Inca alpaca and its long neck made an ideal handle.

You could almost hear the thump of their hearts in the still room. Argyll recognized whose body it was. 'Phyllis Remington!'

'Your model!'

He touched the girl's hand. It was warm and limp. She had just been killed.

Linda hear a movement in the hall behind her. She made one terrified leap to Argyll's side.

In the doorway appeared a roly-poly little man with a baldish head and gleaming eyeglasses on a wide black ribbon. He wore striped pants and what Senator Banner called a come-to-prayer coat. As he stood there poised, his legs bent backward at the knees like sabres. He was George Honeywell, founder and director of the Galleries. His wrinkled forehead proclaimed that he was a worrier. And his chief worry was for more money for the upkeep of the Galleries.

He tittered. 'Mrs Carewe! Whatever has happened to you? You're as pale as a—'

'My husband!' she blurted, on the verge of hysteria. 'He's mad! He was just in here! He killed Phyllis!'

'Good Lord, no!' Honeywell's jaw fell slack as he hastened to their side at the desk. He looked down, then away, biting his trembling lip. 'What a loss. She was such a beautiful girl. A trifle tempestuous perhaps, but— Where is Carewe?'

'He disappeared,' said Argyll. 'I know it sounds incredible but he vanished into thin air before I could get in. Maybe you've seen him?'

'Me?' said Honeywell. 'Lord, no. I've been in the other office across the hall ever since coming back from a Judo lesson. Nobody came my way.'

They looked around the square room. There were no windows. It was air-conditioned. The door was the only opening.

Argyll's eyes rose to the nearly life-size painting hanging flush with the back wall. It was one of his own recent works. It was a vividly realistic subject called *Werewolf and Victim*. In the shaggy face of the pawing werewolf, with its prominent incisors and lancet canines, no one could fail to recognize DeWitt Carewe.

Argyll had used Carewe and Phyllis Remington as his models.

Honeywell shook himself like a wet poodle. 'Wait for me in the Seventeenth Century Gallery while I phone the police,' he said. 'We've got to stick together.'

It was hours after the discovery of the murder. Linda and Honeywell huddled outside the phone booth in the drugstore while Argyll, inside, dialled.

Argyll, half listening to the buzz in the receiver, was saying to them, 'While Senator Banner was sitting for the oil I made of him during his last political campaign, he talked a blue streak about impossible murders. He must have cited at least four cases he's solved where a person left a room *unseen* through a watched door. The answer to each one was a simple magic trick. There was nothing supernatural about it.'

Linda said tremulously, 'DeWitt is capable of anything evil. Anything.'

Argyll spoke into the phone. 'Ninety-one Morningside Drive? I want to speak to Senator Banner. Is he home?'

The switchboard girl said, 'No, he isn't, sir. Have you tried the Sphinx Club? He's probably playing bezique there, or pulling rabbits out of hats. This's one of his nights.'

Argyll called the Sphinx Club on Fifth Avenue. The desk clerk said 'He hasn't been in tonight, sir. He may be banging away at clay geese at the shooting gallery on Broadway and 42nd Street. That's one of his hangouts.'

Argyll called the shooting gallery. A beery voice said, 'The Senator? He looked in while passin' and said somethin' about goin' to a bowling alley.' The voice broke off while someone in the background did some coaching. Then the beery voice resumed. 'Beg poddin! You'll catch him at Shell's Billiard Parlor playin' snooker.'

United States Senator Brooks U. Banner could not have been more at home in Shell's Billiard Parlor if they had built the place around him. Cue in hand, he was bending his girth over a pool table, studying the layout of the balls. The cuffs of his peppermint-striped shirt were folded up and his red Hercules suspenders made a blazing crisscross on a back as wide as a cement walk.

He was playing a thin, dark, nervous man with eyes like a blacksnake's. The dark man agitatedly chalked a cue, watching Banner.

Argyll, rain dripping off his hat brim, led Linda and Honeywell through the smokiness and chatter of the pool room. Some of the men whistled approval at Linda and that made Banner abandon the game for a moment to turn around for a look-see.

Linda got the full impact of his blue watered-steel eyes. He knew that to her he looked like a slovenly archangel who enjoyed consorting with blackguards. He was a King Kong in size with a mop of grizzled hair and black-lead eyebrows. His string tie looked greasy, as if it had trailed in his soup. And it had.

Banner's eyes stabbed away from her and at the others. 'Borden

Argyll!' He held out a palm the size of a welcome mat. 'Howzit, paint-slubber? How're all the paintings?'

Argyll shook hands and introduced his companions. 'We came to see you, Senator,' he said hesitantly, 'about the murder.'

Banner shuffled with interest, like a performing bear. 'What murder?'

Linda started to say, 'The ghost in the gallery—'

'Jumping hop-toads! *That* one! I read the headlines. That's all I looked at. Wait'll I finish off this game.'

Briskly calling his shots, he pocketed one red ball, then a pool ball. His dark opponent stopped chalking his cue. Banner pocketed another red ball, another pool ball. The dark man, disgruntled, put his cue back in the rack. He couldn't bear to look at the table as the last ball rolled out of sight.

Banner wet his big thumb and counted his winnings, a sheaf of red seal U.S. notes. Then he struggled into his antique frock coat and grinned.

'He doesn't know I'm an international pool shark. We'll all go to the Sphinx Club. You're my guests. I want to feed the elephant—meaning, yours truly. Then we'll talk about the murder.'

Banner, waving at everybody, selected a table in the centre of the dining room. He ordered one of his favourite rare Spencer steaks and a scuttle of black coffee. 'Make the dessert a rhubarb meringue pie.'

The others said they had already dined at the rotisserie. But they ordered drinks. Banner attacked his feast as if it were Fido's dinner; he cut the whole steak into small chunks, salted his string beans, stuccoed a whole potato with butter, and buried everything under a volcanic eruption of gravy.

Argyll cleared his throat. 'We three have been together ever since we discovered the murder.'

Banner lifted a plastered fork to his mouth. 'Sail into this easier, lad. I'm gonna be quiz master in a game of cross questions and crooked answers. First off, in what order did you people go into the Galleries?'

Honeywell said, 'McPherson, the man at the front door, tells us that I was the first one in this afternoon, then came Phyllis Remington, the dead girl, then Carewe, then Argyll, and lastly Mrs Carewe.'

Linda clutched Argyll's arm. 'DeWitt knew about our meetings!' She seemed as if she were just finding that out.

'We didn't try to hide it very well,' said Argyll.

Banner kept his eyes on Linda. 'You don't ask like a native New Yorker, kitten. Where'd you hail from?'

'Pawtucket, Rhode Island.'

'What'd you do before you married Carewe?'

'I was a dancing teacher.'

Banner brightened. 'Can you do the Paris cancan?' She looked at him frosty faced. Banner crowed. 'If you can, don't be bashful about 'fessing up.'

'This is neither the time nor the place for anything like that,' she said heatedly. 'I want to tell you what kind of man my husband was—is . . . Oh, I don't know. Have I killed him or not?' she ended in a whimper.

'He's not dead,' said Argyll stiffly. 'We saw and heard him.'

'All right,' she said, trying to convince herself. 'He's not dead. But he might easily be. I don't know—it's all so puzzling, so mysterious.' She paused and shuddered in the warm comfortable dining room. 'Borden, how old would you say DeWitt is?'

'About forty,' said Argyll without hesitation.

'He *looks* forty,' she whispered. 'But he has an old Bible with a metal clasp. He always kept the clasp locked. I'd never seen him open it. He told me to keep my hands off it. The other day I broke the clasp. His birthdate is on the flyleaf. *He's fifty-nine years old!*'

The clatter of dishes seemed far away. Centuries away. The Dark Ages yawned again for an instant and they seemed to hear a thin, tortured cry of 'Witchcraft!'

Argyll put his hand on Linda's for a moment to calm her. Then he drained his whisky glass to steady himself. Honeywell sat rooted there, fascinated. Banner covered a burp with his serviette to his lips.

She went on, 'I'll never forget the first day of our married life when I stepped into his vast studio apartment. It has crimson curtains and black drapes and brass ceremonial gongs. The place always reeks of incense. It doesn't seem real. It doesn't seem as if these things could happen in New York. That very same night he asked me if I would go with him to a celebration of the Black Mass.

'I was stunned. He said, "Phyllis will be there. She'll act as assistant—my scarlet-robed acolyte." His animal teeth seemed to grow longer as he grinned at me. I tore away from him and locked myself in my room. He called through the door that if I wanted him I would merely have to draw a pentagram—a five-sided figure—in chalk on the black oak floor and he would reappear . . . And then there were other things, like the books about werewolves in his library. And the lampshade of human skin. Today'—her words stumbled—'I wanted to finish with him. I made a meal for him and put five grains of arsenic in his milk. I saw him take it. But he didn't die! He's—he's the devil.'

Banner thoughtfully sipped his coffee with the spoon standing in the cup and almost poking him in the eye. Another of his Bannerisms. He said, '*Three* grains would kill an adult. Where'd you get the arsenic? By soaking flypaper?'

'No, no. I found it in his medicine cabinet.'

'Mebbe it wasn't arsenic.'

'It was, Senator. My friend has rats in her basement. I tried it on them. They died.'

Honeywell stirred and spoke with a frog in his throat. 'Only Beelzebub could vanish the way *he* did.'

'I wanna hear about that,' said Banner.

Argyll told the story up to the time he started for the blackened glass door with the match flickering in his hand.

'Now whoa right there!' Banner halted him. 'Could Carewe have flown the coop in the instant of complete darkness before you struck the match?'

'No' said Argyll positively. 'Those glass doors make a noise when you open and close them. Aside from that, the doorknob rattles when you turn it. He had no time to do it silently and we never heard a sound.'

'All right. So he was still in the room as you barged in.'

Argyll said, 'I touched the light bulb. It was warm.'

'The light had just been turned out. Did he wriggle out of the door before you lighted the floor lamp again?'

Linda said, 'I was in the doorway. He couldn't have got out without crowding me. Besides, I could see the whole room vaguely. There was illumination from Borden's match.'

'No other exits but the door?'

'None,' said Honeywell, chiming in.

'No place in the room to hide?'

Argyll shook his head.

Banner frowned at all three of them in turn. 'Against which wall is the lamp?'

'To the left and rear as you go into the office.'

'And that's the only wall, or portion of wall, that you can see when you stand at the turn of the corridor?'

'Yes,' said Honeywell.

'Can you solve it?' asked Linda impatiently.

'Can you?' countered Banner.

She said no in a little voice.

Banner said, 'I'm just another Boobus Americanus. What you people have done is handed me a lemon on a tray . . . Forget about Carewe for a minute. I'm keen on models. Has anyone got a good word for Phyllis?'

Honeywell looked sideways at Linda. 'Mrs Carewe,' he said embarrassedly, 'there are unpleasant things that I'm aware of that have to come out now. I happen to know that Phyllis and Carewe were in love before he married you.'

'The old billy goat,' chuckled Banner.

Linda kept her eyes on the salt cellar.

Honeywell continued, 'They'd been in love for several years. Then Carewe quit her abruptly to marry you. Phyllis pretended to take it as a woman of the world should, but in her heart I knew she was jealous and embittered. She sunk her teeth in Carewe. She strafed him with extortion. She bled him for huge sums of money under the threat of telling you about them.'

Argyll beamed. 'That's why Carewe killed Phyllis. That's the motive.'

'Sounds possible,' agreed Banner. 'Going back to Carewe, let's grant that he got out of the room without harping too much on the *how* of it. Did he get out of the Galleries?'

'No,' said Linda.

'Yes,' said Honeywell.

'Which is it?'

'To tell the story in proper sequence,' said Argyll, 'Linda and I waited in the Seventeenth Century Gallery for Honeywell to join us after he'd phoned the police.'

Linda interrupted, 'Then I heard something strange. Remember I told you, Borden?'

Argyll frowned doubtfully. 'I'm not sure.'

'I am,' she said. 'It was a rapid clicking sound—a whirring—like a window blind being pulled down.'

'A window blind?' Banner juggled his furry black eyebrows.

'There aren't any in the whole building,' said Honeywell.

'No,' said Argyll, shaking his head. He looked at Linda as if to tell her to stop being so silly.

Honeywell continued, 'I joined Mrs Carewe and Argyll after I'd phoned for the police. "We must stick together," I said. And we did. We went first to the back door of the building. It was locked from the inside the way it generally is. The only other door is the front.

We went there and found the door attendant, old McPherson, talking to a newsboy. Both of them swore that Carewe—nor anyone else, for that matter—had not gone out that way.'

'The windows,' suggested Banner.

'All of them burglar-proof,' said Honeywell promptly. 'No one can use them to get in or out without setting off an alarm. Before the police came we made a hasty but thorough tour of the whole building. It's a fairly easy place to search. Nothing but paintings and small art objects. *Carewe was not in the building!*'

'Ha!' chortled Banner. 'I know where he's hiding!'

'Where?' cried all three at once.

'In a suit of armour!'

Honeywell sighed with disappointment and shook his head. 'There's no armour in the Galleries.'

Banner's ruddy face was wry. 'I've always wanted to get on a case where somebody hid in a suit of armour. No such luck.' He started picking his teeth meditatively with a raccoonbone toothpick on the end of a tarnished silver chain.

Honeywell said, 'There we were up against it. Carewe had not only escaped from the room when he turned out the light—he disappeared bodily from the entire Galleries!'

'Did the police hunt for him when they came?'

'They certainly did. They looked into everything that could conceal a live man.'

'Yass, yass.' Banner leaned back and jabbed a cigar into his mouth. He didn't light it. He never did. He gnawed it. 'Carewe committed the murder, then dissolved. That's the picture.' He looked sweetly at Linda. 'Do you think you'd melt, sugar, if you went out in the rain again with me? Of course not.'

Linda merely looked at him, puzzled.

Honeywell said, 'Where are you going?'

'To the Galleries. All of us.'

'At this time of night?' said Argyll, shocked.

'I'm gonna make one last stab at finding Carewe and doping out how he escaped.' He started to look around for his white campaign hat and finally discovered that he was sitting on it. He punched it back into shape.

'I wonder,' he mused, 'if I oughta take some chalk with me to draw a pentagram. Mebbe it'd help us materialize Satan.'

A policeman in a glistening poncho had replaced McPherson at the front door. He shined a heavy duty flashlight in their eyes, then Banner showed him his special salmon coloured police card.

The policeman let them into the Galleries.

Banner said to them, 'That's Coyne, the cop who sot it out last month with Four-Finger Flannigan the vice czar.'

They stood dripping in the dark main hall until Honeywell found a switch and threw it, lighting their way. Their heels rang eerily on the cold bare marble.

First, Banner had a look into the Trustees' office, whence Carewe had vanished. He posed by the floor lamp and had Argyll and Linda go out to the corner of the corridor. Then he had Argyll stand by the lamp and went to the corner himself for a look.

He trotted back. 'See anything wrong with it, Argyll?'

'No, Senator,' said Argyll.

'That's the trouble. That's what's giving me the screaming meemies.'

He led the way to the Director's office. It was fifteen farther down the corridor, across from the Trustees office.

The furnishings were similar to the first office, but arranged differently. The floor lamp in here was deep on the right.

Banner said, 'This's where you were, Honeywell, when it all happened?'

'Yes,' said Honeywell.

'Here in the dark?'

'Huh?'

'Linda and Argyll say that when Carewe turned out the light in the other room the whole corridor went dark. This room has a plate glass door too. If your light was on, it would've shined out.'

'Of course it wasn't on,' said Honeywell, a trifle pettishly. 'As I told them, I'd had a Judo lesson late in the morning. And I was lying on that studio couch'—he pointed—'resting. I wasn't asleep. Just relaxing here in the dark.'

'Carewe never disturbed you?'

'Not today.'

Banner strayed to Honeywell's desk. There were a variety of objects on it. Banner began to toy with some coloured glass squares. 'What're these used for?'

'They're stereopticon slides for our magic lantern,' said Honeywell. Those you're handling are pictures of Oaxaca pottery.'

'Magic lantern?' said Banner. 'Then you have a movie theatre.'

'You can call it that. Very small one.'

'Is it located near the Seventeenth Century Gallery?'

'Close to it,' said Honeywell, his brows knitted together over his beribboned eyeglasses.

'We'll go there.'

They filed slowly into the miniature theatre. Looking down over the slope of seat-backs, they saw the screen. It was pulled.

Banner ambled to it. It hung about eleven inches out from the wall. He grasped the lower edge and gave it a sharp jerk, then released it. It started to roll itself up rapidly on a spring.

As it went up it made a rapid clicking sound—a whirring—like a window blind.

And they saw a man with a face like Satan!

He was hanging there. But he was dead. His neck was in a noose. The rope ran up over a hook, then down again to be fastened at the baseboard. All covered by the screen.

'Sweet Marguerite!' grunted Banner. 'What d'you think of that?'

'He hung himself,' gasped Argyll.

Linda put her hands up to her face to shut out the sight.

'We never thought of looking—*there*,' murmured Honeywell.

'Neither did anyone else,' said Banner. 'You were looking for a *live* man. Not one hanging. And the screen looked innocently close to the wall. Only about eleven inches clearance. But you'd be surprised how little space you take up hanging that way. We've all been obtuse. Something else was obtuse today too. I'll tell you later. Honeywell, skip out and fetch Coyne, the cop on guard.'

Honeywell didn't skip out. He plodded.

'But how, Senator?' pleaded Linda. 'How has he been able to do all this?'

'You wondered,' said Banner slowly, 'why you didn't kill him when you flavoured his milk with five grains of arsenic. You've heard of men taking more than that without harming them, haven't you?'

'Addicts!' cried Argyll.

Banner nodded. 'Yass. Was your husband on record as ever having a skin disease, Linda?'

'A skin disease? Oh yes. He once mentioned having had psoriasis. But he was cured long ago.'

'Oh sure. The baker's itch. The cure is *arsenic*. That started him off. Another thing. Arsenic puts the youthful bloom in your cheeks. Does that answer another question?'

Linda stared. 'That's why he looked so young!'

'I'm still bothered,' muttered Argyll. 'How—?'

Honeywell returned with Coyne. Seeing the hanging corpse, Coyne crossed himself religiously and exclaimed, ' 'Tis the divil hisself!'

Banner scowled. 'No. Just a poor sap with buck teeth.' He lifted his voice. 'Lemme finish. Ready for the surprises? I told you something else was obtuse. It's an obtuse angle. Every schoolboy knows that the angle of reflection is equal to the angle of incidence.'

'What are you talking about!' said Linda irritably. She studiously kept her eyes away from the wall.

'Ever notice what you see when you look in a mirror?'

Argyll answered. 'My reflection, of course.'

'Is it accurate?'

'Naturally.'

'No, it ain't,' said Banner. 'When you move your right hand, the *left* hand in the mirror moves. It's completely the reverse.'

'I see what you mean,' said Argyll. 'But how does that apply?'

'When you stand at the corner of the corridor,' said Banner, 'and look toward the door through which you saw Carewe, an obtuse angle is formed. It's fifteen feet from you to the Trustees' door. And then the line rebounds off that door to go another oblique fifteen to the Director's door across the hall. Get it? The floor lamp in the Trustees' office, you said, is deep on the *left*. The floor lamp in the Director's office is deep on the *right*. But if you saw a reflection of the Director's office in a mirror, the lamp'd be to the left and rear—exactly the way it is in the Trustees' office!'

'You can't mean that what we saw was—' Argyll started to blurt.

'Carewe was never in the Trustees' office! He vanished, because he was never in there. It was the floor lamp in the *Director's* office that he turned out. What you saw was his reflection on the glass door, made to a perfect mirror with a black room behind it. The way you can often see passengers up ahead in the same car when you look out a train window at night.' He turned suddenly with an alarming gesture of accusation. 'Honeywell, you lied!'

'My God!' said Honeywell piously. 'You're not accusing me of being in league with that devil.'

Banner nodded. 'Worse than that, Honeywell. You killed Phyllis. You know too much about her blackmailing of Carewe not to have a whole hand in the pie. You drove her to it. When she got sick and tired of being your cat's paw, you killed her to stop her from blabbing to Carewe about you.'

'You don't know what you're saying,' cried Honeywell.

'Today she told you to go find another pigeon. You had to think fast. You told her to wait in the Trustees' office, that you had to have time to think it over. You had to have time, all right—to calculate her murder. You chawed your nails alone in the Director's office.

Then Carewe burst in on your maledictions with the story of how his wife had tried to poison him so that she could fly off with her Skeeziks.

'Carewe was full of sly tricks. He wanted to put the fear of the devil into these two with an idea he'd formed by his observation of the way the doors on that corridor were arranged. He told you all about it. You fell in with it. It was like the final piece in a jigsaw puzzle. While Carewe was off spooking Linda and Argyll in the gallery, you were murdering Phyllis with the silver alpaca. You turned off the Trustees' light. That's why Argyll found the bulb still warm when he touched it less than three minutes later. You'd left Phyllis's body lying there and you'd gone into the Director's office. That light you left burning. Carewe returned to you breathlessly, never suspecting that you'd committed a murder in the meantime. His spoof was working like a charm. Linda and Argyll had the wind up and they were tailing a ghost. Carewe stood near the lamp by the right wall, looking diagonally out toward the Trustees' office door.

'When Linda and Argyll poked into sight, they saw his *reflection* in the office door for a moment before he plunged the whole place into darkness. Argyll crashed into the wrong room. And Carewe had every opportunity in the world to slip out of the other, unwatched office and into the little theatre.

'Honeywell, you sent Linda and Argyll into the Seventeenth Century Gallery ahead of you. You took a moment to call the police, then dodged into the theatre to see Carewe. You knew that as soon as he heard about the murder he'd tell how he really disappeared, to save his own skin. You had to kill him too. You knocked him out with a plexus blow. You know all those pretty tricks. You practice Judo. Then you strung the unconscious Carewe up. Linda heard you pull down the movie screen to hide the body . . . Watch him, Coyne! I didn't bring my revolver! He's a bone breaker!'

'So'm I,' grunted Coyne. As Honeywell made a lunge, Coyne broke a clawing arm with his alert nightstick.

Honeywell dropped, groaning.

As they went out into the rainy night, Linda said to Banner, 'Why did Honeywell go to such lengths to get money in the first place?'

Banner snorted. 'Having these Galleries was enough to keep him broke. How a guy can expect to get a nickel back on a Siwash outfit like this beats me.'

Art, to Banner, was just a man's name.

EDGAR WALLACE

# The Missing Romney

*Four Square Jane was just one of many female characters, created by that phenomenon Edgar Wallace, who was a crook. Or at least seemed on the surface to be a crook. In fact it was usually (though not always) the case that the female in question was taking revenge on society for one reason or another, often on one particular member of society, usually high-born, who had ruined her family or her (though never with a fate worse than death) years before. And if it had been proved conclusively that a female was, say, a jewel-robber, it would later turn out that she wasn't, or that the jewels were hers anyway.*

*It's often said that Wallace's women characters were typical of the fictional heroines of his time (i.e. feeble and wishy-washy), but in truth they had a good deal of get-up-and-go about them, and if they did swoon in a book it was rarely more than once and then only after the most gruelling experience. Indeed, a good many of them (remember Cora Ann Milton, witheringly sarcastic wife of the Ringer?) were wonderfully hard-boiled and feisty.*

*And how often was it the case that his female crooks had an American background or an appropriately American or semi-American* nom de guerre: *Denver May, for instance, in the series 'The Man Who Killed X', California May in 'Lord Exenham Creates A Sensation', Chicago Kate in 'Her Birthday'. And, of course, Four Square Jane. There was a reason for all this. Back in the mid-1900s Wallace had fallen under the spell of a genuine female villain, the notorious May Churchill or—as she was known in America, France and England—Chicago May.*

*Chicago May was the Real Thing, an authentic, and entrancing, underworld character who'd been involved in all kinds of villainy from bank robbery down to the badger game (sexual blackmail). She was at that time attached to an equally fascinating crook, the infamous Eddie Guerin, the man who in 1902 had blown the American Express vaults in Paris (in the planning and staging of which May herself had been closely involved) getting away with over fifty thousand dollars. Guerin was subsequently pinched and sent to Devil's Island, from which he then proceeded to escape, causing something of a sensation.*

*Wallace was immensely attracted to the kind of women then known as 'adventuresses'. Some years later he came into contact with Evelyn Thaw, the ex-chorus girl whose somewhat unhinged millionaire husband had shot her lover in Madison Square Garden Roof theatre restaurant in New York*

138

*in 1906. While by no means a hardened criminal Evelyn Thaw was still a pretty tough nut.*

*Even when he was at the height of his fame and five million copies of his books were being sold per year worldwide (a million and a quarter in the UK alone), Wallace was still fascinated by the breed, now nominally updated to 'gangsters' molls'. Four Square Jane was not a gangster's moll, but she was certainly clever, took risks, and when an opportunity presented itself to baffle the law she grabbed it with both hands—as the following story relates.*

JACK ADRIAN

Chief Superintendent Peter Dawes, of Scotland Yard, was a comparatively young man, considering the important position he held. It was the boast of his department—Peter himself did very little talking about his achievements—that never once, after he had picked up a trail, was he ever baffled.

A clean-shaven, youngish looking man, with grey hair at his temples, Peter took a philosophical view of crime and criminals, holding neither horror towards the former, nor malice towards the latter.

If he had a passion at all it was for the crime which contained within itself a problem. Anything out of the ordinary, or anything bizarre fascinated him, and it was one of the main regrets of his life that it had never once fallen to his lot to conduct an investigation into the many Four Square Jane mysteries which came to the Metropolitan police.

It was after the affair at Lord Claythorpe's that Peter Dawes was turned loose to discover and apprehend this girl criminal, and he welcomed the opportunity to take charge of a case which had always interested him. To the almost hysterical telephone message Scotland Yard had received from Lord Claythorpe Peter did not pay too much attention. He realized that it was of the greatest importance that he should keep his mind unhampered and unprejudiced by the many and often contradictory 'clues' which everyone who had been affected by Four Square Jane's robberies insisted on discussing with him.

He interviewed an agitated man at four o'clock in the morning, and Lord Claythorpe was frantic.

'It's terrible, terrible,' he wailed, 'what are you people at Scotland Yard doing that you allow these villainies to continue? It is monstrous!'

Peter Dawes, who was not unused to out-bursts on the part of the victimized, listened to the squeal with equanimity.

'As I understand it, this woman came here with two men who pretended to have her in custody?'

'Two detectives!' moaned his lordship.

'If they called themselves detectives, then you were deceived,' said Peter with a smile. 'They persuaded you to allow the prisoner and one of her captors to spend ten minutes in the library where your jewels are kept. Now tell me, when the crime occurred had your guests left?'

Lord Claythorpe nodded wearily.

'They had all gone,' he said, 'except my friend Lewinstein.'

Peter made an examination of the room, and a gleam of interest came into his eyes when he saw the curious labels. He examined the floor and the window-bars, and made as careful a search of the floor as possible.

'I can't do much at this hour,' he said. 'At daylight I will come back and have a good look through this room. Don't allow anybody in to dust or to sweep it.'

He returned at nine o'clock, and to his surprise, Lord Claythorpe, whom he had expected would be in bed and asleep, was waiting for him in the library, and wearing a dressing-gown over his pyjamas.

'Look at this,' exclaimed the old man, and waved a letter wildly. Dawes took the document and read:

'You are very mean, old man! When you lost your Venetian armlet you offered a reward of ten thousand pounds. I sent that armlet to a hospital in need of funds, and the doctor who presented my gift to the hospital was entitled to the full reward. I have taken your pearls because you swindled the hospital out of six thousand pounds. This time you will not get your property back.'

There was no signature, but the familiar mark, roughly drawn, the four squares and the centred 'J.'

'This was written on a Yost,' said Peter Dawes, looking at the document critically. 'The paper is the common stuff you buy in penny packages—so is the envelope. How did it come?'

'It came by district messenger,' said Lord Claythorpe. 'Now what do you think, officer? Is there any chance of my getting those pearls back?'

'There is a chance, but it is a pretty faint one,' said Peter.

He went back to Scotland Yard, and reported to his chief.

'So far as I can understand, the operations of this woman began about twelve months ago. She has been constantly robbing, not the ordinary people who are subjected to this kind of victimization but people with bloated bank balances, and so far as my investigations go, bank balances accumulated as a direct consequence of shady exploitation companies.'

'What does she do with the money?' asked the Commissioner curiously.

'That's the weird thing about it,' replied Dawes. 'I'm fairly certain that she donates very large sums to all kinds of charities. For example, after the Lewinstein burglary a big creche in the East End of London received from an anonymous donor the sum of four thousand pounds. Simultaneously, another sum of four thousand was given to one of the West End hospitals. After the Talbot burglary three thousand pounds, which represents nearly the whole of the amount stolen, was left by some unknown person to the West End Maternity Hospital. I have an idea that we shall discover she is somebody who is in close touch with hospital work, and that behind these crimes there is a quixotic notion of helping the poor at the expense of the grossly rich.'

'Very beautiful,' said the Chief drily, 'but unfortunately her admirable intentions do not interest us. In our eyes she is a common thief.'

'She is something more than that,' said Peter quietly; 'she is the cleverest criminal that has come my way since I have been associated with Scotland Yard. This is the one thing one has dreaded, and yet one has hoped to meet—a criminal with a brain.'

'Has anybody seen this woman?' said the Commissioner interested.

'They have, and they haven't,' replied Peter Dawes. 'That sounds cryptic, but it only means that she has been seen by people who could not recognize her again. Lewinstein saw her, Claythorpe saw her, but she was veiled and unrecognizable. My difficulty, of course, is to discover where she is going to strike next. Even if she is only hitting at the grossly rich she has forty thousand people to strike at. Obviously, it is impossible to protect them all. But somehow—' he hesitated.

'Yes?' said the Chief.

'Well, a careful study of her methods helps me a little,' replied Dawes. 'I have been looking to discover who the next victim will be. He must be somebody very wealthy, and somebody who makes a parade of his wealth, and I have fined down the issue to about four men. Gregory Smith, Carl Sweiss, Mr Thomas Scott, and John Tresser. I am inclined to believe it is Tresser she is after. You see, Tresser has made a great fortune, not by the straightest means in the world, and he hasn't forgotten to advertise his riches. He is the fellow who bought the Duke of Haslemere's house, and his collection of pictures—you will remember the stuff has been written about.'

The Chief nodded.

'There is a wonderful Romney, isn't there?'

'That's the picture,' replied Dawes. 'Tresser, of course, doesn't know a picture from a gas-stove. He knows that the Romney is wonderful, but only because he has been told so. Moreover, he is the fellow who has been giving the newspapers his views on charity—told them that he never spent a penny on public institutions, and never gave away a cent that he didn't get a cent's worth of value for. A thing like that would excite Jane's mind; and then, in addition, the actual artistic and monetary value of the Romney is largely advertised—why, I should imagine that the attraction is almost irresistible!'

Mr Tresser was a difficult man to meet. His multitudinous interests in the City of London kept him busy from breakfast time until late at night. When at last Peter ran him down in a private dining-room at the Ritz-Carlton, he found the multi-millionaire a stout, red-haired man with a long clean-shaven upper lip, and cold blue eyes.

The magic of Peter Dawes' card secured him an interview.

'Sit down—sit down,' said Mr Tresser hurriedly, 'what's the trouble, hey?'

Peter explained his errand, and the other listened with interest, as to a business proposition.

'I've heard all about that Jane,' said Mr Tresser cheerfully, 'but she's not going to get anything from me—you can take my word! As to the Rumney—is that how you pronounce it?—well, as to that picture, don't worry!'

'But I understand you are giving permission to the public to inspect your collection.'

'That's right,' said Mr Tresser, 'but everybody who sees them must sign a visitors' book, and the pictures are guarded.'

'Where do you keep the Romney at night—still hanging?' asked Peter, and Mr Tresser laughed.

'Do you think I'm a fool,' he said, 'no, it goes into my strong room. The Duke had a wonderful strong room which will take a bit of opening.'

Peter Dawes did not share the other's confidence in the efficacy of bolts and bars. He knew that Four Square Jane was both an artist and a strategist. Of course, she might not be bothered with pictures, and, anyway, a painting would be a difficult thing to get away unless it was stolen by night, which would be hardly likely.

He went to Haslemere House, which was off Berkeley Square, a great rambling building, with a long, modern picture-gallery, and having secured admission, signed his name and showed his card to an obvious detective, he was admitted to the long gallery. There was the Romney—a beautiful example of the master's art.

Peter was the only sightseer, but it was not alone to the picture that he gave his attention. He made a brief survey of the room in case of accidents. It was long and narrow. There was only one door—that through which he had come—and the windows at both ends were not only barred, but a close wire-netting covered the bars, and made entrance and egress impossible by that way. The windows were likewise long and narrow, in keeping with the shape of the room, and there were no curtains behind which an intruder might hide. Simple spring roller blinds were employed to exclude the sunlight by day.

Peter went out, passed the men, who scrutinized him closely, and was satisfied that if Four Square Jane made a raid on Mr Tresser's pictures, she would have all her work cut out to get away with it. He went back to Scotland Yard, busied himself in his office, and afterwards went out for lunch. He came back to his office at three o'clock, and had dismissed the matter of Four Square Jane from his mind, when an urgent call came through. It was a message from the Assistant Chief Commissioner.

'Will you come down to my office at once, Dawes?' said the voice, and Peter sprinted down the long corridor to the bureau of the Chief Commissioner.

'Well, Dawes, you haven't had to wait long,' he was greeted.

'What do you mean?' said Peter.

'I mean the precious Romney is stolen,' said the Chief, and Peter could only stare at him.

'When did this happen?'

'Half an hour ago—you'd better get down to Berkeley Square, and make inquiries on the spot.'

Two minutes later, Peter's little two-seater was nosing its way through the traffic, and within ten minutes he was in the hall of the big house interrogating the agitated attendants. The facts, as he discovered them, were simple.

At a quarter-past two, an old man wearing a heavy overcoat, and muffled up to the chin, came to the house, and asked permission to see the portrait gallery. He gave his name as 'Thomas Smith.'

He was an authority on Romney, and was inclined to be garrulous. He talked to all the attendants, and seemed prepared to give a long-winded account of his experience, his artistic training, and the excellence of his quality as an art critic—which meant that he was the type of bore that most attendants have to deal with, and they very gladly cut short the monotonous conversation, and showed him the way to the picture gallery.

'Was he alone in the room?' asked Peter.

'Yes, sir.'

'And nobody went in with him?'

'No, sir.'

Peter nodded.

'Of course, the garrulity may have been intentional, and it may have been designed to scare away attendants, but go on.'

'The man went into the room, and was seen standing before the Romney in rapt contemplation. The attendants who saw him swore that at that time the Romney was in its frame. It hung on the level with the eyes; that is to say the top of the frame was about seven feet from the floor.

'Almost immediately after the attendants had looked in the old man came out talking to himself about the beauty of the execution. As he left the room, and came into the outer lobby, a little girl entered and also asked permission to go into the gallery. She signed her name "Ellen Cole" in the visitors' book.'

'What was she like?' said Peter.

'Oh, just a child,' said the attendant vaguely, 'a little girl.'

Apparently the little girl walked into the saloon as the old man came out—he turned and looked at her, and then went on through the lobby, and out through the door. But before he got to the door, he pulled a handkerchief out of his pocket, and with it came about half a dozen silver coins, which were scattered on the marble floor of the vestibule. The attendants helped him to collect the money—he thanked them, his mind still with the picture apparently, for he was talking to himself all the time, and finally disappeared.

He had hardly left the house when the little girl came out and asked: 'Which is the Romney picture?'

'In the centre of the room,' they told her, 'immediately facing the door.'

'But there's not a picture there,' she said, 'there's only an empty frame, and a funny kind of little black label with four squares.'

The attendants dashed into the room, and sure enough the picture had disappeared!

In the space where it had been, or rather on the wall behind the place, was the sign of Four Square Jane.

The attendants apparently did not lose their heads. One went straight to the telephone, and called up the nearest police station—

the second went on in search of the old man. But all attempts to discover him proved futile. The constable on point duty at the corner of Berkeley Square had seen him get into a taxi-cab and drive away, but had not troubled to notice the number of the taxi-cab.

'And what happened to the little girl?' asked Peter.

'Oh, she just went away,' said the attendant; 'she was here for some time, and then she went off. Her address was in the visitors' book. There was no chance of her carrying the picture away—none whatever,' said the attendant emphatically. 'She was wearing a short little skirt, and light summery things, and it was impossible to have concealed a big canvas like that.'

Peter went in to inspect the frame. The picture had been cut flush with the borders. He looked around, making a careful examination of the apartment, but discovered nothing, except, immediately in front of the picture, a long, white pin. It was the sort of pin that bankers use to fasten notes together. And there was no other clue.

Mr Tresser took his loss very calmly until the newspapers came out with details of the theft. It was only then that he seemed impressed by its value, and offered a reward for its recovery.

The stolen Romney became the principal topic of conversation in clubs and in society circles. It filled columns of the newspapers, and exercised the imagination of some of the brightest young men in the amateur criminal investigation business. All the crime experts were gathered together at the scene of the happening and their theories, elaborate and ingenious, provided interesting subject matter for the speculative reader.

Peter Dawes, armed with the two addresses he had taken from the visitors' book, the address of the old man and of the girl, went round that afternoon to make a personal investigation, only to discover that neither the learned Mr Smith nor the innocent child were known at the addresses they had given.

Peter reported to headquarters with a very definite view as to how the crime was committed.

'The old man was a blind,' he said, 'he was sent in to create suspicion and keep the eyes of the attendants upon himself. He purposely bored everybody with his long-winded discourse on art in order to be left alone. He went into the saloon knowing that his bulky appearance would induce the attendants to keep their eyes on him. Then he came out—the thing was timed beautifully—just as the child came in. That was the lovely plan.

'The money was dropped to direct all attention on the old man, and at that moment, probably, the picture was cut from its frame, and it was hidden. Where it was hidden, or how the girl got it out is a mystery. The attendants are most certain that she could not have had it concealed about her, and I have made experiments with a thick canvas cut to the size of the picture, and it certainly does seem that the picture would have so bulged that they could not have failed to have noticed it.'

'But who was the girl?'

'Four Square Jane!' said Peter promptly.

'Impossible!'

Peter smiled.

'It is the easiest thing in the world for a young girl to make herself look younger. Short frocks, and hair in plaits—and there you are! Four Square Jane is something more than clever.'

'One moment,' said the Chief, 'could she have handed it through the window to somebody else?'

Peter shook his head.

'I have thought of that,' he said, 'but the windows were closed and there was a wire-netting which made that method of disposal impossible. No, by some means or other she got the picture out under the noses of the attendants. Then she came out and announced innocently that she could not find the Romney picture—naturally there was a wild rush to the saloon. For three minutes no notice was being taken of the "child".'

'Do you think one of the attendants was in collusion?'

'That is also possible,' said Peter, 'but every man has a record of good, steady service. They're all married men and none of them has the slightest thing against him.'

'And what will she do with the picture? She can't dispose of it,' protested the Chief.

'She's after the reward,' said Peter with a smile. 'I tell you, Chief, this thing has put me on my mettle. Somehow, I don't think I've got my hand on Jane yet, but I'm living on hopes.'

'After the reward,' repeated the Chief; 'that's pretty substantial. But surely you are going to fix her when she hands the picture over?'

'Not on your life,' replied Peter, and took out of his pocket a telegram and laid it on the table before the other. It read:

'The Romney will be returned on condition that Mr Tresser undertakes to pay the sum of five thousand pounds to the Great Panton Street Hospital for Children. On his signing an agreement to pay this sum, the picture will be restored.

'JANE."

'What did Tresser say about that?'

'Tresser agrees,' answered Peter, and has sent a note to the secretary of the Great Panton Street Hospital to that effect. We are advertising the fact of his agreement very widely in the newspapers.'

At three o'clock that afternoon came another telegram, addressed this time to Peter Dawes—it annoyed him to know that the girl was so well informed that she was aware of the fact that he was in charge of the case.

'I will restore the picture at eight o'clock to-night. Be in the picture gallery, and please take all precautions. Don't let me escape this time—The Four Square Jane.'

The telegram was handed in at the General Post Office.

Peter Dawes neglected no precaution. He had really not the faintest hope that he would make the capture, but it would not be his fault if Four Square Jane were not put under lock and key.

A small party assembled in the gloomy hall of Mr Tresser's own house.

Dawes and two detective officers, Mr Tresser himself—he sucked at a big cigar and seemed the least concerned of those present— the three attendants, and a representative of the Great Panton Street Hospital were there.

'Do you think she'll come in person?' asked Tresser. 'I would rather like to see that Jane. She certainly put one over on me, but I bear her no ill-will.'

'I have a special force of police within call,' said Peter, 'and the roads are watched by detectives, but I'm afraid I can't promise you anything exciting. She's too slippery for us.'

'Anyway, the messenger—' began Tresser.

Peter shook his head.

'The messenger may be a district messenger, though here again I have taken precautions—all the district messenger offices have been warned to notify Scotland Yard in the event of somebody coming with a parcel addressed here.'

Eight o'clock boomed out from the neighbouring church, but Four Square Jane had not put in an appearance. Five minutes later there came a ring at the bell, and Peter Dawes opened the door.

It was a telegraph boy.

Peter took the buff envelope and tore it open, read the message through carefully, and laughed—a hopeless, admiring laugh.

'She's done it,' he said.

'What do you mean?' asked Tresser.

'Come in here,' said Peter.

He led the way into the picture gallery. There was the empty frame on the wall, and behind it the half-obliterated label which Four Square Jane had stuck.

He walked straight to the end of the room to one of the windows.

'The picture is here,' he said, 'it has never left the room.'

He lifted his hand, and pulled at the blind cord, and the blind slowly revolved.

There was a gasp of astonishment from the gathering. For, pinned to the blind, and rolled up with it, was the missing Romney.

'I ought to have guessed when I saw the pin,' said Peter to his chief. 'It was quick work, but it was possible to do it.

'She cut out the picture, brought it to the end of the room, and pulled down the blind; pinned the top corners of the picture to the blind, and let it roll up again. Nobody thought of pulling that infernal thing down!'

GERALD FINDLER

# The House of Screams

*Imagine a junk-shop. Or even a genuine bookshop but one at the seedier end of the range, that no one really should contemplate entering without the kind of protective clothing worn by the SAS in chemical-warfare exercises. This, to me, is Paradise.*

*Neat ranks of fashionable authors with equally fashionable prices do nothing for me. Give me shops piled with dusty and forgotten periodicals and bowed shelves creaking with the weight of turn-of-the-century fiction. In emporia such as these the real nuggets are to be found.*

*Such as* Some Cases of Sherwood Lang, *say, published by Henry J. Drane in the 1920s, publication no doubt subsidized by the author, one C. Delves Warren. That emerged from a basement in Leicester. Or it might be R. Thurston Hopkins's scarce paperback* The Valentine Vaughan Omnibus, *chronicling the exploits of a ghost-hunter, which turned up in a black plastic sack in the back-room of a shop on the Isle of Wight (and I shudder to think what other fate awaited it). Or perhaps the copy of Eden Philpotts's* My Adventure on the Flying Scotsman, *which just happened to be in the dealer's raincoat pocket when the conversation veered in Philpotts's direction.*

*Then there are those wonderful magazines, some celebrated, others long forgotten and obscure—the* Ludgate, Royal, Premier, New, *a few score more—all stuffed to the gills with short fiction, much of it never collected, by authors who range from the famous to the infamous. And let's not forget other kinds of publications.* Printer's Pie, *published quarterly, lavishly illustrated, with tasty morsels of fiction thrown in for good measure. The* Help Yourself Annual, *published under the auspices of the Stock Exchange Operatic and Dramatic Society from 1927 to 1940 and featuring first publication of top-quality stories by authors such as Dorothy L. Sayers, Edgar Wallace, P. C. Wren and Rafael Sabatini. Or* Bart's Annual. *Or* The British Legion Poppy Annual. *Or* Phil May's Annual. *Or* The Snark. *Or* The Magpie.

*Or even* Doidge's Western Counties Annual — *which is probably as obscure as one is likely to get. Yet Doidge's published their yearbook over many decades, digest-sized and full of almanacs, timetables, pictures (later it was photographs), articles, adverts and, of course, fiction. In the main the authors were quite unknown outside of, I suspect, the columns of the local weekly papers, though there were exceptions where syndicated material—the romance writer Ruby M. Ayres, for instance—or famous local*

149

*sons—Eden Philpotts or Sir Arthur Quiller Couch—appeared on the Contents pages.*

*As for Gerald Findler, the author of our next story, I can, alas, tell you nothing. He had at least one more story to his credit (probably in another Doidge's), but seems to have slipped back thereafter into total obscurity. Which is a pity, for the following tale shows inventiveness and originality, and a flair for the dramatic that leaves one wishing he had written more.*

ROBERT ADEY

I had been on a walking tour through Cumberland when I discovered this House of Screams.

Hidden among a clump of trees—there it stood: a mysterious looking building . . . windows and doors overgrown with green creeper . . . garden and lawn badly requiring attention.

The nearest house must have been two miles away, and I can quite understand the 'To Let' board not appealing to those who were on the look-out for a residence near the Cumberland lakes and fells.

To me, however, this house did appeal. Here was a house wrapped up in solitude—far from the noise and bustle of industrial Britain. Here was the very place I had often searched for, and had now found.

By spending three months alone, I could write the book which I intended to be my great success. No noise—no servants—no conventions to upset my work—just to write, write, and write.

I made my way back over the course I had come, and found the owner of the house was abroad, but his agents were in Penrith. By going on another mile I should be able to phone from a village Post Office.

I reached the Post Office and General Store, and phoned the house agents in Penrith, who seemed delighted to accept my own terms as to rent. They informed me that the house had never been occupied since the owner had left to go abroad some years ago. It was well furnished, and they would send the key out by messenger immediately.

I arranged to stay the night in this old world village, and then take possession of my newly acquired house. First thing next morning, I engaged two women to go out and clean and air the rooms, so that I could occupy it that evening.

The village store also were asked to deliver groceries and necessaries every three days—and not being used to sudden increases in trade they willingly complied with my request.

At 5 o'clock the cleaning and airing (such as it was), of the house was finished, and after tipping my two cleaners sparingly, I was left alone to commence my work.

As I had previously stated, the house was hidden in a clump of trees—and except for an occasional bird pouring forth its twilight song, the world was quiet.

I made tea, and ate up a portion of cake I secured in the village, and then I settled down to work writing my book.

It is surprising how time flies when one is deeply interested in some work or hobby and what appeared to me to be a few minutes was close to five hours, because my watch said it was ten minutes past eleven o'clock.

The day to me had been a busy one so I decided to give up my writing and toddle off to my bed.

My chosen bedroom was large, but contained rather too much furniture, and the only means of lighting the room was by an old fashioned oil lamp, the glass of which was unusual in shape, very finely made, and of a peculiar green shade.

You can imagine, then, how dull a bedroom would look—green lights—large ugly furniture—crowding any available space. Two windows were draped with heavy curtains, which I had drawn to the side, for the air seemed damp and thick. I tumbled into bed and left the lamp burning, for I have lately got into the habit of waking in the early hours, and reading a chapter of some favourite book.

Outside, the wind was blowing a little stronger than it had done for days—and the dark skies foretold of a coming storm.

As soon as my head touched the pillow I was asleep, and I remembered nothing more until I was awakened by a horrible scream which seemed in the very room where I was lying. The lamp still threw its flickering green light about the rooms and I felt every limb of my body shaking nervously.

I got out of bed and slipped on my dressing gown, lit a cigarette to steady my nerves, and looked around the room for the person whose persistent screaming was unbearable, but not a sign of anyone could I see.

I plucked up courage and started to search every room in the house, thinking perhaps some poor girl had got lost and had entered the house in fright, but room after room only contained horrid shadows that seemed like ghosts flying past me. I have never believed in things supernatural, but now that belief was getting badly shaken. The perspiration was standing like beads on my forehead.

Towards the front of the house I made my way, and in the hall I lit another lamp—much the same kind of lamp that was still burning in my bedroom.

No sooner had I left the hall than a second lot of screaming started. It seemed to me like a girl in mortal agony—but where she was I could not tell.

The wind was whistling through the trees—and the two lots of screaming seemed to delight in making every sound.

I had searched every nook and corner, with the exception of an attic room, of which the door refused to open. I made up my mind to explore that room at daybreak—to solve the mystery of this House of Screams.

After half an hour enduring this ghostly serenade, the storm outside began to break, and strange though it may seem, the screaming started getting fainter too, until it gradually died away.

It was now 4 o'clock and the strain of this haunted house was telling on me, so I wrapped a rug around myself and quickly went to sleep in an easy chair. I did not waken until 10-15, and found the sun peeping in through the window. My head throbbed—as though I had a horrible nightmare after too great a supper—but the peculiar green lamps still burning were sufficient proof to me that my experience was more than a ghostly dream.

I made a jug of coffee, but could not eat anything, for my appetite had deserted me with my courage. After my necessary toilet, I found a large hammer and a wood chopper and made my way upstairs to the attic—the only room I had not been in.

For ten minutes I battered and hammered at the door, until slowly it moved under the weight I had applied. When the door opened, a terrible sight met my eyes—for sitting on a chair by a small table was a skeleton.

Had I solved the mystery of those screams? I walked nervously towards the table, which was thickly covered with dust. I picked up a small bottle from the floor, and faintly written on a red label was the word 'Arsenic.'

A leather wallet lay on the table, and I opened it. An envelope first caught my eye, and it was addressed 'To the finder of my body.' I opened the envelope with shaking fingers, and pulled out the letter which I now have in my possession. It is getting worn with being continually shown, but it reads thus:—

'To Whoever You May Be.'
'My end is drawing near, and the screams of my late wife continue. I have stood this horror as long as I dare, and now my

brain is on the verge of snapping. My lawyer believes me to be going abroad, but the last few hours the spirit of Muriel will not leave me— but still goes on screaming—screaming—screaming. Before I die I must confess that my jealousy caused me to ill-treat my wife, who was both young and pretty.

She was 21 when we married, and I was in my sixtieth year, and because of the many admirers she had, I bought this house and brought her here.

Most of my time was spent in drinking—and when under the influence of liquor, I have thrashed her unmercifully.

No wonder her ghost screams. She died a year after our marriage—a broken heart was the cause of it, but the village doctor said it was lung trouble.

I thought that when she was gone that I would be rid of her incessant screams—but no, she has left them to torture my very soul.

This attic is my only refuge, and I have boarded up the door— and now intend to prepare for my . . .

Screaming again.—My God how she screams.'

The letter remains unfinished, but it unfolds both romance and tragedy.

Somehow I felt that the late owner of that skeleton had earned his deserts. His own actions had brought about his own end.

Surely after hearing the screams of the ill-treated girl the previous night—and finding the skeleton of her brutal husband—no man could settle to write a book. So I packed up my few belongings, and walked into the village to notify a somewhat dull constable of my experience.

He laughed at my idea of a screaming ghost and enquired the number of drinks it took to get like that, but when I told him of the skeleton in the attic, he thought he had better ask his Sergeant to come through.

I had kept the wallet in which the letter was found, and in searching among its various contents, I came across a portrait of a beautiful girl. Her eyes seemed to be dark and bewitching, her face full of noble character and beauty, her lips were lips that most men would move heaven and earth to kiss. Was this the young girl who was the victim of that brute who believed in torture instead of love.

This girl's face has fascinated me ever since. Perhaps it is because I have heard her screams, and know her story, that one will understand how a few years ago I made my way back to the House of Screams.

The building was in a bad state of repair, the furniture all removed. An old road-mender told me the house was haunted, and how the villagers imagined ghosts flitted through the trees every night at twelve o'clock.

At the village where I had previously stayed the night, I was informed about the young bride who was ill-treated, and how she was buried in the little churchyard nearby. The village postmaster described her as a girl with dark eyes that fascinated man and beast, and I concluded from his description that she and the girl of the photograph were one and the same.

I made my way to the churchyard, and found a stone bearing the name of Muriel Dunhurste, aged 22 years, over a small grave. A lump seemed to swell in my throat—I again pictured such a sweet innocent girl being ill-treated by such a drunken sot as he confessed to be.

I made up my mind to leave the place forever; it seemed the uppermost thought in my mind. Just as I arrived at the little white gate of the churchyard, a big touring car pulled up and a young man got out, and made his way into the churchyard. At first I was filled with surprise, for this young man was the very image of the dead girl whose grave I had just visited.

He made his way to the very spot where a few minutes previous I had stood, and I noticed he placed a small wreath of white lilies on the grass mound. By this I concluded that he must be the girl's brother—and this proved to be correct, for when he came back to his car, I asked him if he was going towards Penrith, and if so would he give me a lift. He replied he would be delighted with my company.

We had not gone far on our journey, when I showed him the portrait from the wallet. He recognised it immediately, and inquired from where it came, as it was a portrait of his late sister, whose grave he had just visited, taken before she married.

I told my story carefully, and after thinking for a few minutes he smiled. 'Well, friend,' he said, 'I owe you an apology. But let me tell you my side of the story—that of a self-confessed murderer.

'I always loved my sister, and she wrote to me after her marriage and told me of her husband's brutality—well, I arrived too late—for she had died.

'Now I acted in a friendly way to her husband, and one night he admitted when under the influence of drink, that her screams upset him. I left him alone in his house, only to return a fortnight later, with two peculiar shaped lamps which I said were keepsakes of my late sister.

'At that time I was on the variety stage as an Illusionist, and these lamps I had specially made to my requirements. They were manufactured so that if the lamps were lit these peculiar shaped lamp glasses would get hot. Now by making a whistle or scream of a special range nearby these lamp glasses would act as reproducers, and throw out a weird increased volume of the original sound.

'A day or so before I gave him the lamps, I experimented with them in such a way that it was only when the wind was very rough—and caused a high whistle through the trees that surrounded the house—that the lamps screamed. By filing little bits of the lamp glass, I was able to get a sound as near to my sister's scream as possible.

'The lamps evidently did the work intended, and drove my sister's husband to take his own life.

'As for your experience, my friend, I regret you spent a night under such weird circumstances, but I gathered from your conversation that you were an author. If that is so—why not write a true description of the House of Screams.'

EDWARD D. HOCH

# The Impossible Murder

*It's not easy to come up with new information about Ed Hoch. So let's start by repeating some of the old. Ed was born in Rochester, NY, in 1930. He became an avid mystery fan before he was ten and lists Ellery Queen and Sherlock Holmes among his favourite authors. He sold his first story in 1955 while in an advertising agency, where he continued to work for another dozen or so years before regular story-sales convinced him he should turn to writing full-time. All in all, a wise decision.*

*Ed has gone on writing short stories ever since and is something of a legend in his own lifetime, a literary throwback to the great days of the Pulps—a writer who actually earns his living by writing short fiction (a form which, as publishers continue to tell us, doesn't sell). Now he's all but reached the almost unbelievable number of 800 short stories, published in books, magazines and newspapers—not to mention a handful of novels, Introductions to books, and various editing tasks. A phenomenal hit rate.*

*And Ed is certainly no stranger to the Impossible Crime. In 1981 he edited the collection* All But Impossible, *featuring stories by the Mystery Writers of America, and of those 800 stories he's penned no less than 78 (pretty well 10 per cent) have featured Impossibles, nearly half of which starring the same sleuth. I speak of course, of Dr Sam Hawthorne, the retired New England medico who tells, invariably over a small libation, of the crimes he solved in his adopted town of Northmont. Sam Hawthorne (can the initials he shares with an even greater detective really be a coincidence?) related his first tale in the December, 1974, issue of* Ellery Queen *and his last appeared as recently as May, 1990.*

*Of the remaining half of Ed's Impossible canon, a fair number of stories are singletons with non-series sleuths. As well, Sir Gideon Parrott (delightful name) stars in two, as do Rand of the Department of Concealed Communications, and Sebastian Blue and Laura Charme of Interpol. That most urbane and unusual of thieves Nick Velvet has had four brushes with miraculous thievery, while the Coptic priest Simon Ark (surely Ed's most original creation) features in no less than nine Impossible tales.*

*However, it's from the annals of police detective Captain Julius Leopold, solver of six crimes of the Impossible (out of a roster of just over 40) that our selection is taken. The 1985 volume* Leopold's Way, *with an excellent Introduction and Checklist by Francis Nevins, Jnr, gathered nineteen tales from the Leopold saga. Here's one that—happily for us—wasn't included.*

ROBERT ADEY

'Automobiles!' Leopold was to remark long after it was over. 'I never had a case involving so many different automobiles! The crime, the clue, the capture, the confession—each involved a different car. There was an auto driven by a dead man, and another that hadn't been driven by anyone in thirty years. It was one hell of a case!'

It began at dusk on a November afternoon when Leopold's own car was in the garage for some minor repair work. Lieutenant Fletcher had offered him a ride home, and they'd chosen the Eastern Avenue route to avoid the rush-hour traffic on the expressway. But the usually deserted street was jammed with cars, and as they approached a familiar curve by an embankment Fletcher spotted some trouble ahead.

'Looks like we gotta go to work, Captain. One driver's out of his car. It could be a fight.'

'All right,' Leopold sighed. 'I wasn't hungry anyway. Turn on your flasher.'

They left the car and walked up to the scene of the trouble. A sandy-haired young man, standing at the open door of a late-model hatchback was gesturing wildly to a motorist in the next car. 'What's the trouble here?' Fletcher asked. 'We're police.' Leopold followed behind him, feeling just a bit like a traffic cop.

The young man turned in obvious agitation. 'I think this driver is dead!'

Fletcher bent inside the car to feel for a pulse. 'What happened?'

'We were caught in this traffic jam for like twenty minutes, just inching along. Finally, when it began to clear up and move, he just sat there ahead of me. I got out of my car after honking a few times, to see what the trouble was. God, I think he's dead!'

Fletcher straightened up and glanced at Leopold. 'I'll radio for an ambulance.'

Leopold lowered his voice. 'Is he—?'

'Dead as he'll ever be, Captain.'

'Heart attack?'

Fletcher shook his head. 'He's got a cord wrapped around his neck. Somebody strangled him.'

Leopold's eyes widened. 'In the middle of a traffic jam?'

'You figure it out, Captain.'

The young man's name was Sam Prowdy, and he told a straightforward story. He was a plumber, employed by a building contractor, and he'd been on his way home from work along with everyone else when an accident on the expressway forced them into a traffic jam on Eastern Avenue. He'd noticed nothing unusual about the little green car ahead of him, and certainly hadn't seen anyone leave it in the middle of the traffic jam.

'Sure, I'd have noticed,' he insisted back in Leopold's office. 'Somebody gets out of a car ahead of you, you notice it, don't you?'

'It was just getting dark,' Leopold pointed out. 'You could have missed it.'

'I didn't miss a thing! The guy was alone in the car, and he was driving it. Then we were stuck for about five minutes and he stopped moving. I honked and got out to check on him and that's when you guys came up.'

'Did you know the dead man?' Leopold asked.

'Hell, no! I still don't know him. Who was he?'

'His name was Vincent Conners. Thirty-two years old, with a wife and two children in the suburbs. Worked as a stockbroker with Bland and Burnett.'

'Never heard of him!'

'All right,' Leopold said with a sigh. 'We'll probably be contacting you again, but you can go now.'

When he was alone with Fletcher he said, 'There was nothing to hold him on. A woman in the next car confirmed that he'd just opened the door of Conners' auto when we arrived. He couldn't have done it. Besides, Conners had already been dead anywhere up to half an hour according to the preliminary medical report.'

Fletcher snorted. 'Where does that leave us? With a dead man driving a car around town?'

'I don't know,' Leopold admitted. 'But I guess we have to talk to Mrs Conners.'

The home was in a suburb touching Long Island Sound, the sort of area in which local stockbrokers were expected to live. Lights burned in every window, and a neighbour opened the door as Leopold and Fletcher approached. 'Mrs Conners is in the kitchen,' the woman said. 'The children are over at my house.'

Leopold nodded and went into the brightly lit kitchen. A few others, neighbours and relatives, stepped aside to let them pass. It was a gloomy setting for all its brightness, and the heavy atmosphere was one he'd encountered too many times before. Sudden violent death had a way of settling over lives like a sombre fog.

Linda Conners was small and fragile-looking, with long dark hair and high cheekbones. Only one man chose to remain in the kitchen while Leopold spoke to her, and that was one of her husband's employers, Frank Bland. He looked like a stockbroker too. He might have been another Conners, ten years older and forty pounds heavier. 'She's had a great shock,' he explained to Leopold. 'They were very close.'

'I'm sure they were. Mrs Conners, I hate to bother you at a time like this, but I know you want to help in finding your husband's killer.'

She took a sip of coffee and gazed up at him with pale eyes. 'There's nothing I can tell you. No one had a reason for killing Vince. Everyone liked him.'

'It must have been a car thief,' Frank Bland suggested. 'Someone Vince caught in the vehicle, who strangled him from behind.'

'We have a bit of a problem because no one was seen leaving the vehicle,' Leopold said. 'Yet your husband couldn't have driven it after he was strangled.' Even as he spoke the words, he was aware of how incongruous this suburban kitchen setting was with talk of an impossible crime.

'He once told me he'd probably die in his car, the way his father did.'

'You needn't get into all that, Linda,' Frank Bland cautioned. 'The Captain is only investigating this case.'

But Leopold was interested. 'What happened to Vince's father?'

She tried to take another sip of coffee but the cup was empty. Bland refilled it from a nearby pot. 'Well, he was shot in a hunting accident. Thirty years ago.'

'What did that have to do with a car?'

'He bled to death on the back seat, while he was being rushed back to town. The car belonged to one of Vince's aunts, and they never used it again. They've still got it, up on blocks in their garage.'

'You say this happened thirty years ago?'

'Yes.'

'Then your husband would have been around two years old.'

'Yes.'

'Is his mother still living?'

'She remarried, moved out West somewhere. He never sees—saw her.'

'Is this aunt still alive?'

'Oh, yes. There are two of them. They live together in the family homestead.'

'They're his closest kin in this area?'

'*I'm* his closest kin. And the children.'

'Of course,' Leopold corrected himself. 'I meant besides you.'

She nodded. 'Yes, Aunt Gert and Aunt Flag.'

'Aunt Flag?'

'That's what they've always called her.'

'Perhaps you'd better give me their address.'

'Certainly. Frank, could you hand me a piece of paper?'

She wrote out the address and handed it to Leopold. 'I hope you find the killer,' she said quietly.

When they were outside, Fletcher asked, 'We going over to see the aunts now, Captain?'

Leopold looked at his watch. It was already after ten. 'No, it's a bit late to be upsetting a couple of old ladies. We'll see them in the morning.'

Connie Trent was in the office before Leopold, checking out a shooting at an all-night restaurant. 'I heard about last evening,' she told Leopold. 'You and Fletcher just manage to drop right into them, don't you?'

Leopold nodded. 'Can't even get home at night without finding a murder on the road. How about it? Any ideas how a man can be strangled to death in a car in the middle of a traffic jam? While he's alone?'

She thought for a moment. 'If the window was open someone could have lassoed him.'

'The window was only open a couple of inches, and none of the other drivers saw anything like a lasso. But thanks anyway.'

'Any time,' she said with a smile, and went back to typing her report.

Leopold and Fletcher reached the Cónners homestead just after eleven and went up the crumbling sidewalk to the front door. The woman who answered was not as elderly as they'd expected, but she moved slowly, with a hint of some hidden disability.

'You'd be the police,' she said without looking at Leopold's identification. 'My sister and I have been expecting you, ever since we heard about poor Vincent. Come in—I'm Gert Conners.'

'We're sorry to bother you like this, Miss Conners. But outside of his wife and children you're the closest kin. We don't mind admitting we're baffled as to a possible motive.'

Gert Conners pushed back a stray wisp of grey hair. 'They said on the news he probably surprised a car thief.'

'Well, that's one theory. But it doesn't cover all the facts.'

She'd led them into a musty sitting room with lace curtains on the windows. A second grey-haired woman was seated in a rocking chair, busily knitting something long and blue. She smiled as they entered but didn't rise. 'This is Aunt Flag,' Gert Conners said.

Aunt Flag nodded as Leopold and Fletcher introduced themselves. 'I know you'll find out who killed our nephew,' she said. 'He was a good lad. Always came to see us.'

Aunt Flag was perhaps ten years older than Aunt Gert, and obviously feeble. 'You have an unusual name,' Leopold commented.

'It's really Flagula, but that's a terrible name for a person. I've been called Flag all my life. We were always Aunt Flag and Aunt Gert to Vincent.'

Leopold had taken a seat at one end of the claw-footed couch, and Fletcher gently lowered himself into position at the other end. 'Do either of you ladies know any reason why Vincent might have been murdered? Any troubles, any enemies? Perhaps a feud from long ago?'

'There was never anything like that,' Aunt Flag assured them. 'He was always very honest and open, even as a child. We saw a great deal of him as a child, because of course his father died when he was only two.'

'That would be your brother?'

Aunt Gert nodded. 'Our brother George—our only brother.'

'Just how did George die?'

There might have been a look that passed between the sisters before Aunt Gert replied. 'It was a hunting accident, one of those foolish things. They were out shooting pheasants and George dropped his shotgun somehow. It went off and hit him in the stomach. His wife helped him back to the car and put him on the rear seat. They hurried back to town as fast as they could, but poor George was dead by the time they reached the hospital. He'd bled to death on the back seat of the car.'

'It was your car?' Leopold prompted her.

Aunt Gert frowned. 'Who told you that? No, actually it was Aunt Flag's car. It was right after the war and cars were still scarce. George didn't have one of his own, so he borrowed it.'

'We never used it again,' Aunt Flag said. 'It's back in the garage.'

So both father and son had died violent deaths in automobiles, separated in time by 30 years. Leopold wondered about it, wondered what effect the father's death might have had on the son. 'Thank you,' he said. 'You've been very helpful.'

Aunt Gert walked outside with them, kicking a stone from the crumbling walk. 'I really must get this fixed,' she said.

'Is Aunt Flag confined to her chair?' Leopold asked.

'Oh, she gets around but she's very feeble since her stroke. I do all the shopping and I take care of her.'

'That must be hard on you.'

'She's my sister.'

'Of course.' Leopold looked up at the dappled sky, wondering if the sun would break through. 'When did you last see your nephew alive, Miss Conners?'

'Oh, it must have been about a week ago.'

'When he came to visit you, did he ever go out to the garage and look at the car his father died in?'

'Why would you ask a question like that? Of course not! He came to see us, not to stir up memories of the past.'

'Did his wife come with him last week?'

Aunt Gert avoided Leopold's eyes. 'Not last week, no.'

'But she did come sometimes?'

'Not often. She has no use for old people.'

'You're not old,' Leopold reassured her climbing into his car while Fletcher got behind the wheel.

'Thank you. You're very kind.'

'Just one other question. Who was with your brother George the day of the hunting accident?'

'With him? No one was with him, only his wife. There were just the two of them out there when it happened.'

It was Connie who tracked down the information and brought it to Leopold's office later in the day. 'I ran up a small fortune in long-distance phone calls for this,' she said. 'I hope it's worth it.'

'If it helps solve this damned case it's worth it. What have you got, Connie?'

'George Conners served in the European Theatre of Operations during World War Two, and took part in the D-day invasion of Normandy. He met and married a British girl named Jean Hemmings. Apparently it was a rush marriage—their only child Vincent was born two months later, near the end of 1944. Conners and his wife returned to America in the spring of '45, when the European war ended. It was the fall of 1946 when he was killed in the hunting accident, just after Vincent's second birthday.'

Leopold interrupted. 'Was there any sort of police investigation at the time?'

'Just routine, apparently. Anyway, the widow Jean remarried soon after—within a year—to a car salesman here in town. I don't think Vincent was ever close to his mother and stepfather. When he was eighteen he went off to college and they moved out West. Except for occasional brief visits he never lived with them again.'

Leopold grunted and stared out of the window. 'What are you

thinking, Captain?' Fletcher asked. 'That his wife shot him?'

'Like in that Ernest Hemingway story,' Connie said. 'The one about Macomber.'

'She shot him and married another man,' Leopold said quietly. 'And thirty years later his son dies in another car. Did his wife kill him too, in order to marry another man?'

Fletcher snapped his fingers. 'That guy Frank Bland! I thought he was being awfully chummy for an employer. Do you think—?'

'Check on him, Fletcher. Talk to Conners' co-workers. See if there was any gossip around the office.'

'But the two crimes are entirely different,' Connie pointed out. 'Knowing about the first one doesn't help us in the least toward solving the second one. How could they possibly be connected?'

'If Vincent suspected his father was murdered all those years ago— suspected it through something he overheard or half remembered— he might have mentioned it to his wife. That might have planted the idea in her mind.'

'It's all guesswork,' Connie said.

Leopold agreed. 'But in this case we've got nothing to go on but guesswork.'

Both Connie and Fletcher had duties involving other cases, and after Fletcher's report on Frank Bland the following day the investigation was left pretty much in Leopold's hands. Fletcher hadn't come up with anything concrete about Bland. He was divorced, and he occasionally dined at the Conners' home—but this could have been nothing more suspicious than the time-honoured custom of having the boss to dinner.

With the Conners funeral only a day away, the medical examiner still had not ruled on the cause of death. Speaking with Leopold, he was inclined to rule it a suicide, simply because 'It couldn't be murder, could it, Captain?'

To which Leopold replied, 'Doc, did you ever hear of anybody committing suicide by strangling himself with a cord while driving in a traffic jam?'

'I guess not,' the medical examiner agreed.

Leopold picked up the murder weapon and examined it once more. It was a loop of knotted cord that they'd had to cut away from the dead man's neck. It fit the most likely newspaper theory of the case— that a car thief had been trapped in the back seat by Conners' unexpected return and had strangled Conners from the rear.

But that left one big question mark.

If the thief left the car immediately, how did a dead man drive the automobile for nearly a half hour? And if the killer was still in the car when it was caught in the traffic jam, how did he leave it without being seen?

It was as close to an absolute impossibility as anything Leopold had ever encountered.

So he went back the medical examiner again. 'Doc, can't you be more precise as to the time of death?'

'We're talking about minutes here, Captain. Remember it was nearly an hour after you found him before I saw the body. I'd be inclined to say he died twenty to thirty minutes before you found him, but if you say that's impossible I'll cut it to a shorter period.'

Leopold accepted that and went in search of a new lead. In the police garage where the murder car was impounded he had a mechanic sit in the front seat while he sat in the back and went through the motions of strangling the mechanic. But that didn't satisfy him. It was all wrong. Finally he decided to follow up Fletcher's investigation by calling on the dead man's employer.

Frank Bland greeted him with a wan smile. 'Still at it, Captain?'

'Still at it.' He glanced through the glass wall of the office at the lighted display board of noon stock quotations. 'I imagine this is a profitable business.'

The stout man shifted uneasily. 'We have our good years.'

'I mean, Vincent made a comfortable living here.'

'The salary and commissions are good, and we have a generous life-insurance programme which will benefit his widow. He had no reason to complain.'

Leopold chose his words carefully. 'He gave no hint of anything wrong on the day he was killed?'

'Nothing. He left early, right after the market closed. I was surprised he wasn't home long before he was killed. But there was nothing else unusual.'

'And you say his wife would benefit from the insurance?'

Frank Bland half rose from his chair. 'Surely you're not implying that Linda had anything to do with this terrible thing!'

'No, no—don't misunderstand me. I was only thinking that Conners was well off financially. I visited his aunts and they would seem to be part of a monied family. And you've confirmed that Conners had a good income here. Of course if his wife divorced him she'd lose most of that.'

'I can assure you Linda was happily married. I saw a great deal of them and they were very close.'

'Were there any tensions among his fellow workers? Any clients he steered onto a bum stock?'

Frank Bland sighed. 'I thought your Lieutenant Fletcher had been all over this matter. As I told him I can contribute nothing to the investigation.'

'All right,' Leopold said. 'One more question and I'll be on my way. Did Vincent Conners ever mention his aunts to you? Or the hunting accident that took his father's life?'

'Nothing was ever said about the accident. He may have mentioned his aunts in passing once or twice. I remember asking him one time if he couldn't bring them in as clients.'

Leopold rose to leave. 'Thank you, Mr Bland. I hope I don't have to trouble you again.'

He got his car out of the parking lot across the street and went back to visit the aunts. On the way he thought about Bland's denial that Vincent had mentioned the hunting accident. Bland had seemed to know about it earlier, and that indicated he'd heard it from Linda.

It was one of those sunny November days when it seemed as if summer was staging a comeback, and he found Aunt Gert trimming rosebushes in the side yard of the house. 'So it's you again,' she said by way of greeting.

'It's me again. I don't mean to interrupt your work.'

She straightened from her task, brushing some loose soil from the knees of her slacks. 'The garden takes a great deal of time. Aunt Flag used to help me with it when she was able to.'

'I'll try not to take up too much of your time,' Leopold said. 'But we've come up against a dead end in trying to trace Vince's mother and notify her of his death. Do you have any idea at all where she might have moved out West?'

Aunt Gert shook her head. 'We've lost all track of her. I know for a time they were in California, but then Vince told us once his mother had moved to New Mexico. He never said where, though. Doesn't Linda have an address?'

'She claims not. We've asked the police to check the last-known address in Los Angeles.'

'It was too bad about Vince and his mother. But it was his stepfather's fault they drifted apart. He never took to the lad.'

'I was wondering, Miss Conners—as long as I'm out here again, do you think I could have a look at that old car in your garage? I'm something of an antique-car buff—'

'You'd hardly call it an antique,' she said. 'It's a 1941 Packard, made just before the war.'

'Could I see it anyway?'

She hesitated a moment. 'I'll get the key to the garage.'

When she opened the garage it gave off a musty odour even more overpowering than the one in the house. It was a cramped one-car garage, separated from the house as all garages had been back in Leopold's youth. The car was a dull shade of green. Its tyres had been removed at some time in the distant past and its axles rested on concrete blocks.

'It seems in good condition,' Leopold observed. 'You could probably still drive it.'

'Never had a licence. Never wanted one.'

There was no overhead light, but the sunlight coming through the side window was strong enough for him to study the vehicle. He opened the rear door and looked at the back seat, where Vincent Conners' father had bled to death 30 years ago. There were two large bloodstains on the upholstery, about a foot apart. The one on the left was slightly larger.

'You should have sold the car,' Leopold suggested. 'It does no good remembering.'

'He was our brother. Some things have to be remembered.'

'Did he really shoot himself, Miss Conners?'

'She said so.'

'What do *you* think?'

She was silent for a long time, staring out the driveway at a playful dog across the quiet street. Finally Gert Conners said, very softly, as if it was the first time her tongue had dared give voice to the words, 'I think she killed him.'

Leopold took a deep breath. The air in the garage seemed suddenly even closer. 'And Vincent? Your nephew?'

She looked up at him puzzled. 'How could—?'

There was a noise from the house, a tapping on the rear window. They could see Aunt Flag motioning. 'She wants me,' Aunt Gert said. 'I must go now.'

He waited while she locked the garage door, then said goodbye and went back to his car.

Two deaths, with 30 years between. Different, and yet somehow the same.

That afternoon he told Fletcher to put a tail on Linda Conners. 'The funeral is tomorrow morning. For the next few days I want to know where she goes and whom she sees.'

Oddly enough, Linda Conners phoned Leopold less than an hour after he'd issued his order. Her voice was firm and she seemed in good control of herself. 'Captain, I'm calling from the funeral parlour. I understand you've been trying to locate Vincent's mother.'

'That's right, Mrs Conners.'

'I've found an address that may be her current one. I'll read it to you.'

Leopold copied down a street address in Santa Fe, New Mexico. 'Do you want to try calling her, Mrs Conners, or should we contact her about her son's death?'

'I wish you would, Captain. I've only met the woman twice in my life.'

'We'll take care of it. Thank you for the address, Mrs Conners.'

Connie was assigned the task of informing Vincent Conners' mother of her son's death. It was not until the following morning, at about the time of the funeral, that Connie managed to reach the woman. 'They certainly weren't close,' she reported back to Leopold. 'She expressed regrets, but that was all. I might have been reporting the death of a distant cousin instead of her only son.'

'She has a new life for herself now,' Leopold said. 'She doesn't want to be reminded of Vincent Conners, or his father.' He was remembering the car in the garage, with its bloodstained back seat—the car that hadn't been driven for 30 years.

'Fletcher says you've put a tail on Linda Conners.'

'That's right. I want to know if she sees Frank Bland.'

'What will that prove, if we still don't know how Vincent was killed?'

'If we know who, we'll figure out how.'

But the two cases—the old one and the new one—were still intertwined in Leopold's mind, and he couldn't help feeling that the answer somehow rested on that bloodstained back seat.

Nothing happened for two days.

Vincent Conners was buried, and Linda Conners cried. Frank Bland attended the funeral and put his arm around the shoulders of the grieving widow.

But you can't arrest a man for doing that.

Finally Leopold telephoned Vincent Conners' mother in Santa Fe. It was late on Friday, and the autumn sun had already set.

Her name had changed from Jean Hemmings to Jean Conners to Jean Quinlan, but she still retained her British accent. After Leopold had identified himself, she asked. 'Is this more about my son's death?'

'Not exactly, Mrs Quinlan. Actually, it's about your husband's death.'

'That was thirty years ago!'

'Yes.'

'Well, what about it?'

'I realize that the shooting was an accident, and we're not attempting to reopen the case, but I have to ask you one question. It'll help us a great deal with the investigation of your son's killing.'

'What is it?'

'Mrs Quinlan, did you shoot your husband?'

'Shoot him? Of course I didn't shoot him! My God, I loved him— he died in my arms!'

'Yes,' Leopold said, 'that's exactly what I suspected.' And then he asked her one more question, although he already knew the answer to that one too.

As he hung up the telephone, Fletcher hurried into the office. 'She's moving, Captain. She left the house by a back door and went through the yards to the next street. Someone picked her up there in a car.'

Leopold was on his feet. 'Damn! Vincent's hardly cold in his grave. Let's go!'

The unmarked car that was following Linda Conners was put into contact with Leopold's vehicle. 'They're heading south on Grand Street, Captain—toward the Sound,' the radio crackled.

'Finding them together won't convict anybody of murder,' Fletcher reminded Leopold.

'No, but if we show up unexpectedly Bland might panic. If she's sneaking around to meet him, she's got something to hide.'

The car had parked for a time on a dark street near the water, but neither of them emerged. And by the time the radio had directed Leopold to the spot they'd started up again.

'We're close to them,' Fletcher said.

'Don't let them spot the car. She might remember it.'

The radio crackled into life again. 'They seem to be just driving around, Captain. Should I keep up with them?'

'Keep with them. Where are you now?'

'Just turning back onto Grand, at Maple.'

'We're only four blocks away. Are they headed north again?'

'Right.'

'We'll join a few blocks up.'

Fletcher was driving Leopold's car, and he turned onto Grand Avenue a block and a half behind the red tail-lights of their quarry. 'Looks like they're heading back toward her neighbourhood,' Fletcher remarked.

The car turned off Grand and before long Leopold could see that

Fletcher was correct. He was taking her back home. If it had been a lovers' meeting it was a brief one.

'He's stopping a block from the house,' Fletcher said. 'Must be letting her out.'

The door on the passenger side opened and Linda Conners appeared. She bent down for a final goodbye and then slammed the door shut. Something gnawed at Leopold's memory as he watched.

Then he had it.

'That car, Fletcher! That car!'

'What is it, Captain?'

'Head him off! Don't let him get away!'

Fletcher cut across the lawn of a corner house to beat the car around a corner, then slammed on the brakes to block the narrow street. The other car screeched to a halt as the driver hit his brakes. Then his door came open and he tumbled out, trying to run.

Leopold and Fletcher were on him then, with guns drawn.

It wasn't Frank Bland.

It was the man who had found the body—Sam Prowdy.

Leopold pulled the car up before the Conners homestead the following morning and tapped lightly on the horn. Aunt Gert looked up from her task of tying the bushes in burlap, recognized him, and walked over.

'My, you're getting to be a regular visitor here!'

Leopold smiled. 'Could you get in the car for a minute, Miss Conners? Then we can stay warm while we talk.'

'I saw in the papers that you caught the man who killed Vincent,' she said, opening the door and sliding into the front seat next to him. 'But I still don't understand it all.'

'His name is Sam Prowdy,' Leopold explained, 'and he's been Linda Conners' lover for some time. They killed her husband for a large insurance policy on his life. It's the oldest sort of crime, but at first we didn't recognize it for what it was. A bizarre chain of circumstances made it look like an impossible crime.

'You see, Prowdy strangled Vincent with a cord in the Conners garage, and then put him behind the wheel of his car. He sat next to the dead man and drove over to Eastern Avenue with Linda following in his auto. Then they stopped for a minute while he tied the steering wheel of Vincent's car and got back into his own vehicle. Linda walked over a few blocks and caught a bus. Then Prowdy simply started pushing the car with Vincent's body in it down the straight road—pushing Vincent's car with his own car.'

'And nobody noticed it?'

'Well, it was getting dark. And that portion of Eastern Avenue is rarely travelled since the expressway opened parallel to it. Prowdy's plan was to pick up speed until he reached the point where Eastern Avenue curves to the left, then take the curve with his car while Vincent's went straight ahead and through the guard rail. They were hoping Vincent's car would burst into flames going down the hill, burning both the cord on the steering wheel and the one around your nephew's neck. Whether they could have covered up the signs of murder completely is doubtful, but they might have pulled it off. What they didn't expect, though, was the traffic jam.'

'It was caused by an accident?'

Leopold nodded. 'An expressway accident that shifted all the rush-hour traffic over to Eastern Avenue. Sam Prowdy hadn't figured on that of course. The traffic was bumper to bumper, with no chance for him to pick up speed or push Vincent's car through the guard rail unobserved. It was easy for him to keep nudging the other car along on a straight road, but with the curve coming up he knew he had to do something else.

'So he simply stopped pushing it, honked his horn, and got out in all innocence to see what the trouble was. When he opened the car door he had time to unknot the rope from the steering wheel and hide it under his coat in the near-darkness, but we arrived before he could get the rope off the throat. He should have removed that after he killed Conners, of course, but murderers don't always think of everything.'

'And you figured all this out?'

Leopold smiled. 'I wish I could take credit for it. I never bought the newspaper theory of a back-seat strangler, because late-model cars have a head-rest making it extremely difficult to strangle someone from behind and knot the cord around his neck. After I discounted a car thief as the killer I naturally shifted focus to Linda. We followed her when she met a man, but it wasn't till I finally recognized Prowdy's car that the whole method tumbled into place in my mind.'

'I appreciate your coming out here to tell me about it,' Gert Conners said.

'To be honest, that wasn't the only reason I came. It's been stuck in my mind all along that there was some connection between the deaths of Vincent Conners and his father.'

'That was a long time ago,' she reminded him.

'Of course. And obviously the same person couldn't have been responsible for both deaths.'

'Responsible? Nobody was responsible for my brother's death. He shot himself.'

'It's difficult to shoot yourself in the stomach with a shot gun, even when dropping it—though of course it could have happened that way. But then I looked at the car and saw those bloodstains, and they told a different story.'

'What do you mean?'

'There were *two* bloodstains, Miss Conners, on the back seat of that car. Next to each other, but separated by about a foot.'

'There might have been a blanket under him.'

Leopold shook his head. 'On the long trip back to town that much blood would have soaked through the blanket. He was lying on the back seat, so if the blood simply trickled down his sides from the wound the stains would have been at the front edge and the back of the seat, not side by side.'

'Then how do you explain it?'

'My first thought was that he was held in someone's arms during the car trip, that he bled to death in someone's lap. That would explain the twin stains—on either side of the seated person. I finally located his widow yesterday and spoke to her on the phone. She confirmed that George died in her arms.'

'As I remember,' Aunt Gert said, 'that's the way it happened.'

'But if they were out there alone, and he died in her arms on the way back into town, *who was driving the car*'

She was silent.

'They weren't alone, Miss Conners. They couldn't have been. And that means you lied about it when you said they were. If your brother really shot himself—or even if his wife shot him— there would be no reason to lie.'

'All right,' Gert Conners said very quietly. 'I did it. I shot him. I was aiming at his wife, and I hit George instead.'

In one of the trees overhead two squirrels were hard at work on a winter nest of leaves. Leopold watched them and wished he was in some other line of work. He turned to her and said, 'The lies never cease, do they? Thirty years of it and the lies never cease.'

'What do you mean?'

'The other person out hunting that day, the one who shot your brother, was obviously the one who drove the car back to town while Jean Conners held her dying husband in the back seat. And you told me you never had a driver's licence.'

'I—'

'It was Aunt Flag who shot him, wasn't it? It was Aunt Flag you've been protecting for thirty years. It was her car, after all, and she was driving it that day. That was why she put it up on blocks and never drove it again. No use denying it—Jean told me on the phone that Flag was there, though she never knew exactly how the shooting happened.'

Gert Conners was sobbing now. 'God, it's like a family curse! First George and now Vincent! I asked Flag what happened that day and she told me. It was Jean she was trying to kill, of course—Jean who even then was cheating on our brother by having a sordid little affair with that man she later married. Flag said she deserved to die. But somehow George stepped in front of the gun. Perhaps he knew what was in Flag's mind.'

Leopold glanced toward the house. 'She's tapping on the window. You'd better go in.'

'You won't take her away, will you? Lock her up?'

'She needs someone to watch over her, to confine her and make certain she never hurts another person.'

'She's already got that,' Gert Conners said. 'I've been doing it for thirty years.' She brushed away the tears.

Leopold watched her get out of the car.

'Yes,' he said, 'I suppose you have.'

GEORGE LOCKE

# A Nineteenth Century Debacle

*George Locke is a bookseller of the old school. That is, he can read (and without moving his lips) and he actually knows about books—and one has the distinct impression these days that not a great many booksellers can or do.*

*To be sure, some booksellers of the old school could be stubborn, purblind, curmudgeonly, downright rude, and prone to sudden acts of violence (one of your editors was virtually frogmarched out of a shop in a town not unadjacent to the River Thames for the crime of spotting P.G. Wodehouse's* The Swoop *mistakenly marked at ten shillings, and a mutual friend was once felled to the floor by a volume of the DNB wielded by a bookseller for mildly querying a book's price), but in the main they had a feel for and cared about books. Most, however graceless and misanthropic, knew about such things as signatures, folios, collections, issue-points. They were, in a word, bookmen.*

*Over the past decade—thanks to the intense upsurge of interest in the financial aspects of genre fiction and the collecting of authors such as Wodehouse, Agatha Christie, Raymond Chandler, Ian Fleming, W.E. Johns and so on—a new breed of instant bookseller has appeared and bookselling itself has become (to use an already outdated word) yuppified. Specialist collecting magazines, edited and written for the most part by people who probably think an issue-point is where babies come from, have sprung up with a strong emphasis on hard cash rather than knowledge or research. In such magazines Grosset & Dunlap is invariably noted as a publisher of new American fiction, advertisements may be found for signed First Editions which turn out not only to be reprints but reprints issued after the author's death, and dealers, for the most part, seem unaware that a First Edition, however scarce, by a collected author is essentially worthless if it looks as though it's been stored in a Dutch barn for 20 years.*

*George Locke will have no truck with any of this nonsense. Cock an eyebrow as one may at some of his prices and barring the odd hiccup, what you get from George is the real McCoy, with 30 or more yearsworth of book-lore and hard experience behind it.*

*However, we are not here to puff George's wares but quite another aspect of him. Over the years he's written, and published himself,* Search & Research, *various Ferret Fantasy Christmas Annuals,* Science Fiction First Editions, *and (surely his* magnum opus*) the mammoth* A Spectrum of Fantasy, *all of which are invaluable reference tools without which no serious collector or dealer should be. And on occasion, to describe or elucidate* *some arcane bibliographical point (the three variants of R. C. Sherriff's* The Hopkins Manuscript, *say, or the nine variants of Wells'* The Time Machine*), or simply for amusement, he has resorted to fiction—specifically parody. Here is his bibliographic sleuth Morlock Tomes with a tale sparked off by an entry in that indispensable guide* Locked Room Murders And Other Impossible Crimes—*which just happens to be the work of one of your editors.*

JACK ADRIAN

---

'Come in, my dear Clotson!' Morlock Tomes cried. 'Your visit is most timely. My memory is severely taxed. I hope you can help me.'

'As your chronicler, I'm sure that I can,' I said.

He waved at a set of galley proofs on his desk. 'What do you make of those?'

I examined them. 'Why, very fine proofs indeed—printed on imitation vellum.'

'*Genuine* vellum,' Tomes said. 'I don't mean that.'

I could see that, taxed memory or not, Tomes' penchant for forcing his faithful confidant to extract every piece of information as though it was a peculiarly deep-rooted molar was unimpaired. I had to play along with him. 'The title is *Locked Room Murders and other Impossible Crimes*,' I said. 'A bibliography, by one Robert Adey. On a subject that should interest you immensely.'

'It does—particularly one of the entries. See here. Item 1221. Louis Zangwill's *A Nineteenth Century Miracle*. What do you make of it, Clotson?'

I studied the entry very carefully. 'The detective has a name very similar to yours.'

'Indubitably. What else?'

'Why—er—I don't see anything else.'

'Does nothing strike you as familiar?'

'No.'

Tomes smote his fine, high brow in anguish. A regal bruise appeared. Absently dabbing witch hazel onto it, he said, 'There is something hauntingly familiar about it, but I cannot recall what it could be.'

'Is it perhaps the nature of the puzzle? The mystery of a man being washed from the deck of a steamship in the English Channel simultaneously with the appearance of his drowned corpse through the skylight of a house in London. That, surely, is the kind of case you would have essayed to solve in the old days.'

'*Essayed* to solve? No two ways about it—I *would* have solved it. Clotson, *did* I solve it?'

I reached far back along the dark, often noisome, corridors of my memory. A recollection, fleeting and grey like a rat in a sewer, came briefly within range.

'Yes, I think I do remember. I chronicled that tale. It was in the early years of our literary association, not long after *A Study in O'Hara* and *The Sign of the Just* were published. We thought that a new periodical called The Chesil Magazine might prove to be a rewarding outlet for my accounts of your adventures. Do you remember now—I sent off a specimen. A minor piece, I recall . . .'

'Yes, yes! It's coming back. The editor praised your style yet rejected the tale. It was too parochial, he said. He didn't think his readers would be interested in such a minor affair in such a remote part of the world . . . Did he ever return your manuscript?'

'No!' I cried. 'And this Louis Zangwill stole the plot and transplanted it to a British setting. I seem to remember that the correct solution to the mystery could not, for some reason, be applied to the new, British setting. So Zangwill substituted the pitifully unimaginative one recorded by Mr Adey—that the dead man had never been on board.'

'Mr Zangwill may not have been guilty of plagiarism,' Tomes said. 'After all, the case did receive some publicity in the Press. So why don't you restore your wounded pride to its usual high state of egotism with some witch hazel tea while I think.'

He sat back and lit a leisurely pipe, content now that a lacuna in his memory was filled. Presently, he started to talk, meditatively.

'We first learned of Titus Q. Goonhilly in Singapore. I recall receiving a letter, forwarded from Hong Kong. He expressed great fear for his life. Forces were bent on destroying him. Professor Andreas Abelman Veeblefetzer (whom I knew to be the fourth most dangerous man in Barnsley) had flown to the area in his balloon. He was engaged upon a devilish scheme to induce a local volcano to erupt by emptying four tons of Mexican red peppers into its crater. But Goonhilly, a chili baron, had learned of his scheme and threatened to expose him. Consequently, he was a marked man. Stealthy gentlemen in black overcoats followed him wherever he went.

'He needed help. Would I protect him? He was travelling to Savai, in Western Samoa, and he would expect me to meet him there at my earliest convenience. Goonhilly was a wealthy man, and had considerable influence with his country's government. He would, he said, be travelling under the alias of Athanasius Brown.

'Don't you remember, Clotson? I had sent you out to buy a newspaper while I read the letter, and when you returned and I mentioned Athanasius Brown, you told me that there was a report of his death in the paper.

'We were too late!

'I remember the report clearly; a remarkably competent piece of work considering the area. Mr Brown had been at Savai for a couple of days. On January 7, 1883, he decided to take a trip in a small boat, to go fishing, despite the fact that there was a strong wind blowing, from a quarter a little south of west. Two white people—their names I forget—accompanied him. They were later identified as first generation Americans. According to them, at 3.25 pm on January 7, a freak wave struck the boat. Although it did not founder, Mr Brown (who by all accounts was a poor swimmer) was washed overboard. His body was not found, although later some shreds of clothing were identified as having belonged to him. The not unnatural conclusion was that a shark had partaken of his reportedly ample bulk.

'Despite the fact that clouds were low and grey, witnesses on the shore were able to confirm the wave and the time; the boat was only half a mile out to sea.

'In the same newspaper, I found the report of another death—a very strange death indeed.

'At about 3.30 pm of January 7, in the grounds of an American merchant's house on Wallis Island, nearly 300 miles to the east of Savai, the naked body of a man fell from the branches of a large tree. It struck a large stone ornament. It was assumed that the fall, which split his head open, had killed him. The report identified the man, known in the area, as Goonhilly. The editor did not link the two identities (which was left to me, reading the newspaper) and contented himself with speculating long and fruitlessly on where Goonhilly had come from and where his clothes had gone.

'Now, how was it possible for Brown to have been swept overboard a mere half mile from the coast of Savai, yet almost simultaneously make violent impact with a marble replica of George Washington nearly 300 miles away?

'There was no way, in 1883, in which such a crime—for crime it was—could have been committed. Even in 1979, with helicopters and all 20th century technology at our disposal, it could not have been done.'

Tomes relit his pipe and gazed at the ceiling. I could see that he was now luxuriating in the reliving of one of his triumphs.

'Do you recall in what manner I solved the problem, Clotson?'

'Not entirely, Tomes.'

'When we arrived at Savai, we located the witnesses. Gradually, from the mists of their memories of a murky afternoon in January, we learned that Professor Veeblefetzer, pursuing his nefarious schemes, had launched a balloon from a headland jutting out to sea shortly before 3.15. It was a hazardous undertaking. At times, the balloon was swallowed up by the billowing bases of the clouds as it was blown across the wide bay by the strong wind.

'I now reconstruct what happened. The balloon flew unerringly to its prey—the little fishing boat. As it passed over, Professor Veeblefetzer cast a hook down. It caught in Goonhilly's clothing, ripped part of it away—the part which was later found in the water nearby. A second hook caught Goonhilly fair and square. He was hoisted up into the basket of the balloon, which promptly ascended into the clouds, all the while that Goonhilly's companions (who had been angling from the other side of the boat) thought that he had been washed overboard by the co-incidental freak wave.

'I do not know what happened in the balloon. I can only presume that Professor Veeblefetzer permitted it to be carried for many hours north-east by the strong wind. Perhaps at the given time he saw Wallis Island beneath him and threw Goonhilly out of the basket then.Perhaps he simply tossed him blind over the side and the body fortuitously alighted, if that be the word, on Wallis Island. It is of little moment.

'What *is* important is that Goonhilly was thrown overboard almost exactly twenty-four hours after he had been snatched from the boat.'

'But—but—' I stuttered.

'Yes, my dear Clotson. Twenty-four hours later, but on the same date. You see, like Jules Verne's Phileas Fogg, the vile Professor Veeblefetzer had crossed the international date line, which runs between Savai and Wallis Island.'

'You are a genius, Tomes,' I said.

'That is precisely what you said at the time.'

'Well, it was one of your greatest triumphs, after all.'

Tomes shook his head sadly. 'A minor triumph only. We were unable to prevent Professor Veeblefetzer from succeeding in his scheme. Krakatoa erupted in that very same year.'

JOHN DICKSON CARR

# A Razor in Fleet Street

*Received wisdom is that plays and playlets don't work. Not as reading matter, at any rate. The reader, the argument goes, cannot take continuous dialogue . . . cannot take the different typefaces used to distinguish between speech and scene description . . . will be irritated by the jumps in the narrative flow that will surely occur every time he or she checks which particular character is speaking.*

*All nonsense, of course. And, come to think of it, remarkably similar in bossiness to the reason publishers give when asked about the dearth of short-story volumes on the market: they don't sell because no one reads short stories—or the excuse offered by second-hand booksellers when you wonder why they have so little fiction in stock: it doesn't sell because no one reads fiction (this latter never fails to drive both your editors wild).*

*In the hands of a master-storyteller the play or playlet can be as entertaining, indeed as riveting, as a short story or a novel. When read, that is, as opposed to listened to. A certain amount of imagination is of course needed to fill in, say, undescribed location details, but, really, not so very much more than is required when reading the average text story.*

*John Dickson Carr, the undisputed master of the miracle problem, was a storyteller par excellence. He was also an expert, and prolific, radio dramatist in the British rather than his native American tradition, although he brought to the plays and documentaries he wrote for the BBC during the War a good deal of the atmospheric sound-colour, special effects and musical histrionics (e.g., sudden harsh cords struck at moments of high tension or crisis) that were obligatory in American radio drama.*

*Radio suspense, if it is to work at all, needs a special type of mind. The hints and clues must be simple and fairly presented, but not facile; too, although Carr enjoyed bamboozling his listeners (just as he enjoyed bamboozling his readers) there was no point in baffling them utterly. His technique was to lay on the atmosphere, to lead his listeners into (as Dorothy L. Sayers once wrote about his books) 'the menace of outer darkness', yet at the same time drop into conversation ambiguous words and phrases which will later prove to be crucial had the listener interpreted them correctly. In his classic 'The Dead Sleep Lightly' there is a daytime scene in a cemetery to a background of falling rain. The rain FX is useful since it lends a note of dreariness to the proceedings, but still the locale could be anywhere*

178

*until a character speaks of a 'nightmare of tombstones'. Instantly a whole series of eerie and disturbing images is conjured up. However, in the same scene there are at least three highly significant lines and one whopping verbal clue which the listener—and for that matter the reader—takes in then passes over simply because he or she is so wrapped up in the strange and unsettling situation. On the other hand, Carr did not invariably need an eerie atmosphere to get over his effects. In the crucial opening scene of his famous 'Cabin B-13' the reader/listener is hoodwinked by the very normality of the events taking place.*

*In 'A Razor In Fleet Street' there is an outright impossibility . . . which of course is no such thing. Readers are warned that every word, whether in scene description or dialogue, is important—although some are more important than others. Readers are also advised to use their imaginations . . . to picture each scene, or tableau, in their minds.*

JACK ADRIAN

## TABLEAU ONE

*T*he scene is London. *The curtain rises on a private sitting-room in a small, old-fashioned, expensive hotel in a small, old-fashioned, expensive street that runs down to the Thames from the Strand. Fleet Street, lined with huge newspaper buildings and small shops, is close by, as you can partly see (when there isn't a fog) by crossing the road to stand by the statue of Dr Johnson in St Clement's churchyard. Hampden's Hotel is dingy, self-consciously dingy, like a certain famous shop in St James's. The carpets are old, but of the best quality, like the staff. Some of the staff have been there longer than the oldest regular visitor can remember. The atmosphere is redolent of friendly deference and easy courtesy. Even the lift is a vintage one. Without doubt, the oldest lift in London, it rises and descends so slowly, and with such creaks and tremblings, that it is no wonder rumour tells how it is pulled up and lowered by a mysterious boy turning a windlass in the cellar. Two new patrons have just ascended to the second floor of Hampden's and been shown to their rooms by an ancient porter. They are Bill Leslie, an American, on his first visit to London, and Brenda, his English wife. Bill is romantic about London, and London, always polite, obligingly tries to live up to Bill's notions of what it ought to be. As a start, London provides him at once with that rarity, a thick fog, and from the shrouded river the deep notes of ships' sirens sound melancholy warnings. As the porter, well tipped, closes the door, Brenda Leslie laughs delightedly.*

*Brenda:* Bill, darling, don't look so bewildered!

*Bill:* Was I looking bewildered, Brenda?

*Brenda:* I *know* the furniture is red plush and dates back to the eighteen-sixties! I know we can't get a private bathroom!

*Bill:* By George, the waiters look as old as the furniture!

*Brenda:* But if only we'd gone to Torridge's or the Hautboy, or—

*Bill:* Brenda, you don't understand.

*Brenda:* No?

*Bill:* Who the devil *wants* to go to those swank hotels? This is London!

*Brenda:* Bill, I'm afraid I still don't understand.

*Bill:* I've been in the Diplomatic Service for seven years. I've been stationed in three capitals. But I've never been here.

*Brenda:* It's a lovely old town. It's—home.

*Bill:* It's home to me, too, in a way. It's put a spell on my imagination ever since I was a boy so-high. Sherlock Holmes! Dr Fu-Manchu! Hansom-cabs rattling through the fog . . .

*Brenda:* Darling, you don't think we still ride about in hansoms?

*Bill:* No, but it's the spirit of the thing! Here! Look out of this window!

*Brenda:* Yes?

*Bill:* Grey-and-black buildings. A lovely fog. Night falling. And—yes! Listen!

*Brenda:* What? I don't hear anything.

*Bill:* It's one of your famous barrel-organs. What's the tune, Brenda? Do you know it?

*Brenda:* Something about 'She's a lassie from Lancashire.' It's an old one.

*Bill:* But it's *right*, don't you see? Everything's right. And if I crane out of the window—sideways, like this—I can see down to the river. At least, I could except for this fog. That's where the bodies fall from the wharfs, and the police launches—

*Brenda:* Bill! Please listen to me!

*Bill:* Yes?

*Brenda:* I love you terribly, Bill. But of all the romantic Americans I've ever met, you have the most fantastic ideas about England. You don't really expect to find Scotland Yard men, in bowler hats, trailing your every step, do you?

*Bill:* That wasn't the point, Brenda! I only said—

*Brenda:* When you think about it, just remember that barrel-organ. Safe. Stodgy. Comfortable. That's London, Bill. Will you remember?

*As Bill gives his wife a friendly hug, the telephone rings. Bill, in mocking tones, exclaims as he goes to answer it:*

So they've got telephones here! Hallo, Bill Leslie here. What's that? The police! Must be some mistake. What? Well, I guess you'd better send the gentleman upstairs. Thank you.

*Brenda:* What on earth's the matter, Bill?

*Bill:* Search me! A Scotland Yard man is on his way up to see me. What price safety and stodginess now, Brenda?

*Brenda:* You're joking, Bill. What can the police want with you?

*Bill:* About six hours in England, and—

*Brenda:* Oh, this is ridiculous! There must be some mistake!

*Bill:* There probably is. All the same, come to think of it, I don't feel very keen about facing one of these C.I.D. bowler hats in real life.

*As he speaks there is a rap on the door, a firm, official knock, not loud but determined.*

Come in, please, come in.

*The door opens, and Chief Inspector Radford enters. He is wearing a well-cut dark suit and carries a brief-case and the latest model in bowler hats. Yes, he has a neatly cropped black moustache. He has an affable manner and keen grey eyes. He bows slightly to Mrs Leslie. Then turns quickly to business.*

*Radford:* Mr William Leslie? Sorry to have to trouble you, sir. I'm a police-officer. Metropolitan C.I.D. Here's my warrant-card.

*Bill:* I see. 'Chief Inspector—'

*Radford:* Radford, sir. And I'm bound to tell you I'm here about a serious matter.

*Bill:* How delightful—I mean, how surprising. Please sit down, Inspector.

*Radford:* Thank you, sir.—Now . . . don't mind my notebook. It's a mere formality . . . You and your wife arrived this morning by the *Maurevania*. Your wife is British, and carries her own passport. Correct?

*Bill:* Yes. That's correct . . .

*Radford:* A week from to-day you leave, by the same ship, for Lisbon. At Lisbon you take up a new diplomatic assignment at the American Embassy. Correct?

*Bill:* | Yes! But . . .

*Brenda:* | What's wrong?

*Radford:* Just a moment! I'd like you to look at this snapshot I have here . . . Who is it?

*Brenda:* But—it's Bill! No, it isn't. Look at that awful shirt and tie! It's your double, Bill!

*Bill:* So help me, I never had that picture taken. It must be my double. I never wore a shirt like that!

*Radford:* I know you didn't, Mr Leslie. That's Flash Morgan. Ever heard of him?

*Bill:* Never. Is he—*wanted* for something?

*Radford:* He's wanted for several murders. Also bank robbery. Also he's a ripper, if you know what that means. Uses a razor, and—likes it. Never has a gun. That's Flash in a flash, so to speak.

*Bill: Me?* The image of a murderer?

*Radford:* They don't look so different from the rest of us. Do you realize, sir, you can't leave this hotel without being nabbed, as Morgan, by the first copper you meet? It isn't just a likeness you'll agree. You're his double. You're the dead spit of him—as we say.

*Bill:* But I can prove who I am! I've got my papers!

*Radford:* You've got your papers. Right! Suppose Morgan gets 'em?

*Bill:* Morgan?

*Radford:* The *Maurevania* sails a week from to-day. Somebody called William Leslie, carrying diplomatic immunity, sails with her. What's to prove it's really you?

*Bill:* You mean he might—

*Radford:* I do.

*Bill:* That's impossible! He couldn't get away with it!

*Radford:* No, I don't think he could. But I'll give you ten to one he *tries* it. This is a small country to hide in, and he can't get away. He's desperate. This is his last hope.

*Bill:* What about—Brenda here?

*Radford:* There are several things that might happen to Mrs Leslie. All unpleasant. There's just one more matter I'm bound to warn you of. Morgan may try to get into this hotel.

*Bill:* But look here, Inspector! This ripper, or whatever he is, couldn't possibly know there's a man in town who looks like him!

*Radford:* He couldn't, eh? Have you seen the evening papers?

*Bill:* No.

*Radford:* Some fool took a picture of you getting off the boat-train. It's been published, with comments on the resemblance in all the evenings! You'll find Morgan's story in the *Evening News*. With pictures.

*Bill:* So I've made the front page at last!

*Brenda:* Don't laugh about it, Bill. But haven't you got *any* idea where this man is, Inspector?

*Radford:* No, ma'am; we haven't. He used to have a hangout at 996 Fleet Street, up over a barber's shop. But he won't go there now. He's loaded with money from the Whitehall Bank job. He's got a razor, and he's ready to use it. And now, if you'll excuse me, I must go. But for your own sakes I want you to stay in this hotel, both of you, until that boat sails.

*Bill:* Cooped up here for a week? Just in case?

*Radford:* Yes, Mr Leslie. Just in case.

*Bill:* Suppose I do go out?

*Radford:* I can't stop you, sir. The guard I'm leaving here can't stop you. But I might send you some photographs of people with their throats cut. Sorry to have to upset you. Good night.

*As the bowler-hatted representative of England's Criminal Investigation Department closes the door behind him, Bill and Brenda sit down on a sofa covered with red plush. For a few moments they simply stare at each other. From the street below the barrel-organ is playing 'The Lambeth Walk,' accompanied in the bass register by hoots and toots from the fog-covered Thames.*

*Bill:* Brenda! What price romantic London!

*Brenda:* Don't, dear. This is serious. I'm scared, Bill.

*Bill:* What was the number of that address Radford gave us? Where Morgan used to hang out?

*Brenda:* I don't remember.

*Bill:* You mean, darling, you won't remember. Nine hundred and ninety-six, wasn't it? 996 Fleet Street?

*Brenda:* Why do you want to know?

*Bill:* Because I'm going there. And I'm going now.

*Brenda:* Yes, I thought that was it. Bill, you can't! You mustn't! You can't do anything there!

*Bill:* I know.

*Brenda:* Bill, come back here! You're not to go!

*Bill:* Where's my overcoat? Now, this address—

*Brenda:* If you go, I'm going with you.

*Bill:* Oh no. This isn't a woman's kind of dare; and you know it.

*Brenda:* It's as much my dare as yours!

*Bill:* 996 Fleet Street. Up over a barber-shop. How do I get there?

*Brenda:* I don't—

*Bill:* If you don't tell me, Brenda, I can easily find out.

*Brenda:* Oh, all right, I give up. It's not very far from here. You could walk it in ten minutes.

*Bill:* That's better! That's much better!

*Brenda:* What about your identification papers?

*Bill:* I'm throwing 'em out here on the bed. Morgan won't get *those*.

*Brenda:* But if you haven't got those papers, you won't be able to prove who you are!

*Bill:* I'll risk it, Brenda. I'll risk it. See you later!

*Brenda:* Bill, come back! It's idiotic! Don't leave me! Please come back! *Please* . . . If you don't, I'm coming, too . . .


# TABLEAU TWO

*Fleet Street on a foggy October evening is not the easiest place in the world for a stranger to find a particular building. London street numbering is so eccentric that it seems arranged on purpose to puzzle, and Fleet Street is no exception. Bill Leslie has passed Temple Bar without seeing it, and is now stumbling across Fetter Lane. As he stares at the lighted windows of Peele's Coffee House (one of the street's noted taverns) the slow booming bell of St Paul's strikes seven, followed by the harsh clang of St Dunstan's. Bill bumps into someone as he reaches the narrow entrance to 'The Cheshire Cheese,' and a cheerful Cockney voice shouts 'Sorry, guv'nor.' Bill feels his throat apprehensively and begins to wish he had a Londoner as a guide. He mutters to himself:*

*Bill (soliloquizing):* Can't see the numbers. Those I can see seem to be in the wrong order. Fool stunt to come out alone in a fog. Wish I hadn't started. Supposing Morgan with his rip-throat razor is following me! But can't turn back now. Who's afraid? Mustn't be afraid. Might walk a little faster. No harm in walking a little faster. There! Number nine thirty-four. Can't be far off now. Was that a policeman's helmet? Doesn't matter. Police mean safety. Nobody can see my face. Another policeman's helmet! Swear to it! Over in that alley. A little faster . . . Take it easy, now; don't run. They can't possibly . . .
*Man's Voice:* You, there! Stop!
*Bill:* Mustn't get panicky. How do you stop panic? Got to find that address; got to justify myself; got to—
*Bill's soliloquy is interrupted by the shrill blast of a police whistle. As he begins to run, he stops abruptly. By a staircase open to the street Bill has noticed the number 996. Then he sees a notice: 'Henry S. Todd, Barber.' As the police whistle blows again, he goes upstairs.*


# TABLEAU THREE

*Bill Leslie enters a large room, not too clean, with a cork floor giving back no sound. Facing him is a window. On the left is another door. On his right, a wall of mirrors with two white barber chairs and another door*

*at the end. That is what Bill Leslie sees. What he can smell is the thick
odour of hair-tonic. On a white stool sits a little old man with yellow-
white hair and a reddish nose, peering up from an evening paper with
Cockney friendliness* . . .

*Bill:* I—I beg your pardon. I didn't mean to crash in like this.
*Todd:* Not a bit of it, sir! Nobody 'ere, sir! Glad to 'ave you come
up any way you like!
*Bill:* I've come about something important. I want—I want a shave,
please. And I'll just close this door.
*Todd:* Shave, sir? *Very* good, sir! If you'll just come over 'ere . . .
that's it . . . Your overcoat, sir; allow me . . . and in *this* chair, please.
Now we'll just whip out the cloth and get busy.
*Bill:* Wait a minute! Don't tilt me backwards yet! Are *you* Mr Todd?
*Todd:* Me name *is* Todd, and that's a fact. But mostly the gentlemen
call me Old Scratch.
*Bill:* Old Scratch?
*Todd:* It's only their joke. If they call me Old Scratch, or as it might
be Old Nick, it's 'cos they know I *won't* nick 'em. Never miss with
a razor, *I* don't. There now! We'll just tip the chair back. And I'll
bet this lather is as comfortable as—well, as going 'ome to tea and
kippers on a night like this. It's remarkable, sir, 'ow comforting.
*In the mirror Bill Leslie is suddenly aware that his double has just slipped
into the room and vanished again through the glass-panelled door on
the left of the street door. The barber, busy with his razor, has seen and
heard nothing.*
*Bill (whispering):* Mr Todd, listen carefully. Keep on lathering, and
don't speak any louder than I do.
*Todd (whispering):* Wot is it, sir? Wot's up?
*Bill:* Flash Morgan has just come in.
*Todd:* 'Oo?
*Bill:* Flash . . . Morgan.
*Todd:* Never 'eard of 'im.
*Bill:* He's a killer.
*Todd:* But there's nobody 'ere but you and me. Lift your 'ead up
and look!
*Bill:* You didn't see him. You were looking at the shaving-mug. I
saw him come in by the door from the stairs when you moved the
chair. He went through the other door.
*Todd:* Swelpmearry!
*Bill:* He's a killer. Wanted by the police.
*Todd:* The police, 'ere now, are you—

*Bill (loudly):* Finished with the lather? Then start shaving (*softly*), but make it quick. Get a razor! That's it. He didn't look at either of us. He didn't make a sound. I saw him in the mirror. I heard him bolt the street door on the inside. Look over and see if it isn't bolted.

*Todd:* Blimey—so it is!

*Bill:* He walked to that door there. Behind me. Where does it lead? Upstairs?

*Todd:* No, sir. There's no upstairs on this side of the 'ouse.

*Bill:* But there's got to be! Morgan lives at 996!

*Todd:* Don't move your chin like that! Keep your 'ead where I put it!—if you was looking for nine-nine-six proper, you must 'a made a mistake.

*Bill:* What do you mean?

*Todd:* Nine-nine-six is under the arch and round the back, like a lot of these old 'ouses. This is nine-nine-six B.

*Bill:* Then where *does* the door lead?

*Todd:* Only to a cupboard, sir. A big cupboard. Blimey! And 'e is *'iding* there now.

*Bill:* That's right. Hiding there—with his razor.

*Todd (loudly):* That's the end of the shave, sir. 'Ot towel?

*Bill:* Yes, thanks. Hot and steaming. (*Softly.*) Hang on to your nerve, Old Scratch, and we'll get him in two minutes!

*Todd:* Towel satisfactory, sir? (*softly*) I'm a peaceful man, guv'nor. I don't want no trouble.

*Bill (whispering):* Now listen. When you take the towel off, go to the shelf under the mirrors and mess around with the bottles. Ask if I'd like some kind of lotion, and edge towards the glass door. When you get near it, run like blazes and yell for the police. The whole neighbourhood is full of cops. Morgan will come out fighting when he hears you run. I'll pick up that high stool and try to hold him off. The cops didn't find me, because I went to the wrong number . . .

*Todd (urgently):* Sir! That door behind you!

*Bill:* Well?

*Todd:* The knob's moving.

*Bill:* Then we'll have to do it when I count three.

*Todd:* I *can't*, sir. I just ain't up to it.

*Bill:* You can run, can't you? One! . . . Two! . . . Thr—

*The street door bursts open, and Inspector Radford enters, accompanied by a sergeant of City police and two constables.*

*Radford:* Better stay where you are. Both of you.

*Bill:* Well, well! Do I hear Chief Inspector Radford?

*Radford:* You do. Sorry to break the door, Old Scratch; but why is it bolted?

*Bill:* Inspector, don't you recognize me? I'm Bill Leslie!

*Radford:* Yes. You probably are. Where's Morgan?

*Bill:* He's in that cupboard over there. *I* don't want to handle him. Where's your gun?

*Radford:* We don't carry guns. Sergeant!

*Sergeant:* Yes, sir?

*Radford:* Guard that window. Constable stay here. I'll take the wasp out of his nest. Coming out, Morgan? No? All right. Have it your own way. I'm turning the knob, and—Lord Almighty! It's Morgan, all right. But he won't give any trouble. His throat's cut! . . .


## TABLEAU FOUR

*The scene is Chief Inspector Radford's room at New Scotland Yard. The fog has penetrated even this official sanctum, which overlooks the invisible Thames. The river traffic is still hooting and tooting as it noses its way upstream or down. Big Ben, on the opposite side of Westminster Bridge, is striking eight o'clock as Chief Inspector Radford, flanked on one side by an official shorthand writer and on the other by two young policemen, continues his interrogation of Bill Leslie and the barber.*

*Radford:* Mr Leslie, why don't you tell us the truth?

*Bill:* Inspector, I have told you the truth. So has Old Scratch here.

*Todd:* Ah! Every word of it.

*Radford:* Let's face it, Mr Leslie. I suggest that you killed Morgan, and you don't seem to understand the law here.

*Bill:* How do you mean?

*Radford:* To kill a wanted man, even a murderer, is just as bad as killing the Prime Minister. I can't help you if you say you didn't kill him! But I *can* if you admit you did it in self-defence.

*Bill:* Look, Inspector, I never set eyes on Morgan except when he walked through that shop. Scratch never saw him at all. I never stirred out of the chair for one second. Scratch never left me, never even took his hands off me, for a second. Neither of *us* did it.

*Radford:* Then who killed Morgan?

*Bill:* I don't know!

*Radford:* I suggest that you and Morgan met at the barber's. There was a fight and you killed him, unintentionally.

*Bill:* I killed him with what?

*Radford:* With his own razor. We found it in the cupboard. Then you bribed Old Scratch to keep his mouth shut.

*Todd:* 'Ere now, Inspector. I—

*Radford:* Morgan was loaded with money. Carried a thousand quid in an oilskin tobacco-pouch. It wasn't on his body. If you gave it to Scratch, and Scratch hid it in the confusion after we broke in—

*Bill:* You know, Inspector, I've been wrong about this whole thing.

*Radford:* That's better!

*Bill:* Not in the way you mean!—*I* thought my trouble would be to prove my identity. But you don't doubt my identity. Or do you?

*Radford:* I don't, no. But officially, until your wife identifies you—

*Bill:* That's what I've been asking all night; and you won't answer! Where *is* Brenda?

*Radford:* Well, sir. The fact is—

*Bill:* You haven't got her locked up somewhere?

*Radford:* No, of course not! The fact is—we can't find her.

*Bill:* Isn't she at the hotel?

*Radford:* No. Your wife left the hotel just after you did.

*Bill:* Brenda left the . . . Where did she go?

*Radford:* To 996 Fleet Street!

*Bill:* How do you know that?

*Radford:* The real entrance to 996 is at the back. Up a flight of stairs past the barber's window. One of our men saw her there. Then lost her.

*Bill:* You mean, Morgan may have seen her before he came into the shop and attacked her. Brenda's dead! That's what you're saying! Don't start to object. That's what you're intimating! And if Brenda's dead . . . I'm the cause of it.

*There is a knock at the door and a sergeant enters.*

*Sergeant:* Chief Inspector!

*Radford:* Sergeant, keep out of here! I told you—

*Sergeant:* Yes, sir. But I couldn't help it. Mrs Leslie's here. She says she wants to give herself up. Here she is.

*Brenda:* Bill! Bill! Oh, Bill!

*Bill:* Brenda!

*Radford:* Please stay where you are. Mrs Leslie. You want to—give yourself up?

*Brenda:* Yes. I saw the murder.

*Radford:* You saw it? From where?

*Brenda:* From the back stairs, through the window. It was dark there but I could see into the lighted room quite easily. Bill, I got there before you did. You had to ask your way. I didn't. I—I saw you come in.

*Bill:* Into the barber-shop?

*Brenda:* Yes! But I think I'd have *known* what happened, even if I hadn't seen it.

*Radford:* Are you one of our women detectives, Mrs Leslie?

*Brenda:* Please! It's because I *am* a woman that I'd have noticed. You're too used to it. Bill *thinks* that . . . that man you call Old Scratch was never out of his sight for a moment. But he's forgotten something.

*Bill:* Forgotten what?

*Brenda:* You've forgotten there were thirty seconds when you had a hot towel over your face and eyes.

*Radford:* Sergeant! Grab our friend Scratch's arms! Quick!

*Brenda:* Keep him away from me! *Please* keep him—!

*Sergeant:* Got him safe, ma'am!

*Radford:* Go on, Mrs Leslie!

*Brenda:* He went to the cupboard. He opened the door only partly, and—and *slashed* inside and dropped the razor. He came back with an oil-skin pouch. He put the money under a trap in the cork floor. It was done in seconds.

*Todd:* It's a pity I ain't got another razor. Old Scratch never misses with a razor.

*Radford:* Better put the cuffs on him, Sergeant!

*Brenda:* You see, I already guessed he was an accomplice of Morgan's . . .

*Bill:* You . . . *what?*

*Brenda:* Bill, you're so romantic you won't use common sense. He was reading an evening paper. With pictures of Morgan and you too on the front page. But he said he'd never heard of Morgan. You spoke first, so he knew you were the American. And he saw a way of killing Morgan for the money. If he just dropped that razor in the cupboard, the police would think it belonged to Morgan. I was so paralysed I couldn't even scream. Somebody chased me; maybe it was the police; and I fainted in some old woman's room. I—(*falteringly*) Inspector, may I go to my husband now?

*Radford:* You may, Mrs Leslie. With the apologies of Scotland Yard.

(CURTAIN)

LEONARD PRUYN

# Dinner at Garibaldi's

---

*'Dinner At Garibaldi's' is a fine example of a story that hovers on the borderline of fantasy but (despite its central gimmick) doesn't quite cross over. Which is why we like it so much.*

*Not that either of us has anything against fantasy, or indeed science fiction—our respective shelves are stuffed with books of all genres, including those (incidentally, one of the few real arguments your editors have ever had has been on the merits or otherwise of Randall Garrett's* Too Many Magicians:*One thinks it's excellent, the other thinks it's punk—although not, to be fair, because of the Impossible gimmick itself). Early on, however, we decided to banish all entirely unrealistic elements from* The Art of the Impossible—*emphasis on 'entirely'. If it hadn't been reprinted so often, we'd both have enjoyed including Anthony Boucher's wonderful 'Elsewhen'. But that features a time-machine, and although, in theory, time-travel is practicable—at least, if time, as one theorist has it, may be likened to a boat drifting down a winding river (and thus you ought to be able to step off the boat at one of the bends and walk either backwards or forwards along the bank)—in practice, forget it. But if in a story an author makes out a good case for a particular impossibility and the gimmick works within the rules the author has laid down, and if, moreover, the gimmick in the end delights you because of the author's sheer brass neck—well, why not?*

*Leonard Pruyn certainly had cheek, whoever he was. Alas, he's proved untraceable, even though, back in the mid-1950s when the story was published, an editorial blurb referred to him as a full-time writer. Not in the mystery field he wasn't (although he did later collaborate on a straight novel with the mystery writer Day Keene).*

*Which is a pity because he had pace, style and, on the evidence of this story, a fertile imagination. As for the gimmick itself, is it feasible? Who knows? Who cares! Feasible or not, the story works. 'Dinner At Garibaldi's' is a little gem.*

JACK ADRIAN

---

I hated to admit it—but I had to. This was a case for Joachim.

It wasn't Edmond Leffington's body slumped in the bathtub that bothered me. In the insurance game you see a lot of bodies, all just as dead—hanging from rafters, smashed to hamburger on city streets, black, bloated bodies dragged up from the bay—old ones, young ones, short, tall.

I guess you get to take a suicide for granted—or murder with a hatchet in the skull. Even the mean torture deaths don't bother you too much. It's all dirty and sticky. You get used to it: the smell of it and the touch of it.

And the reasons don't bother you either. You just find them out—because that's your job. Murders for loot, murders for love, hate. Suicides for the same. People who seem to have everything and cut their wrists in the bathroom, beautiful women with stomachs full of cyanide. Edmond Leffington's death wasn't strange there. Most people seem to die in the bathroom, or the bedroom.

It was the way he died.

I'd heard of rich men dying of starvation. But Leffington wasn't only rich—he was one of the best known gourmets in the country! And now he sat in a bathtub—dead, of malnutrition.

He had been our biggest client—worth almost fourteen million. The insurance coverage in this one man alone nearly built our company. And yet a mealy-mouthed butler had just 'phoned to say Edmond Leffington was dead . . .

I took a taxi to the big brown-stoned house and showed my I.D. to the cop at the door. The place seemed different from six months ago—guess I just missed Leffington. A nice guy, you couldn't help but remember how he looked: tall and friendly and red-cheeked—like a skinny Scotsman. A man who loved good food—and plenty of it. Leffington never gained much weight and we considered him a good risk.

Now I followed the butler through the large dark rooms, still filled with those big antiques and paintings. There was money everywhere: in the thick oriental rugs, the leather chairs, and the high timbered ceilings.

The coroner hadn't arrived yet, and Leffington still sat propped up in the tub. The skin on his face and arms was emaciated, and the water against his bloated stomach. I put fingers to the grey flesh and closed his mouth.

When I asked the butler about the family doctor, he said there was none. I had forgotten that the old boy hated doctors. The servant handed me a routine medical report by the emergency physician. I scanned it quickly and couldn't believe what I read.

*Starvation.*

I went into the bedroom and sat on the bed—trying to figure this one out. I'd brought Leffington's file, and pulled it out of my briefcase. The butler was able to help a little, but none of it made too much sense.

Seems Leffington ate out most of the time—even breakfast. Our company examiner had put the kibosh on his eating anything between meals, so the old man had to depend on restaurants for nourishment. He was known to have gone over the deep end on this gourmet kick, and I actually believe he *would* have starved to death before he'd eat a bad meal. Leffington was a friendly guy, in his own way—but getting on, and a little eccentric. He'd inherited a mint of dough, played the stock markets, built up some real loot. A pretty solid character—and he liked to have his own way. He'd written a book once, called 'The Gourmand's Delight,' and every now and then he'd do a special food article for some small magazine or other. He was really considered an authority in the field. At home, though, he'd usually putter with an old vase, or something else in his collections—maybe catalogue those weird masks he had. His wife died years ago, and he didn't have many friends.

Spent most of his time, it seems, at a gourmet's club called The Epicure—sort of a hangout for old men and connoisseurs. The club was also a union for high-class chefs and restaurant owners. Very exclusive place—the incomes of its members reported to run in six figures.

That's all I learned. It added up to anything but starvation.

Then I searched the house, but there wasn't much to find. Nothing that made sense, anyway. Just the antiques, the vases and the masks, a make-up kit, and some pretty good disguises. I wondered about the camouflage too—but, so what? It didn't fit together: eccentric old men never do.

That's when I first decided to see Joachim.

When they told me Joachim was out of town for the weekend, I went to the Epicure myself.

The club was downtown, near Wall Street, and very hard to get in. When the doorman found out I was representing Leffington's estate, however, he sent me straight to the director's office. It was an English job (which I knew Joachim would like), smelling of saddlesoap and silver polish. A large brick fireplace stood in one corner.

Reginald Sims was the name of the director, and he sat behind a big oak desk covered with those German beer steins you saw before the war. The guy seemed to like me and tried his best to cooperate.

Told me Leffington was considered the expert of the association and was always willing to experiment with new foods. I tried to follow a lead there—but that's no way to starve. Also the doctor's report had made no mention of toxins or poisons—and, anyway, the autopsy had taken place the following day and confirmed the cause of death: *malnutrition*, pure and simple.

Sims said one thing, though, that made a lot of sense. Said for three months, Edmond Leffington had been eating at the same place. A restaurant called Garibaldi's.

I told Joachim about it the next morning.

Joachim Andreas is a guy you have to know to like—because he makes some people feel stupid. Also, he's not easy to describe—sort of a squashed face, with big black horn-rimmed glasses and cropped hair. He wears expensive flannel suits, but floppy—and *always* a red tie. He's a corporation lawyer—gets good money, but doesn't need to work. Likes the good things in life, and has a taste for them.

He's also the smartest guy I ever knew.

He was in his workshop that morning, carving one of those tall skinny statues he does. After pushing aside the plaster and putty, I sat down on one of his work benches and told him the story. He listened patiently to everything I said, nodding occasionally, those big hands of his messing with some clay.

Joachim—like I said— is a strange guy. He didn't feel like talking. 'We'll discuss it at dinner,' he said. 'I'm busy now.'

That's all. *I'm busy now.*

He even burned *me* a little at times—but I knew he'd crack it. It was a matter of principle with him—not the pay. 'Where?' I asked.

'Garibaldi's, of course,' said Joachim.

And to think I'd considered The Epicure exclusive! This was like Tuxedo Park—not only expensive, but particular. It took every wheel I'd ever known to get us that reservation at Garibaldi's—even Reginald Sims couldn't do it. Actually, Joachim got us the reservation. But I'll bet he had a time too.

We arrived at eight o'clock, and were both bowled over to find it was only a twelve table room. Don't get me wrong—it was big—very big, and beautiful.

Garibaldi met us at the door. He was a short little man, with thick black curly hair and probably the longest moustache I ever saw. It was his eyes you noticed first, those deep Italian eyes, then the olive brown skin and the white teeth. He greeted us in a kind of syrupy European voice and led us through a gold and red velvet vestibule.

It reminded me of those huge empty villas of Florence. That was 1945—just after the war. But Garibaldi's—*that* was something: like the inside of a small cathedral right in Wall Street's high rent district. I checked around later and none of the tickertape boys had ever heard of it. Like prohibition days—that's what Garibaldi's was. The dining room had a black and white marble floor, great pillars supporting the ceiling, tables along a railing on one side, looking on a big photograph of Venice. The tables, on the other hand, were small and intimate— like little boats bobbing on a big ocean.

I followed Joachim and Garibaldi to one of the little tables across the room. It was covered with fine embroidered linen, cut glass and expensive silver. Garibaldi clicked his fingers and a captain appeared from almost nowhere. Then Joachim ordered a light Johannisburger.

When I turned about I was surprised to find only four other people in the restaurant besides ourselves. Joachim looked at me. 'I spoke to Sims this afternoon,' he said. He allowed the captain to pour the wine. It sparkled in tall Czechoslovakian crystal. 'We'll have to search Leffington's place.'

I told Joachim I had.

'Then I'm afraid you must have missed something,' he said. He caressed the stem of his glass with the tips of his fingers—like that English actor Ralph Richardson would do. Joachim's a lot like him, in ways. Then he ordered dinner from an immense menu: Pheasants and turtle soup and soufflés and foods with foreign names I'd never heard of.

'Do you think he starved himself purposely?' I asked.

Joachim leaned forward slightly. 'You know about Garibaldi, of course . . .'

'Yes—Sims said he was kicked out of the union—'

Joachim rubbed his nose and tasted the wine. 'There's more than that,' he said. 'More than mere professional pride—'

I was a little confused and waited for him to go on.

'The restaurant,' Joachim said. 'It has a reputation.'

I never got a chance to ask him what kind of a reputation. We were interrupted by the waiter as he rolled the tray to our table. It was the first time I'd ever had *foie gras* smothered in truffles—and it made the quick sandwich at the corner drugstore seem a little sad. You don't forget the food they served at Garibaldi's.

Joachim ordered a special sauce; and I looked across the table at him, thinking what a mysterious bird he really was. Never have completely figured the guy out. Maybe I'll start on him, I thought, after this Garibaldi case is wrapped up. Sure—he was right—it *was* the restaurant. But how?

'We'll come here every day if necessary,' I said.

'That's just it,' Joachim said, with a flourish of his napkin. He pushed his soup aside and settled to a cigarette. 'We *can't* come here tomorrow.'

I was pretty surprised. 'Why not?' I asked.

'It's Garibaldi's gift,' Joachim said, with a trace of real admiration. 'He refuses to serve the same person more than once a week.'

'How exclusive can you get!'

Joachim laughed. 'Quite. But taste the wine again, my friend. And the hors d'oeuvres. I should judge the prices somewhat less than inexpensive.'

He always talked that way—the biggest snob you ever met. Highbrow, egghead—but smart, real smart. He always had to run things—a born ninety day wonder—the most selfish character I've ever heard of. But you let him, and like it. You end up respecting Joachim.

About ten-thirty or eleven we were out on the street again, in those empty stone canyons. Wall Street is a lonely beat at night, you know. Joachim and I stood on the sidewalk for a long time, just talking and remembering the first experience of Garibaldi's. I could still taste the lavender sweet flavour of that Crème Yvette.

It was when we moved down the street toward the light of a magazine stand that I noticed I was hungry. Seemed strange after such a big dinner—but I soon forgot it. Had a sandwich before I went to bed. Wondered what Joachim *really* thought about all this by now. He had rejected the idea of suicide.

We returned to Leffington's house next morning. It looked more cheerful now, with the big rooms full of sunshine. Joachim said he'd look upstairs, and I left him to return again to that famous green tub. The bathroom was empty, however—and I wandered about the first-floor rooms, looking at Leffington's pictures. Then, in the back hall, I stumbled into a sort of library, or study—a dark and creepy place, like being in a wax museum with nobody around. There was some Swedish stuff Leffington had collected. All along the walls and shelves he had them piled: old wooden drinking bowls and strange looking coffee pots. At one corner of the room I found some of that famous Scandinavian glass they talk so much about—hand-cut wine glasses and decanters, and some bowls and vases that looked very modern. I was amusing myself with rocking an old cradle, when I heard something behind me . . .

I turned around quickly and saw what looked for all the world like a short arrogant Russian count, standing in the open doorway. He wore a high hat, cutaway morning coat, striped trousers and the most dignified goatee you ever saw. But he also had on thick horn-rimmed glasses, and I began laughing. Joachim could be very corny at times.

He took me through the rooms and we found disguises in places you'd never look. Not the amateurish junk I'd found first visit. But inside the false bottom of a grand-father clock, for example. Here there was the entire outfit for an Indian prince—complete with red turban, silk robes and shoes.

'I guess we can have lunch at Garibaldi's tomorrow, after all,' Joachim said, stroking that beard he'd put on.

I, of course,—being stupid—asked why. He explained that we could go in disguise—as maybe old Leffington had done. And since Joachim didn't care, Mr Bartlett, department head at my insurance company, was very impressed with this my latest discovery.

'By the way,' my sculptor friend said, as we were leaving. 'It wouldn't do any harm to study up on the culinary arts this evening.' He scratched that Ukrainian goatee. 'We may be spending a good deal of time at Senor Garibaldi's.'

Much to the alarm of my wife, I studied recipes that evening.

I met Joachim at Roth's the next morning and we had vodka martinis before going to Garibaldi's. Joachim sat next to me and I watched him in the mirror across the bar. He looked a little tired and beat, and his hair wasn't combed flat. Joachim always looked sloppy in the mornings—pale and unhealthy, about ten years older than 35. But me, well, I'm eternally young. Like my wife, Martha, says—all I need is Joachim's brains. We've had him over to the house for dinner a few times, but he turns down most invitations. My wife's always nice to him, but I also think she's a little afraid of him, calls him 'a strange duck.' She had a real weird dream about him once in which he beat her up. The loony boys would say she's in love with him—but I don't think so. Kind of glad Martha *doesn't* like him too much, understand he's death on women.

Anyway, we had this drink, then went over to Leffington's place and got into our costumes. Joachim was dressed as a bigshot Texas oilman, with white boots and a hundred dollar Stetson. He got me fixed up as a pinched little Boston tycoon—pin-striped suit, even complete to watch chain. I really felt silly until I looked in the mirror; they were good disguises. Anyone would have thought I was sixty, at least. Joachim told me to act like sixty—and to remember enough about fancy menus to read them right. Then he made a 'phone call about the reservation's at Garibaldi's and we left.

Luncheon was something to remember—I remembered enough about Europe to know that. First, it was exotic. Like the snails they tried to serve us on furlough in Paris. Only this was *good*.

I started lunch off with a bottle of Spanish muscatel—that real cool sweet wine I'd had once in a little town just outside Barcelona. Joachim told me sweet wines are not fit drink for meals—but I didn't care. I'd carted Martha all over New York and never could find that wine. This was the real thing. I made up my mind right then—next visit to Garibaldi's I'd have some of that white Orvieto wine we'd bought from a little old lady at a station, when we were on the military train to Rome. I'd searched for that too. As I said, Garibaldi's was *really* something. But let me tell you about the luncheon.

Joachim ordered a bottle of dry German Riesling for himself, of course. Big snob—the guy really makes you so sore at times that it almost ruins your appetite. That's unless you eat at Garibaldi's, of course. First there was soup, called aux Marrons, a warm chestnut broth that would have been a meal for anybody. Joachim—needless to say—ordered something called Potage Creme de Potiron—a kind of pumpkin soup. Then Garibaldi brought us a fisherman's dream of flaked mackerel with gooseberry sauce. For the light entree I had stuffed artichokes. Joachim had kidney saute in white wine. But it was the main dish that was really worth waiting for. The head waiter rolled up a tray of roast guinea fowl, floating in its own rich brown juices. It was a meal to drive you crazy. Even Joachim was impressed, and believe me—*that's* something.

Anyway, about halfway through the meal, Joachim pulled the joker. He asked Garibaldi if we could see the kitchen. I really thought that was *it*. But the old pud didn't seem to mind—just waltzed us down the shining marble floors to a couple of big swinging doors. Inside, we walked past a blend of aromas like you've never smelled before. No wonder Leffington loved this place, no wonder he had invented a couple of dozen disguises to come everyday, three times a day.

It still beat me though, and I wondered if I'd ever figure this one out. *How could a gourmet like Leffington eating at a place like this starve to death?* Joachim and I walked the entire length of the kitchen—past row on row of what seemed a thousand different dishes, each one smelling and looking more delicious than the last, Joachim all the time keeping up a lively conversation with Garibaldi about the better Dallas restaurants. What a kick—I guess I made a pretty corny tycoon.

Anyway, Garibaldi let us see it all—the shining pots, the white refrigerators, the oyster bar and pantry, the rare imported foods from at least two dozen different countries. Garibaldi never took those sparkling brown eyes off you, and you got to like him after a while. Matter of fact, I thought we were barking up the wrong tree. I told Joachim so at dessert.

Joachim delicately punctured the Oeufs a la Neige Garibaldi had brought him and looked up at me, his eyes cold hard. 'Just what do you think Leffington's trouble *was?*' he asked, sarcastically.

'Starvation,' I said. 'So what?'

'So what,' Joachim repeated. 'And just where did Leffington dine, may I inquire?'

'Here, of course!' I told him.

'Ah,' he said, making a wry smile. 'Then where is the logical place to look for Edmond Leffington's murderer?'

'*Murderer!*' I whispered. 'But—'

'Come now,' Joachim said, twirling his silver cigarette holder in my face, 'lets get down to fundamentals.' He belched and took a bite of his Oeufs a la Neige. 'As you once so sagely remarked—famous gourmets just don't starve to death. That's the only clear-cut thing about this case.'

Joachim gave me a dirty look and ordered the cheque. We sat a few minutes longer—in silence—over a demi-tasse and a thimble full of Crème Yvette, which (as I mentioned) is the speciality of the house. But don't get any ideas about the cordial—we knew it wasn't poisoned or anything. Joachim had taken a mouthful of it home the previous night, and the lab boys at the office had analyzed it that morning. It was just Crème Yvette. Very good—but Crème Yvette.

One thing bothered us though. A half-hour after we left Garibaldi's we had that tremendous hunger again. Although we could still taste the liqueur, we were just as hungry as though we'd had no lunch at all. We went immediately to Child's and ordered steaks.

That's when Joachim really started thinking.

Next day Joachim was changing into the outfit of an Italian duke. He seemed pretty confident, and it made me a little sore that I didn't too.

'It's all so embarrassingly easy,' he explained.

I asked him what he meant.

'Garibaldi and his fabulous entrees, Leffington's demise,' he said, 'All of it.'

Leave it to Joachim—he refused to say anymore. Had to take all the credit himself.

When Garibaldi met us in the vestibule, Joachim was wearing sun glasses. *This* was it. The effect on Garibaldi was shattering. Somehow all the showmanship seemed to drain out of the old boy's performance. He led us to our table like a sleepwalker.

I was fully prepared to order the menu this time—determined not to leave Garibaldi's hungry again. I ordered the most expensive items on the menu: Crisp hearts of Sardinian Hummingbirds in Almond Sauce; Paté des Rana Pipiens served on Croustade with Asparagus tips and Carrots Vichy. For wine, I ordered a Hungarian tokay called 'Hegyaljai.'' Then for dessert, I chose two real jawbreakers: Pizza Figliata and poussé-café. Wonderful place—it improved your vocabulary as well as your appetite.

Matter of fact, I was enjoying the meal so much, I had completely ignored Joachim. When I happened to look up between pigeon livers, I was surprised to find he had touched none of the food before him. He sat there, with his dark glasses, chain-smoking cigarettes. Matter of fact, he was behaving very strangely—not even seeming to see the waiter or the captain when the various dishes were served, and once addressing the waiter as 'Garibaldi,' even though the two looked as much different as Joachim and me.

It was not until the after-dinner Crème Yvette, that Joachim touched a thing. He sipped it slowly and seemed really to enjoy it. He inhaled deeply on his cigarette, and smiling, told me I was making a dope of myself.

I pushed the Pizza Figliata aside and asked him what he thought he was talking about.

'Don't you think it's a little silly to scrape an empty plate?' he said, looking over at the heaping of Figliata on my dish.

'Maybe those glasses are ruining your eyesight,' I suggested. I put them on, and the Figliata was still on my plate.

'Just wait,' Joachim said. Then he told me how he'd taken a wing of guinea fowl home in his handkerchief the previous day. His hand had never left the coat pocket where the greasy wing was hidden. On his arrival at Child's, however, the handkerchief was empty and spotless.

I stopped listening to him long enough to look through the green glasses at the head waiter approaching our table. You can imagine my surprise when he turned into Garibaldi right on the spot—even worse when my Figliata just plain disappeared.

I guess Garibaldi saw my expression, because he hightailed it on through the kitchen doors, Joachim and me right after him.

It was when we were both in the kitchen that we got the meat-axe.

Ever visit an empty house? A very empty house? That's what this room was like now that the shining pots and refrigerators were gone.

We looked the entire length of the emptiest kitchen either of us had ever seen—just bottle after bottle of that Crème Yvette lining both walls on wooden shelves—and at the far end of the pantry—behind some garbage pails—Garibaldi cringing like a two-bit hood.

The weatherbeaten trunks under the kitchen told us the story of Garibaldi. They also answered the strange death of Desmond Leffington. Garibaldi wasn't a murderer—he was just a cheat.

**LUIGI GARIBALDI**
Munich—Florence—London
**CONJUROR—MAGICIAN—
HYPNOTIST**
A Full Course Dinner in the
**MIND'S EYE**

Joachim called the police. I went down the street to Nedick's and had a hamburger. With.

JOEL TOWNSLEY ROGERS

# The Hanging Rope

*In 1945 the American publishers Simon & Schuster issued in their Inner Sanctum Mystery series a book that is surely one of the dozen or so finest mystery novels of the 20th Century, Joel Townsley Rogers'* The Red Right Hand.

*It's a book impossible to summarize, impossible to describe. Perhaps the best thing, to give all those unfortunate enough never to have read it a flavour of what is on offer, would be to list a few of the basic ingredients: an ugly little red-eyed murderer with a torn ear called Corkscrew who doesn't seem to exist . . . a psychopathologist, soon to die, who specializes in aberrant mentalities (notably the split-personality) . . . a speeding car with a wailing horn and a dead passenger that vanishes . . . a narrator who just possibly might be implicated in the murders, just possibly might be going out of his mind . . . a hacked-off hand . . .*

*But no, that won't really do. All of those elements—give or take a bloody ear or hewn-off hand—may be found elsewhere. And such a list may well hint at the nightmarish atmosphere, the hallucinatory nature of what takes place, but it certainly takes no account of what is in fact one of the most extraordinary aspects of the book—indeed, of Rogers as a writer—which is his torrential, unstoppable prose. Having gotten up a full head of steam on the very first page, he doesn't let up for even a paragraph throughout the book's 65,000-word length, and one is carried along in this unrelenting spate to a climactic and bloody confrontation that is quite unforgettable. It is, in all ways, a genuine tour de force.*

*Almost as breathtaking (especially in its construction) is his last novel* The Stopped Clock *(1958) which begins powerfully with an atrociously beaten woman left for dead by her would-be murderer, crawling in agony, and with agonizing slowness, around her house trying desperately to lock all doors and windows because she knows he's coming back to finish the job—and ends just a half hour later in an astonishing blaze of violence. A half hour in real-time, that is, for in between beginning and end lies a 100,000-word novel detailing the woman's life and the events that led up to that frenzied assault.*

*One invariably leaves Rogers' fictional worlds in a state of high tension—but a word of warning to those who, on the strength of this encomium, might be contemplating taking him up. Rogers is not for the speed-reader. He is not for those who scan the page, extracting the juice but not the pith. You need (to mix the metaphor) to keep your eye on the ball when reading him, for he had a nasty habit of sliding crucial information into his torrential text when you least expected it.*

*As here, in this forgotten tale that I and my co-editor are particularly proud to have had a hand in resurrecting.* The Hanging Rope, *a 30,000-word novella, bears all the hallmarks of Joel Townsley Rogers at his best and with all cylinders firing. Pulp-writing of the very highest order, it careers along at a breakneck pace and ends with an awe-inspiring twist. In a phrase, sheer class.*

JACK ADRIAN

# CHAPTER ONE

### The Beanpole Man and the Cat Man

If Kerry Ott, the playwright, hadn't detested a bad play with all his mind and to his dying breath, the murder in the Royal Arms apartment house that night might have been written off as unanswerable. Or at best have been ascribed to some vague, intangible, amorphous third visitor who old Dan McCue had had, in addition to the bean-pole and the cat man—the lawyer and the priest—after they had both made their departures.

And yet there was nothing complicated about the killings. They were actually one of those classics of crime simplicity, with a definite place where they occurred, a limited number of men who could possibly have committed them, and the police already at the door before they were completed. Practically every detail about them was apparent at a glance, except how the killer had got away.

We'll take the scene, first.

The murders took place in the fourth floor rear apartment—apartment 4C, consisting of large library living room, dining room, kitchen, bedroom and bath, hallway, and four or five closets—of Mr Daniel McCue, the wealthy retired contractor and political sachem. The weapons used were a wine bottle and a fireside poker for the first killing, and sharp steel for the second—crude and simple weapons, with more blood than was necessary spilled and spattered about. Old Dan McCue himself was done to death at three minutes after midnight; the terrified girl within the next dozen minutes, according to those who heard her scream.

It was as simple as that. A dozen minutes, a locked apartment, and two dead. The killer must have been present to do his killings, at the time they were committed. Up to the last terrible minute he must have been there, desperate and cornered, with the alarm raised before he had completed his work, and the police already at front and back.

And yet there was no one who saw him. He might have been as invisible as smoke or mist. As transparent as the highball glass he finished off before he killed old Dan McCue. As thin and sharp as the steel he used on that girl's warm throat.

Perhaps in that moment in the hallway as he pushed past the doorway of the murder bedroom, in the flash of the silver blow that fell, Tuxedo Johnny Blythe had seen his face. Yet the vision was so quick, he fell so suddenly, he could not be sure of what had struck him. The big blue-clad cop had fled by then. The rustling in the kitchen had ceased. Tuxedo Johnny lay there dazed, the only living thing, as far as he knew, within that death apartment. And there was no answer to how the murderer had got away.

He said to Big Bat O'Brien of homicide, going through the murder apartment afterwards, 'We were within thirty feet of her when he killed her. Right at the door. It must have been only a matter of seconds. But he wasn't there. Nobody. There just had to be some way.'

'Front door locked on the inside, Johnny,' Big Bat enumerated. 'Fire escape window locked on the inside. Bars on all the other windows. He couldn't have, but he did. And unless someone turns up who saw him and can identify him, there's not a thing in God's world to pin it on him, either. The damned cup of custard must have been wearing gloves. He didn't leave a print.'

Not a print that could be identified as belonging to a murderer exclusively. The homicide men had dusted everything by then. There were Paul Bean's prints (the lawyer's), of course, and Father Finley's (the purring priest's), as was to be expected, since they had both visited old Dan McCue that night. But they had both left before the murders.

'He was smart,' said Tuxedo Johnny. 'He was smart, and I played it dumb—you're right, Bat. Still I'd like to be able to figure out, just for my own personal satisfaction, how he could have got away. There had to be a way.'

Well, there was a way of escape, though they were a little late in discovering it . . . There had to be a way, and so there was. Only one, but one was all he needed.

At half past eleven that night, according to his later statement to the police, Paul Bean, old Dan McCue's lawyer, had decided that it was

time for him to say good night. He had set down his highball glass,
put his cigar butt in the tray on the smoking table beside his chair,
glanced at his watch and unfolded his long stilt-like legs.

'Time for the hay, Dan,' he remarked in his profound and
lugubrious voice. 'I've always got a load of work at the office in the
morning. I'll try to drop in with a tentative will draft tomorrow
evening for you to look over.'

'No need to rush it,' said old Dan. 'Plenty of time before I die.'

'That's what you think,' said Paul Bean. 'I'll be around again soon,
anyway.'

'Here, boy, you haven't finished out your drink,' old Dan said.
'You've left the half of it.'

'Put a tag on it, Dan, and save it for me the next time,' said Paul
Bean.

He opened the lid of the silver humidor on the satinwood desk and
selected another corona before departing. He picked up the magnum
of champagne with a pink ribbon around its neck, which he had
brought under his arm, unwrapped, and had given to old Dan for
his birthday tomorrow. He examined the label again, then set it down.

Old Dan McCue, in his green silk dressing gown and easy slippers,
with his glass and cigar, did not bother to accompany Paul Bean to
the front door. Paul Bean frequently dropped in of evenings for a short
visit, living only three or four blocks away on Park Avenue as he did,
and the formality wasn't necessary.

With his cigar in his mouth, the tall attenuated lawyer had gone
along the hall towards the front door, past the doorways of dining
room on the left and bedroom on the right. He had not opened the
coat closet, not having even a hat to bother with in the warm
September night. He had opened the front door of old Dan McCue's
apartment, and had gone on out, closing the door behind.

Paul Bean was better known, of course, as Pole Bean. It would have
taken a man with a great deal of originality not to have called him
that. In college twenty years ago, where he had been a pole-vaulter,
there had been a comedy pretence of being unable to distinguish him
and his bamboo apart; and he had never cleared the bar without some
wit in the stands yelling a protest that he had merely dug his heels
into the ground and heaved his pole across.

That is known as a sense of humour to those who have it. He had
none himself. He was a cautious and careful lawyer, however. Besides
being old Dan's counsel, he had been his son-in-law for a dozen years,
having been married to Dan's late daughter Sue.

She had died six months ago in a rather tragic and hideous way, of a cat scratch which had developed into tetanus, and for which serum had been used too late. It had been an event shattering to old Dan, not to speak of Paul Bean himself, following as it had the death of Dan's only son, by drowning, a few years before. It was for that reason that Paul Bean made it a point to drop in once or twice a week for a brief visit. With the added reason tonight of bringing old Dan the bottle of birthday champagne.

He had brought up, just incidentally, the matter of Dan's making a will, which Dan had never done. Perhaps with a subconscious superstition, like many men, that to do so was a kind of invitation for death. Or perhaps out of mere procrastination, not believing that he, with his great powerful body and long-lived ancestors, at a mere sixty years of age would not have still another thirty years to go.

Paul Bean, being a lawyer, realized better the uncertainties of life, however. He knew that there were various hospitals and other charities which Dan would like to have benefit by moderate bequests and probably some personal friends, like harmless and slightly demented Father Finley. It would be a good thing too, to have himself as executor, since he was acquainted with all of Dan's affairs. Old Dan had seemed not unacquiescent to the idea, Paul Bean thought. If he had not agreed, at least he had not disagreed.

Paul Bean had left that scene, which was not yet a murder scene, at half past eleven. He had paused in the corridor outside to light his cigar, with his shadow long and thin on the marble floor.

He had rung for the slow little elevator, but it had not replied at once. He had decided to walk down the stairs, and had done so, not meeting anyone on the way. In the lobby he observed the gilt scroll-work top of the elevator cage down in the basement. The operator was probably having supper, and had not heard his ring.

He had gone out into the night, walking west towards Park Avenue. A block away he passed a fat-bellied policeman moving slowly down in the shadows of the building line, who adjusted his cap with a deferential gesture when Paul Bean spoke a gloomy, 'Good evening, officer,' to him. A block farther on a couple of half-grown youths, playing some kind of wild chase-tag game on and off the sidewalk, tripped Paul Bean as he tried to angle his way between them, and he fell sprawling in a tangled knot, like a giraffe, scraping his palms and the pads of his fingers, and tearing his pants knees.

With expressions of regret, the boys got hold of him beneath the armpits to help him up, and just as he got his long legs untangled and was starting up from all fours, kicked him in the pants, sending him sprawling again and running away down the street laughing.

Considerably hurt, both in skin and feelings, and with his cigar mashed and lost on the sidewalk, Paul Bean got himself up once more. The boys had ducked around some corner, and the policeman he had passed a block before was no longer in sight. Holding his palms up like a melancholy Airedale, and limping slightly, Paul Bean proceeded on to Park Avenue, and down it to his own large and lofty apartment building.

The elevator man was still on duty—after midnight there was only a small self-service elevator for tenants. Paul Bean rode up to the fourteenth floor, where he got off, with an exchange of good nights, and was unlocking the door of his apartment opposite before the doors were closed.

Having arrived home, where he lived alone now that he was a widower, and with his step-daughter Jennie away at summer camp, Paul Bean proceeded into the bathroom off his bedroom, where he washed the dirt and skinned blood from his hands, and soaked them in hot water. He applied a soothing lotion when he had dried them, after which he wrapped surgical gauze with adhesive tape on his fingertips. At his bureau in his bedroom he removed his jacket, with some clumsiness because of his bandaged hands, and examined the dirt upon it.

He took out his watch from his pants fob pocket and wound it. It said five minutes and thirty seconds of midnight, he observed.

He began to remove the other items from the various pockets of his pants and jacket, putting them on the bureau with his watch, to have his suit ready for the cleaners in the morning. He paused a moment, standing before his mirror motionless, looking at the reflection of his dark green eyes in his small dark bony face, with his bandaged hands pressed to his hollow ribs, meditating. He continued his undressing, stepping out of his light-coloured suit pants. He went to his clothes closet, where his robe and pyjamas hung on a hook, next to a hook on which hung a pair of dark baggy slacks and a dark golf pullover and reached in . . .

But Paul Bean was not the last man to see old Dan McCue alive.

At a quarter of midnight, or a few minutes later, the pan-faced elevator operator of the Royal Arms opened his gates on the fourth floor for the little shadowy man who stood there, having rung to go down.

He was a slight little man, not more than five feet two inches in height and weighing perhaps not more than ninety pounds, dressed in a dark grey, silk-like alpaca with a clerical collar, and a stiff straw hat which had been dyed black and varnished. He had a vague, wistful face, which he was rubbing with his fingers as the elevator arrived, in the way of a man who feels a new shave. He pulled out a tobacco pouch and pipe as he stepped into the elevator, with an apologetic, sidewise gesture.

The Royal Arms elevator men knew him by sight—Father Finley, as he called himself, a friend of Mr McCue's. He lived somewhere in the neighbourhood, and came in frequently to see Mr McCue, or just to wander around the corridors or down in the basement—though Swede Rasmussen, the janitor, always chased him out when he got down there—looking for some stray cat to feed.

The pan-faced elevator man, whose name was Boaz, didn't particularly like to have Father Finley riding in his car. That wasn't because the little man was probably demented, and might some day pull out a hatchet from underneath his coattails and maybe chop him from behind, but because he smoked a bad-smelling shag tobacco, and had also about him a somewhat disagreeable meaty odour, in spite of his clean and well-bathed look.

The goof had probably just come from Mr McCue's, thought the elevator man.

'Mr McCue still up, Padre?' he said, closing the cage doors, although he knew that old Dan McCue never went to bed before one or two o'clock.

'I believe so,' said Father Finley. 'I believe that he was up, or sitting down. I just dropped in to have a shave. Did I get it clean enough? I had a drink with him, too. Or rather, he poured out a drink for me. I'm not sure if I drank it. We were discussing philosophy, and I smoked my pipe. Have you seen a cat wandering about by any chance?'

His voice was soft and purring and quite inoffensive. Boaz, the elevator man, thought it disagreeable, however, like his smell. The sound of it always lifted the bristles on the back of his neck.

'What kind of a cat, Padre?' Boaz said.

'A grey Maltese cat,' said Father Finley, with his vague eyes lighting for the instant. 'More precisely, perhaps, a kitten. A grey half-grown cat about five months old, with a short tail, a white breast, and three white feet—all except the left hind one. I saw it on the sidewalk out in front an hour ago, but before I could reach it it had disappeared, either into the building here or down the alley. It was homeless and hungry. It was crying. I shall not sleep tonight, worrying about it. You haven't seen it, you say?'

'No,' said the elevator man. 'Maybe it went down into the basement, and Swede Rasmussen caught it to make a stew out of it. If I see it

I'll tie a brick to its tail and heave it out the door for you, though, Father Finley.'

'How brutal—how bloody—some men are!' said the little man in grey sadly. 'It is such a cruel world. A hard and cruel world. The things that some men have in their hearts are inconceivable.'

'Yeah,' said Boaz. 'Ain't it awful? It busts my heart, too. Was Mr McCue alone when you left him, Padre?'

'I believe he was,' said Father Finley vaguely. 'Yes, I am sure of it. Dan mentioned that Paul Bean had just gone.'

'I just wondered,' said Boaz.

He took another bite of the half-finished sandwich in his hand as they reached the lobby floor. He hadn't seen Mr Bean go, though he had taken him up at about eleven. He hadn't seen Father Finley come in, for that matter, either. However, he was seeing him now, going out.

Boaz, the pan-faced elevator man, strolled after the little man in thin whispering silky grey to the doorway of the Royal Arms, which stood open in the warm late summer night. Father Finley turned left, and Boaz looked right down the street, towards Third Avenue and Park beyond. The fat blue bulk of a patrolman was coming down the midnight street from there, having just emerged from a doorway, it looked like. Boaz recognized him as Ignatz Slipsky.

The little man in grey went down the sidewalk, past the entrance of the black alley which separated the Royal Arms from the old brownstone tenement next door, where he lived. He mounted the worn sandstone steps and went in through the heavy walnut doors with their small ground glass panelling, on which was lettered ARGYLL HALL in peeling gilt script. He went up the worn creaky wooden stairs inside, under dim bulbs above each landing, past snoring doors and dead deserted doors on the second and third floors, pausing momentarily to listen and look around him. At the top floor he paused again a moment.

He looked toward the door of the rear flat on the right. On tiptoes he moved toward it.

That right rear flat had been shown to him before he had moved in a month ago. However, he had preferred the front with its view of the street and southern exposure, even at two dollars and fifty cents more a month.

As far as he knew, the rear flat was still empty. No truckload of broken furniture had been moved into it that he had observed. There had been no garbage cans at the door, no swarming children erupting from it, no sounds of yelling voices behind it, or any other normal indications of life and occupation. Father Finley listened a moment, with his head bent to the door panel, quietly pulling a pair of grey silk summer gloves on his delicate small hands, just as the great bonging bell in the clock tower around the corner on Third Avenue began the slow stroke of midnight . . .

But this was not the murder scene, of course. This was in Argyll Hall, next door, across the alley. The fact was that Father Finley, like Paul Bean before him, had departed from that murder scene, from old Dan McCue's apartment, before the murders began. Both the two known visitors whom old Dan had had that evening had departed. And the murderer, when those murders took place, was in the Royal Arms. He was in old Dan's apartment.

## CHAPTER TWO

### Twelve Minutes

That was the murder scene—old Dan McCue's apartment. Entrance hallway, dining room and kitchen to the right, bedroom and bath to the left, and down at the end of the hall, across the back of the building, the large library living room, furnished with bookcases filled with tooled leather, grand piano, a huge rug, satinwood desk, Old Masters and easy chairs grouped around the fireplace. Front door and fire escape in back. All windows of all rooms with bars on them, except the fire escape window, and one little bathroom window.

Old Dan was in the living room. Maybe he had been sipping and smoking, garbed in his green silk dressing gown, thinking of his birthday, which would be tomorrow, thinking of all the years of his life. Maybe he had just arisen from his chair, hearing a ring at his door—maybe the black-eyed girl in that moment was at his door, waiting to be let in.

Or may be the doorbell didn't ring at all and she came in with a key old Dan had given her—there was the key on the bathroom shelf, and it might have been hers, not Finley's. Or maybe old Dan had arisen, instead, to pour himself a fresh drink at his mahogany cellarette—and looked around and his murderer was there.

Maybe the murderer said, 'Hello, Dan.'

'When in hell,' maybe old Dan said in startlement, 'did you come back? I thought I had got rid of you for good.' Or, 'How in hell did you get in?' with sudden suffused rage. 'Sneaked in, did you?'

Maybe the murderer said, 'It's a long story, Dan. I'll tell you about it.'

And maybe he picked up a half-emptied highball glass then, that stood on one of the pieces of furniture, and half sat on the arm of one of the easy chairs, reaching in his pockets nervously for something to smoke.

'I've heard enough of your long stories and tall tales,' maybe old Dan said. 'I don't like you, boy, I've told you. I think you're sneaking, scheming, and too smart for your own breeches. I think you're a swine and greedy and money-mad. Ay, by God there are times when I think you might be a murderer. You know who. And I've wrestled with me soul whether or not to take it up with Big Bat O'Brien at homicide. Yet it's not in me to give any man a dirty name without the proof, and I know Big Bat would say there was no proof. And even if there was aught of proof, it would not bring back the dead. If you have done murder and got away with it, let it be between you and your God . . .

'Here, let me get you a fresh glass,' maybe old Dan said. 'The liquor in that is stale. Help yourself to a cigar, if you've a mind to, too. Damned if I like you or anything about you, and this sneaking way of coming has a dirty look to me. But no man will be a guest of Dan McCue's without a show of hospitality. What kind of a story is it that you have to tell me, that brings you so quiet? About me money, maybe, that you'd like to get your hands on?'

Maybe old Danny said words like that. Or maybe he said something different. Or maybe he just turned to the cellarette to mix a highball for his murderer, and the murderer carefully and quietly picked up the heavy fireside poker from the hearth, or the champagne bottle with the pink ribbon around it which stood on the desk, and crept two steps towards old Danny, behind his back.

Maybe old Danny saw the gesture of that skull-crushing blow, and reached for his telephone then. Or maybe the first furious blow had struck him before he knew it . . .

That was the scene, anyway. Old Dan's living room. And the murderer was there, in it, when he killed old Dan McCue at three minutes after twelve that night, and a dozen minutes later when he killed that black-eyed girl.

Kerry Ott, the big deaf playwright, was never on the scene of those murders in the Royal Arms, like Paul Bean and Father Finley and, of course, the murderer. He would never, therefore, have to make any explanations to the police.

He did not know the murderer. He did not know Paul Bean or Father Finley. He did not know old Dan McCue. He had never seen or heard of that black-eyed girl who died fifteen feet from him. He was even quite unaware that murder was happening near him in that quarter hour after midnight.

He had nothing to do with it and wanted nothing. Still it wasn't particularly fortunate for him that the killer would be able to escape only over his dead body . . .

A few minutes after the clock had struck, Kerry Ott came back to life.

Something—the reverberation of the ponderous bell, perhaps—had penetrated his remote absorption. He looked up at the peeled, discoloured wallpaper in front of him, in the dingy corner where he sat writing. What time was it? What was happening, if anything? And where was he anyway?

He had been working with intense concentration for an incalculable number of unstirring hours on the last act of his new comedy, which he had contracted to have in his producer's hands by the fifteenth of the month, under penalty for delay. Living, while he wrote, in an imagined time and an imagined place, while a set of characters of his own invention made their entrances and their exits before his eyes and spoke their lines to his inner hearing, for the moment he could not have told what day of the week it was, and hardly his own name.

But now something had broken the wall around him, and he was back on earth.

He was in the small side room of the six-room unfurnished railroad flat, on the top floor of the four-story old tenement called Argyll Hall in the East Sixties, which he had rented a few days ago as a hideout while he finished his play. A kitchen table to write on and a kitchen chair to sit on, a dilapidated chest of drawers to hold his necessary shirts and socks, and an army cot in the corner to collapse on when exhausted—he had bought the lot for ten dollars at a secondhand place down on Third Avenue, and anything more would have been only an invitation to ease and distraction.

A hundred watt bulb hanging from the ceiling just back of his left shoulder gave him light. A ream of yellow paper lay on the table, together with a smaller sheaf of completed draft, covered with his large firm black handwriting. The floor around him was littered ankle deep with many times as many crumped and discarded ones, like a strewing of wilted yellow chrysanthemums.

His big awkward frame seemed to have grown to his chair—to have become wood like it, and a part of it. He put down his pencil, and stretched himself. He was tired in every muscle and brain cell.

The only window of the room, beside him, was shut and its heavy green shade was pulled down. He liked to work in small, closed places, with a draftless stillness all about him and by artificial light—as remote as the silent centre of the earth, lit by the flare of the never-setting sun, which burns pallidly and forever at the core of things, and where no wind blows.

No wind blew now. And all around him in the dingy room there was, as always, the silence. But there had been an interruption. The thread of the play had slipped from him. The inaudible voices no longer spoke. The substanceless characters had no more life.

He found he had no remotest idea of the time. His watch had stopped at a quarter after three. It had been ten o'clock of the morning when he had stumbled up groggy-eyed and swaying still from three hours sleep and had sat down, breakfastless, to resume work. He had lost all awareness of the passage of time since—whether it was daylight still, or whether the night had come, or the dawn of a tomorrow.

Somewhere, a minute or two ago, a clock had struck. It must have been that which had disturbed him. The great brazen bonging bell in the clock-tower around the corner on Third Avenue. Once or twice before, during the past days, he had felt its slow repercussions throb through the shut-in atmosphere of his room—at times perhaps when there was no street traffic to dissipate them, or when the wind was right. A thudding faintly felt in the marrow of his bones, like the strike of a muffled hammer on padded wood.

He thought back, counting the echoes of those slow beats in his memory —*twelve*. It was midnight, then. Unless it was noon again.

He pulled aside the shade from the window. A black and yellow spider, with long black legs, had spun its web across the dingy unwashed pane. It looked at him with jet points of eyes, not moving when it saw him.

What thoughts were in its brain, hell knew, at the great bland face and slow mild stare of the maker of plays appearing around the shade edge above it. Perhaps that doom's day had come on it, in its life of hidden, sticky murder. Paralysed, it awaited the blow which would smash it.

But it was no harm to him. He had no interest in destroying it. He was not God.

He looked out, eating crackers.

Outside, darkness lay on the world. Night, then, and the middle of it had been the stroke which he had felt subconsciously. About two or three minutes after midnight now.

Twelve or fifteen feet across an alleyway he looked out on a brick wall set with windows—the side of the six-storey apartment building next door, called by some name such as the Royal Arms, an old-fashioned but still respectable pile, several degrees higher in the social and financial scale than the decayed cold-water old walk-up he was in.

There was a small window with a dark frosted pane, open about six inches from the top, directly across from him—the bathroom window, by its looks, of the rear apartment opposite. There were two pairs of larger windows to the left of it. A light flicked out and a rim of shadow cut across the side wall just above those windows—a rim beneath which was blackness, and above which was blackness, also, though a shade less black. A pair of vague wavering shadows were moving on the wall above that shadow rim—a pair of gargoyle shapes, fantastic and grotesque, one of them resembling a human figure standing on its head and waving its legs in the air, the other a human figure hopping on one foot, holding its thumb derisively to its nose. There was a thin line above them like a shadow of a rope, motionless and horizontal.

The shadows changed shape and position—for a while like boys leaping with upstretched arms, or suddenly swooping and stooping, as if tossing a beanbag back and forth, then both of them suddenly sprang together and merged in a kind of jitterbug dance . . . Kerry Ott watched with mild interest for a full two or three minutes, eating crackers, before the thing finally faded down and vanished.

He looked down into the blackness of the alley four stories below, when the shadow show was over. Two dark shapes of men, more to be guessed at than seen, were hurrying down the alley towards the rear of the Royal Arms. There was something in their agitated stride, and perhaps also a certain ponderosity of bulk they had, which reminded him of a pair of Keystone cops, complete with walrus mustaches, brass-buttoned frock coats, and grey helmets, diligently pursuing a mocking quick-footed shadow all around the barn. He smiled mildly at the suggestion of comedy flatfoot futility.

Light suddenly flashed on behind the little frosted window opposite, as the two dark hurrying figures reached the rear of the Royal Arms, turning back. Through the opening at the top of the window he could see a corner section of midnight blue wall, studded with silver stars, and a portion of chromium shower-curtain bar, with a light-cord hanging from the ceiling near it. A naked arm had reached up and pulled the light on, in that instant.

Nothing distinct—just a moment's glimpse of a cord-grasping hand and a portion of a bare human arm, perhaps a woman's hand and arm, perhaps a meagre man's, undressed for a bath, or in a sleeveless summer garment. As the light went on, the arm had been retracted down. The light remained behind the pane. The smoke of a cigarette came drifting enigmatically up toward the ceiling.

Kerry Ott had finished his box of crackers. He let his window shade drop back into place. He picked up his watch and wound it, setting it at approximately 12:06, and went back to work.

At last he arose ponderously and stiffly, pushing back his chair, wading through the crumpled yellow papers which crushed beneath his shuffling feet with the feel of trodden popcorn. He picked up a cake of soap from the top of his chest of drawers. At the door he took a towel from a wooden horse which stood tilted against the wall, on a pile of three or four paint-smeared planks stacked up against the baseboard—gear left by painters at some date indefinite, together with some buckets of dried paints and a few rolls of dusty wallpaper.

He went out, feeling for the small bulb outside the door and turning it on. He went back down the long dim-lit railroad hall of the flat, past the doorways of black unfurnished rooms, to the kitchen in the back.

He hadn't bothered to supply bulbs for more than his work room light and the one small hall light. In the kitchen he found the iron sink by feel, across the sagging floor. He washed his face and eyes and the back of his neck beneath the slow-running, rusty faucet, in darkness, and dried himself with the rough towel. Picking up his soap again, he went back up the hall to his little room, turning off the hall light in passing.

He draped his damp towel over the tilted sawhorse and tossed his wet soap towards the bureau top. His watch said 12:14 now. He turned off the light above his writing table and felt his way back to his cot in the far corner, where he sat down and pulled off his shoes, then flung himself back, utterly exhausted, with the figures of his play still in his mind.

If beyond his closed and shaded window, across the alleyway, in the fourth floor rear apartment of the Royal Arms, a woman screamed in that moment as swift death struck her, he did not hear it, and he did not know it.

Nor know that in that apartment over there a previous murder had been done, when he had been looking out. And that he had glimpsed the murderer, a man whose face he had not seen, nor would recognize if he should see it.

He knew nothing about it, Kerry Ott. He was never on that murder scene. He was separated from it by a closed window, an alleyway, and a brick wall. He was probably the only man who had a view into that murder apartment while both the front door was chained and the rear window was locked, if that was in any way important. But he had seen nothing.

He was just the man across the alley, not knowing and not hearing, seeing only that vague little, during those twelve minutes of frenzied murder . . .

The third operator from the end on the Harkness-4 exchange board—shuttling her wires with rapid hands, murmuring incessantly with her soft cooing voice into her headphone—saw a light flash on at the left side of her board, connection 1203.

'Ridgewood naine, one-naine-thurree-thurree,' she murmured. 'Deposit fifteen cents for five minutes, please . . . We are not allowed to give out the time, madam. Dial Meridian seven one-two-one-two . . . I will connect you with Information . . . What number were you calling? Harkness four, four-eight-four-three has been changed to Harkness thurree-one-naine . . . I will connect you with Information . . . We are not allowed to give out the time, sir. Dial Meridian . . .'

But the time, as she happened to glance and notice, was just 1203, by the minute-turning electric clock above the board.

There was a red light at 12:03. McCue, Dan'l J.'s number, if she had known it, at 219 East Sixty-somethingth Street. Miles away from where she sat shuttling her loom of wires, weaving the city fates, old Dan McCue had seized his phone in his great thickveined hand and had dialled the operator.

In case of emergency, dial operator, the book says.

It was just one more light in a busy midnight hour to her. She plugged in.

'Operator,' she said.

'Hel—'

A kind of groaning sound followed by a thump, came over the wire. No word beyond that one meaningless syllable, however.

'Operator,' she repeated. 'What number did you want?'

But Harkness 4-1203 gave her no number. There was only the silence in her earphones, after that groaning bump.

She listened efficiently. The red light flashed out at the end of a moment, as the instrument was quietly replaced. So there was no need for her even to report to the trouble desk that Harkness 4-1203 was temporarily out of order. She shuttled her wires with rapid hands, disconnecting 1203 and connecting a hundred other calls, and bothered no more about it.

So whether old Dan McCue had felt that first crushing, paralysing blow crash down on him, and had tried dazedly, with a dying effort, to summon help, or had died totally unwarned, must remain uncertain, like some other items of that scene. He had seized his phone, and jerked the dial round, and uttered that one croaking syllable—that was all. But he might merely have been trying to call a Hellgate number, or Helsinki, Finland.

The uncompleted call fixed the time of his murder, anyway. The coincidence of the phone number and the time had registered on the operator's mind—1203 calling at 12:03—and she would be able to give Tuxedo Johnny Blythe that much information, when he queried her later if she had heard anything. Which information Tuxedo Johnny would pass on to Big Bat O'Brien of homicide, together with all the details that he could remember of every man he had met from the time he left old Dan's door, around that murder time, up to the time of that second murder back up in the dark apartment a dozen minutes later.

After he had recovered his wits a little, and was trying to think it out.

Tuxedo Johnny Blythe had had almost no wits at all, to say the best about it, when he first came cascading down the narrow marble stairs beside the elevator shaft in the Royal Arms from old Dan McCue's door on the fourth floor.

What the exact time was he didn't know. His wrist watch had said around 12:10, he remembered having seen subconsciously, staring at his hand as he sped down. It had been running anywhere from five to nine minutes fast recently, however, as he knew, and so was subject to an indeterminate correction, which he would have no opportunity to make.

It wasn't to consult the time, though, that Tuxedo Johnny was holding up his hand and staring at it with bugging eyes as he rushed down the stairs. There was blood on it—a red slipperiness on his fingers and in the crevices of his palm, which had a still fresh warm, abhorrent feeling.

*Blood!* his Adam's apple seemed to bubble. *My God, it's slippery!* he thought or bubbled. *How in hell did I get all that on me?*

With the instinctive revulsion of a neat, fastidious and well-manicured man—with the inchoate, inane reaction of almost any kind of man in a like moment—he snatched his handkerchief forth from his breast pocket, and pulled at his fingers to wipe them off as he ran. But it would need soap and water. He balled the linen away in his hip pocket as he rounded the elevator shaft on the second floor and poured his agitated two hundred pounds on down towards the lobby.

'Blood!' his throat bubbled.

In spite of his police background, Tuxedo Johnny had had singularly little contact with blood of any kind before, either in accident or murder. He had never been a soldier or even a rabbit-hunter. Even the sight of his own blood always agitated him—a minor cut on the chin while shaving would cause him an anxious and painstaking application of cold towels and styptic collodion, and keep him fingering the place for hours afterwards imagining it still oozing. He had given himself such an invisible nick on the train up from Washington this evening to see old Dan, as it happened, belatedly scraping away his five o'clock shadow outside Baltimore; and he touched the spot now again, with a connection of instinctive thought. But it had dried up as hard as a beetle's shard, of course, hours ago.

There was blood up there on old Dan's doorknob, he thought with horror. Perhaps on the door-frame, also, and the sill—he wasn't sure. Maybe not a great amount, though it seemed to him for the moment that it must be like a huge and pouring tide, which was rushing out from beneath Dan's door and flooding down the stairs after him.

Blood! What else? He must think over every detail. He must keep cool, he told himself—he must not be panicked—being panicked completely.

The slow little gilt elevator in its openwork shaft had gone up, answering that ring from the floor above old Dan's. The car had passed him in its ascent when he was halfway down between the third and second floors, with its bald-headed, pan-faced, operator standing at the control, dressed in a plum-coloured jacket with black frogs and a pair of baggy tweed pants, and holding something to his mouth—a sandwich or a bite of cake—which he was meditatively eating.

He might have been down in the basement having supper. Some new man, the thought flashed to Tuxedo Johnny, whom he had never seen before. But he hadn't been in New York for several months and around to see old Dan, and the whole staff of the apartment house quite possibly had changed.

He hadn't waited for the elevator, anyway. The front door was the only way a killer could get away . . .

That there might be anyone still up there in old Dan's apartment did not occur to him. And whether there was, at that precise moment, was something which would later baffle much better cops than he had ever been.

Tuxedo Johnny Blythe had been, before going to Washington with the F.A.B., old Dan McCue's political lieutenant and right hand man for fifteen years, and had occupied various minor positions in the city government, having a knack for smoothing things over and getting along with people.

He had got his name of Tuxedo Johnny, not because he invariably wore a black tie after six o'clock, but because he had been, eighteen or so years before, one of the famous tuxedo Cops—one of the half dozen graduates appointed to the force by Commissioner Enfield as lieutenants, after an oral examination and on the basis of their athletic records, without going through the ranks. It had been the intention at the time to appoint six more the same way each year, and so gradually build up a nucleus from which future ranking officers could be drawn. The experiment was not continued the next year however, when Waldron succeeded Enfield. Of the original half dozen, two had soon resigned to go into banking, one to join the army, one to become a Trappist monk, and one, of course, is still a star in Hollywood.

Tuxedo Johnny Blythe, who had remained on the force the longest of any of them, something less than three years, had resigned when he married Dan McCue's daughter at the big wedding at St Christopher's. She had Renoed him two years later, taking the kid, and had married Paul Bean, but the arrangement had been friendly, and it had not interfered with his relations with old Dan.

It would not be an overstatement to say that any tough police sergeant who had got his the hard way had never been able to regard the idea of a Tuxedo Cop with anything but an extreme impassivity of face—Tuxedo Johnny Blythe possibly even more than the rest, with his plump, pink-cheeked, surprised and round-eyed look, resembling somewhat the look of a plump good-natured nine-months-old baby examining a feather. No doubt in many ways he was something of a fathead. He wasn't quite a walrus-mustached, heel-clicking comedy Keystone Cop, however, and had never been quite that bad. At least he had had a certain amount of police training and with it he still retained an underlying police awareness, however confused. If there were some things which he didn't think of, and some things which he failed to see—if, as he felt forced to confess to Big Bat O'Brien later with regret, he had played it dumb—it is doubtful if most men would have acted any more intelligently in the circumstances, and perhaps the average not quite so well.

Even in his agitation he was automatically recording everything in the halls and on the stairs, as he went down, but there were no shadows that were tangible. Just empty pockets of darkness. The apartment doors on each floor had been closed—behind one, the murmur of a man's droning voice, perhaps a radio newscaster; behind another, the sound of dance music. Behind all the other doors, what had seemed only a heavy sleeping silence.

The cables of the elevator had ceased vibrating; it had reached the fifth floor, from which that ring had come. The little marble-tiled lobby seemed deserted. The front doorway was open, and there was no sound of car or footsteps out on the quiet midnight street.

Tuxedo Johnny had headed downstairs to reach the front door as quickly as possible, with the one thought in his mind of seeing someone on the way, or possibly out on the midnight street beyond. He did not continue his rush straight for the door now, however. On the bottom step of the stairs, he stopped.

In the quiet and apparently deserted lobby, he had seen the movement of a shadow. There was someone standing back of one of the pillars. He had stepped behind it rather quickly, Tuxedo Johnny thought, just as he himself had come in sight.

The first man he had met since leaving old Dan's door, the thought burned itself into Tuxedo Johnny's mind. He must remember every detail—not forget one.

The pillar didn't hide the man behind it completely. He was a big man, dressed in a blue patrolman's uniform. He had fat hands and wrists beyond the ends of his blue sleeves, and white socks beneath the bottoms of his blue pants.

After a moment, as Tuxedo Johnny Blythe remained halted on the bottom step, looking at him, the man behind the pillar came on out. He swung his stick with measured ease. He had a big hooked nose and a broad face, set with small green sliding eyes. One of the buttons of his tunic was unfastened over his belly, and he made a gesture of buttoning it.

'Evening, Lieutenant Blythe,' he said, adjusting the cap.

There were twenty thousand on the force, thought Tuxedo Johnny. He couldn't know them all. The patrolman knew him, anyway.

'Slipsky, sir,' said the big patrolman, sliding his eyes. 'I used to be on the—under you for a while in the old precinct back in 'twenty-nine, Lieutenant. I'm just, uh, investigating.'

'Someone has sent in an alarm already, have they?' said Tuxedo Johnny.

'An alarm?' said Slipsky, his eyes abruptly motionless. 'About what, Lieutenant?'

'Old Dan! Dan McCue—wait a minute!' said Tuxedo Johnny

haggardly, as Slipsky half wheeled, glancing over his shoulder, as if to bolt headlong out of the door. 'Where the devil are you going?

'No need of going off half-cocked,' he added, catching his breath. 'We'll have to see what it is first. I may have got a little excited. But he didn't answer the doorbell, and there's blood—blood on the doorknob! But maybe it's not murder. We'll have to see.'

'Murder?' said Slipsky, as if he had never heard the word before. 'Mr McCue? When?'

'Someone must have just come from there—'

'I hadn't heard anything about it, Lieutenant,' said Slipsky. 'I only just came in the lobby a minute ago. I was just asking Sam Boaz, the elevator man, how things was, only he got a call up. I was just waiting for him to come back down.'

'You've been here only a minute?' said Tuxedo Johnny. 'Someone might have gone out then—'

'Only a couple of minutes, anyway, Lieutenant. I came in just at midnight, and it's only eleven-fif—well, I guess the clock here's not running. I thought it was. But not more than seven or eight minutes, anyway, Lieutenant.'

His wrist watch said 12:12, Tuxedo Johnny saw now, looking at it finally. Even though it might be those five or nine minutes fast, Slipsky must have been here in the lobby for an appreciable number of minutes. The fat patrolman was endeavouring to minimize the time, he realized somewhat tardily. He might have been in here since around 11:50, the time the lobby clock said, or he would have noticed when he came in that it had stopped.

It had probably been just a sense of uneasiness at having been caught loitering with the elevator man which had caused him to step back of the pillar, it occurred to Tuxedo Johnny somewhat belatedly, as well. Just for a moment, in the movement of that shadow, he had thought he had seen something sinister . . .

He recalled Slipsky now vaguely, back over the years. A younger and much thinner cop, though with those same sliding green eyes. His nickname had been Slippery or Slippy. Not a particularly good record, Tuxedo Johnny had an impression—a back-room crap-shooter. Slipsky had once come to him for help in getting himself out of some jam, he thought. Still that made no difference now.

'Forget it, Slippy,' he said, taking a breath. 'No one could have gone out while you've been here without your seeing him, I suppose?'

But it was an automatic question. The answer was obvious. Bad cop though he had been and still might be, Slippy would have seen anyone going out.

The elevator had come rattling down again. There was no passenger in it. The bald-headed, pan-faced operator stopped it jerkily at the lobby floor and opened the grilled doors.

'That Kitty Weisenkranz's damned brats again!' he said, with a flat glare, stepping out. 'They're always sneaking up and ringing the bell from the fifth floor and then beating it down again, or setting fires in the halls or dumping garbage down the shaft, or some other dirty trick like that, damn their slippery hides! Why in hell couldn't their mother have kept them in Chicago? McCue doesn't like them, neither, living right across the hall from him. Some day I'll catch them and carve my initials on them. You know me, Slippy.'

The second man he had seen; Tuxedo Johnny ticked him off. Or had met—he had glimpsed the elevator man ascending in the cage as he came down, of course.

'No one on the fifth floor?' he asked automatically.

'That's what I said, sweetheart! Are you waiting to go up?'

'You mustn't mind old Sam, Lieutenant,' said Slipsky, sliding his eyes. 'Greatest dead-pan kidder you ever saw. A heart of gold. Him and me was roommates for two years at—at a place we used to live at. Lieutenant Blythe belongs to the cops, Sam. He used to be at the old precinct back when I was. He's just been up trying to get into Mr McCue's apartment, but nobody answers. And there's blood all over the doorknob. He's afraid it looks bad.'

'McCue!' said Boaz. 'You mean somebody had done him in? Why, God a'mighty, if that ain't tough! You mean you want me to go up and see? I got a pass key, but I'm not supposed to use it without permission—'

'I have a key myself!' said Tuxedo Johnny. 'For God's sake, you're new here, or you'd know it. The door is chained on the inside! I couldn't get in. Then when I saw the blood—'

He tried to think. They would have to get in by the back.

'You mean there's somebody still up in the apartment?' said Boaz uneasily. 'Do you think we ought to call the cops? Well, hell, of course you're one yourself, Lieutenant. And Slippy Slipsky here—ain't you, Slippy?'

'He must have got out some other way,' said Tuxedo Johnny—beginning to get calmed down a little and to think about it. 'I'm not a cop myself. I just used to be. When Dan didn't answer and I saw the blood, the first thing I thought of was the front door, to see if I could catch him. But Slipsky's been here, and he couldn't have come out this way. The door chain answers that, anyway. I guess I didn't think. Who's been up to see Mr McCue this evening?'

he added as an afterthought—it was the police thing to inquire.

'Why, Mr Bean was up to see him about eleven, but he left some time ago,' Boaz said. 'He's been his only visitor.'

'Paul Bean, his lawyer?' Tuxedo Johnny asked mechanically.

'That's the guy. He brought Mr McCue up a bottle of champagne. I didn't see him go out, but he generally stays only about half an hour. Father Finley said he had gone, anyway—I forgot about him. I don't know what time he went up. I brought him down maybe twenty or twenty-five minutes ago, though, about a quarter of twelve—he said he'd stopped in for a shave. He's a kind of goofy little guy that's nuts on cats, a friend of Mr McCue's. He isn't a real priest, I don't think, but that's what he calls himself. He isn't there any more, either, anyway.'

'I know him,' Tuxedo Johnny said. 'He gave Mr McCue's daughter a cat last year that scratched her and gave her blood poisoning. What other ways are there that anybody could have got away, Boaz? Can you think?'

'Well, there's the rear fire escape. A guy could climb down that, if nobody was out in back to see him.'

'Or up and across the roofs, perhaps,' said Tuxedo Johnny—never having been up to the Royal Arms roof, but trying now to get a picture of all other possible ways.

'Not that way,' said Boaz. 'There's an alley between us and the old dump next door that would take a goat to jump. Its roof is two stories lower, anyway. The Susskind loft's on the other side, ten or twelve stories high without a window. If there's been anybody in Mr McCue's apartment all evening besides Mr Bean and Father Finley, I guess he either got away down the fire escape, or he didn't get away at all.'

'That's what I was trying to get the picture of,' said Tuxedo Johnny, drawing a deep breath. 'Looks like we'll have to go ahead and get in the backway, Slippy. You've got your gun?'

'Well, Lieutenant,' said Slipsky, sliding his eyes, 'that's one of the things— As a matter of fact, I was sort of thinking it might be a good idea for me to kind of go up and keep watch on the front door, or something, while you went around—'

'For God's sake, are you afraid?' said Tuxedo Johnny, not able to believe that Slipsky really was, that even a bad cop could be afraid of anything, though afraid enough himself. 'Of course not! You're the patrolman on the beat. You'll have to make entrance with me, to see what we find.

'Perhaps you'd better ring up headquarters right away, Boaz,' he added, with an additional flash of police thought, as he was starting for the door. 'Get hold of Inspector Bat O'Brien of homicide. Say you're calling for Tuxedo Johnny Blythe, who's just got in from Washington. Tell Big Bat that I'm breaking in with the beat patrolman into Dan McCue's apartment, to investigate what looks like some bad play, after finding the door chained on the inside and no response. Say that I just wanted him to be alerted, in case something has happened to Dan. I'll call him again in a few minutes from Dan's apartment, if it turns out to have been murder.'

With no idea that it would be two murders up there. With none that, before very long, there would be a third body lying in the black alley down which he and Slipsky were hurrying in a moment more, towards the fire escape in back.

## CHAPTER THREE

### Over Whose Dead Body

A scant three or four minutes, or perhaps less, had elapsed since Tuxedo Johnny had left old Dan's door and come rushing down the stairs, with the feel of blood on his hands that was slippery and still warm.

So far he had done and was still doing, it seemed to him, the only thing he could have. Having encountered Slipsky and ascertained that there was no possibility that anyone could have got away out the front door of the building. To have inquired who Dan's visitors had been tonight, and what other ways out of his apartment there might be. To hurry back to break in with Slipsky. It was just what Big Bat himself would do, he thought, if confronted by blood on a door knob and a chained door.

As yet he had encountered only Slipsky and the pan-faced elevator man. But the whole apartment house couldn't be all asleep. There had been a man's muffled voice behind one door, he remembered, and the sound of dance music behind another. There had been the silences behind the other doors which had almost seemed to shout.

Who lived behind all those doors, those compact and hidden walls, above and below and across from Dan's? Had one of them, on the fourth floor across from Dan's been open just a crack? For the life of him, he could not remember now. He could only remember releasing the knob, with a wild glance around him, looking at his hand with horror, and fleeing.

The anonymity of a city apartment house, where no one knows who lives across the hall! Like the dead within a cemetery. Yet when the trumpet of murder blows, out of their graves they swarm, with staring eyes.

Kitty Weisenkranz's boys, Chicago—suddenly, as he went down the alley, that name which Boaz had spoken clicked in Tuxedo Johnny's mind. Why, she must be Kitty Kane! Kitty Kane—diminutive, black-eyed, and utterly alluring—of the *Jollities* and the Nestor Club, almost twenty years ago.

He had not forgotten her, with her look of a shy young woods dryad and her loving, sinful heart. Eighteen years old, and old as Egypt. He had been wild about her, romantic young sap that he had been. Once, when he had been a young lieutenant, he had jeopardized his career for her, bluffing and bulldozing a visiting Texas oil man into withdrawing a blackmail charge against her which had her caught cold. He had protected her and loved her, though knowing that there were a dozen more. At least she had always cared for him more than the others, who had been just men with dough.

Years ago she had passed out of his life, marrying O.K. Weisenkranz, the big cloak-and-suit man out in Chicago. Weisenkranz had cut his throat a year or two ago in a fit of depression—had been found lying before his bathroom mirror with his jugular severed and a razor beside him. And though there had been some question as to whether he had been right-handed, and also as to whether a man could so nearly decapitate himself, the verdict had ultimately been suicide. Tuxedo Johnny Blythe had heard the details from Big Bat O'Brien, who had known Kitty, too.

A vital image—a still remembered flame. She would be thirty-six or seven now, and with her two boys by Weisenkranz. But her slender burning beauty could have hardly changed. She was the sort of girl who would never grow old. She must have come back to New York fairly recently, to live in the Royal Arms here, right across the hall from old Dan's apartment, Boaz had said. At this very moment not far away from him, perhaps, alive and breathing and awake.

*I wonder if she would remember me still?* thought Tuxedo Johnny Blythe, with a pounding of his heart. And knew the answer as he asked the question: *Of course! Of course she would . . .*

'Jeez!' Slipsky croaked behind him, stumbling against an ash can with a bang. 'There goes another one! I don't see how you can see, Lieutenant. It's darker than the bottom of the ink. Cripes! Was that another dead cat?'

Kitty Kane!

*     *     *

They had come to the spiked iron fence that enclosed the rear areaway of the Royal Arms. Tuxedo Johnny Blythe found the latch of the gate. With Slipsky at his heels, he pushed on through.

The small high silver moon, just tipping past the edge of the tall surrounding roofs, shone down on the pavement in a crazy rhomboid design, with sharp rectangular edges of blackness. There was a square of yellow light from the rear basement door, standing open, with a vista of rows of ash cans and a boilerroom inside. A grilled fire escape zigzagged up the rear brick wall, its bottom ladder moored by chains to hooks against the wall.

A red eye seemed to brighten and glow a moment in the black edge of the areaway, near the light of the basement door.

'Rasmussen?' said Slipsky, in a croak.

'Ya.'

'What are you doing there, Swede?'

'Smoking mine pipe.'

'How long have you been out here?'

'About ten minutes.'

'Swede Rasmussen, the janitor, Lieutenant,' said Slipsky, panting. 'He's a friend of old Sam Boaz's, too. He lives on the ground floor at the back.'

'The janitor? That's who I thought it probably was,' said Tuxedo Johnny, with an unavoidable croak himself.

The janitor of the Royal Arms came forward into the yellow basement door light—a small hunchbacked figure, dragging one leg after him, with a slow deliberate twisting of his hip. He had a dark ridge of hair like a clipped horse's mane, and a dish-shaped face set with deep sockets, out of which peered his burning eyes, behind slow smoke.

*The third man*, thought Tuxedo Johnny Blythe, *I've seen since leaving old Dan's door.*

'This is Lieutenant Blythe, Swede,' said Slipsky. 'He thinks we ought to climb up to Mr McCue's apartment and investigate. There's blood on his doorknob and nobody answers. The door is chained on the inside.'

'Ya?'

'You've been out here fifteen minutes, Rasmussen?' said Tuxedo Johnny, watching those burning eyes. 'Happen to see anything?'

Rasmussen sucked his pipe to a red glow.

'Vot sort of ding?' he said.

'Anything particular. I thought if there was something wrong with his apartment—'

'Dere is nutting wrong vit' McCue's apartment dot I know of,' said Rasmussen, smoking. 'Maybe a faucet vasher needs fixing, dot iss all.'

Tuxedo Johnny looked at him a moment. 'All right.'

'Lieutenant Blythe means about the old man himself, Swede,' said Slipsky uneasily. 'I know you, you cagey old coot. You like to have it dragged out of you. What do you know about Mr McCue?'

'McCue?'

'For hell's sake, Swede!'

Rasmussen took his pipe out of his mouth.

'McCue iss dead,' he stated.

'How do you know?' said Tuxedo Johnny. 'Have you been up there? Where have you been?'

'Here,' said Rasmussen, putting his pipe back in his mouth. 'Yoost here, Mr Policeman. Out smoking mine pipe and looking up at det moon. But I see McCue's lights go out not fife or six minutes ago. And den I see dot deffil flying out det vindow.'

'What devil?'

Rasmussen sucked his pipe to a glow.

'I see det vindow slide up vidout no noise,' he said. 'I see dot deffil creeping out on det fire escape, like he vas going to fly away. *Ya, ya,* I say to mineself! *Ya, ya, I know who you are yet, Mr Deffil, and I know vot you haf been doing!*'

Tuxedo Johnny Blythe felt a coldness rushing down his spine. The burning eyes of the hunchbacked man were uncanny and inhuman. His thick guttural voice wasn't man-like. He looked like a demon himself. Like the living fiend. 'You saw some man you knew leaving Mr McCue's apartment a few minutes ago, Swede?' said Slipsky uneasily, asking the question which Tuxedo Johnny Blythe might have asked but for the coldness of his tongue.

'*Nei,*' said Rasmussen, smoking.

'I thought you said you knew him, Swede—'

'Ya.' He pulled on his pipe once more, deliberately. 'It vass neider man nor voman,' he stated. 'It vas nuttings human, but it vass det Old Vun out of hell dot had come to get his own. "He valketh up and down like a raging lion, seeking vot he may devour," det Book says. Det soul of dot bad old man has belonged to him already. And ven I see him coming from det vindow, dere is someding comes and tells me inside here—' he rapped his knuckles—'dot old Dan McCue vill nefer bodder mine daughter Hulda, and try to make her take a drink vit him ven she goes up to clean his apartment. Climb up, and break in all you vant, if you do not belief me. You vill find der Old Vun inside vit him, munching on his bones. It iss too late, yentelmen.'

He put his pipe into his mouth and puffed contentedly, with his hands behind him.

*Cracked!* thought Tuxedo Johnny Blythe. He felt a crazed desire to laugh, on the rebound. The janitor's weird portentous manner and glaring eyes had almost made him believe in the devil, himself. But Rasmussen was just a crackpot with a religious streak, enjoying being important and the centre of attention. The preposterous exaggeration of the gnome man was a relief in itself. It mustn't be anywhere near as bad as he had thought, Tuxedo Johnny told himself. He felt himself, for the first time, curiously steadied.

'You mean he's still in there?'

'Ya. He did not fly away. Ven he looked down and saw me standing smoking mine pipe and vatching up at him, he yumped back in, vidout no sound, and closed det vindow quick. Vy? I had mine Testament in mine hip pocket. It took det vind out of his sails. He could not pass it. He vent pack to finish his meal and vait for me to go away. But I haf been vatching.'

'How do you reach the fire escape, Swede?' said Slipsky, looking up uneasily.

'I don't,' said the lame janitor. He took his pipe out of his mouth. 'You can go in det basement and up to mine apartment, and out through Hulda's vindow,' he said. 'She hass gone to midnight church, so it iss all right. If you do not belief me.'

But Tuxedo Johnny Blythe had already turned to the high spiked fence that enclosed the areaway, where it joined the rear wall. He stepped up on the horizontal crossbar of the fence halfway up, and reached up to the bottom of the slanted iron escape ladder, which overhung the building corner.

Holding it by his finger tips to steady himself, he stepped to the top of the fence, from where it was only another four-foot stretch up onto the moored-up ladder. He made it, with a voiceless little grunt, and went along the edges of the ladder steps to the first floor landing. Slipsky, as a qualified flatfoot, though a few years older than he was and overbellied, could make it with even less effort, he thought.

Slipsky didn't, though. As Tuxedo Johnny Blythe paused on the landing, he saw the shoulders and padded hindquarters of the overgrown patrolman disappearing into the basement doorway underfoot.

'Iss too fat,' said Rasmussen below. Pulling on his pipe and looking up, he followed Slipsky in. 'Slippy iss afraid he vould split his breeches. Iss going up t'rough mine apartment, mine girl Hulda's room. He vill make it yoost as quick.'

The lame gnome went in, closing the basement door behind him. Without that yellow light it was dark as pitch now in the areaway, though the escape above was visible against the lighter sky. Tuxedo Johnny sweated.

Slipsky did make it as quickly, perhaps, or quicker than he could have climbed the fence. After thirty or forty seconds the door of a bedroom, beyond the dark open window beside the first floor landing, was flung open, emitting a strafe of light from a hall beyond, and Slipsky's bulky form came tiptoeing across the semi-obscurity of the room, with the gnome janitor standing smoking at the door behind him.

If Slipsky had quit, if he had fled, Tuxedo Johnny would not have gone on up alone. He would have quit, would have fled with him—his tautened nerves cried out to. But Slipsky, though uneager, was the solid blue-clad law. To Slipsky, he was still to an extent the law himself, he understood in part, though not too comprehensively. As the overbellied patrol man stepped out over the window ledge with a sighing groan, Tuxedo Johnny Blythe was already starting on up.

No one shouted out at him; no one, awakened previously by any sound from Dan McCue's above, was starting forth in terror. Incredible that anything had happened to Dan within the last half dozen minutes. Tuxedo Johnny Blythe had a crazy feeling that he had been fantastically mistaken, that it was all a dream. But the feel of the blood was still upon his hand, and on his mind the terrible silence there had been in old Dan's apartment.

Half a flight behind him, the iron steps punged to Slipsky's more solid tread and Slipsky's blue-clad form was a black bulk in the night. He was real, anyway. Slipsky at least was real. He was not a dream walking up the iron stairs.

His wrist watch said 12:18 when he reached the fourth floor landing, outside old Dan's dark moon-gleaming library window. Tuxedo Johnny pressed his face against the glass. He could see something white upon the floor inside, like a man's white face . . . No, it was a piece of paper or a cocktail napkin, probably. Dead men's faces are not as white as that.

There was a silence beyond the window. He could hear only the *thump-thump-thump* of his own pulse. Yet for an instant he had a ghastly feeling of some living, creeping presence beyond the dark glass. Of something breathing mutely, with strangled breath, more terrible than the dead.

Slipsky had mounted up beside him. 'See anything, Lieutenant?'

'It looks like Danny lying on the floor over by the desk,' Tuxedo Johnny muttered with a dry croak.

'Think someone's still in there?' Slipsky breathed.

'Not a chance,' muttered Tuxedo Johnny putting on a show of steadiness he did not feel. 'For a moment I had a sort of notion—but there isn't anybody. Take your stick and smash the pane above the glass. We've got to get in.'

'It mayn't be locked,' said Slipsky.

He pushed the edge of the sash with his big pudgy fingers, trying it. But it was locked. Gripping his nightstick by the middle, he drove the end of it at the lower edge of the upper pane. The glass crashed, with a sharp, momentous sound, as a third of the pane fell away in shards. Slipsky reached in, turning the catch.


# CHAPTER FOUR

### A Cutting Kill

Old Dan McCue's body lay sprawled on his five thousand dollar Bokhara rug inside in the darkness, beside his eighteen hundred dollar inlaid satinwood Louis Quinze desk. Tuxedo Johnny Blythe knew that he was dead. He stopped three feet away in the darkness only for a moment, to be careful to skirt him, on his way across the room.

'Beside the desk!' he said with a croak. 'There's glass on the rug. Come on in, Slippy. Watch your step. I'll find the light switch. There's a telephone on the desk. You can call up police headquarters. I'll see if the front door's still chained.'

He had gone on across the room to the doorway out to the hall. He found the light switch beside the door and snapped it on. He glanced back over his shoulder in the flood of light which filled the room now. Old Dan lay on his face in his green silk dressing gown. His big freckled hands clutched at the rug. The blows had all struck the back of his head. Any one of them should have been enough to have dealt death, it would seem, but perhaps the first one or two hadn't stopped his tough old heart completely. So there had been a torrent of furious blows and now his grey hair mingled with bone and blood and with the marks of other ill-aimed senseless blows which, missing his occiput, had ripped his jawbone from behind and almost torn off one ear.

The neck of the heavy wine bottle was lying beside him, still with the pink ribbon on it, and the brass fireside poker at his feet. The thick glass had shattered into a score of segments, spilling champagne over the desk and blotter. The poker had done the most of it.

The dark stain seemed to be still spreading into the rug, soaking wider. There he lay. It was worse than Tuxedo Johnny had imagined. Slipsky looked green about his carp-like gills.

'Call up homicide and make it official,' repeated Tuxedo Johnny, swallowing. 'We can't touch anything. Let Big Bat get the picture as it lies.'

He went out into the hall, partially lit by the living room light, toward the front door, stepping swiftly on the waxed mirror-like parquet floor scattered with small silky rugs. The doorways of the dark kitchen and dining room were to his left, of the bedroom to his right. They were all open and unbreathing as he passed, and there was darkness beyond them. There was a faint rustling from the blackness of kitchen or dining room, but that was all.

There was a door chain, which he had not been certain of. It was hooked across the door.

Tuxedo Johnny stood staring at it from three feet away. There must be other ways out of the apartment. He felt and heard the hot breathing of Slipsky on his neck. The overgrown patrolman hadn't paused to telephone, but had dogged him out, in sheer funk at being left alone in that room of rich, quiet death.

'What's the matter, Lieutenant?' Slipsky breathed. 'Chain's still on, is it?'

Tuxedo Johnny put out a hand and felt it, tugging at it. It was metal, and tight within its groove.

'Yes,' he said. 'It seems to be—'

There rose a scream, shrill, terrified and appalling, from somewhere near. From one of those black doorways they had passed.

'Oh, cripes!' said Tuxedo Johnny, with sagging knees.

The stillness of the death apartment rang with that appalling shriek. It was enough to wake the dead, it would have seemed. There was a crash, as of glass shattering, after what seemed an incredible time, yet which must have been immediately.

'Did you hear that, Lieutenant?' mouthed Slipsky. 'Lieutenant, did you hear that? He's still in here!'

Did he hear that! The dead in hell could hear it. Tuxedo Johnny turned, stiffening his knees. 'Try the kitchen, Slipsky!' he managed. 'I'll try the bedroom.'

He put a hand on Slipsky's jellied chest, half pushing him out of the way. He plunged back down the hall, skidding and staggering as one of the small rugs slipped out from underneath him. With his left hand fending out, he struck against the gilt rope-framed mirror that hung on the wall, banging his cheek against the glass and knocking it askew. Half sprawling, recovering balance, he veered left into the blackness beyond the bedroom doorway.

There was nothing moving in the room, it seemed. Yet there was something breathing in it with him. The scream had come from in here. There was a liquid gurgling sound. He went swiftly, feeling with his hands, as in a terrible game of blind man's bluff. Across the room, beyond the foot of the massive bed, near the threshold of the bathroom door he felt something intangibly soft crush beneath his feet, and smelled the terrible fragrance of roses. He heard a bubbling or a breathing from the floor. His foot touched, with a sense of uncontrollable horror, the soft yielding body of the woman who had screamed.

The window shades were drawn, and the bedroom was all in blackness. But in the bathroom there was a small high frosted pane without a shade, open a little at the top. The dim obscurity which came in through it could not be called light. It was only the darkness of the midnight sky without, over the roof of the next building. Still over a brief area of the floor around the threshold it was a little lighter than nothing.

She was lying across the bathroom threshold—her slender body in some kind of silk Chinese lounging gown—her ghostly bloodless face and black mop of hair upon the white tiles of the bathroom floor. There was the feel of broken glass, that gurgling sound, the terrible smell of white roses, as on a bier.

*Kitty Kane!* thought Tuxedo Johnny Blythe, with a spasm of unparalleled horror. Beautiful, alluring Kitty Kane.

For an instant he had dropped on one knee beside her, feeling the broken glass and a wetness through the fabric on his kneecap. Her pale face was in shadow, all the rest of her in darkness. But there was something remembered in her pose which would have told him who she was even without the faintest light at all, even in the blackest blackness. Some line of the outflung arm, of the curved flung hip, the straight graceful silken legs—even now.

Her dark staring eyes were on him. His lips were half parted; her throat seemed to be pulsing and breathing, as if to cry out again at the horror she had seen. And was perhaps still seeing.

His hands reached swiftly for her. How warm, how warm she was! Kitty Kane. Like a girl still in the darkness. Like the girl with warm remembered breath that she had been at eighteen. Moments of hot youth flashed swiftly back to him. But she would never know him now. Never again . . .

'Found her, Lieutenant?' gasped Slipsky from the doorway of the room. 'Where is he? O God, I feel him creeping! Hello, Lieutenant Blythe! Are you in there? Where are the lights?'

'She's—dead,' said Tuxedo Johnny.

He got himself under control. For the moment he had forgotten everything else but her. Had forgotten that there was anyone else in the apartment, even blue-clad Slipsky. On his feet again, his mind working, he turned towards Slipsky, who stood warily crowding the doorway with his big-bellied bulk.

'Hall light switch by the front door, Slipsky!' he managed. 'I'll try to find a light in here. Could he—'

He had started to ask, 'Could he have got out of the bedroom past you?' But he knew the answer to that, he thought. Slipsky had been right there.

There must be a lamp somewhere in the room. Two or three, or maybe half a dozen. One of his swiftly groping hands struck the shade of a standing bridge lamp as he swept them out, back of a lounge chair within arm's length of him.

'Something's the matter with it, Slipsky! Bulb's been unscrewed, it looks like—'

That terrible smell of roses, that terrible gurgling.

Slipsky flashed on the hall light outside. He had found the switch by the front door with palsied hands. The blackness in the bedroom of death seemed to split apart in shadows that leaped and rushed in headlong frantic race, like a flock of shadowy greyhounds, like wild horses rushing darkly. Over huge bed, bureau, dark silver gleam of mirrors, an open closet door with dark suits hanging, those shadows rushed. A glimpse, Tuxedo Johnny had from the edges of his eyes, of that motionless, bloodless form lying on the floor just back of him. . . . He had got the lamp bulb screwed in then at eternal last, though it had been only seconds. He snapped the switch. A flash and again the blackness.

The fuse had blown. The hall, too, was in blackness. The library lights still seemed to be on, though, on a different circuit, down at the end of the hall.

He heard the wail of sirens out in the night. From blocks away, and nearer. They were coming wailing up from all directions. The scream of brakes, the slam of opening car doors. Men's voices, and the thud of feet down the black alley below, towards the back.

Boaz, the pan-faced elevator man, calling Big Bat O'Brien at headquarters, had not merely alerted homicide, but summoned it. The police were here.

Slipsky hadn't remained by the front door. At that sudden blackness he had bolted. As Tuxedo Johnny Blythe came out of the bedroom, he heard the panic-stricken tread of the big-bellied man thudding down the fire escape in back.

He ran back through the lighted library to the fire escape window. He saw Slipsky's vague dark bulk descending like a galumphing elephant a flight and half below, with a flash of white socks beneath his flapping pants legs, with a spreading white slice down his back where his tunic had split apart.

The death still lurking in old Dan McCue's apartment, or else those howling sirens, must have drained the last drop from Slipsky's heart. Tuxedo Johnny didn't blame him. He would have liked to flee, too. But he had fled once already, from the front door, even more brainlessly. He picked up the telephone from the desk edge, above old Dan's sprawled head, and dialled the operator with a swift finger flick.

A thought flashed to him. Perhaps she had heard something over the phone placed so quietly on the edge of old Dan's desk, just above his head.

'This is the police,' he said. 'There's been a murder here. Do you remember noticing any calls over this phone in the past fifteen minutes?'

'There was an uncompleted call at twelve-o-thurree,' she said alertly. 'I don't know what number they were calling, though. A man just said "Hello," and then there was a sort of moan and bump. The phone was hung up again two or three seconds later, so I thought it was all right. I just happened to notice the time—twelve-o-three. It seemed sort of coincidence, the number being one-two-o-thurree. If that helps—'

'Thanks,' he said, and set the instrument down again.

The precise time to the minute could hardly make any difference. Big Bat might like to have it, anyway. His wrist watch said twenty-two minutes past midnight now, but the actual time was probably not much more than a quarter after. Two murders within a dozen minutes.

There was a ringing of the doorbell. He ran down the semi-lit hall to unhook the door chain, which he had failed to slip off. As he passed the doorway of the dark bedroom he felt his feet slip again on one of the misplaced little rugs, and more violently than before.

He sprawled sideways, thrusting out his right hand. Against his palm he felt something like a rope. Something heavy and flashing silver bright came down and struck the side of his head a blinding blow, and he fell headlong to the floor, with the crash of shattering glass about him.

Within seconds, it seemed, the police had come all around the Royal Arms.

Running back down the alley from their cars, some of them were out in the rear areaway before Slipsky, breathless and sweating, had delivered his carcass down the fire escape. They swarmed up from the fence at the corner of the building to the moored ladder, and along it to the first floor landing of the escape, pushing aside the lame gnome janitor who stood on it, baffled, smoking his pipe, and catching Slipsky by the splitting seat of his pants just as he was heaving his fat bulk into the janitor's daughter's window. Others, plainclothesmen who had come from the precinct house around the corner on Second Avenue, had actually been in the lobby down below, looking for the elevator man who had phoned in the alarm to headquarters, when that mortal scream had sounded. Piling into the elevator or running up the stairs, they were at the door or near it when Tuxedo Johnny fell in the hall inside, with that crash of glass.

The squad car men who swarmed up the fire escape let in the precinct men at the front door. They weren't homicide men. They were men with guns, however. They made an immediate search of the apartment, using flashes in the bedroom and turning on all lights in dining room and kitchen.

Room by room, and closet by closet—the two bedroom closets, the rather large and deep hall coat closet, the linen closet, the broom closet in the kitchen. Behind the couches in the living room, behind all chairs. But there was nothing larger than a mouse in the wastepaper basket in the kitchen. It leaped out, with the cunning and terror of its rodent kind, when the hunt drew near the basket, but one of the squad car men snapped his foot down on it as it hit the floor, and it died with a thin shriek.

There was the front door, and there was the fire escape window. But there had been no one on the escape when they had hurried back except the lame janitor on the first floor landing smoking his pipe and looking up, and Slipsky, frantically descending. As for the front door, its chain had been on.

There were the various windows, of library, dining room, and kitchen, as well as of the black murder bedroom itself. There were fifteen of them altogether, facing the side alley and the rear of the building and an air-shaft in the kitchen, but all had bars. They tried even those that were closed, slamming them up and shaking the solid bars, but all were immovable. There was the little frosted bathroom window without bars, but it was only about sixteen inches wide, and high up, and open only about six inches from the top. Even at the widest, either pane would give a clearance of only about twelve inches.

They played their flashes on it from the bedroom, and all around inside the bathroom, at the shower curtain, and through the crack of the door, not crossing that black-eyed woman's body lying on the threshold. But there was no one in the bathroom, and no way out of it, just at sight.

No way out, it seemed, at all.

'No dumbwaiter? No fire door into the next building or apartment?' said Tuxedo Johnny Blythe with dazed eyes. 'No bars loose at all?'

'It doesn't look that way, Johnny.'

'But you'd think there would be something. The chain was still on the front door?'

'In the groove.'

'Maybe he got to the rear of the building while Slipsky and I were fumbling for the lights.' He tried to think. 'When Slipsky flashed the hall light on, there was a rush of shadows. He might have been among them, if he was quick. Got out and down the fire escape ahead of Slipsky, before you and the boys got out back.'

'This guy Rasmussen was down on the first floor landing, watching up, Johnny. Nobody came out the window here from the time you and Slipsky climbed up and broke in till Slipsky came busting out and down, he says. It's black as sin down there, and you can't see much of anything, looking down. If it hadn't been for Slipsky's split tunic and white socks, you mightn't have seen him yourself. But this Rasmussen could see a figure against the lighter sky, looking up. He's one of these kind of guys that if he had one less brain cell he'd be an idiot. But if he had one more, you might figure he had maybe been looking away just a minute, thinking about something else. When he says nothing came out the window, you know nothing did.'

'I guess that's right,' said Tuxedo Johnny dazedly.

They had helped him to his feet after they came in. Sitting sprawled on the slippery floor, slammed against the wall. The skidded rug, the shattered mirror.

'He's not here, anyway. You don't think it was him that banged you, Johnny—or did you just slip?'

'I didn't see him. Maybe I slipped, Jim. He must have been gone by then. He must have got away right after he killed her. There must have been some way.'

The heavy mirror had grazed his head and the side of his face with a thudding blow. He wiped his palm over his temple and cheek again. Sore and contused, but with no feel of blood. His watch crystal had smashed, and its minute hand had snapped off. But the hour and minute made no difference. It was the seconds, the bare seconds that had passed, from the time when she had screamed and he had found her, to the wailing of the sirens and those rushing feet.

There had to be some way.

'I wouldn't worry about it, anyway, Johnny,' said the man named Jim. 'He just got away, that's all. Most guys do get away, when you get down to it. It's not one in a hundred that's caught cold—a guy has to be pretty dumb to wait around till the cops come. And this guy looks as if he might have been damned cool-headed and smart. Still he must have left his tracks somewhere—even the smartest do. Big Bat's homicide boys will find them.'

They had searched the whole apartment, but there was no one there. They took care to disturb nothing. They did not touch old Dan McCue and they did not touch Kitty Kane, lying supine with flung hip in the darkness where she had fallen, in her red silk Chinese dressing gown, with the ideograph embroidered on it which means 'Good Luck'—with the old-fashioned ebony-handled straight razor from the bathroom shelf above her head lying beside her black hair in the warm red pool that was still creeping on the tiles.

## CHAPTER FIVE

### The Face

Big Bat O'Brien appeared with his cohorts in a few minutes more.

'Bring in Paul Bean and Father Finley,' he gave his commands as he came highballing in the door. 'Any other visitors that Dan may have had tonight that anybody knows about. Any men that Kitty's been playing around with lately. Maybe letters in her apartment. Get the pass-key off that elevator man, Boaz, who was picked up lamming down the street. Or maybe the janitor has one.

'When I think of it,' Big Bat added, 'Kitty has probably had her two boys living with her recently. A couple of mug-faced brats about fifteen or sixteen, jive-happy little hellions. They were up before the judge out in Chicago for petty thieving and sending in false alarms, before Kitty came back East. Were under investigation in connection with their old man's death two or three years ago, too. Pretty young then, but some boys can be damned bloody to their fathers. They've made Kitty's life a hell. Get the little darlings up and see if they know what time she left her apartment, if they aren't out themselves violating the Cinderella law at some jivehole.'

With his hat pushed on the back of his crisp red curls and shiny pate, carrying his big paunch nimbly on the balls of his small feet like a man eternally tiptoeing, Big Bat paused to slap Tuxedo Johnny Blythe on the shoulder on his way to the living room.

'Stealing my stuff, Johnny?' he gibed. 'You always wanted to be a homicide sleuth. Now you're it. Headquarters got word that you were busting in with the patrolman on the beat. Precinct reported that the beat patrolman was at his box on Park. Didn't you even notice that Slipsky's uniform wouldn't button around his belly? White socks! A fat cop spreading out of his pants, without a shield! And you had to call on him to help you break in on murder!'

'Do you mean, Bat—' said Tuxedo Johnny palely. 'But he knew me. And I remembered—'

'Hell, the guy hasn't been on the force for fourteen years. He's done time up the river. He was with you when Kitty got it, anyway, like he claims—you're sure of it? Yeah, I guess he must have been. Anybody would sure remember it if he had been left alone at a time like that, with one murder already in the apartment. He couldn't have been in on it. He's just a fat punk. In some lousy shakedown racket with this bird Boaz, it sounds like, from the squawk he made. This janitor, Rasmussen, thought that Dan was trying to get gay with his daughter, it seems like. Rasmussen is a nut. Dan may have offered the cock-eyed dame a drink and pinched her cheek, as he would with any colleen. But Boaz believed the nut, and thought he saw a chance to ring in his old cell-mate Slipsky in his outgrown moth-eaten uniform for a shakedown. Hell, Dan would have pitched them both out the window. But you had to swallow the clown. Didn't you know he didn't even have a gun? But for the grace of God and there being two of you, you might be lying here in the dark yourself with old Dan and Kitty!'

Tuxedo Johnny Blythe's face was filled with wax. 'I played it dumb, Bat.'

'That's all right, Johnny. You got the boys here quick, anyway. You did fine. I always said you'd make a cop some day.'

Swiftly and nimbly on his small feet, Big Bat proceeded on to the doorway of the living room. His eternal smile was on his shrewd shiny face. His tiny green eyes twinkled like emeralds, bright and hard. The fingerprint men and police photographers had already set to work.

'What's the print picture so far?' he said.

'Four highball glasses, inspector. One on the cellaret top with a fresh drink in it, ice not yet all melted, as if Dan had just mixed it. One beside it, empty, with only his own prints, too. One on the little smoking table beside one of the fireplace chairs, half empty, with his fingerprints on it and somebody else's—A's. One on the rug by the chair, on its side and empty, with his fingerprints and another guy's—B's—smeared over.'

'Smeared over—you mean somebody tried to wipe his prints off?'

'No. You can still make out enough so that they can be identified. They were just overlaid. It looks more like three people had handled the glass—old Dan and this guy B who had the partial prints, and then some guy with gloves. There's a white ring on the desk like maybe he had picked up the glass from there.'

'Gloves, eh?' said Big Bat, frowning. 'That's the picture?'

'It looks that way, inspector. We aren't going to get any prints that matter, it looks like. Just A's and B's, and this guy with gloves.'

'Get at the pieces of the champagne bottle and the poker handle. At that razor, too.'

The prints on one glass, A's or B's, must be Paul Bean's, Big Bat thought.

'Let's see,' he mused. 'Three visitors, and the third one was the killer. He must have been some guy Dan would expect to wear gloves for some reason—even on a warm September night. Or maybe they were bandages—he could explain to Dan that he had hurt his hands. So he picked up some other guy's drink and gulped it down before he killed him, with his gloves or bandages on. And dropped it, and picked up the bottle.'

He would have used gloves or bandages with that razor, too, thought Big Bat.

He examined the ashtrays in the room, moving about swiftly, touching nothing. One had four of old Dan's own Havana butts and a little hill of white ashes in it. The other ashtray had a Happy cigarette butt lying on a lump of pipe dottle.

The cigar butt at the bottom would be Paul Bean's—one that Dan had given him. He had been here first and he smoked cigars. The dottle would be Finley's who had been in next, and smoked foul shag. The cigarette might have been Kitty's, but wasn't. No lipstick on the Happy. It had been smoked by a man. A man who smokes cigarettes doesn't smoke a pipe or cigars. Though a man who smokes a pipe or cigars may occasionally smoke a cigarette, particularly when the time is brief, and he is keyed up or tense. Keyed up to murder.

'Hey, Cark!' he said. 'Pick up this butt and see what you can get from it, will you?'

But there would be no fingerprints on the butt.

Big Bat threw his cigar stump away in the ashes of the fireplace. With his thumbnail he flipped up the lid of the silver humidor on old Dan's desk and selected a corona, fingering it for texture. He didn't like to picture, he didn't try, what had been happening in those intervening minutes, in the black apartment, before Johnny and Slipsky had broken in.

'Let's see her now, boy,' he said to Tuxedo Johnny.

'I can give you the exact time of Dan's murder, Bat,' Tuxedo Johnny said apologetically, as they went down the hall. 'It was just three minutes after midnight. Dan tried to put in a phone call for help at that time. The operator heard a kind of groan and bump as he dropped it, but that was all. It was hung up again in a couple of seconds, and she didn't think enough of it to report it. But she did happen to notice the time—One-two-o-three calling at twelve-o-three.'

Big Bat nodded absently.

'Good boy,' he said. 'You'll make a homicide man yet, Johnny. You and the operator. Probably doesn't make any difference, the exact minute. But it does no harm to know.'

He was thinking of something else, however, as he chewed old Dan's corona. Of that prize pair, Slipsky and Boaz. Johnny had played it dumb.

There were cops in the areaway out back, and cops in the alley, and cops down in the basement and in the lobby and all the halls. There were cops looking over the water tank and chimney-pots of the roof, two stories up. For twenty minutes the Royal Arms had been cut off, from within a few seconds of that second murder. The police were completing the work of arousing those denizens who, thanks to deafness or sleeping pills or drink, had been spared the hearing of that appalling scream.

The blown fuse had been replaced, and the bedroom was bright with lights now. All bulbs had been removed and substituted. Only the bridge lamp nearest to that murdered girl, which Tuxedo Johnny had groped for desperately and found, had been tampered with, however—with the burnt penny in the socket that had been expected. A scattering of three or four small coins about upon the rug might indicate that the killer had intended to fix more, but that there had not been time. They might, though, merely have been spilled from a hasty, fumbling glove or bandage—that one lamp had been enough to flash the lights out for his getaway.

Only, nobody had yet figured how.

Adjacent to the lamp there was only one of the barred bedroom windows, however, closed and locked. It was near the bathroom door, too, of course, but there had been no one in the bathroom and no egress from it, the precinct men had decided, probing it with their flashlights from beyond the sill.

Yet he must have been here, within reach of that lamp, with hot murder in him, ready to flash it if necessary—only Tuxedo Johnny had saved him the effort, by finding it and doing it for him.

A plainclothesman was sitting on an ottoman, reading a comic. He stood up. Tuxedo Johnny Blythe took off his hat, which had saved him in part from the force of that crashing mirror blow, and brushed his thin brown, neatly parted hair on his plump head.

Big Bat O'Brien squatted on his hams, pushing his own hat farther back on his tonsured red curls. He looked down, with Tuxedo Johnny standing beside him, at the woman who had once been Kitty Kane, little Kitty Kane of Jerome Street, Kitty Kane of the Nestor Club and the *Jollities*, with the broken glass beside her on the waxed hardwood floor edge, and the spilled white roses. With her gaping throat upon the white tiles just across the threshold, and her black eyes staring up yet at some unnamed terror, at the terror in the blackness which had taken her off.

Staring, staring with her dead eyes up at Big Bat O'Brien and Tuxedo Johnny Blythe. But she did not speak.

'She used to play with my kid sisters,' said the murder man heavily. 'Right down the next block on Jerome Street. Her mother was black-eyed Kitty Shawn of Shannon, that was a friend of Dan McCue's. She died when Kitty was born. Bill Kane, her old man, worked for Dan. He took to the drink. Was she an eyeful as a kid! God, were all the boys nuts about her in the old days! But you had all the play, Johnny. You were the only one she ever really loved. You were honeymooning, and you never knew, but she went on the tear for a month after you married Sue McCue. The Tenderloin boys used to pick her up in the gutter. She didn't care what she did; she was crazy. But that's the way things go.

'Kitty Kane!' he repeated heavily. 'She was wild, she was wild all through. The wildest kid on Jerome Street. But she was always a square-shooter with her friends. She never let a pal down, or did him dirt. Whatever she was or did, she never deserved this. It was as damned hellish a piece of business as I've ever run up against, and I've seen plenty. It was a black way for Kitty Kane to die . . . God, but the way she keeps looking up at you!'

'If she hadn't screamed!' said Tuxedo Johnny. 'It was the way she screamed!'

'I know. I know, Johnny. You might sort of hope she hadn't known what she was up against here in the dark, if it hadn't been for that. I'm glad I wasn't where I could hear her. I'll always be glad. But I'll be gladder yet when I meet the black son of hell who made her scream like that. It must have been an awful moment for you when you found her, Johnny.'

'The worst I've ever known, Bat.' Tuxedo Johnny said with a constricted throat.

With hard bright eyes Big Bat O'Brien had taken in the shattered amber vase glass, the water pooled on the hardwood floor, and the wet stems of the roses. The hollow-ground straight razor lying near her head, across the threshold, with its red blade open. The pool of blood on the white tiles.

'Looks like she knocked the vase off from somewhere when he got her,' he said. 'White roses were always Dan's favourite flower. I remember the blanket of them he had for Kitty Shawn of Shannon. That was all of thirty-six years ago, and I was only a boy of eight then, but I still remember them. They were the talk of Jerome Street, Dan's roses, and Mrs Kane did look beautiful. He couldn't have had much money then, Dan couldn't, and what he had he got the hard way, with his hands. But he went all out for those white roses for her who had been Kitty Shawn of Shannon.'

One of the fingerprint men had come in to take the razor. Big Bat arose and inched on past that red-clad form into the bathroom, pulling on the light cord with a big red-haired hand. Tuxedo Johnny followed him.

'Where do you suppose the razor came from, Bat?' Tuxedo Johnny said with a dry throat.

'Danny always used a straight razor—didn't you ever notice, Johnny? You must have seen him a hundred times. He had a case of them that his father had brought from the old country. He would generally keep one out and use it till it had lost its edge, then put it away and use another one, before sending four or five of them to the barber to be honed. Probably it was lying here on the glass shelf right beside the brush and soap. Maybe he picked it up as she came out of the door, and he grabbed her wrist and forced it across her throat. Or . . .

'No, they couldn't have been struggling very long,' he amended it. 'She didn't have it in her hand at all. She had that bowl of flowers in her hand, Johnny. There isn't any table or anything else around where it could have been knocked from. It just comes back to me, too, that tomorrow would have been old Dan's birthday—the 17th of September, he'd have been sixty-one or sixty-two. That's it! Dan's birthday. Maybe Kitty brought those roses over to give him after Finley left, before the murderer came in and chained the door.

'Maybe old Dan gave her the vase to put them in, or maybe she had come into the bedroom first and picked one up, one she knew about, and gone on into the bathroom here to put them in water, before giving them to him. She must have been in here, anyway, almost up to the moment of her death. A woman can spend a lot of time in a bathroom, if maybe she happens to look at herself in the mirror and decides to put another curl in her hair. She didn't know the killer had come in, and he didn't know that she was here.

'She was in the way of the killer's escape, it looks like. He had probably come in off the fire escape, the same way you and Slipsky did, Johnny. It was easy and natural, so long as there was no one out there to see him. He had probably expected to get out the same way, too. He doused the lights after killing Dan, and started to. He was that devil Rasmussen saw starting out on the fire escape. When he saw the light of the basement door down below and the glow of Rasmussen's pipe in the blackness near it, he bolted back in, though, and closed and locked the window if Rasmussen should come up to investigate.

'He had another way figured out to get away, of course, just in case there might be somebody down below like that. Even a goon would have another way figured out, a little harder one, maybe, but still a sure way. And he was smart as hell. He shows it by the way he did get out. Having the lamp fixed to douse the lights if necessary, right here by the bathroom door. Maybe he was just fixing it when Kitty came out. No way of saying just when he did it. But right there he met her, at the door. She was in his way, and he killed her.

'You're right, Johnny. You're right as hell, and you've been right all along. How did he get away? That's really the one question.'

Big Bat looked up at the little frosted bathroom window, measuring it dubiously with his eyes.

## CHAPTER SIX

### The Moaning Ghost

Tuxedo Johnny Blythe had been following all the murder man's reflections with strained attention. These horrors were his first experience with red bloody murder, and he hoped sickly that they would be his last. Old Dan had been terrible enough, but Kitty . . .

He had had enough of it, and he was afraid Big Bat would see how sick his nerves were. He had lost his head. He had played it dumb. Perhaps it made no difference what symptoms of calm or panic he showed, of brilliance or dumbness. Big Bat would continue in any case just to think him a tuxedo clown. Still he couldn't just walk out, or collapse like a woman.

He had followed, with a sense of amazement and even awe, the work of the fingerprint men, whose thoroughness and skill were even more intensive than he had believed possible. He had been baffled by some of the obvious things Big Bat had seen, which he himself had missed, and the uncannily accurate pictures which Bat had drawn from them—Big Bat might have almost been there himself, the way he had now figured out that Kitty must have been carrying that vase of flowers, and hadn't just knocked it off some table. And that the flowers had been a birthday gift for Dan—he had forgotten himself that Dan's birthday would have been tomorrow.

The problem still remained of how the killer could have got away. Dumb as he had played it, Tuxedo Johnny had seen that from the beginning. Now Bat himself had come to it, as sooner or later he must.

With his baffled gaze, Tuxedo Johnny Blythe followed the murder man's hard emerald eyes up to the little frosted bathroom window. It was too small, it was high up, with its lower sill more than six feet above the floor, and open only those six inches at the top, for ventilation.

Nevertheless, Tuxedo Johnny stepped up on the rim of the lavatory basin beneath the window, pushing up both panes to the top. With a dry throat, he started forth.

It was a straight drop down to the alley, and must be dismissed as a possibility. There were no similar windows of other apartments below, he remembered—this apartment of Dan's, the owner's suite, was built on different dimensions from the rest. And the squad car men had been hurrying down the alley within a fraction of a minute after Kitty's murder. They would have seen any man who might have cat-climbed down the bricks, or slid down a rope.

Opposite, a dirty window pane showed blank and bare. No shade, no curtains, back of the glass. The opacity of years of dust seemed on it. An emptiness lying behind it. An unbreathing silence.

Tuxedo Johnny felt his stomach muscles knot. There was something inexplicably dismal about that window. Like a great rectangular inhuman eye. Like the blank face of nothing. Like the shape of a grave that is filled with dark earth and a dark water.

With dry lips and knotted muscles he stared.

'How does it look, Johnny?' said Big Bat.

'Empty window across, Bat,' Tuxedo Johnny said, taking a quiet breath. 'He was small enough to squirm out the one here, that's all. He crossed over on a ladder or a board. The precinct boys played it dumb, too. They didn't even step up and look out. He may have been still crawling across it when they got here. But that's the way he did it.'

Big Bat stepped up on one light-balled foot beside him. Tuxedo Johnny bent his head aside for Bat to get the picture, too.

'Empty window,' mused Big Bat, rubbing his chin, staring with emerald eyes. 'A ladder or a board. A little catlike man, or a long thin man with eel hips and rubber bones.

'Yes, that's got it, Johnny. He hid behind the door or shower-curtain in the bathroom while you were stumbling in and finding her. When you blew the lamp that he had fixed, and went running out again, he stepped out, quick and cool. My God, I take off my hat to him. He thought of everything. He even closed the window part way behind him, to look just natural—a panic-stricken man would have left it open, or would have closed it all the way. And across and in through the window of that empty room, pulling his plank in after him. Then out a deserted flat and down the stairs, and out the entrance next door, while we had the building here surrounded. It's the way he must have done it. It's the only way.'

He stepped down to the floor again, did Big Bat, a little heavily.

'Get hold of Jorgensen,' he said to the plainclothesman in the bedroom. 'Find out if Paul Bean has come back to his apartment yet. If they've traced where Father Finley moved to when he moved out of that dump over in Hell's Kitchen where he was living with all his cats up to a month ago.'

One of the fingerprint men had come into the bedroom to report. 'We've got the story on the murder weapons, inspector. A's prints are on the neck of the bottle and some of the broken pieces. Smeared over. Dan's and B's prints are on the razor. Smeared over. No prints on the poker except bloody smudges.'

'A was Paul Bean, of course,' said Big Bat wearily. 'He brought the champagne bottle, this bird Boaz says. B was Finley. He came in and got a shave. And one of them, at least, has an alibi that's wonderful and good. Unless there was a living witness.

'Okay, he played it smart. As smart as hell. It happened after he had gone. It was some other guy. He was so damned innocent he even left his prints on one of the murder weapons. Before he put on the bandages or the gloves. And there's no way short of hell of telling from the prints which one he was . . . Here's a cake of soap and a towel to give the boys, Fulheimer. But they won't get any prints from them. He probably even washed his hands in gloves, he was that smart. We've found the way he got away, anyway. If that does us any good.'

Tuxedo Johnny Blythe gave a last glance at that bare dirty window opposite, before stepping down.

By every look, the room back of it was unoccupied, and had been unoccupied for months, and perhaps years. As empty as the grave. Or more so. Yet as he gave his final glance now, he thought he saw a pallid face looming slowly into view in the depths of darkness back of the glass.

Tuxedo Johnny paused upon one foot, staring, with knotted stomach muscles. It was a face—an apelike ghostly face, with a wide grinning mouth, with juglike ears, with a pair of great moist glistening eyes like the eyes of a lemur. The face swam toward the dirty window pane, staring back at him as he stared out.

The dim face gibbered, grimacing at him. It twisted up in a hideous, formless snarl. It stretched its mouth and twitched its ears. It mocked him, laughing hideously.

'In the name—' Tuxedo Johnny whispered, with his knees like water beneath him.

'What have you got there, Johnny?'

Big Bat O'Brien sprang up beside him again, staring forth, but the leering face had vanished. There was only the blank glass across, dirty and bare.

It had been only an illusion of his febrile and excited brain, Tuxedo Johnny told himself. A phantasm of his racing heart.

'See anyone over there still, Johnny?' Big Bat repeated.

Tuxedo Johnny Blythe drew a deep quiet breath. 'No,' he said. 'No one, Bat.'

He could not confess having seen that phantasm to Big Bat. He stepped down to the floor again. Yet even in hell he would remember the look of that gibbering, mocking face behind the dingy window across the black alley.

*   *   *

Kerry Ott, who knew a scene when he saw one, never saw that murder scene. He was never on it. He had not known that there had been murder.

The lights behind the shaded living room windows, down at the back of that apartment across from him, which had gone out when he had been looking forth a few minutes after midnight, had not told him that it was murder. The shadow show upon the wall, the two dark bulks of hurrying Keystone Cops down the black alley, the light which had flashed on behind that frosted little bathroom window opposite, with the glimpse of hand and bare arm he had seen, had had nothing in them of murder.

He did not know that he had had a kind of fluoroscopic glimpse into a murder apartment during a brief period of time while its front door was chained and its rear window was locked, and that he was the only person alive who had had such a glimpse. He did not even hear that girl's mortal scream, within twenty feet of him, when it sounded, though he was even nearer to it in feet than Slipsky and Tuxedo Johnny, and though people five hundred feet away, and down on the next street, heard it.

How long he had been lying on his cot Kerry didn't know. His tired and overstrained mind had been racing with his play . . . Still he must have been asleep, for a brief time, anyway. Something had brought him back into the world of reality in which all men must live, into the world of silence where he always lived, the world of darkness where he was lying now.

Had he felt the faint jar of a footstep on the worn floor? A door-latch click, a window going up? Sounds that he could never hear. He lay with eyes open. The molecular corpuscles of the darkness swam before his eyes like the eyes of deep sea fishes. All the darkness was filled with nothing. With dark grey eyes of nothingness, which floated, and drifted, and paused to stare, and swam on by.

The room was impalpably lighter than when he had lain down. It was still black, but not with an utter blackness. The kind of blackness from which the adage comes, that all cats are grey at night.

His window shade was up—that was it. It could have snapped up, with a worn roller catch, and its jerk could have awakened him. The windows of the apartment across the alley must be lighted now—though he could not see them where he was, recumbent at the back of his room—since a certain amount of dim light came in his window from across.

He lay motionless, watching. Against the dingy lustre of the pane he saw the shadow of the spider, moving and weaving. No living thing visible in all the darkness with him except her, Arachne, shuttling her laddered silk all through the night.

Still there was something else.

He had heard no door click, he had heard no board creak, he had not heard the shade go up, in his eternal silence. Still he had been awakened . . . And then he knew it had been the vibration of a human voice in the closed, unstirring air of the room. Someone was in the darkness with him, and had spoken.

That was always a lost hollow feeling. When he could see a man's lips and face, he had no handicap in his deafness. But the vibration of a voice in darkness, not knowing whether it had spoken to him, or to another. Not knowing what had been said . . . then, only then, he felt like a man in a world of fourth dimensions, surrounded by an oral world which he could not know.

A head rose up above the dim window pane which he was watching. It was in the room with him, on this side of the window. It was moving away from him, toward the window. A broad, flat-topped head with jug ears. Someone was creeping toward the window at a crouch, or on hands and knees.

A foot or a yard away from the dingy pane it paused. It was spying out at the lighted windows of the apartment across. The top of its flat head seemed to ripple and slide. Its jug ears twitched.

It put its thumbs to its ears, waggling its fingers. The darkness, vibrated with a voice again—perhaps with laughter.

Kerry Ott pushed himself up on an elbow.

'Will you,' he said in his clear, deliberate, rather high-pitched voice, 'kindly get the hell out of here?'

The head vanished. He arose in his dark corner, stumbling and still groggy, reaching out an arm. He felt something rushing towards him. A touch of hair, of cloth, of sweating human face with a large moist mouth, was mingled with his blind palm. Teeth sank into his hand, and he jerked it back. A blow from behind him, from someone else, punched him in the kidneys, hard.

He surged with a formless bellow, groping with both arms. The edge of his room door, standing open, banged into him as he made towards it. He went into the long railroad hall, following the vibration of fleeing feet, the smell of terror, towards the front door of the long flat. Ahead of him the door was jerked open, and two-jug-eared figures darted out into the dim-lit hall beyond like bats.

He surged to the door. Fleeing towards the cracked plaster corner of the stairs, headlong and frantically, were a couple of half-grown jug-eared boys, in loud sport coats and baggy pants, with red hair and freckled necks.

'Woooo!' He sent a bloodhound howl after them.

Sheer heedless panic had hold of them—for a few moments more, flight by flight, the ancient building seemed to vibrate to their headlong frantic descent. They must have reached the front door then, and out into the night.

Kerry Ott had halted at the doorway of his flat. He couldn't catch them, and if he could, he didn't think they would be good to eat. He put his palms upon his naked chest and rubbed his pectoral muscles meditatively, with a grim mouth.

He glanced down towards the end of the corridor, where there was a ladder going up to a trapdoor to the roof. The trapdoor was open—he had thought so. They had probably been that pair of heat-standing, nose-thumbing, jitterbugging shadows which he had watched on the side wall across the alley, when he had been looking out a little after midnight, just above the dim shadow line cast by the roof parapet of Argyll Hall, beneath the shadow of the long clothesline which was stretched above. Tossing a beanbag back and forth, and all of that. Though maybe it hadn't been a beanbag they had been tossing, but a dead cat.

Funny—but not too damned funny. Unpleasant little hellions. Probably spying from his window on someone they knew in the apartment across, just for the hell of it. Peeping toms, and junior members of the thugs' union in good standing. That had been a vicious bite on the hand that one of them had given him. A filthy punch in the kidneys, the other. He could still feel it.

They had probably used the flat at other times, he thought. They had seemed to know their way around. He remembered a bunch of trashy pictures and a couple of empty whisky pints which he had found in the kitchen when he took the place. There wasn't any lock on the door. Anyone could come in.

That pair would be telling each other about the moaning ghost in the haunted flat on the top floor of Argyll Hall for a long time to come, he had the feeling. They wouldn't be back again. Still he didn't like to be disturbed. He had better get a bolt for the door tomorrow, if he wasn't finished with his play and out by then.

He fumbled with the latch mechanism before closing the door, to see if there was any way to make it catch. He noticed something flat and black lying on the worn dirty floor of the railroad hall back of him, about five feet in from the door. He stepped towards it and picked it up, examining it in the light from the hall. It was a man's black morocco purse, with gold corners, which didn't belong to him, and which he had never seen before.

It was stamped, 'P. O. B.' There was no money in it, but there was a draft identification, a driving licence, and various cards: 'Paul O. Bean, Bean, Halsey, Pardee & Bean, Counsellors at Law, 50 Exchange Place'—'Mr Paul Ormond Bean, Six Hundred Ninety-nine Park Avenue.' He stuck it in the hip pocket of his pants. He would phone Mr Bean tomorrow that he had found his purse in his flat. Or perhaps just mail it to him.

He closed the rickety front door, having found no way to secure the latch. In his sock feet he felt his way back down the long black railroad corridor towards his room. He had reached the doorway of it before he became conscious of that faint catty and meaty odour again.


## CHAPTER SEVEN

### The Cat Man

He had noticed when he awoke a vague catty smell somewhere in the darkness and the odour of shag tobacco. He didn't smoke himself. He was sensitive to it. With his senses of smell and touch and sight which had always to be a little keener and more keyed up because of the silence in which he dwelt.

He paused in the doorway. Against the dingy pane across the room he saw the silhouette of a small grey figure stepping down to the floor with cat lightness. Still outlined against the window it came vaguely towards him. There was some gesture it was making—of pulling off gloves, he thought.

He had an idea that he was being seen, though he could not see more than that vague approaching outline. The air stirred a moment as a voice purred at him. Or was it his imagination? Very small and soft.

'I'm deaf,' he said. 'I can't talk in the dark. If you'll just stay where you are, I'll find a light.'

He advanced. The vague figure stepped aside, became invisible— no longer outlined against the dingy window. Just for an instant he had a feel of silk.

He reached his writing table beside the window, feeling the crumpled balls of paper crunch beneath his shoeless feet. He found the hanging bulb and turned it on. Looking over his shoulder mildly, he pulled down the window shade.

'What did you say?' he said.

A small grey man in stiff black straw hat and grey silky clerical attire stood apologetically in the centre of the room. His shoulders were hunched. There was something bulging in one of his pockets, which sagged his thin coat down. Delicately and carefully he continued pulling off his grey silk gloves, and stuffed them towards his other pocket. The gloves were rather soiled; Kerry saw a reddish stain at their fingertips, and a few small particles of some reddish stuff adhering to them, like flesh. Like hamburger. The little meek grey man's hands, however, were very white and clean.

'I am sorry, sir,' his lips moved vaguely. 'I didn't know anyone was in the flat.'

Kerry looked at his writing table with a mild frown. The little man had stepped down from it, he thought. There was a piece of crumpled wax paper on it, with some of those same tiny pieces of red meat. The top page of his script had a wrinkled and torn look, as if it had been stood or sat on. These signs of disturbance of his sacred desk were distinctly annoying. However, in face of the little man's vague look and soft humility, he forbore.

'I heard her crying, and came in,' said the little man in vague apology. 'I looked for her in the front room, but she wasn't there. It was all quite dusty and empty, sir. I didn't realize that anyone had moved in. Someone came out of the rooms down the hall, and turned on a light and went back to the kitchen, and ran water, and then came back again. Perhaps it was you, sir? I called out if they had seen a grey cat, but they did not reply.

'I came out of the front room and down the hall. I heard her then. She was playing with the papers in here on the floor. I could hear her rustling them I knocked, sir, but there was no answer. I came in, and asked you if you minded. You were lying on your cot and didn't answer. I didn't realize that you were deaf—I thought you were asleep. I don't see very well in the dark, unfortunately. Not half so well as they do, it seems. I found her playing underneath the table, and picked her up. Then those boys came bursting in, and I got up on the table with her out of their way, crouching back against the wall. I was really quite badly frightened. They are quite bad boys, really, Oscar and Willie. They do cruel things to cats. But they didn't see us, happily—most people, it seems, have extraordinarily blind eyes. I was quite relieved when you chased them away, sir. They would certainly have killed her if they found her. Isn't she a lovely thing?'

He had pulled forth a bundle of grey fur from his sagging pocket—a grey half-grown kitten, with three white feet.

Its pink tongue yawned. Its belly was full and fat. He held it in the crook of his arm, while he fumbled for tobacco pouch and pipe, which he filled with a small delicate finger.

'I always carry a packet of meat for them,' he said in soft apology, striking a match on his thumbnail and lighting his pipe with little puffs. 'It's horrid stuff, and I can't stand the feel of it, but they love it. My name is Finley, by the way—Father Finley, or did I introduce myself? I live across the hall. I have quite a little family at present—she makes twenty-three. Of course I don't keep them very long. When I have found a loving home, I give them away. Some day I hope you will drop in and visit us. Turn about's fair play.'

'That is kind of you,' said Kerry courteously, ushering the little silky grey man towards the door.

He went with Father Finley to the front door of the flat, and ushered him on out. Smoking his pipe, with his cat cradled in his arm, the little man wandered vaguely cater-corner down the hall. Kerry fiddled with the broken lock another futile moment, then closed the door once more.

Back in his room, he saw one of the grey bloodstained gloves lying on the floor. The meek little man must have dropped it when he was stuffing them away. Kerry picked it up by the cuff edge, and deposited it in his bureau's empty bottom draw. He dropped Mr Paul Bean's purse in with it. He would return both items to their respective owners perhaps tomorrow, if the little grey man didn't come back for his glove before.

There was no likelihood that Mr Bean knew where his purse was, of course, or would come for it.

He was thoroughly awake, now, and keyed up. The last act of his play, on which he was stalled, was organizing itself in his mind. He sat down, crumpling the waxed hamburger paper and throwing it to the floor. In his large firm and round black handwriting he began to write the last act.

Men and women moved before his eyes. He saw their entrances and their exits on a stage. He heard them speak. He heard even their most secret thoughts go round, behind the masks or grief or smug cold virtue on their faces . . . He was launched again in that timeless and speechless world of the imagination where no wall is impenetrable and no clock ticks, that free and unlimited world where everything is possible, because nothing ever was.

So it was, rapt in that immeasurable and unimmurable world, he was not aware of the men who entered.

ENTER (he wrote) THE MAN-HUNTERS, WITH STERN
BLOODHOUND FACES
　　1st Manhunter: I thought the place was empty.
　　2nd Manhunter: Well, there's nothing invisible about this bird,
anyway.
　　1st Manhunter: . . .

He was not aware of anyone standing just behind him, speaking
to him. He didn't hear the good-humoured, slightly bewildered voice.
He didn't see the slightly baffled face. He was out of this world and
out of all reality.

He wouldn't know till the hands fell on him.

Tuxedo Johnny Blythe shook his head. 'Excuse me, brother,' he
said. 'That must be damned interesting tripe, whatever you are
writing. But there just happen to have been a couple of small murders
committed across the alleyway from you within the past hour or less,
and the killer just happens to have escaped through your room here.
We'd like to have you tell us if you saw him.'

The big half-naked man with the bland mild face sitting at the
rickety old table in the dingy room here across the alley, beside the
window whose shade had been pulled down, wrote on. Tuxedo Johnny
looked with a helpless belly laugh towards Detectives Jorgensen and
Cark behind him.

'Out of this world,' he said. 'Anybody could have crawled right
over him, and he wouldn't have known it. Maybe they did. Hey,
brother! Wake up! It's murder!'

It was, Tuxedo Johnny was sure, the right room. He had come on
into the empty rear flat with Cark and Jorgensen to locate the escape
room and look it over, while Big Bat had delayed a moment, turning
back to give a last look into Father Finley's cat-filled front flat across
the hall.

It had been an extraordinary break of luck, finding Finley vaguely
wandering, grey and small and silky, with a grey cat on his arm,
smoking his shaggy pipe, in the dim, mouldy hall. His place of
residence hadn't been traced yet, and it would have been some time
tomorrow at the least, and maybe several days, before the little
unobtrusive man would otherwise have been located.

He hadn't known where he had been during the last hour, or all
evening, when they asked him. Perhaps he hadn't known where he
had been for the past several years.

He had left Dan's apartment at one or two o'clock, he thought.
But it wasn't quite one o'clock yet. He had thought, then, that he

might have left at nine or ten. But actually it had been a quarter of twelve, just eighteen minutes before Dan's murder and thirty minutes before Kitty's, when he had taken the elevator down, according to Boaz, the elevator man, who was sweating to tell the truth.

He didn't know where he had been in the meantime. He had been looking for a cat—a half-grown cat, or rather a kitten, grey, with three white feet. And here he was, smoking his pipe, with the grey kitten with the white feet, that he had found at last, in his arm.

*Isn't she lovely, Bat?*

Behind a door, near where they had found him, there had been the inaudible silky rustling of his innumerable cats, throatily, inaudibly thrumming, walking around in slow cat-patterns on padded feet. This was where he lived now, therefore. Here on the fourth floor of the old tenement across the alley from Dan McCue's. This was where he had probably been living for the past month, since he had unobtrusively left Hell's Kitchen. Laying what plans, making what cunning catlike stalks preliminary to murder, God knew.

*Dan's dead, Michael.*

*Oh, dear, I do hope he remembered to leave me his money for my cat foundation. Paul Bean promised to see to it that I should have some of it. But I really could use it all. One doesn't realize how many hungry cats the world is filled with . . .*

*Dan was murdered, Michael. In his apartment. He was beaten to death with a bottle and a poker, by some friend of his, who came to visit him.*

*Oh, dear, oh goodness me! How bloody, how cruel, some men can be . . .*

*Kitty Weisenkranz, her that was little Kitty Kane of Jerome Street, that was the daughter of Bill Kane the bricklayer and Kitty Shawn of Shannon, was murdered, too, Michael. Wild and beautiful little black-eyed Kitty. Remember how when you were younger and were clerking in the bookstore, living with your wife and kid, before they were burned up in the fire and you went kind of off, you used to tirade against her, Michael! Saying she was sinful, full of sin, and would be better off dead. You were younger and hotter then, of course, Michael, against the sins of the flesh. But she had her throat cut with a razor, Michael.*

*Dan's razor was a little dull tonight. He never strops them. I like a razor with a good clean stroke. My skin is very tender. But he always has plenty of hot water . . .*

*Yes, the water is hot, Michael. Wouldn't you like to go along down with one of the boys? Perhaps you had better go along, and collect your thoughts a little, Michael. Perhaps there will be something you can remember.*

*I remember I heard the crying beyond the door. I put on my gloves, and went in. I think she was afraid of me and trying to hide from me. But I knew she was there. Then I found her.*

He's got a glove, just one, in his pocket, boys. May have dropped the other in the vacant room, or in the alley. If we find it, that will clinch it. Take him along, Fulheimer. Just tell the boys to go easy with him. Nothing rough. He wouldn't know what they were doing to him, anyway . . .

So they had found Father Finley, by a lucky break, wandering in the hall here on the top floor of the old tenement across the alleyway from Dan's. And Big Bat had paused, after the little grey man had been taken unprotestingly away, to look for a moment into that front flat of his, filled with pad-footed, silkily weaving, lambent-eyed cats, to see if the ladder or the board he had used was there, while Tuxedo Johnny Blythe and Jorgensen and Cark had gone on to look for the glove, or anything else, into the old empty flat without a lock in the rear, which faced Dan's, and which must have been the way he came through.

'It's murder, brother!' said Tuxedo Johnny good-humouredly, though baffled. 'The boys think they've probably got the man, but there's just a chance it might have been the other one. He got away through your window here, anyway, whichever one he was. All we wanted to know was just whether you happened to see him . . . My God!' he said, with a helpless quiver of his belly muscles. 'Clear out of this world! I wonder how they do it?'

The two detectives laughed with him as the big unconscious man laid a page aside and wrote on.

Big Bat O'Brien came down the hall.

'Boards!' he said, with his quick eyes darting to the baseboard just inside the door. 'A pile of painter's planks! And he needed only one! That's what I wanted! Have you found his other glove here? . . . Who's that bird?' he shot, advancing. 'Does he live in this dump? Was he in here? Did he see him? Why, for the holy love of the whispering son of Brian of Carney!' he said in a whisper, on tiptoe. 'It's Mr Ott!'

'Do you know him, Bat?' Tuxedo Johnny said with a bewildered chuckle. 'Does he think? Does he breathe? Is he human? I thought maybe he was the original mechanical man. So help me, I've told him five times that it was murder, and five times that the guy escaped right through his room here, and five times I've asked him pointblank if he saw him. And he just sits here writing. He's out of this world. He's nowhere. Anybody could have come in and walked right over him.'

'He's Kerry Ott, the playwright,' said Big Bat in a whisper, tiptoeing. 'He doesn't know anything you're saying unless he's looking at you, Johnny. He's deaf as the grave. There's only one thing that makes him mad, and that's to be disturbed while he's writing, too. He may have been out or asleep when the killer came through, of course, and not seen him at all, or be able to tell us anything about him. But if he saw him well enough to identity him, and it *wasn't* poor Michael Finley, I'd like to know it, and quick. We've got poor Michael where he can't do any more harm, and for as long as we want him. But Paul Bean's a lawyer, and we can't hold him three hours unless we've got some proof. And if we let the wrong man loose, he's just too smart, and he's liable to kill again on us. I don't know what to do.'

'I was just thinking of giving him the hotfoot, to see if he could feel it without his shoes,' said Tuxedo Johnny Blythe good humouredly. 'I'd have liked to see his face. But if he's a friend of yours, Bat, we'll do it the soft way.'

'Johnny, you'd better not—'

But Tuxedo Johnny Blythe had already put his smooth plump good-natured, chuckling hands on the sides of the big concentrated man's face from behind, with a slight, soothing barber's stroke.

'Wake up out of your dreamland, brother! It's murder!'

Kerry Ott turned his bland mild face around, pushing up his knees, in bland glaring rage. He stood up, knocking his chair backwards, filled with glaring thoughts of murder. He snapped his pencil in two and squeezed the pieces in his fists.

'Who did that?' he said. 'Damn him, who did that? That broke it! Who are you with your slick polished hands and the dumb fat grin like a bewildered nine-months-old baby examining a feather?

'What do you mean by coming in here and rubbing me?' he went on in his high outraged voice. 'Haven't you got brains enough to leave me alone while I'm working on a play? If you think that writing one is simple work, trying to make something impossible seem possible, and something seem real that never happened; just try and do it some time! Damn it, that broke it! That broke it all apart!'

He exhaled an outraged breath.

'What are you doing in here, Arthur?' he said to Big Bat O'Brien, glaring. 'Who is this dumb friend of yours with the baffled look? Who is responsible for this insufferable intrusion?'

## CHAPTER EIGHT

### The Cobweb

Oh, it was terrible!

Wrenched out of that timeless and spaceless imaginary world, where he had been ranging, back into this small limited world of obviousness and reality, by a stroke of offensive familiarity. Light and smooth as the touch of a beetle's wing, perhaps, but he was sensitive to touch, and had an antipathy to being handled. He would almost sooner have been hit with a hammer. Damn the fool!

Emerald-eyed, red-haired, bald-pated Big Bat O'Brien of homicide—whom nobody else in God's world had ever called or even thought of as Arthur, even his mother having called him Bat—from whom Kerry had got at times an idea for a play or two, and to whom perhaps he had given an idea, was in here, with a couple of his prize bloodhounds, it looked like, and this fourth bird, who had given him that startling brush of hands. Just as his play was finishing. They broke it.

He took another breath, calming down. The man who had done it looked completely baffled, startled, hurt, and anguished to the death.

'All right!' Kerry said, leaning back against the table. 'I didn't mean to hurt you. I don't like to hurt men. Let's leave it there . . . What is it, Arthur? Spill it, and get it over.'

He leaned back against his table, with his bland mild face, watching the movement of Big Bat O'Brien's lips, a little sick. Oh, it was terrible! Terrible . . .

Big Bat O'Brien had clenched his teeth in his cigar.

'Mr Ott,' he said, 'the light was out and the shade was up in this room a little while ago, when we looked across. It had the appearance of being an empty room. But it's your room, I take it. Could you just tell me whether you have been here since fourteen and a half minutes after midnight, and if you saw a man, who was either a little unobtrusive grey cat man, or a thin, tall beanpole man, coming in through your window from the small bathroom window in the building across the alley, on one of those painters' boards which are stacked up along that baseboard and making his escape out through your door?'

'What is it, Arthur—the It-pays-to-be-an-idiot program? If so, I bite.'

Make a joke out of it, he might. But it was terrible, really.

Big Bat O'Brien had clenched his teeth more firmly into his cigar. Standing wide planted on his light and nimble feet, rocking his stomach quietly. Looking at Kerry Ott, the playwright, who knew a scene when he saw one, or a play when it had been described to him, with his hard emerald eyes.

'Mr Ott,' he said, 'a man and a woman—Mr Dan McCue, the eminent philanthropist and political leader, and Mrs Kitty Weisenkranz, a friend of his, who lived across the hall from him— were murdered in his apartment in the Royal Arms, directly facing you across the alley, during the quarter hour after midnight. The front door was chained and the rear window was locked when the place was broken into, and there were bars on all the other windows. There was only one way the killer could have escaped, and that was out the little bathroom window and through this room, by crossing the intervening space on a ladder or board. Shake hands with Johnny Blythe of the Federal Aid Bureau, who's just up from Washington, who used to be Dan's right hand man for fifteen years, and who is one of the most popular and best-liked guys you ever met. Johnny used to be a cop himself. If he had stayed, he might have made a good one. The boys just inside the door are Detective-sergeants Cark and Jorgensen of homicide, two of the smartest men in the department, who are agreed with Johnny and me that the killer could have escaped in no other way than this.

'Dan was killed in his library at three minutes after midnight with a champagne bottle that Paul Bean had brought to him, and a poker that was there. Kitty was killed at fourteen and a half minutes after midnight with a razor that Michael Finley had used to shave himself with a half hour before—he had dropped in before, off and on, to do it, using Dan's hot water, and had done it tonight, as he mentioned to the elevator man. So both Bean and Finley had prints on one of the murder weapons, but whichever killed him later wore gloves.

'We just picked up Michael Finley, and he had no explanation or alibi at all for his whereabouts during the murder time. We found one bloodstained glove on him. He lost the other somewhere. If he had lost it in your room here, we would know we had him. However, since apparently he didn't, there is an element of doubt about him, which leaves Paul Bean still in it.

'Paul Bean was picked up about half an hour ago, fifteen minutes after the murders were completed, on the street about a block away from the Royal Arms, dressed in a pair of dark slacks and an old dark golf pullover, and with his fingers wrapped in bandages, looking for a purse he had lost when some boys tripped him up, after he left Dan, earlier in the evening. Or that's his story. But if we had found his purse lying on the floor in this room, it would have been the clinching thing against him, like the glove against Michael Finley. Or if you saw one of them close enough to identify him, that would close it. You get the picture, Mr Ott?'

Oh, it was terrible, really. It would have been a terrible play.

'Motive, Arthur?' said Kerry tiredly. 'There must be some motive.'

'Both men had a motive, a money motive,' said Big Bat O'Brien, 'for killing Dan. Kitty Kane, it looks like, was just in his way as he escaped. But Finley thought—and still thinks, it seems—that Dan was going to leave him a big chunk of money in his will, if not all of it. He's laying plans to feed ten million cats. Dan hadn't made a will though, as Bean knew. And without a will Bean's thirteen-year-old-stepdaughter, Dan's granddaughter, will inherit everything—little Jennie Blythe. She was Johnny's daughter here, but Sue McCue Renoed him a dozen years ago, and married Bean. Which means Bean would have control of the money for eight years till she comes of age. And that is all the time a lawyer needs to have his hands on money.'

A terrible play, still.

'Time, Arthur?' said Kerry tiredly. 'How do you know the time so precisely of the murders?'

'Fifty people heard Kitty scream,' said Big Bat O'Brien. 'Some police were already downstairs in the building—Johnny here had them called. The time was fourteen minutes after midnight, or fifteen. The phone operator clocked the time of Dan's murder. He had tried to call for help as he was being killed— at twelve-o-three.'

'My God,' said Kerry Ott. It was even more terrible than he had thought.

'Scene?' he said, staring incredulously at Big Bat O'Brien's hard bright emerald eyes. 'Chained door and locked windows? Who discovered the murders, Arthur?'

Big Bat told him about that, too. About how Johnny had come rushing down the stairs, with the front door of the Royal Arms the only way he could think of for a murderer to get away, but watching for anybody he might see on the way, too. Without realizing, till he met that phoney cop, Slipsky, and the elevator man had come down to join them and had offered to get into Dan's apartment with the pass-key that he had, that with a chain on the door no murderer could have got away out in front, and that if there hadn't been a chain he could have got into Dan's himself with his own key.

Big Bat wore a brief grin, while Cark and Jorgensen joined in a laugh again at poor Tuxedo Johnny. Big Bat told about how Johnny had then gone around to break in the back, taking Slipsky with him, and had met Rasmussen, the janitor, and heard about the devil himself. And how Johnny and Slipsky had gone on up and broken in the locked window and found Dan's body; and how Johnny had told Slipsky to phone homicide while he went on to see if the chain was still on the front door, which he didn't expect to find, it having now occurred to him that it was probably off and should be off, as that was the way the killer had probably got away. And how Slipsky hadn't phoned, but had followed him out. And how Slipsky and he had both seen that the chain was still on the door, which meant that somebody was still in the apartment. And how then they had heard Kitty scream, and Johnny had gone rushing in.

'Johnny thinks it may have been only a few seconds before he went in,' said Big Bat O'Brien gibingly. 'But he may have just stopped to tie his shoelace, or figure up his insurance policies. I know I would, myself, without a gun. There she was, anyway. She must have died within a second. However long it was, it gave him time, with the fuse that blew, to make his getaway someway. By the bathroom window, as we found out, and across here. It was the only way.'

Great God, it was incredible! Kerry Ott turned his bland mild face on the pink-cheeked man with the round blue eyes, with the look of a fat nine-months-old infant examining a feather.

'My God!' he said.

'It may have been more time than I thought before I found her,' the dumb-faced man's lips moved to him, with a swallowing of his Adam's apple. 'A man gets mixed up at a time like that. Maybe it was as long as forty or fifty seconds. I was just trying to gauge the probabilities. She was dead, anyway. He got out that bathroom window, that's all. He came through your room, that's all. He got away.'

His fat dumb eyes were on that drawn window shade, before that dingy window, straining.

'Oh, impossible!' said Kerry tiredly.

'Impossible?' said Big Bat O'Brien.

'The hell it was impossible!' said Tuxedo Johnny Blythe. 'What does this bird know about it, Bat? Anyone could have come in here and walked right over him.'

He strode to the window shade and ripped it off. He said something with his back turned, but Kerry didn't see.

'The spider web,' said Kerry wearily. 'Not any slipshod haphazard web thrown up helterskelter in fifteen minutes by a theridiid, but the patient work of an argiopid—octagonal, geometric, flawless, with four rays of laddered silk. A work of time. A work of highest art. Moored from the window ledge across the pane, to every corner. That web wasn't spun since twelve-fourteen. She has been spinning that web all night.'

Tuxedo Johnny Blythe tore the geometric net of thin and sticky threads to tatters with one sweep of his arm. He smashed the black and yellow spider as it ran, with one blow of his fist. He gave the window a violent tug. But it didn't budge. His shoulders heaved. There was sweat on his smooth-shaved neck. Big Bat O'Brien went over and helped him. They both heaved.

Big Bat O'Brien turned his puzzled face around.

'Nailed,' he said. 'In solid, and there's paint and dust on the heads. They've been in years. What's the answer, Mr Ott?'

Kerry Ott's mild face looked tired. The obviousness of reality. The walls which no one could have gone through. The one actor on the scene. But he was not one to smash even a spider, which had not harmed him. He was not God, or even a policeman.

'Perhaps you had better go back to your fingerprints, Arthur,' was all he said.

He watched them going out the door, before he sat down to work again. Big Bat had his big red-haired paw on the shoulder of that dumb-eyed man, with his look of a nine-months-old infant examining a feather. And Kerry thought that Big Bat had understood . . .


## CHAPTER NINE

### Killer

That Kerry Ott, the big deaf maker of plays, had any idea that his death was near him, even in the most submerged recesses of his mind, seems unlikely.

There he was, a man who was always sure that he knew the way men's minds work, and the probability of their actions in a given situation. He knew that Big Bat O'Brien was intelligent, strong, and relentless. He knew the killer looked dumb and had acted dumb.

It seemed to him that he was finished with it. It had been just a bad play, a terrible play, conceived and acted out in a hysterical, addlepated, confusedly ad-libbing way by a fatheaded murderer. That was the terrible thing about it. An actor must have entered a stage somehow before he can exit from it, in any play. But there that brainless fat-headed goon had been seen by an audience exiting at a wild hysterical rush from a stage, without an explanation of how he had ever got onto it.

Rushing down the stairs from Dan McCue's door. That had been his first appearance on the scene—getting off it. No one had asked him when he had gone up to Dan McCue's door, or how else he had got there, except by going up the stairs, and he had not explained, since there would have been no explanation. Slipsky had been in the lobby for at least fifteen minutes, and the elevator man, too, and would have seen him coming in, if he had come in that way. He hadn't been a man who had come in. He had been a man who had been leaving, by the nearest and quickest way that he could think of, with that yellow light and red pipe glow which he had seen down below the fire-escape out back. Maybe he hadn't thought of the need of explaining how he had come in, with his need to explain how he must have got away. And nobody had asked him.

It made a play, Kerry thought, beginning, 'Exit, murderer.' Like Alice through the looking-glass, where everyone runs backwards. A very bad play indeed. If the guy hadn't been such a dumbbell, someone would have asked him just where he came in, and he would have never got away as far as he had. Which had been only as far as here, to a spider's web and a nailed window across the alley, seeking a way out.

The one bright thing he had done, apparently, had been to rush up to the fifth and ring the elevator bell, before rushing down. But even a moron has one brain cell. He had hidden on a landing of the stairs, behind the elevator operator's back, as the cage arose. Except for Slipsky, he would probably have gotten away unseen. It must have been a dreadful moment for him when he saw that form in blue watching for him quietly behind the pillar in the lobby.

A dreadful moment, in a different way, when he learned that Slipsky hadn't been a real cop, and that he might have made him and Boaz the goats for Dan McCue's murder, if he had only played it a little differently.

A ham actor, who had done a terrible play. It had been awful to watch Big Bat O'Brien's lips reciting the crudities of it, and project it before his eyes. But it was finished. Big Bat was keen and intelligent, and certainly must have got it. He had had his hand on that feather-eyed killer's shoulder when they went out.

Only Kerry failed to take into calculation the strength of an established idea. The idea that a tuxedo cop could be anything more than comical in any connection with police work would never occur to Big Bat O'Brien. Particularly Tuxedo Johnny. He was just a laugh. Unless Big Bat had seen those vicious murders being done before his eyes by that pink-faced man with the bewildered eyes, it would quite likely have been impossible for him to believe that Tuxedo Johnny could do them. Even if he had seen them, he might have regarded them as an optical illusion, and gone down to see the eye-man, rubbing his pupils.

'I don't get it, Johnny,' Big Bat had said, with his big, red-haired paw on Tuxedo Johnny's shoulder as they went out the door of the little room and down the long railroad hall. 'Ott is usually smart in seeing things in a scene that you describe to him. Where this actor is, and where that. He says a playwright has to be. He calls it constructive imagination. He seemed to hint that I was something of a boob for not seeing for myself. But, by God, as I can see it, it leaves nowhere for him to have got away to at all when the boys came in at front and back, not more than two minutes at the most after Kitty had screamed. That must mean that he—was right.'

'Rasmussen!' said Tuxedo Johnny Blythe, sweating. 'Rasmussen, the gnome janitor, Bat!' With the most brilliant thinking he had done all evening, and perhaps in his life. And thinking for his life.

'That's who this bird Ott, who doesn't know where he is at, meant it must have been, Bat,' he said, thinking fast, and sweating. 'I can see it all plain now, dumb as I am. Rasmussen was in the apartment when I was there at the door. He unchained it and followed me down when I went rushing down the stairs. He took the lobby stairs into the basement, while I was talking to Slipsky, ran through to the back, and was out there smoking his pipe when Slipsky and I arrived. Can you imagine how smart he was?

'After telling us that crazy story of having seen the devil on the fire escape, he followed us up the escape, got in the window just behind us, rushed across the living-room into the hall and into the bedroom before I had got the library lights turned on, and killed Kitty. Fixed the bulb, too—he'd have had time for that—it could have been longer that I thought. He had all the motive in the world, too. He thought Dan had been getting gay with his daughter. My God, why didn't I think of him before?'

'He's lame, Johnny.'

'It's only a disguise. Don't let him fool you. He's probably fast as lightning. Don't let any doctor tell you any different either. A guy as smart as that can fool any doctor.'

'Would he have had time, as he was rushing from the living-room into the bedroom, after you and Slipsky had entered and before you got the lights on, to have stopped and put the chain on the door again, Johnny? He had had to take it off to get out and follow you down, you know. And it would have made a jangle as he put it on which you should have heard. And so on.'

'Why, Kitty put the chain on the door, Bat,' said Tuxedo Johnny quietly. 'Hadn't you got that figured out, Bat? She came in after old Dan had been killed, I've got it figured out, with the key she had, with those birthday roses for him. It was all dark, and she thought he had gone to bed. But she wanted to arrange the roses in water and put them in his bedroom where he could see them in the morning. She just slipped the chain on the door for the few minutes she would be in, so none of the different friends that he had given keys to might come in and wake him up while she was arranging them. She tiptoed through the bedroom into the bathroom, thinking he was sleeping in the big bed, picking up a bowl that she knew of from his chiffonnier in the darkness and went into the bathroom. She arranged the roses, and maybe waited till she had finished smoking a cigarette. Then she came out, and saw—*him*. And suddenly she knew—she knew he was a murderer, and she went hysterical, and let out that scream—'

Tuxedo Johnny swallowed.

'I've got it all figured out, Bat,' he said. 'I got it figured out some time ago.'

As indeed he had.

'It fits,' said Big Bat slowly. 'It fits. She was the one who put the chain on, after Dan was dead. The killer went out, and in again. That was one thing that was puzzling me—What he was doing in those eleven and a half or twelve minutes. But that answers it. Rasmussen was the killer. Johnny, you'd have made a cop yet, if you'd stuck to it. You aren't so dumb.'

He came up the worn old dusty stairs of Argyll Hall soundlessly and obscurely, hugging the poor, torn wallpaper against the staircase wall. The dwellers in the dingy flats were all asleep in this black hour of morning.

There was no pan-faced elevator man in front, no gnome janitor with burning eyes in back, in Argyll Hall. People here minded their own business. They were not prying. They kept their eyes down when they moved up or down the stairs. And they were all asleep.

He saw no one. No one saw him. An obscure figure in his suit of cobweb grey, with his coat lapels turned up above his neck, with his hat brim pulled down above his eyes. He even simulated in part a drunken man's uncertain tread. The worn wooden flights had been mounted or descended by many such vague figures in the many years they had stood here, in the old building. Perhaps by some on the same errand. His right hand was jammed in his coat pocket as he mounted softly upward, pressing against the dingy stair wall beneath the dim infrequent bulbs.

He was on the fourth floor now. He went down it, tiptoeing, past the door with silent padding cats behind it, which was the door of Michael Finley, stepping no less silently than they, towards the trapdoor ladder at the end.

He mounted up it. This time he would have another way out, just in case. As Big Bat had said, even a goon would think to have another way. There was the clothesline stretched above the parapet, which he had observed as he stood on the first floor escape landing of the Royal Arms, waiting for Slipsky, waiting to go up and discover Dan dead, and put the chain upon the door. Not knowing that she was in there, that the chain was on already. Not knowing that to have the chain on would leave him no way out.

He had noted that rope, as he noted a great many things, with his round eyes of an infant examining a feather. As he noted, a few years ago at Nantucket, while swimming with Dan, Junior, that the boy was floundering a little, and was not a good swimmer, afraid of water. And so, the next time he had taken him out in a rowboat, in his bathing suit, a mile off shore, had asked him to lean back and fetch that painter dangling off the stern; and just accidentally with a crabbing oar had given the boy a nudge, which had knocked him out into the water—for a long time, it seemed to him, for a long, long time, the boy had followed him, floundering, gasping, sobbing, calling out to him, as he had pulled hard for shore. He had been afraid the boy would make it, and indeed, he had made it more than three-quarters home.

With his round feather-filled bewildered eyes, that noted a great many things—that had noted the tetanus culture in the laboratory of his old college-mate, the research biologist, one day last autumn when he had been on a bumbling visit. Finding the time, in his bewildered way, while Doc Joe explained it to him and he examined it, to impregnate a pin with it.

He had gone to Sue and Paul that evening, to see Jennie. The divorce of twelve years before had been friendly; they were modern people and he and Paul both worked for Dan. He had surrendered none of his rights over Jennie. The right to see her at any time. He had picked up and been fondling the cat which Finley had given Sue for Jennie, a tortoiseshell with a milk face, while he had been standing talking with Sue and Paul right in the hall. And Sue and Paul had turned their faces for a moment, as Jennie had called goodnight to them from the doorway of her bedroom. Suddenly the cat in his arms, which was brushing against Sue's arm, had scratched her, with one claw, thrusting deep.

Oh, it must have been a cat. Cats scratch. And it had been in his arms, brushing her. He wouldn't have stuck a pin in her, would he, with his round bewildered eyes? Right before the eyes of Paul and Jennie. So it was just the deep dig of a cat's claw, and nothing to go to the doctor for. And tetanus serum must be used quickly.

A drowned boy washed up on the beach, with water-filled lungs and a burst heart, but with his face quiet and at peace—calmed by death, calmed by the sea, after all his agony. A woman, placid, middle-aged, who had loved him once, though wisely not for long, who had died of tetanus—not a pleasant way to die. The doctors and nurses hadn't liked to talk of it—too tragically preventable. But that look of last agony had been wiped out on her face, too, by death, or by the undertaker's art.

Two quiet murders, when the opportunity had been presented. But never red bloody murder before tonight. It was his first contact with it. He didn't like it. It had been the only way to get old Dan, though. You couldn't drown him. You couldn't scratch him. He was too tough and strong. From behind, with all strength and fury, that had been the only way to do it to old Dan. Any one of those blows should have killed him, but still he had reached his phone. He had been tough, it had been bad. Bad old Dan.

The blood that he had got upon his hands, without knowing it till he was outside the door! He must have left prints of it on the doorknob, he had realized, and perhaps on the door frame. A huge and flooding tide pouring down the stairs after him as he fled. But there couldn't have been much blood on the door knob. Kitty couldn't have noticed it. The precinct men who had come in hadn't seen any. They had just laid it down to his imagination—poor dumb bewildered Johnny.

He had washed the blood off his hands with soap and water in the bathroom, swiftly, when Slipsky had fled, stepping in the darkness over that dead form lying on the bathroom threshold, with her dead staring eyes. Had she fainted when she collapsed in terror, with that scream at sight of him, and had her head struck the hard tiled floor, and she known nothing more? Or had she been awake, and knowing him, when he had reached her in three seconds, swift, swift as a leaping tiger in the darkness, falling on a knee beside her and stifling any second scream that might come from her warm soft throat, reaching up with his other hand to old Dan's bathroom shelf?

Whether she had known him, or not known him, in that last swift dreadful second, he would never know, with her black eyes upon him. But she had known that he had murder in him long ago. A woman knows that about the man she loves.

Terror at the sight of him with his bloody hand, at old Dan's door, as she came out of the bathroom! Sheer terror, and she had screamed, collapsing. And he had been in there with her, swift, swift as a tiger, in three seconds more. The tiger on the bound moves swift and straight. The paralysed doe awaits its death.

Tuxedo Johnny Blythe, with his bewildered eyes which saw so much. With the well-kept, well-fed, gymnasium-conditioned muscles beneath his plump pink hide . . .

On the roof of the old tenement he cut the clothesline stretched above the parapet which he had seen. It was good, new stuff—he ran it swiftly through his slick fingertips—with a tensile strength of all of three hundred pounds. He bent one end of it with a bosun's knot around an iron stanchion set in the brick parapet, just opposite that little frosted bathroom window of old Dan's, and let the end drop down into the alley, past the window of the playwright straight below.

It was another way out, if necessary, if the stairs down should be blocked. He estimated that the chances were not one in a thousand that he would not be able to get out of the building down the stairs and clear away before the bang of a shot in the upstairs of the old tenement would rouse anyone. Still it was better, as he had found, to have a way out. Always one possible way.

He had paid the rope out. It reached down to the alley, or near it. The shade had been replaced at the window below again. The man inside could not see it.

Tuxedo Johnny Blythe went down the ladder again from the roof. He went quietly along the hall to that rear flat, and through the door that had no lock. He went down the long black railroad hall, to the door of the room halfway in back.

He listened without a breath. He heard the rustle of a sheet of paper being crumpled and thrown to the floor. He heard the brief momentary sharpening of a pencil—*snick-snick-snick*. He heard the creak of chair legs as the man in there shifted position slightly. He heard the smallest sounds—to the pounding of his own heart. The man in there could hear no sound. He would never know what had hit him.

Gripping the gun in his pocket Tuxedo Johnny opened the door.

He watched carefully.

The big man sat at his table across the room, beside the shaded window, beneath the bright bulb hanging from the ceiling, writing and writing on. He was out of this world. He was nowhere. A man could walk right up behind his shoulder, and he would not know it.

Still with a soft quiet step Tuxedo Johnny put a foot across the threshold. The big deaf man with the bland mild face made a sudden gesture as if to push his chair back, or turn around.

From the threshold the killer fired straightway . . .

'CURTAIN,' Kerry Ott had written, jabbing his pencil down.

Putting a period to the play. The thing was finished. He eased his shoulders back with a relaxing gesture. It was a movement purely involuntary and reflexive, which contained in it the split second, the inch of life, for the man who had fired that gun had a steady hand and eye. Diagonally beside him the wall spouted plaster dust from a hole suddenly bored there. In the silence in which he dwelt.

He was not quite the bland sophisticated type that he aspired to be, nor even completely the inspired man-of-letters type which he appeared to be; and no doubt there would always be many subtle civilized situations where his large and somewhat ungainly presence would be at a loss. But he had a more primitive type of awareness than a bland sophisticated man or an inspired literary man may be supposed to possess. For he had come from the Ozarks, from a feud country, and he knew what bark means when it flies from a tree or plaster from a wall.

His reaction was something more than instantaneous, hurling his body to one side, gripping the back of the chair behind him and swinging it above. He hit the floor and rolled as the light above him went out in a shower of shattered bulb glass, struck by the chair legs, with the wood in his grip splitting to the blast of the second shot.

He saw the flash of the third shot in the blackness as the killer came rushing at him, firing. He was no longer the maker of plays, out of this world, in spaces unwalled and time-less. He was in this little room, in quick and black reality. He had respect for a gun—in the hand of a madman all the more.

*He killed O'Brien!* the thought flashed to him. *No! O'Brien didn't get it! No one knows. If he kills me, he's safe!*

There was only the blackness, and the thudding rush of the killer's feet towards him. The vibrancy of a voice, with oaths or threats or triumph that he could not hear. He was on hands and knees. He hurled himself in a blind silent tackle, as a flash streaked at him again and his right arm went numb with the anodyne of shock which blots out pain.

He missed at first. But he caught hold of the killer's gun wrist in the next moment. With his left hand, in silence. A flash went upward. A hand was at his throat, choking. He could not feel his right arm. He butted with his head and broke that grip. They struggled over the floor. He felt fist blows rain against his face. He held that gun wrist, he struck with his head again, in silence.

He was strong, this dumb-faced man, with his round eyes dim in the darkness for the moment, six inches from Kerry's own. Two hundred pounds of him, and full of murder, fighting now for his own life. Kerry had his thumb jammed beneath the gun hammer, but he could not hold that wrist. His sprawling feet stumbled. The hammer of the gun almost tore his thumbnail off as it was ripped from him. The killer was out of contact with him again.

In the silent blackness. Perhaps it was filled with oaths of gibbering, he wouldn't know. Shoeless, he had leaped aside, in silence. The killer had no more shots to waste. He was waiting to locate the target now. Kerry felt a piece of wood, a leg or rung of the shattered chair, he thought, touching his foot. He rolled it lightly, leaping aside.

Sound! In the world of silence where he lived there was no sound. He did not know what it was to have it or to miss it. But to men who lived in a world of sound, there is a dreadfulness about a silent struggle in a black place, and their nerves may be betrayed by a small rolling sound. Kerry did not hear it, but the killer did. His gun blazed at it. In panic again.

The last shot in that gun, he knew. And the killer knew that he knew. Kerry felt the floor thud with the rush of feet. Rushing for the unseen door.

He reached it first. He stood backed to it. He took a silent breath. 'You won't get out!' he said in his clear and careful voice. 'I'm going to murder you right now! You asked for it.'

It was the first word that he had uttered. The first sound, except for the rolling of that chair rung, which he had made. But he had got his breath now, and that murderous gun was empty.

Whether the dumb-faced man answered him he did not know. Nor what terrors were in that man's mind, over the struggle in the black silence, and now the word of death. Kerry felt the sawhorse standing on the pile of planks beside the door. He planted his right foot against a leg of it, and ripped at it to pull it apart with his left hand. The two-by-four leg came off, a two-foot length, with nails at the end of it. Perhaps the ripping wood had cried and the pulled nails had screamed—he wouldn't know. But the killer knew—though perhaps not from what those sounds had come. Let him guess.

He himself was a killer now. In the darkness he advanced.

His eyes were swimming, swimming, through the darkness . . .

Suddenly, half across the room from him, the window shade was ripped from its roller. Against the dark dirty window glass he saw the silhouette of the killer then. He rushed. There was a rope hanging beyond the window. But the pane was filled with the killer's bulk and was sharding outward in a burst of glass within the instant. The killer had gone through.

He had gone at last through the dark and dingy window of that room across the alley, the only way out for him that there had been, as perhaps he had known from the beginning. The only way out at all. And he had found it now, going through the window.

Kerry Ott was two strides behind him as he went bursting out, with the glass splintering. Just for an instant Tuxedo Johnny seemed to be floating motionless in space, with his hands reaching for the rope. Just for an instant the sharding glass was motionless around him—a flat piece of it, a foot in diameter, with ragged edges, sitting horizontal in air beside his throat. Then he had caught the rope, and one of his legs was twisted in the slack of it, and the flying shards of glass went on, to drop below. Beyond the window that he had gone through at last, Tuxedo Johnny Blythe looked at the playmaker with his bewildered eyes, like the eyes of a nine-months-old infant examining a feather. Baffled by the mystery and strangeness of it. By the mystery and strangeness of life and death.

Kerry had not seen that flat sheet of glass strike him, or him strike it. There are things much too quick to see. Quick as the stroke of a razor, it had gone across his throat, and on.

He looked at Kerry Ott with his bewildered eyes for an instant, and then his mouth opened, in what was perhaps a scream, or might have been no sound at all. The blood was coming from his throat. He put up his hands, and fell backward, with his leg caught in the bight of the rope. He had always been horrified by his own blood so. But he could not hold it in with both hands now.

For what seemed a long moment he hung head downward. Then the rope whirled and straightened, and he was gone. Kerry Ott shoved his feet into his shoes, and put his shirt around him.

He left his flat, and went down to the street. The grey false dawn at the end of the summer night was beginning to lighten in the east. The air was cold and thin.

Some men had gathered back in the alleyway already. More were going down. There had been those shots; a gun being emptied in the old tenement. There had been, perhaps, yells, and oaths which Kerry had not heard, and just as well. A milkwagon and two or three taxis had stopped beside the curb, at the alley's mouth. A patrolman was going down it at a run. Soon there would be dozens, and perhaps hundreds. But the man who had been frightened that the gnome janitor might see him, and had been paralysed with terror when Slipsky had seen him, did not care how many might see him now. He had gone through the window at last. He had found the way out, as he had known that he must do from the beginning.

A taxicab drew up in front of the Royal Arms as Kerry reached the alley's mouth. Big Bat O'Brien got out of it. He caught sight of Kerry and came towards him, his steps deliberate.

'I was thinking about what you said about going back to the fingerprints,' he said a little gravely, with his external meaningless smile gone from his face. 'None on the phone, when I knew that he had used it. But I just couldn't imagine that even Johnny could be quite dumb enough to tell me, practically out loud, what he was trying so hard to hide.'

'I wonder if he was so dumb,' said Kerry, 'if most of us would have played it any better, or even half so well. Being caught red-handed, trying to escape, by the blue arm of the law and still trying to bull it through. At least I'd hate to have to try, myself, to do it any better. You would have come to the fingerprints sooner or later yourself, Inspector. A man can't think of everything. Even having no prints at all can be a betraying thing.'

'Collodion, I suppose,' Big Bat said. 'There was a spot on his chin, where he had given himself a little cut. Maybe it was that that made him think of doing it. Started him off on thoughts of blood. Maybe he didn't play it so bad, when he got started.'

'He played it well,' said Kerry. 'It was just the play that was terrible.'

'So it had to come to this for Johnny, did it?' said Big Bat gravely, a little heavily, as they went down the alley.

He pushed his hat on the back of his head. He clasped his hands behind his back. His emerald eyes were dull, full of the shadow of many remembered things.

'I had just made my first grade the hard way when he was taken on as a lieutenant,' he said. 'He didn't know much, but he was always a nice guy. I remember the day when he married Sue McCue, a big fine healthy wholesome girl, Dan's daughter, and it looked like his world was made. The big wedding at St Christopher's, and the mayor and all were there.

'It's too bad that the days of our youth and joy can't go on forever, isn't it, Kerry? But perhaps we'd get tired of them if they did, too.'

JEFFREY WALLMANN

# Now You See Her

*Jeffrey Wallmann is not exactly a household name. But he is one of the many authors who has helped to provide the backbone for two of the longest-running mystery digests produced*—Mike Shayne Mystery Magazine *(which finally folded in 1985, alas, after nearly thirty years) and* Alfred Hitchcock Mystery Magazine *(started in 1956; still going strong).*

*Wallmann has never been a prolific writer of mystery fiction but in the early-1970s he published over 30 stories, around half of them in collaboration with the indefatigable Bill Pronzini. One of the latter, 'Day of the Moon', was expanded into a novel and published in the UK in 1983 under the joint-pseudonym 'William Jeffrey' by Robert Hale: an excellent and fast-paced pulp-thriller, inexplicably it never found an American publisher.*

*Wallman's short stories are well worth seeking out. There was a short-lived series about a PI called Sam Culp, but the remainder take a look at crimes from an unusual angle and go out of their way to close with a neat little twist. And you don't usually see the twist coming. But then neither does the victim in the story. And the victim is not always the dead man.*

*Jeff Wallmann has two Impossible Crimes to his credit. The later one, the intriguingly-titled 'The Half Invisible Man' contained a neat locked room gimmick that he and Bill Pronzini dreamed up (and one wonders how they came to concoct it; but then the untold sagas behind the triggering-off of half the most ingenious Impossible ideas would probably fill a book in itself—and a fascinating book at that). The other story appeared a year or so earlier and perfectly illustrates that the Impossible Crime can (indeed must) move with the times and doesn't have to depend on a snowbound mansion or an eccentric detective or a technical explanation you'd need a degree in quantum physics to understand.*

*Wallmann is clearly a man who, rather sinisterly, sees immense criminous possibilities in normal, everyday objects and, I think you'll have to agree, uses them to murderous effect.*

ROBERT ADEY

Mrs Ibsen backed away from the window. 'He's still in there,' she said, with a shudder, letting the drapes fall into place.
Detective second grade Hal Devlin stood at the window next to her

and continued to peer at the window in the apartment house across from them. He was a big man, with a barrel chest and thick arms and legs. He had black crew-cut hair and brown eyes and a nose which had been mashed to his face by a baseball bat when he had been a patrolman.

'I can see the reflection of his binoculars,' he said.

His partner for the week, Detective third grade Worth, stubbed his cigarette out in a nearby ashtray. He wasn't much of a contrast to Devlin, for he had brown eyes and black hair as well. But somehow people kept taking him to be the senior partner, which always rankled Devlin a bit. He eyed Mrs Ibsen and said, 'And you say you have no idea who the person is?'

'None,' Mrs Ibsen replied. 'I don't even know all the tenants in this building, much besides those in South Tower. You know how it is—so many people together, privacy is sacred. All I can tell you is that I saw him spying on us two days ago, and he's never stopped. I don't even think he sleeps, just sits in that window and watches.

'I would have reported him sooner, but I wanted to make sure before I accused one of the tenants of being a Peeping Tom.'

She sat down in a chair heavily, a middle-aged widow about twenty pounds overweight, with dyed silver hair rolled into a bun and bland, round features. She was wearing a sleeveless spring dress, and the meat under her arms swayed as she talked, for she gestured with her hands in quick, jerky motions.

'You understand, don't you?' she continued. 'The Acreage is supposedly a model community, with security guards and screening of applicants and very high rent. I wanted to be positive.'

Devlin understood. The Acreage was less than a year old, one of those planned oases of respectability in the middle of an urban wasteland called a city.

He fingered the fine material of the drapes and recalled his first impression of sterile good taste when he had entered her apartment fifteen minutes before. He was pretty sure all the apartments in The Acreage were exactly like hers, right down to the furniture arrangement.

A person moving into The Acreage forsook his individuality, his identity, his memories, for there was nothing in one's past worth salvaging. The past was a jumble of clash, of worry and strain. Here, life was ordered and safe. One belonged, like cubes in an ice tray.

Devlin was glad that his family and he still lived in that white elephant of a house. He liked having a past.

Worth turned to Devlin. 'I'll talk to the super.'

'Do that,' Devlin replied. He let the drapes fall. 'And get a pass key from him, too.'

'Right.' Worth paused to light one of his chain link cigarettes, then left. Devlin smiled at Mrs Ibsen, trying to reassure her that she had done the proper thing by reporting the man, and then he said, 'About this other matter. You want us to investigate it?'

'I don't know,' Mrs Ibsen said, frowning slightly. 'I—'

A bell sounded from the kitchen. Mrs Ibsen rose from the chair. 'Excuse me. My pie is done. We can talk in the kitchen.'

Devlin followed her into the small kitchen which was at the rear of the eighteen-by-twenty-four living room. The other end of the living room was all glass and drapes and was where the woman and he had been standing moments earlier. Next to the kitchen were a small hall, the entrance foyer, and another hall leading to the two bedrooms and the bath.

Mrs Ibsen opened the oven door and removed a steaming pie. 'All I can tell you is that Lenore Grimond seems to have disappeared.'

'Disappeared,' Devlin echoed. He watched as she placed the pie carefully on the counter, using the empty frozen pie box as a pad.

The rest of the kitchen looked as though it was unused. The stainless steel sink was spotless, the counters shone, and the pseudo walnut cabinets and trim were as though waxed and buffed. Even the inside of the warm oven gleamed, and Devlin realized it was a self-cleaning model.

'Yes. Lenore is probably my oldest and dearest friend. We've known each other long before we moved here. In fact, it was my doing that her husband and she came to The Acreage. They live in seven-twelve, which makes it very convenient. Anyway, I was supposed to meet Lenore for lunch on Monday at the beauty shop she manages. She wasn't there and none of the girls had seen her since closing on Saturday. Here it is Wednesday, and I haven't heard from her.'

'You spoke to her husband?'

'Yesterday. I don't get along too well with Peter Grimond. Few people do. He's a CPA and uses his apartment as an office, so he's home all day but gets very upset if he's interrupted. Last night I went up there to see Lenore or find out what had happened, and he said the strangest thing. He said that she had left him.'

'Many women leave their husbands, Mrs Ibsen.'

'Not women our age, officer. Not that we don't consider it, but after being with one man for so long, there just isn't any place to go. We might make the man leave, get a divorce and settlement, but not walk out. And Lenore wasn't the type. She was quiet and patient, a plodder. When she got angry it was over something important, and she wasn't the least bit flighty or emotional. She was everybody's friend.'

'What do you think has happened to her, then?'

'I couldn't begin to guess. I know that there wasn't another man in her life, though I think Peter plays around a bit. But then that's to be expected of a man, I suppose.'

Devlin wouldn't know about that. Rose had always been enough of a woman for him. 'Did she leave any kind of word at her salon?'

'No, none. I called there this morning, and when I found out that she hadn't left any instructions for its management, I really began to get worried. That salon is very important to her, and I can't believe she would leave without some kind of plans for its continuation.'

She shook her head. 'I can't accept the idea that Lenore just up and left.'

'I'll speak to her husband, Mrs Ibsen,' Devlin said. 'Perhaps he's heard from her by now, and everything is all right.'

Worth returned then, and Devlin thanked Mrs Ibsen and left.

'The super's not the cooperative kind,' Worth said as they walked down the hall to the elevator. 'Practically had to drag him outside to see which apartment I meant. Then he called the owners before he'd part with a pass key.'

'Who's the Tom?' Devlin asked.

'Young man named Osgood, in apartment seven-forty-seven. The funny thing is that the super swears Osgood left for work this morning, said he saw him drive away in his sports car.'

'Maybe he came home early,' Devlin said, and they stepped out of the lobby into the brilliant sunlight. There was a crushed oyster shell path between the centre court building where Mrs Ibsen lived and the south tower where Osgood lived.

There were three other apartment houses to The Acreage, the others like south tower, at each corner of the property, ell-shaped, and ten floors high. The centre court building was in the middle, also ten floors high, but square in shape. The ground floors of the buildings were open and paved for parking, with the lobbies at the end where the cars could drive in.

The Acreage was stone-wall enclosed, with only four entrances, one near each of the tower buildings, and the grounds were well gardened grass, shade trees, flower beds, paths and wooden slat benches. It was a complete world unto itself, and to Devlin, an alien one.

They waited a moment before the door to 747, listening. They couldn't hear anything inside the apartment, so Devlin unholstered his .38 Special and Worth slid the key into the lock. He jiggled the key until the tumblers fell silently, and then nodded. Devlin shouldered the door.

The blond-haired man at the window spun around in his chair, a pair of binoculars in his hands 'Wha—'

'Freeze,' Devlin ordered. 'Police.'

The man froze, still in a half crouch. Devlin crossed to him and motioned him to place his hands against the wall, then step back until his weight was fully on them. Then Devlin frisked him, pulling out the contents of his pockets as he went. The man was clean. Devlin let him stand and then show identification. He proved to be a Mr Oscar Dortmund, 112B Yancy Street, married, five-eleven, 185 pounds, blond hair and blue eyes. He also proved to be a licensed private detective for A-Acme Investigators, Inc.

'What are you doing here,' Devlin asked.

'Stake-out.'

'Does Osgood know you're using his apartment?' Worth asked, lighting another cigarette.

'Of course,' Dortmund said. 'We're not stupid. We're paying him twenty bucks a day for its use, plus whatever food we eat.'

'Who's we, Dortmund?'

'Me and my partner, Ed Bagley. He's asleep in the bedroom.'

Worth rousted Bagley, then started checking out Dortmund's story on the phone while Devlin continued questioning them. Bagley sat on the couch, his eyes half lidded and puffy, mostly yawning.

'Who were you staking out?' Devlin asked.

'Man across in the big building. Name of Grimond. Peter Grimond.'

Devlin and Worth looked at each other with surprise. Worth said, 'Huh!' and flicked his ash, and Devlin asked, 'Why?'

'The usual,' Dortmund replied. 'Divorce evidence. We were hired by Mrs Grimond for two weeks' surveillance. She was right about him; a big redhead's been visiting him most every afternoon. That is, until Saturday. Haven't seen her around lately.'

Bagley yawned and added, 'Haven't seen our client, either.'

'What?' Devlin asked.

'Lucky thing we got paid in advance,' Dortmund said. 'We've been reporting to her twice weekly at her beauty shop, but when Ed went over there Tuesday, she wasn't there. And she hadn't been, not since Saturday from what we can gather. We decided that if she didn't appear by our next meeting, we'd notify you.'

'Of course we saw her Sunday, when she was in the apartment,' Bagley said. 'She and Grimond had a fight about seven in the evening and she stalked off to the bedroom. Pulled the curtains and we haven't seen her after that. Of course, the way we're situated, if the bedroom door or curtains are closed, we can't see the entrance, so we can't tell when she left.'

'And Grimond?' Worth asked.

'Has been in the apartment ever since. He has a desk in the living room and he works there most of the day. Walks around a lot. On Monday, I think, he cleaned up the apartment, vacuuming and everything, but he hasn't gone out and nobody's visited him. Except for one old lady Tuesday night, and she only stayed for a minute.'

'I thought you couldn't see the entrance from here,' Devlin said.

'Well, the curtains and door have been open most of the time,' Bagley said. 'Moreover, we can see the building's entrance from here, and Grimond's car stall is right next to the lobby. We've been watching that place like hawks, and I can swear that he hasn't left centre court. He's been out of our sight maybe fifteen, twenty minutes at the most, except at night when he's been sleeping.'

Devlin thought for a moment and then said, 'There's one thing which puzzles me. You say that Grimond couldn't have left his apartment house at any time without you spotting him. Right?'

'I'll stake my rep on it,' Dortmund said.

'Then how did Mrs Grimond leave?'

Neither Dortmund or Bagley could answer that one. Devlin left them with a warning to stay further back from the windows, and then Worth and he returned to centre court. They went directly to apartment 712.

Peter Grimond was irritated at the interruption.

'What is it?' he snapped when he opened the door. He glowered first at Worth and then at Devlin, then back at Worth. He was tall and lanky, with thinning grey hair and sagging jowls. He was dressed in a white shirt and suit pants, but the pants were baggy and wrinkled and the shirt was coffee-stained and almost as grey as his hair.

Devlin identified himself and Worth.

Grimond seemed to flinch at the mention of police, blinking rapidly as an owl does. He allowed them in, however, shutting the door and following them into the living room. The main difference which Devlin could see between Grimond's and Mrs Ibsen's living rooms was in the choice of carpet colour.

As Dortmund had noted, in one corner of the room was a paper-strewn desk, a pipe turned over in an ashtray on the floor beside it.

'We're here about your wife, Mr Grimond.'

'Lenore?' Grimond scowled. 'Has something happened to her?'

'That's what we'd like to know,' Devlin said. 'A number of people are concerned for her.'

'Oh.' Grimond slumped in a chair and leaned forward, clasping his hands in front of him, a picture of morose despondency. 'She left me, you see. After eighteen years, she left me. I thought when you mentioned her name she'd been in an accident, or something like that. I had no idea—'

'When did this happen?' Worth asked.

'We had a fight Sunday night. A spat over nothing, but it was the straw, she said. The final straw. Out she went, bang, like that.'

Devlin started walking around the apartment, not touching or opening anything, but not letting anything skip his attention. He saw that the apartment was getting a bachelor's patina; there was one shoe on the coffee table holding down a sock, dust on the credenza, magazines and cushions and books askew.

The sink was half full of dishes, and there was a large sack full of garbage in one corner. One bedroom had been turned into a combination office and storage room, though Devlin could understand why Grimond chose to work in the living room, where it was sunnier. The bedroom facing the yard was a mess. The bed was unmade and clothes were strewn on it and the floor. The dresser was littered with odds and ends, including a large brown alligator handbag with a black handle.

Devlin asked: 'What did your wife take with her?'

'Nothing,' Grimond replied. 'She left everything behind, saying she didn't want anything to remind her of me or her life here. She didn't take a suitcase or a toothbrush.'

'Strange,' Devlin said.

'Yes, it is, but that's what happened.'

'And she didn't say where she was going?' Worth asked.

'No, only that I would be hearing from her lawyer in a few days concerning the money.'

'Money?' Devlin said.

'Settlement would be a better word.'

'So you haven't seen or heard from your wife since Sunday,' Devlin said. 'You have no idea where she is, yet you didn't report her missing.'

'She's not missing,' Grimond protested.

'Then you know where she is?' Worth demanded.

'No, no. I mean she knows where she is. She just doesn't—'

'What was she wearing when she left?'

'A suit. A double-knit, with a belt and buttons up the front. A light blue. And a frilly white blouse underneath.'

'Purse?' Devlin asked.

'Of course. Matching blue leather. Blue shoes, too.'

'Do you have a picture of her?' Worth asked.

'What is this, officers? I am in the middle of a terrible domestic crisis, true, but I can't understand why you would be concerned. It is a private affair, I assure you, and—'

'A picture, Mr Grimond,' Worth repeated. 'Please.'

Grimond fumbled for his wallet, his fingers shaking badly. He had trouble removing a small snapshot from the milky plastic window.

'You act as though I did something to Lenore,' he mumbled, handing the picture to Devlin, who was closer.

'We'll return this,' Devlin said and studied the woman. It wasn't a good shot of her, accentuating Mrs Grimond's slide from youth. She was in a one-piece bathing suit with some unknown hotel in the background.

It was a colour snap, and showed the paleness of her skin, except for two strips of sunburn up her thin legs. Her hair was piled on top of her head like some Egyptian queen, and she was squinting at the sun and showing large buck teeth.

'And did you?' Devlin prodded as he handed the photo to his partner.

'Did I what?'

'Do something to your wife?'

Grimond grew very red in the face, and he sucked in his breath sharply.

'We were happily married. Or so I thought, officer,' he said stiffly. 'I don't care for your insinuations. Please go.'

Devlin shrugged. He had done about as much as he could without a search warrant or more evidence of some crime. At the door he handed Grimond one of his business cards with his name and the precinct phone number printed on it.

'When you hear from your wife,' he said, 'call us.'

Grimond studied the card. 'Why should I?'

'It would save us a trip back here,' Devlin replied.

Grimond didn't respond. He shut the door firmly after them, firmly and loudly.

'Well?' Worth asked as once more they walked down the hall to the elevator. 'What did you find while you were looking around?'

'Nothing.' Devlin punched the elevator button. 'Not one damned thing. And I don't see how he could have hidden her, either. There's only one linen closet and the clothes closets in the bedroom, and the cabinets are out unless he cut her up. Besides, if she was still there after three days, our noses ought to have led us straight to her.'

'He could have frozen her,' suggested Worth, and then he shook his head. 'No, the refrigerator is too small. Perhaps the waste disposal in the sink?'

'Disposals have been tried. They won't take the bones and they burn up. Only large commercial jobs can handle such a load.'

'Those cartons in the bedroom. Maybe he shipped her out in one of those.'

'Doubtful,' Devlin said. 'We should have seen the stack of papers and records he had to have taken from the carton, and on top of that, Dortmund would have spotted the truckers when they came to pick it up. And,' Devlin added for good measure, 'there would have been the problem of decomposition.'

'Yeah,' Worth said. He paused, smoking reflectively, then he said, 'Maybe she's in the building somewhere.'

Devlin thought hard about that as he rode down to the lobby. As the doors to the elevator slid back he said, 'Let's find that super again.'

The superintendent was in the basement, painting a piece of wrought iron. His name was Saunders, and he was bald, squat, with an ugly mouth and cold, suspicious eyes. He wiped his hands on a rag, and Devlin wondered if there was something in Saunders' past which, unlike the tenants, he hadn't been able to leave behind.

He took the pass key Worth returned and put it on the ring of keys hanging from his belt, and when Devlin asked him about Mrs Grimond, he replied that he didn't know nothing.

'Didn't see her on Sunday or any other day. Got enough to do around here without playing nursemaid.'

'Are there any vacancies here? Any empty rooms?' Devlin asked.

'Nope. We have a two-year waiting list, in fact.'

'What about closets?'

'There's a tenant storage room and a building supply closet on each floor of the building. Oh, and another storage room in the basement.'

'We want to check them,' Devlin said.

'Go ahead. Be my guest. Just don't ask me to come along. I've got a job to keep. There's stairs to sweep and incinerators to clean, and—'

'Incinerators!'

'One in each building,' Saunders said. 'Got chutes which open on each floor, and the tenants throw their garbage down and it gets burned up. Wednesdays are my shovelling days.'

Devlin turned to Worth. 'Get Trimm on the phone and have him authorize a lab crew to be sent out here. I want those ashes sifted.

Then you search the storage and supply rooms, and I'll start talking to the guards.'

The security offices for The Acreage were on the second floor of the centre court. The only person there when Devlin arrived was a young secretary who looked as though she had just finished her schooling. She told Devlin that each of the four gates were manned by a guard and that there was one roving guard on duty at all times, and that there were three shifts a day. The fifteen men rotated positions and times according to a weekly schedule, which she supplied, along with a list of their names, addresses, and phone numbers. Devlin thanked her and left.

None of the five guards then on duty had seen Mrs Grimond leave Sunday or since then, though they all knew her by sight. Part of their job was to recognize who were the tenants and who were visitors, and they all prided themselves in their ability. Devlin asked about any delivery trucks stopping at centre court, just to make sure that Worth's idea about the record-keeping cartons wasn't true. Again, none of the guards had seen anything which couldn't be accounted for as normal.

Devlin returned to the security offices and used the phone there to contact the remaining ten, off-duty, guards. He drew a complete blank.

At five o'clock, when Worth returned, Devlin and he had the lab crew around the incinerator in the centre court basement and pooled their information. Nobody had seen Mrs Grimond leave centre court or The Acreage either on foot, in a private car, or in a taxi. Nor had there been any trucks stopping beyond the ones which were expected and explainable.

Worth was dirty and dusty and empty-handed. The supply and the storage rooms had produced nothing and Worth was sure that he had checked every other conceivable hiding place in the five buildings. The lab crew had collected three tin cans, some silverware, the metal backs to a set of buttons, and a bent shoehorn, but no teeth, bones, or residue.

'How sure are you that there wasn't a body burned in there?' Devlin asked the head of the crew.

'As sure as I can be without analyzing every ash,' came the answer. 'I'd think that if one had been burned, the smell would have been terrible. It's not a very good incinerator. It burns slowly and incompletely and really doesn't get all that hot.'

Devlin thanked him and his men, told them they could go, and then Worth and he returned to the precinct house. Shortly afterwards Devlin went home thoroughly disgusted. He crabbed at his wife, snapped at his children, and tossed around the bed, bothered by the vanishing Mrs Grimond.

Around midnight, his wife could stand no more. She switched on the bedside lamp and demanded an explanation for his behaviour.

Devlin told her, concluding with, 'And she's still in that building, Rose. I know it.'

'But isn't there the chance that the guards and those private detectives overlooked her, and she did leave Mr Grimond as he said she did?'

'The chance is very slim. Both the guards and the detectives are trained, and if one missed her, I can't see the other missing her as well. Besides, no woman would walk out and leave everything she owned behind, including a thriving business.'

He slid down further under the covers and folded his hands over his chest. 'No sir, he did away with her for that redhead. I don't know what he did with her afterwards, but that's what happened.'

'I certainly hope you find out before I have to do away with you,' Rose Devlin said.

'I intend to,' he muttered. 'Now shut off the light so I can get some sleep.'

The next morning Devlin and Worth began anew. They talked to the two private detectives again. This time Dortmund was asleep, and Bagley merely reiterated what had been said the previous day. He added that Dortmund had seen them in Grimond's apartment, but that nothing strange had happened since. Grimond had worked the balance of the day, watched television, and gone to bed.

Bagley also said that they had been paid up until Friday, and Mrs Grimond or no, they were going to finish their job and then leave.

There were five different guards on duty, though they all remembered Devlin's phone calls. Seeing the picture didn't change their memories any. That left five guards who hadn't seen the picture, and on an off-chance, Devlin sent Worth in the squad car to personally interview the five, and then stop at the beauty shop and talk to the operators there.

Devlin located Saunders and again the superintendent was reticent and uncooperative.

'I tell you,' he said to Devlin, 'I ain't seen nothing. Leave me be.'

Devlin took the pass key again and went through the supply and storage room again. Worth was a good conscientious man, but there was always the chance . . .

Worth found Devlin just before one in the afternoon, on his hands and knees on the fourth floor of the east tower, looking at baggage tags. He was hot, grimy, and in a foul humour. Worth didn't help matters any.

'The guards are positive Mrs Grimond didn't pass them, or that a truck picked up anything at centre court. The girls at the salon all say they haven't heard from her. Just to be on the safe side I checked the logs at the cab companies, and neither Yellow or Checker has picked up a woman of her description within ten miles of here.'

'Great,' Devlin said sourly. 'Just great.' He sat down on a steamer trunk and rubbed the bridge of his nose, his eyes shut. He was developing a headache. 'She isn't in centre court. She isn't in any of the other buildings. She never left here, alive or dead, and the last person to see her was her husband, who hasn't moved from his apartment.'

'What now, Hal?'

'Help me finish this building. It's the last one. Then we'll have lunch, and afterwards—' He paused, then said, 'afterwards we're going to tear Grimond's apartment to shreds. It's the only spot left, and the last place she was seen.'

'And if there's no sign of her?'

'Don't say that,' Devlin replied grimly.

Grimond called his lawyer when Devlin served him the search warrant. The lawyer advised him that there was nothing he could do and to just sit tight and not say anything, even when queried. Grimond took his advice and sat at his desk and stared at Devlin and Worth as they went through his apartment.

One hour later they hadn't found anything. They compared notes in the hall so that Grimond couldn't hear them, then went back inside and started all over again. Two hours later they were still without anything.

'And don't come back,' Grimond said, his only words the whole time, and slammed the door.

Devlin stormed down the hall, seething with frustration and smarting from Grimond's smug expression, contempt evident in his eyes.

When he got back to the station house, he sat at his desk and brooded, cupping his face in his hands. His wife called, telling him he was overdue for dinner and that she had fixed his favourite casserole and it was drying out in the oven, and even that failed to cheer him. He continued to sit, and then he began to talk to himself.

Worth wisely kept on typing reports and didn't interrupt. He knew that Devlin only talked to himself when absolutely furious.

So Devlin spoke unhindered about how he knew damned well that

Grimond had murdered his wife following the argument Sunday night, and that Grimond knew he knew it, but that until the method of disposal was discovered, Grimond was safe.

He went over every detail, starting with his visit to Mrs Ibsen's, the surprised detectives, and the sullen superintendent. He reviewed the search of the buildings and the incinerators and Grimond's own apartment. He hit upon everything he could think of, right down to his sitting in his chair, missing his wife's casserole. He sat and stewed, turning and twisting the facts, and it was painful, like pulling teeth.

All at once some minor things started to fit into place, and he knew he had the answer.

The grin on his face was more one of determination than elation. He swivelled around and said to Worth, 'Get the lab on the phone. We're going back to see Grimond.'

'What now?' Worth asked. 'Why?'

'I'll tell you on the way,' Devlin said, and then turned back to call his wife. Rose was going to be mad, but he wasn't going to be home tonight.

The formal arrest of Peter Grimond didn't come until mid-morning of the next day, after a messenger brought Devlin the lab report. Devlin had been up all night, but as he read the typed report, he suddenly felt fresh and full of energy.

The report was, so to speak, his second wind. He handed it to Grimond, who had been sitting beside the desk for many hours, and asked, 'Do you want to tell us about it?'

Grimond scanned the report and something seemed to escape from him. It was as if he deflated a little; his shoulders sagged, his head lowered, and he let out a tremendous sigh. His lawyer tried to caution him, but he waved him away and started to speak.

'We fought over Joanie, this girl I've been seeing. Lenore said she had proof, that there were detectives watching the apartment from south tower. She was going to divorce me, and I couldn't stand that— my own business hasn't done too well, and hers was lucrative—she would have taken it and the apartment—everything.' Grimond licked dry lips and Worth brought him a cup of water from the cooler.

Grimond drank greedily and continued. 'When she went into the bedroom and pulled the drapes, I saw a way of killing her. The detectives couldn't see me then, so I strangled her and stripped her and took her into the bathroom.'

In spite of the detailed contents of the lab report, Grimond couldn't bring himself to mention his method of disposal. He coughed delicately and brushed over it by saying, 'Afterwards, I stayed in the apartment, knowing that the private detectives would be my alibi. They would have to testify that I never left the apartment, had never done anything suspicious, had never been out of their sight for more than a few minutes at a—'

Devlin picked up the lab report and thumbed through it again, smiling. Grimond had been smart to turn his wife's trap around to serve his own purposes. But Devlin had thought it strange that Grimond hadn't gone out for three days, and he had wondered why, and then he recalled that at certain times the bathroom, bedrooms, and kitchen were out of sight to the detectives.

The death had to have occurred in those rooms, as well as the disposal, and Grimond couldn't afford to move from the apartment, not while there were two men ready to testify to his behaviour.

The lab crew had found microscopic blood samples on one of the large kitchen knives and around and in the bathtub drain, evidence that Mrs Grimond had been dismembered after having been killed. There was still some ash stuck to the fibrous bag of the vacuum cleaner and some along the edges and around the heating coils of the oven.

Devlin was a little chagrined at not having tumbled sooner to the significance of Ed Bagley's words, '. . .on Monday, I think, he cleaned up the apartment, vacuuming and everything.' Especially after he had seen the condition the apartment was in.

Grimond had used the vacuum cleaner on Monday, all right, but not to clean house. He'd sucked up the residue left in the oven, then reversed the machine and blown the contents out of the window, to be scattered forever.

Devlin was going to have to thank his wife tonight. Maybe take her out to dinner. Her casserole was ruined, but she had inadvertently made him think of ovens, and then he had recalled Mrs Ibsen's pie, and the fact that the ovens at The Acreage were all the self-cleaning kind. Self-cleaning ovens work by intense heat, burning the grease off the sides and bottom—quick, tremendous blasts of heat, getting up to 900 degrees.

That's much hotter than a crematorium.

# The Blind Spot

Barry Perowne (r.n. Philip Atkey, 1908-1985) is the classic example of a writer who rose up steadily through the authorial ranks to become a medium-echelon entertainer, and then had a single idea which thrust him far higher up the ladder of fame than he, or anyone else, might reasonably have expected.

As a teenager Perowne worked as secretary to his uncle Bertram Atkey, the novelist, comedy-thriller writer and creator of the popular little Jorrocksian crook Smiler Bunn, later marrying Atkey's daughter Marjorie, his cousin. He joined the publishers Newnes to work as a lowly sub-editor on magazines such as the Happy (home of Richmal Crompton's boisterous William) and the Sunny, then cut his writing-teeth cranking out Dick Turpin yarns for around 12s (60p) per 1000 words. He then broke into the adult short-story market and at the same time began writing long-completes (25,000-word novelettes) for the Thriller: perfectly competent efforts but with nothing in them to distinguish him from the score or more second- or third-line pulpwriters who also contributed.

Then Perowne had his brainwave. With the permission of the E.W. Hornung estate, he resurrected the gentleman-cracksman Raffles, but updated to the 1930s. This was a huge success which boosted both his confidence and his bankability, and he began selling fiction to the high-paying glossy monthlies in Britain, as well as the 'slicks' in America. Yet he never forgot his old friends in the Amalgamated Press (publishers of the Thriller), and in the late-1930s wrote three very long Sexton Blake thrillers for them (as well as an extended novella for the Sexton Blake Annual) in which he pitted Raffles against the sleuth who, in almost every way, out-Holmesed Holmes.

After the War he resurrected Raffles yet again, this time setting him against an Edwardian backdrop (Hornung's original was pre-Boer War) and transforming him from an amateur safecracker into something of a detective (though one who still indulged in the odd spot of grand larceny when funds grew low). Most of his later Raffles tales were written for Ellery Queen, a market Perowne had cracked back in 1944, although he hadn't known it at the time. Just before setting off for the Normandy beach-head on an Intelligence mission he'd visited his father-in-law and left a manuscript with him. Bertram Atkey found the story intriguing and sent it to EQ where it was pounced on with enthusiasm. And no wonder.

*The story was 'The Blind Spot' and in it Perowne doesn't put a foot wrong.*
*It's a macabre classic in which he created an entirely original and chilling*
*twist to the Impossible Crime.*

JACK ADRIAN

A nnixter loved the little man like a brother. He put an arm around
the little man's shoulders, partly from affection and partly to
prevent himself from falling. He had been drinking earnestly since
seven o'clock the previous evening. It was now nudging midnight,
and things were a bit hazy. The lobby was full of the thump of hot
music; down two steps, there were a lot of tables, a lot of people,
a lot of noise. Annixter had no idea what this place was called, or
how he had got here, or when. He had been in so many places since
seven o'clock the previous evening.

'In a nutshell,' confided Annixter, leaning heavily on the little man,
'a woman fetches you a kick in the face, or fate fetches you a kick
in the face. Same thing, really—a woman and fate. So what? So you
think it's the finish, an' you go out and get plastered. You get good
an' plastered,' said Annixter, 'an' you brood.

'You sit there an' you drink an' you brood—an' in the end you find
you've brooded up just about the best idea you ever had in your life!
'At's the way it goes,' said Annixter, 'an' 'at's my philosophy—the
harder you kick a playwright, the better he works!'

He gestured with such vehemence that he would have collapsed if
the little man hadn't steadied him. The little man was poker-backed,
his grip was firm. His mouth was firm, too—a straight line, almost
colourless. He wore hexagonal rimless spectacles, a black hard-felt
hat, a neat pepper-and-salt suit. He looked pale and prim beside the
flushed, rumpled Annixter.

From her counter, the hat-check girl watched them indifferently.

'Don't you think,' the little man said to Annixter, 'you ought to
go home now? I've been honoured you should tell me the scenario
of your play, but—'

'I had to tell someone,' said Annixter, 'or blow my top! Oh, boy,
what a play, what a play! What a murder, eh? That climax—'

The full, dazzling perfection of it struck him again. He stood
frowning, considering, swaying a little—then nodded abruptly, groped
for the little man's hand, warmly pumphandled it.

'Sorry I can't stick around,' said Annixter. 'I got work to do.'

He crammed his hat on shapelessly, headed on a slightly elliptical course across the lobby, thrust the double doors open with both hands, lurched out into the night.

It was, to his inflamed imagination, full of lights, winking and tilting across the dark. *Sealed Room* by James Annixter. No. *Room Reserved* by James—No, no. *Blue Room. Room Blue* by James Annixter—

He stepped, oblivious, off the curb, and a taxi, swinging in toward the place he had just left, skidded with suddenly locked, squealing wheels on the wet road.

Something hit Annixter violently in the chest, and all the lights he had been seeing exploded in his face.

Then there weren't any lights.

*Mr James Annixter, the playwright, was knocked down by a taxi late last night when leaving the Casa Havana. After hospital treatment for shock and superficial injuries, he returned to his home.*

The lobby of the Casa Havana was full of the thump of music; down two steps there were a lot of tables, a lot of people, a lot of noise. The hat-check girl looked wonderingly at Annixter—at the plaster on his forehead, the black sling which supported his left arm.

'My,' said the hat-check girl, 'I certainly didn't expect to see *you* again so soon!'

'You remember me, then?' said Annixter, smiling.

'I ought to,' said the hat-check girl. 'You cost me a night's sleep! I heard those brakes squeal after you went out the door that night— and there was a sort of a thud!' She shuddered. 'I kept hearing it all night long. I can still hear it now—a week after! Horrible!'

'You're sensitive,' said Annixter.

'I got too much imagination,' the hat-check girl admitted. 'F'rinstance, I just *knew* it was you even before I run to the door and see you lying there. That man you was with was standing just outside. 'My heavens', I say to him, "it's your friend"!'

'What did he say?' Annixter asked.

'He says, "He's not my friend. He's just someone I met." Funny, eh?'

Annixter moistened his lips.

'How d'you mean,' he said carefully, 'funny? I *was* just someone he'd met.'

'Yes, but—man you been drinking with,' said the hat-check girl, 'killed before your eyes. Because he must have seen it; he went out right after you. You'd think he'd 'a' been interested, at least. But when the taxi driver starts shouting for witnesses, it wasn't his fault, I looks around for that man—an' he's gone!'

Annixter exchanged a glance with Ransome, his producer, who was with him. It was a slightly puzzled, slightly anxious glance. But he smiled, then, at the hat-check girl.

'Not quite "killed before his eyes",' said Annixter. 'Just shaken up a bit, that's all.'

There was no need to explain to her how curious, how eccentric, had been the effect of that 'shaking up' upon his mind.

'If you could 'a' seen yourself lying there with the taxi's lights shining on you—'

'Ah, there's that imagination of yours!' said Annixter.

He hesitated for just an instant, then asked the question he had come to ask—the question which had assumed so profound an importance for him.

He asked, 'That man I was with—who was he?'

The hat-check girl looked from one to the other. She shook her head.

'I never saw him before,' she said, 'and I haven't seen him since.'

Annixter felt as though she had struck him in the face. He had hoped, hoped desperately, for a different answer; he had counted on it.

Ransome put a hand on his arm, restrainingly.

'Anyway,' said Ransome, 'as we're here, let's have a drink.'

They went down the two steps into the room where the band thumped. A waiter led them to a table, and Ransome gave him an order.

'There was no point in pressing that girl,' Ransome said to Annixter. 'She doesn't know the man, and that's that. My advice to you, James, is: Don't worry. Get your mind on to something else. Give yourself a chance. After all, it's barely a week since—'

'A week!' Annixter said. 'Hell, look what I've done in that week! The whole of the first two acts, and the third act right up to that crucial point—the climax of the whole thing: the solution: the scene that the play stands or falls on! It would have been done, Bill—the whole play, the best thing I ever did in my life—it would have been finished two days ago if it hadn't been for this—' he knuckled his forehead—'this extraordinary blind spot, this damnable little trick of memory!'

'You had a very rough shaking up—'

'That?' Annixter said contemptuously. He glanced down at the sling on his arm. 'I never even felt it; it didn't bother me. I woke up in the ambulance with my play as vivid in my mind as the moment the taxi hit me—more so, maybe, because I was stone cold sober then, and knew what I had. A winner—a thing that just couldn't miss!'

'If you'd rested,' Ransome said, 'as the doc told you, instead of sitting up in bed there scribbling night and day—'

'I had to get it on paper. Rest?' said Annixter, and laughed harshly. 'You don't get rest when you've got a thing like that. That's what you live for—if you're a playwright. That *is* living! I've lived eight whole lifetimes, in those eight characters, during the past five days. I've lived so utterly in them, Bill, that it wasn't till I actually came to write that last scene that I realized what I'd lost! Only my whole play, that's all! How was Cynthia stabbed in that windowless room into which she had locked and bolted herself? How did the killer get to her? *How was it done?*

'Hell,' Annixter said, 'scores of writers, better men than I am, have tried to put that sealed room murder over—and never quite done it convincingly: never quite got away with it: been overelaborate, phoney! I had it—heaven help me, *I* had it! Simple, perfect, glaringly obvious when you've once seen it! And it's my whole play—the curtain rises on that sealed room and falls on it! That was my revelation— *how it was done!* That was what I got, by way of playwright's compensation, because a woman I thought I loved kicked me in the face—I brooded up the answer to the sealed room! And a taxi knocked it out of my head!'

He drew a long breath.

'I've spent two days and two nights, Bill, trying to get that idea back—*how it was done!* It won't come. I'm a competent playwright; I know my job; I could finish my play, but it'd be like all those others—not quite right, phoney! It wouldn't be *my play!* But there's a little man walking around this city somewhere—a little man with hexagonal glasses—who's got my idea in his head! He's got it because I told it to him. I'm going to find that little man, and get back what belongs to me! I've got to! Don't you see that, Bill? I've *got* to!'

*If the gentleman who, at the Casa Havana on the night of January 27th so patiently listened to a playwright's outlining of an idea for a drama will communicate with the Box No. below, he will hear of something to his advantage.*

A little man who had said, 'He's not my friend. He's just someone I met—'

A little man who'd seen an accident but hadn't waited to give evidence—

The hat-check girl had been right. There *was* something a little queer about that.

A little queer?

During the next few days, when the advertisements he'd inserted failed to bring any reply, it began to seem to Annixter very queer indeed.

His arm was out of its sling now, but he couldn't work. Time and again, he sat down before his almost completed manuscript, read it through with close, grim attention, thinking, 'It's *bound* to come back this time!'—only to find himself up against that blind spot again, that blank wall, that maddening hiatus in his memory.

He left his work and prowled the streets; he haunted bars and saloons; he rode for miles on 'buses and subways, especially at the rush hours. He saw a million faces, but the face of the little man with hexagonal glasses he did not see.

The thought of him obsessed Annixter. It was infuriating, it was unjust, it was torture to think that a little, ordinary, chance-met citizen was walking blandly around somewhere with the last link of his, the celebrated James Annixter's, play—the best thing he'd ever done— locked away in his head. And with no idea of what he had: without the imagination, probably, to appreciate what he had! And certainly with no idea of what it meant to Annixter!

Or *had* he some idea? Was he, perhaps, not quite so ordinary as he'd seemed? Had he seen those advertisements, drawn from them tortuous inferences of his own? Was he holding back with some scheme for shaking Annixter down for a packet?

The more Annixter thought about it, the more he felt that the hat-check girl had been right, that there was something very queer indeed about the way the little man had behaved after the accident.

Annixter's imagination played around the man he was seeking, tried to probe into his mind, conceived reasons for his fading away after the accident, for his failure to reply to the advertisements.

Annixter's was an active and dramatic imagination. The little man who had seemed so ordinary began to take on a sinister shape in Annixter's mind—

But the moment he actually saw the little man again, he realized how absurd that was. It was so absurd that it was laughable. The little man was so respectable; his shoulders were so straight; his pepper-and-salt suit was so neat; his black hard-felt hat was set so squarely on his head—

The doors of the subway train were just closing when Annixter saw him, standing on the platform with a briefcase in one hand, a folded evening paper under his other arm. Light from the train shone on his prim, pale face; his hexagonal spectacles flashed. He turned toward the exit as Annixter lunged for the closing doors of the train, squeezed between them on to the platform.

Craning his head to see above the crowd, Annixter elbowed his way through, ran up the stairs two at a time, put a hand on the little man's shoulder.

'Just a minute,' Annixter said. 'I've been looking for you.'

The little man checked instantly, at the touch of Annixter's hand. Then he turned his head and looked at Annixter. His eyes were pale behind the hexagonal, rimless glasses—a pale grey. His mouth was a straight line, almost colourless.

Annixter loved the little man like a brother. Merely finding the little man was a relief so great that it was like the lifting of a black cloud from his spirits. He patted the little man's shoulder affectionately.

'I've got to talk to you,' said Annixter. 'It won't take a minute. Let's go somewhere.'

The little man said, 'I can't imagine what you want to talk to me about.'

He moved slightly to one side, to let a woman pass. The crowd from the train had thinned, but there were still people going up and down the stairs. The little man looked, politely inquiring, at Annixter.

Annixter said, 'Of course you can't, it's so damned silly! But it's about that play—'

'Play?'

Annixter felt a faint anxiety.

'Look,' he said, 'I was drunk that night—I was very, very drunk! But looking back, my impression is that you were dead sober. You were, weren't you?'

'I've never been drunk in my life.'

'Thank heaven for that!' said Annixter. 'Then you won't have any difficulty in remembering the little point I want you to remember.' He grinned, shook his head. 'You had me going there, for a minute. I thought—'

'I don't know what you thought,' the little man said. 'But I'm quite sure you're mistaking me for somebody else. I haven't any idea what you're talking about. I never saw you before in my life. I'm sorry. Good night.'

He turned and started up the stairs. Annixter stared after him. He couldn't believe his ears. He stared blankly after the little man for an instant, then a rush of anger and suspicion swept away his bewilderment. He raced up the stairs, caught the little man by the arm.

'Just a minute,' said Annixter. 'I may have been drunk, but—'

'That,' the little man said, 'seems evident. Do you mind taking your hand off me?'

Annixter controlled himself. 'I'm sorry,' he said. 'Let me get this right, though. You say you've never seen me before. Then you weren't at the Casa Havana on the 27th—somewhere between ten o'clock and midnight? You didn't have a drink or two with me, and listen to an idea for a play that had just come into my mind?'

The little man looked steadily at Annixter.

'I've told you,' the little man said. 'I've never set eyes on you before.'

'You didn't see me get hit by a taxi?' Annixter pursued, tensely. 'You didn't say to the hat-check girl, "He's not my friend. He's just someone I met"?'

'I don't know what you're talking about,' the little man said sharply.

He made to turn away, but Annixter gripped his arm again.

'I don't know,' Annixter said, between his teeth, 'anything about your private affairs, and I don't want to. You may have had some good reason for wanting to duck giving evidence as a witness of that taxi accident. You may have some good reason for this act you're pulling on me, now. I don't know and I don't care. But it is an act. You *are* the man I told my play to!

'I want you to tell that story back to me as I told it to you; I have my reasons—personal reasons, of concern to me and me only. I want you to tell the story back to me—that's all I want! I don't want to know who you are, or anything about you, *I just want you to tell me that story!*'

'You ask,' the little man said, 'an impossibility, since I never heard it.'

Annixter kept an iron hold on himself.

He said, 'Is it money? Is this some sort of a hold-up? Tell me what you want; I'll give it to you. Lord help me, I'd go so far as to give you a share in the play! That'll mean real money. I know, because I know my business. And maybe—maybe,' said Annixter, struck by a sudden thought, '*you* know it, too! Eh?'

'You're insane or drunk!' the little man said.

With a sudden movement, he jerked his arm free, raced up the stairs. A train was rumbling in, below. People were hurrying down. He weaved and dodged among them with extraordinary celerity.

He was a small man, light, and Annixter was heavy. By the time he reached the street, there was no sign of the little man. He was gone.

*   *   *

Was the idea, Annixter wondered, to steal his play? By some wild chance did the little man nurture a fantastic ambition to be a dramatist? Had he, perhaps, peddled his precious manuscripts in vain, for years, around the managements? Had Annixter's play appeared to him as a blinding flash of hope in the gathering darkness of frustration and failure: something he had imagined he could safely steal because it had seemed to him the random inspiration of a drunkard who by morning would have forgotten he had ever given birth to anything but a hangover?

That, Annixter thought, would be a laugh! That would be irony—

He took another drink. It was his fifteenth since the little man with the hexagonal glasses had given him the slip, and Annixter was beginning to reach the stage where he lost count of how many places he had had drinks in tonight. It was also the stage, though, where he was beginning to feel better, where his mind was beginning to work.

He could imagine just how the little man must have felt as the quality of the play he was being told, with hiccups, gradually had dawned upon him.

'This is mine!' the little man would have thought. 'I've got to have this. He's drunk, he's soused, he's bottled—he'll have forgotten every word of it by the morning! Go on! Go on, mister! Keep talking!'

That was a laugh, too—the idea that Annixter would have forgotten his play by the morning. Other things Annixter forgot, unimportant things; but never in his life had he forgotten the minutest detail that was to his purpose as a playwright. Never! Except once, because a taxi had knocked him down.

Annixter took another drink. He needed it. He was on his own now. There wasn't any little man with hexagonal glasses to fill in that blind spot for him. The little man was gone. He was gone as though he'd never been. To hell with him! Annixter had to fill in that blind spot himself. He *had* to do it—somehow!

He had another drink. He had quite a lot more drinks. The bar was crowded and noisy, but he didn't notice the noise—till someone came up and slapped him on the shoulder. It was Ransome.

Annixter stood up, leaning with his knuckles on the table.

'Look, Bill,' Annixter said, 'how about this? Man forgets an idea, see? He wants to get it back—gotta get it back! Idea comes from inside, works outwards—right? So he starts on the outside, works back inward. How's that?'

He swayed, peering at Ransome.

'Better have a little drink,' said Ransome. 'I'd need to think that out.'

'I,' said Annixter, '*have* thought it out!' He crammed his hat shapelessly on to his head. 'Be seeing you, Bill. I got work to do!'

He started, on a slightly tacking course, for the door—and his apartment.

It was Joseph, his 'man,' who opened the door of his apartment to him, some twenty minutes later. Joseph opened the door while Annixter's latchkey was still describing vexed circles around the lock.

'Good evening, sir,' said Joseph.

Annixter stared at him. 'I didn't tell you to stay in tonight.'

'I hadn't any reason for going out, sir,' Joseph explained. He helped Annixter off with his coat. 'I rather enjoy a quiet evening in, once in a while.'

'You got to get out of here,' said Annixter.

'Thank you, sir,' said Joseph. 'I'll go and throw a few things into a bag.'

Annixter went into his big living-room-study, poured himself a drink.

The manuscript of his play lay on the desk. Annixter, swaying a little, glass in hand, stood frowning down at the untidy stack of yellow paper, but he didn't begin to read. He waited until he heard the outer door click shut behind Joseph, then he gathered up his manuscript, the decanter and a glass, and the cigarette box. Thus laden, he went into the hall, walked across it to the door of Joseph's room.

There was a bolt on the inside of this door, and the room was the only one in the apartment which had no window—both facts which made the room the only one suitable to Annixter's purpose.

With his free hand, he switched on the light.

It was a plain little room, but Annixter noticed, with a faint grin, that the bedspread and the cushion in the worn basket-chair were both blue. Appropriate, he thought—a good omen. *Room Blue* by James Annixter—

Joseph had evidently been lying on the bed, reading the evening paper; the paper lay on the rumpled quilt, and the pillow was dented. Beside the head of the bed, opposite the door, was a small table littered with shoe-brushes and dusters.

Annixter swept this paraphernalia on to the floor. He put his stack of manuscript, the decanter and glass and cigarette box on the table, and went across and bolted the door. He pulled the basket-chair up to the table and sat down, lighted a cigarette.

He leaned back in the chair, smoking, letting his mind ease into the atmosphere he wanted—the mental atmosphere of Cynthia, the woman in his play, the woman who was afraid, so afraid that she had locked and bolted herself into a windowless room, a sealed room.

'This is how she sat,' Annixter told himself, 'just as I'm sitting now: in a room with no windows, the door locked and bolted. Yet he got at her. He got at her with a knife—in a room with no windows, the door remaining locked and bolted on the inside. *How was it done?*'

There was a way in which it could be done. He, Annixter, had thought of that way; he had conceived it, invented it—and forgotten it. His idea had produced the circumstances. Now, deliberately, he had reproduced the circumstances, that he might think back to the idea. He had put his person in the position of the victim, that his mind might grapple with the problem of the murderer.

It was very quiet: not a sound in the room, the whole apartment.

For a long time, Annixter sat unmoving. He sat unmoving until the intensity of his concentration began to waver. Then he relaxed. He pressed the palms of his hands to his forehead for a moment, then reached for the decanter. He splashed himself a strong drink. He had almost recovered what he sought; he had felt it close, had been on the very verge of it.

'Easy,' he warned himself, 'take it easy. Rest. Relax. Try again in a minute.'

He looked around for something to divert his mind, picked up the paper from Joseph's bed.

At the first words that caught his eye, his heart stopped.

*The woman, in whose body were found three knife wounds, any of which might have been fatal, was in a windowless room, the only door to which was locked and bolted on the inside. These elaborate precautions appear to have been habitual with her, and no doubt she went in continual fear of her life, as the police know her to have been a persistent and pitiless blackmailer.*

*Apart from the unique problem set by the circumstance of the sealed room is the problem of how the crime could have gone undiscovered for so long a period, the doctor's estimate from the condition of the body as some twelve to fourteen days.*

Twelve to fourteen days—

Annixter read back over the remainder of the story; then let the paper fall to the floor. The pulse was heavy in his head. His face was grey. Twelve to fourteen days? He could put it closer than that. *It was exactly thirteen nights ago that he had sat in the Casa Havana and told a little man with hexagonal glasses how to kill a woman in a sealed room!*

Annixter sat very still for a minute. Then he poured himself a drink.

It was a big one, and he needed it. He felt a strange sense of wonder, of awe.

They had been in the same boat, he and the little man—thirteen nights ago. They had both been kicked in the face by a woman. One, as a result, had conceived a murder play. The other had made the play reality!

'And I actually, tonight, offered him a share!' Annixter thought. 'I talked about "real" money!'

That was a laugh. All the money in the universe wouldn't have made that little man admit that he had seen Annixter before—that Annixter had told him the plot of a play about how to kill a woman in a sealed room! Why, he, Annixter, was the one person in the world who could denounce that little man! Even if he couldn't tell them, because he had forgotten, just *how* he had told the little man the murder was to be committed, he could still put the police on the little man's track. He could describe him, so that they could trace him. And once on his track, the police would ferret out links, almost inevitably, with the dead woman.

A queer thought—that he, Annixter, was probably the only menace, the only danger, to the little prim, pale man with the hexagonal spectacles. The only menace—as, of course, the little man must know very well.

He must have been very frightened when he had read that the playwright who had been knocked down outside the Casa Havana had only received 'superficial injuries.' He must have been still more frightened when Annixter's advertisements had begun to appear. *What must he have felt tonight, when Annixter's hand had fallen on his shoulder?*

A curious idea occurred, now, to Annixter. It was from tonight, precisely from tonight, that he was a danger to that little man. He was, because of the inferences the little man must infallibly draw, a deadly danger as from the moment the discovery of the murder in the sealed room was published. That discovery had been published tonight and the little man had a paper under his arm—

Annixter's was a lively and resourceful imagination.

It was, of course, just in the cards that, when he'd lost the little man's trail at the subway station, the little man might have turned back, picked up *his*, Annixter's trail.

And Annixter had sent Joseph out. He was, it dawned slowly upon Annixter, alone in the apartment—alone in a windowless room, with the door locked and bolted on the inside, at his back.

Annixter felt a sudden, icy and wild panic.

He half rose, but it was too late.

It was too late, because at that moment the knife slid, thin and keen and delicate, into his back, fatally, between the ribs.

Annixter's head bowed slowly forward until his cheek rested on the manuscript of his play. He made only one sound—a queer sound, indistinct, yet identifiable as a kind of laughter.

The fact was, Annixter had just remembered.

ALEX ATKINSON

# Chapter the Last: Merriman Explains

*Alex Atkinson's first novel* All Next Week *(1951) was a decidedly downbeat, even at times harrowing, social drama about provincial theatre (Atkinson was an actor for a time, with hard experience of the miseries of weekly rep), which featured a suicide in the very last paragraph. And this is odd because Atkinson (1916-1962) was already a leading light in* Punch, *a magazine not noted (at least then; hardly now) for its kitchen-sink approach to social realism, or indeed anything. A later book* Exit Charlie *(1955) was an excellent detective novel, but his fame rests on a number of hilariously acerbic guides to foreign climes produced in tandem with that fine artist Ronald Searle, and if he's remembered at all today (he died tragically young) it will surely be for those. He was also an excellent parodist.*

*The parody is not the easiest of literary jokes. Writers who are on the face of it the most obvious targets (those whose stylistic tics and habits almost poke you in the eye as you read) quite often bring forth the worst in their parodists. There is a fine line between clever and witty caricature and thumping exaggeration, too often stumbled across by the lampoonist.*

*In general parodies of mystery and detective fiction fail dismally because more often than not the parodist homes in on the content rather than the author. Those who poked fun at Edgar Wallace, for instance, dragged in hooded villains, old mansions, secret passages, but rarely came anywhere near capturing his essence, which was his style. On the other hand it is not enough to depend on style . . . not enough when parodying, say, Agatha Christie's Poirot merely to Frenchify the sentence construction and chuck in the odd* Merde alors! *(well, okay—*Zut alors!*).*

*In writing the way he did, and creating such vaster-than-life sleuths as Sir Henry Merrivale and Dr Fell, John Dickson Carr was bound to attract a certain amount of parody and pastiche. When it came it came from varied sources: the anagrammatic Handon C Jorricks (in reality Norma Schier) with the entrancingly-titled 'Hocus Pocus At Drumis Tree'; Jon Breen and his Sir Gideon Merrimac; Arthur Porges involving HM with Stately Homes the Great Detective (two parodies for the price of one!). All had things in common: they were funny, they were affectionate, and they were well-informed.*

*But the laurels for the very best parody—and incidentally the earliest (that we know of)—must go to Alex Atkinson, who clearly knew his Carr very well indeed. Style, content, dialogue, even characterisation—all are superbly mimicked. It is not just funny, but wickedly funny—and supremely clever. It is also (and this is not entirely by the way) tangible evidence of how much value and enjoyment may be gained from sitting in a loft and idly picking through a monstrous accumulation of dusty magazines from a bygone era.*

*What follows is a little masterpiece—and, we trust, a fitting finale to* The Art of the Impossible.

JACK ADRIAN/ROBERT ADEY

---

It must have been a full twelve and a half seconds before anybody broke the stunned silence that followed Merriman's calm announcement. As I look back, I can still see the half-humorous smile playing about his satyr's face in the flickering firelight. I can hear again the hearty cracks he made as he pulled his fingers one by one. I couldn't help feeling that the old fox was holding something back. What lay behind the quizzical look he fired at Eleanor? Did I detect a flutter of fear on her pasty (but somehow curiously attractive) face? What was the significance of the third onion? *Was there a third onion at all?* If so, *who had it?* These and eight other questions chased themselves around in my brain as I watched Merriman pick up his Chartreuse and look round at us with quiet amusement.

It was Humphrey who spoke first, his voice echoing strangely through the quiet room, with its crossed swords, Rembrandts, and jade. 'But—great Scott!—if Alastair Tripp *wasn't there . . .* !'

'Alastair Tripp,' said Merriman, breathing on his monocle (the only time I ever saw him do such a thing in all the years I knew him), 'wasn't, as you say, there. *And yet, in a way, he was.*'

Humphrey gave a snort of disgust, and drained his crème-de-menthe noisily. Even Chief Inspector Rodd gave vent to a half-stifled groan of bewilderment.

Merriman frowned. 'You really are the dumbest crew I ever struck,' he snarled. His gay wit was so infectious that the tension eased at once. He pointed at Humphrey with an olive on the end of an ebony-handled poniard. 'Take your mind back,' he said, 'to a week last Wednesday, at sixteen minutes past seven p.m., in the hall of Mossburn Manor. Haven't you realized yet that the Mrs Ogilvie who flung the grandfather clock over the banisters was in reality her own step-mother—Eleanor's sister's aunt by marriage? Even by the light of a single candle you should have noticed the blonde wig, the false hands, or the papier-maché mask—*the very mask which was found later up the chimney in Simon's bedroom!* Don't you see?'

Eleanor gasped. I could see Humphrey's knuckles whiten as his bony hands tightened their grip on the handle of the lawn-mower. I felt that the pieces were beginning to drop into place like bits of an enormous, sinister jig-saw puzzle. The trouble was, they didn't seem to fit.

'A left shoe, my half-wits,' rumbled Merriman. 'A left shoe with the lace missing. One onion where there should have been three. A half-chewed sweet in an otherwise deserted goldfish-bowl. By thunder, surely you *see?*' He rose to his feet and began to pace the room, with his head bent to avoid the oak beams. Sometimes as he walked he trod on the Chief Inspector, and once as he stood upright to emphasize a point, he brought down the chandelier with a crash. 'It was a chance remark from Lady Powder that tipped me off,' he bellowed, pounding a huge fist on the top of Eleanor's head. Eleanor's eyes widened, and on her face there was a look I hadn't seen before. 'We were on the roof, you remember, trying to find a croquet ball, and all of a sudden she said "It hasn't rained since Monday." ' He stood in the middle of the room, with one hand on the picture-rail and the other in his trousers pocket, and surveyed us. 'From that moment,' he said quietly, 'I knew I was on the wrong track.' He started to walk about again, and some of the floor-boards didn't seem any too safe down at my end of the room.

'But—great Scott!—if Alastair Tripp *wasn't there* . . . ' Humphrey began again.

'I'm coming to that.' Merriman fixed me with his eccentric glare. 'I believe I have told you more than once, my foolish ape,' he said, 'that there are a hundred and four ways of getting into a room with no doors on the inside and no windows on the outside. But that's beside the point. Consider, if you will, the night of the murder. Here we have John Smith taking a nap in the pantry. The door is locked. The window is locked. The cupboard is bare. The carpet—and mark this—the carpet is *rolled up in a corner*, tied round with ordinary common or garden string. Now then, in the first place, as you will have guessed, the lightly-sleeping figure on the camp bed was not John Smith at all.' Merriman fixed Eleanor with a penetrating stare. '*You* know who it was, don't you, *Mrs Anstruther?*'

'Mrs *what!*' The question left my lips before I could stop it. Eleanor turned deathly pale, and tore her cambric handkerchief in two with a convulsive movement. Chief Inspector Rodd stirred slightly in his sleep. A frown of impatience played fitfully over the chiselled features of Humphrey Beeton. Outside the rain whispered eerily against the panes.

'Good Kensington Gore!' swore Merriman, wrenching a handful of stops from his treasured organ and hurling them at the Chief Inspector: 'it was so *easy!*' He sat suddenly in the whicker armchair, and all but flattened Professor Meak, whom we had somehow forgotten. 'Let me take you through it step by step. A bootlace is fastened to one end of the blow-pipe, which has previously been filled with sugar. This whole deadly contraption is lowered down the chimney—oh, there was plenty of time, I assure you: remember that Mercia Foxglove had been concealed in the shrubbery since dawn, and in any case at that time nobody knew that Paul's father was really Janet's uncle from Belfast.'

'But if Alastair Tripp *wasn't there* . . . ' Humphrey's voice was desperate with curiosity. The lawn-mower trembled in his hands.

'I'm coming to that,' said Merriman, filling his pipe with herbs. 'Three onions,' he went on steadily, 'have already been placed midway between the door and the golf-club—which, you will observe, is leaning unnoticed against the wall. Very well, then. Recall, if you will, the evidence of the so-called Alfred Harp—actually, of course, as I will show you, he is none other than our friend the mysterious "milkman": but more of that anon. Where did he find the decanter after—I repeat, *after*—the gardener's cottage had been burnt to the ground? He found it, my pretty dumb-bells, in the pocket of Sir Herbert's dressing-gown—*which was nowhere to be found.*' He beamed expansively. '*Now* do you understand?'

Humphrey rose unsteadily. His face was working, and I thought I detected a fleck of foam on his tie. I reached unobtrusively for my hat. 'But if Alastair Tripp—*wasn't there—*' Humphrey almost shouted.

'I'm coming to that.'

It was too much. With a mighty roar of rage and impatience, Humphrey swung the lawn-mower over his head in a flashing arc.

As I groped my way down the back stairs I reflected sadly that this would probably go down in history as Merriman's Last Case.

# Sources

The stories in this collection originally appeared as follows:

ALEX ATKINSON
'Chapter The Last: Merriman Explains': *Punch*, 15 August 1951.

JOHN DICKSON CARR
'The House in Goblin Wood': simultaneously in *Strand magazine* and *Ellery Queen's Mystery Magazine* (US), November 1947. *The Third Bullet And Other Stories* (1954).

'A Razor in Fleet Street': *London Mystery Magazine*, February/March 1952, as 'Flight From Fleet Street'.

JOSEPH COMMINGS
'Ghost in the Gallery': *Ten Detective Aces* (US), July 1949.

VINCENT CORNIER
'The Courtyard of the Fly': *The Storyteller*, June 1937.

GERALD FINDLER
'The House of Screams': *Doidge's Western Counties Annual*, September 1932.

JACQUES FUTRELLE
'An Absence of Air': *The Storyteller*, December 1922, as 'Vacuum'.

EDWARD D. HOCH
'The Impossible Murder': *Ellery Queen's Mystery Magazine* (US), December 1976, as 'Captain Leopold and the Impossible Murder' in a slightly different form.

W. HOPE HODGSON
'Bullion!': *Everybody's Weekly*, 11 March 1911.

GEORGE LOCKE
'A Nineteenth Century Debacle': privately printed and issued in the first 100 copies of *Locked Room Murders And Other Impossible Crimes* by Robert Adey (1979).

JOHN LUTZ
'It's a Dog's Life': *Alfred Hitchcock's Mystery Magazine* (US), 3 March 1982, as 'The Case of the Canine Accomplice'.

BARRY PEROWNE
'The Blind Spot': *Ellery Queen's Mystery Magazine* (US), November 1945.

ARTHUR PORGES
'Coffee Break': *Alfred Hitchcock's Mystery Magazine* (US), July 1964.
BILL PRONZINI
'Proof of Guilt': *Ellery Queen's Mystery Magazine* (US), December 1973. *Graveyard Plots* (1985).
LEONARD PRUYN
'Dinner At Garibaldi's': *Malcolm's* (US), March 1954.
JOEL TOWNSLEY ROGERS
'The Hanging Rope': *New Detective Magazine* (US), September 1946.
SAX ROHMER
'The Death of Cyrus Pettigrew': *London Magazine*, March 1909, as by A. Sarsfield Ward.
JOHN F. SUTER
'The Impossible Theft': *Ellery Queen's Mystery Magazine* (US), May 1964.
EDGAR WALLACE
'The Missing Romney': *Weekly News*, 27 December 1919. *Four-Square Jane* (1929).
JEFFREY WALLMANN
'Now You See Her': *Mike Shayne's Mystery Magazine* (US), March 1971.

HAKE TALBOT's 'The Other Side' has never appeared in an English language magazine and is here published, in English, for the first time.

# Acknowledgements

Every effort has been made to contact the owners of all the copyrighted stories, and grateful thanks are extended to the copyright holders for allowing them to be reprinted. If any necessary acknowledgements have been omitted, the editors and publisher hope that the copyright holders concerned will accept their apologies in advance.

'The House in Goblin Wood' and 'A Razor In Fleet Street' by John Dickson Carr. Copyright © 1947, 1952. Reprinted by permission of David Higham Associates, Ltd., and Harold Ober Associates, Inc.

'The Courtyard of the Fly' by Vincent Cornier. Copyright © 1937. Reprinted by permission of Mrs Deidre Beatrice Warman.

'Coffee Break' by Arthur Porges. Copyright © 1964. Reprinted by permission of Scott Meredith Literary Agency, Inc.

'Proof of Guilt' by Bill Pronzini. Copyright © 1973. Reprinted by permission of the author.

'The Impossible Theft' by John F. Suter. Copyright © 1964. Reprinted by permission of the author.

'It's A Dog's Life' by John Lutz. Copyright © 1982. Reprinted by permission of the author.

'The Death of Cyrus Pettigrew' by Sax Rohmer. Copyright © 1909. Reprinted by permission of A. P. Watt Ltd.

'Ghost in the Gallery' by Joseph Commings. Copyright © 1949. Reprinted by permission of the author.

'The Impossible Murder' by Edward D. Hoch. Copyright © 1976. Reprinted by permission of the author.

'A Nineteenth Century Debacle' by George Locke. Copyright © 1979. Reprinted by permission of the author.

'Now You See Her' by Jeffrey Wallmann. Copyright © 1971. Reprinted by permission of the author.

306 The Art of the Impossible

'The Blind Spot' by Barry Perowne. Copyright © 1945. Reprinted by permission of Mrs Fernanda Rolle.

Special thanks and acknowledgements to the following for their help and encouragement: Ed Hoch and Bill Pronzini; Peter Tyas (list-maker supreme!); Jan Broberg (who generously passed on a copy of Hake Talbot's original typescript of 'The Other Side'); Bill Lofts and Derek Adley (the old reliables); Dr Stephen Leadbeatter; the staff of the Bodleian Library, Oxford; and Roland and Danièle Lacourbe (for their enthusiasm, particularly in the matter of Joel Townsley Rogers).

JA/RA